CONQUEST
OF A
CONTINENT

4669-BANT

CONQUEST
OF A
CONTINENT

Nine Generations of the
American Frontier

Theodore M. Banta

4669-BANT

To order additional copies of this book, contact:
Xlibris Corporation
1-888-7-XLIBRIS
www.Xlibris.com
Orders@Xlibris.com

CONTENTS

To all of Epke Jacobse's progeny; past, present and to come.

PREFACE

Historical Novel: A form of fictional narrative which recon-
structs history and re-creates it imaginatively. Both historical and fictional characters may appear. Though
writing fiction, the good historical novelist researches
his or her chosen period thoroughly and strives for
verisimilitude . . . (411).
—A DICTIONARY OF LITERARY TERMS,
edited by J. A. Cuddon (Oxford: Blackwell, 1991)

This historical novel is based on historic facts and human figures
which the author, through deductive analysis, brought to life.
It follows a family, the Bantas, seamlessly through twelve
generations, nine in which they lived their lives as frontiersmen
on the edge of civilization on the North American continent.
Names, places and dates in this narrative are as historically
accurate as my knowledge and my sources permit. Most
quotations other than those that are indented are imaginary.
The Paleontologists reconstruct life-like dinosaurs from the remains
of fossilized bones. Even from a partial fossil, they deduce what
the missing bones most likely looked like and then continue
by deduction to cover these bones with muscle and flesh. In
our recent movies, Paleontologists have even put these ancient
beasts in motion. From fossilized foot prints, they have deduced
the most plausible way that ancient extinct animals walked
and ran.
When I first began work on this novel, writing a book was
nowhere in my mind. Instead, my motivation was to study
the genealogy of my family name: Banta. I was very fortunate

in that others before me had dug up most of the bones (historical facts) of the twelve generations. In my research, I also recovered other missing bones needed to build this analogical dinosaur.

When I read what others had dug up in search of our family tree, I realized that these cold historic facts and human figures led through the history of our great nation. With deductive reasoning, I attempted a novel, whose scope would encompass the building of the United States of America. The resulting book is a form of creative non-fiction.

As an example, in this novel, these are the facts: Epke Jacobse was a miller before coming to the New Netherland. When he came to the new world he left his profession behind and became an innkeeper in Vlissengen which was a village of English immigrants located on Long Island in Queens County, New Netherland. Peter Styversant, Governor of the New Netherland, was having trouble with the English inhabitants of Vlissengen and he questioned their allegiance. They had sent him a "Remonstrance" which he believed to be seditious. This happened shortly before Epke took over the inn in Vlissengen. Analytic deduction: Peter Styversant asked the Dutch West Indies Company to send him a Dutch innkeeper so he could keep his eye on the inhabitants of the English village; Epke was recruited for this position because the inn was the center of the town's social life and an ideal place to hear local gossip.

By looking for motives which underlay action, a plausible story can be told. Is it fact or fiction? Are the muscles and flesh the paleontologist put on his dinosaur fact or fiction?

ACKNOWLEDGMENTS

Much of the genealogical information in this book about the first seven generations of the Banta family on the North American continent rely on the information contained in the book "A Frisian Family. The Banta Genealogy" written by Theodore M. Banta, New York, 1893.

To my good fortune, my cousin, Brent Banta, called my attention to a book by Elsa M. Banta written in 1983 and revised in 1985. Mrs. Banta's research not only filled in many questions about the family in America, but it also researched the family through three generations in Friesland prior to their emigration. This permitted me to extrapolate motives that serve as an introduction as to why the family left Friesland and immigrated to the New Netherland, Holland's colony in North America. My sincere thanks to Elsa Banta for the vital information her book provided me.

Vincent Akers series of articles in the The Holland Societies magazine of history, "DE Halve Maen" entitled "The Low Dutch Company. A History of Holland Dutch Settlements on the Kentucky Frontier" was invaluable. Vincent Akers, through his articles and papers, provided me with information from his decades of Low Dutch research. His articles and maps of the Banta's migration to Kentucky, and the founding of the Low Dutch colony there, cleared up many questions as to time line and geography. I am eternally grateful to Mr. Akers for this.

I want to thank those in the small store in Minertsga, Friesland, who helped me find the miller's house in which Epke Jacobse lived with his wife and five sons; the lovely lady who gave me the history and a tour of the Bowne house in Flushing; the librarian in the Long Island Room of the Queensbury Public Library; Charles Markey in the Jersey city Public Library who helped me find the history of Bergen city and Hudson and Bergen county in New Jersey; the sexton of the Low Dutch Reformed Church just off of Bergen Square who helped me find the site of the octagonal church in which Epke Jacobese and his sons worshiped; those who helped us find Hendrick's stone in the Church on the Green in Hackensack; the librarian in Somerset County who led us to the book "An Old Farm"; the lovely lady who owned the log cabin that still stands in Conewago where father Hendrick and his family lived in the 1770s and who was kind enough to let us look through it; the librarians in Kentucky, Eaton Ohio, and Rensellier, Indiana and all the others who made the telling of this story possible.

I relied on many books, articles and newspaper columns. The article, "History of the Low Dutch Colony of Conewago" by Reverend J. K. Demerest, D. D. was most helpful. Nancy Crowell, Preble County Room Librarian, Preble County District Library found the dates and sections of land purchases in Ohio that made that section of the story possible.

Many of the facts about and history of the Imperial Valley and the eighth generation came from the book, "The First Thirty Years in the Imperial Valley" by Otis B Tout, Otis B. Tout, Publisher, San Diego, California. Mr. Tout offers a wealth of information in his book on all aspects of the early history of the valley. His research was heavily relied upon in this historical novel.

My sincere thanks is offered to Don Sperling, who read each chapter in this book as it was written, offering corrections and suggestions for improvement of the text. Without his encouragement, this novel never would have been completed. Thanks to Cesar A. Gonzalez-T, Professor Emeritus, San Diego Mesa College, whose suggestions offered to me after reading an early proof made this a far more readable narrative.

Without his encouragement this book never would have been published.

This novel is the result of seven years of gathering information and writing; I know I have left out people who provided me with vital information that made this book possible. Since I started researching and writing it as a hobby, I never expected to finish the book, or my hobby would have been over. For this reason, my record keeping of all who helped me is incomplete, and I apologize to all the wonderful people I have left out.

The following narrative is dedicated to those nine generations from Epke Jacobse, progenitor of the Banta family, who embarked from Amsterdam for the New Netherland on February 12, 1659, to T. P. Banta, of the eighth generation, his wife Carrie and his sons Earl, Al and George of the ninth generation, who were one of the first four families to settle in the Imperial Valley, sixty miles from the Pacific Ocean. The story ends with the death of T. P. in 1921, when this branch of the family after two hundred and sixty-two years and nine generations, brought to a close their place as frontiersmen on the North American continent.

Part two, which makes up about one half of the pages in this historical novel, is written about T. P. of the eighth generation; for the story of the last frontier in the contiguous United States is a most interesting story and one which could be easily researched from the author's home in Los Angeles County. T. P. is my Grandfather and his youngest son, George, is my father. I, the author, am of the tenth generation and the first of the ten generations on the North American continent not to have lived as a frontiersman. An entire novel could be written about any one of the previous seven generations.

This historical novel is written for all who want to gain insight as to the motivations that kept our frontiers moving constantly westward from the English and Dutch colonies on the east coast alongside the Atlantic Ocean to the shores of the Pacific Ocean a continent away. Why did all those men and women leave behind the safety, comfort and warmth of their family's farm or community to push the harsh and unfriendly edge of the envelope ever forward into the new frontier? The answer to this question is complex, but the following pages will help us understand their motivations.

INTRODUCTION

THE UNITED STATES OF AMERICA

HOW DID IT HAPPEN?

Have you ever wondered as you drove across this great country of ours, who were those guys who wrested this continent from primeval forests, the raging and untamed rivers, the desolate and seeming unconquerable deserts? In short, a threatening, inhospitable and uncivilized land, unexplored, with untold terrors awaiting those foolish enough to take that next step into that vast wilderness. Who were those courageous, fearless frontiersmen who never hesitated to take that next step.

The great American philosopher, Henry David Throeau, said it best when he wrote, "I know of no more encouraging fact than the unquestionable ability of man to elevate his life by conscious endeavor." Think about it. Of all God's creations, from the total universe, to the galaxies with their thousands of stars and great black holes, to our own solar system, and our planet with all its life forms, we humans are the single one of His creations that we know of that has the ability to change in any way our future by our own conscious endeavor. In looking at the universe it is easy to come to the incorrect conclusion that man is insignificant as compared to the entire universe. But we see our significance from a far different viewpoint when we consider our conscious intelligence which permits us to mold our own future.

In Europe, with its landed privileged class and its structured wealthy bankers and men of commerce, the average individual had his ability to elevate his life through his own efforts limited to his philosophical and intellectual life. To raise himself economically and materially was beyond his ability in such limited an economy from the stand point of land and capital. The Spanish and the Portuguese, who were the primary settlers of the new world beyond Canada and the United States, provided large land grants to the wealthy and continued this process. The wealthy were the ones who gained from the success of their venture, not the individual who helped them build their property. The Dutch and English Colonies did it differently, allowing each man to reap the rewards of his own sweat.

This book will examine those rugged individualists who left the comforts of home and family to challenge the unknown frontier. In the words of the great economist, Robert L. Heilbroner, they were what all entrepreneurs are, "rational maximizers." They rationally maximized the personal gain they could achieve from their own resourcefulness. But we will discover as we take this journey through time that personal wealth was but one of many goals that pushed the frontiersman forward to a new untamed frontier.

Perhaps this explains why only the United States and Canada of all the nations in the New World succeeded in becoming the world leaders. The secret of their success was that the individual pioneer was given the freedom to seek what they found most dear, be it temporal or spiritual. In seeking and reaping the the rewards of their work, they created the worlds greatest infrastructures. Both of these countries recognize the value of the individual and his right to seek property, liberty and the pursuit of happiness. Each man was provided the opportunity of reward or loss through individual risk taking. England and Holland let each man reap the benefits of his sweat and labor in hacking out as best he could his place on the new continent.

Epke Jacobse — 1650

BEFORE THERE WAS AN AMERICA

The seventeenth century (the 1600's) is known as the golden age of Holland. During that century, Holland became Europe's center of trade and commerce. She also commanded one of the world's most powerful fleets. Only England rivaled her on the oceans of the world.

Overland commerce with the far east had been seriously restrained and made exorbitantly expensive since the Turks had overrun the Near East. Trade was allowed to continue but only at certain terminals which the Moslems controlled. This caused the decline of the lucrative trade with the Italian city states and the Hanseatic league.

Events leading to the ascent of Holland as the leader of European commerce commenced with the voyage of Christopher Columbus in search of a western sea route to India and China. His voyage resulted in the discovery that an unknown continent stood in the way of such sea route. His voyage was followed by the exploration of the worlds oceans. Two Portuguese navigators proved that trade with India and the far east was possible by sea. Vasco De Gama and his four ships sailed around the Cape of Good Hope at the southern tip of Africa. Then, after sailing twenty-three days across the Indian ocean, he reached India. Ferdinand Magellan, following Vasco De Gamma's discovery, circumnavigated the globe and while doing so discovered a new route to India through the Straits of Magellan near the tip of South America.

Portugal and Spain were the first to gain from the relocation of the trading centers of Europe caused by the change from overland to ocean routes of trade with the far east. Portugal had settlements along the coasts of Asia, Africa and Brazil.

The Portuguese were great explorers and administrators. Their major deficiency was that of a declining population. The hazards of exploring the worlds oceans plus the dangers of sailing the ocean routes to Portugal's far flung empire resulted in a heavy loss of life. Plague, famine and desertion also took their toll. As a result, not one in ten who left Portugal on these dangerous voyages returned to Portugal. During the sixteenth century, Portugal's population declined from two million to just more than one million. Thus, Portugal was pushed to the limit transporting cargoes to Lisbon and had to leave the lucrative financial and distribution matters to others.

The western Hapsburg empire, ruled by King Phillip II of Spain, included the Spanish Netherlands. Antwerp, in the Spanish Netherlands, assumed the role of Europe's center of commerce. The German and Italian bankers, recognizing this shift in the center of trade, came to Antwerp as did merchants and manufacturers from France and England. Antwerp was declared a toll free port and the vast majority of Europe's commerce was transacted there.

Antwerp had held this position for only a short time when Spanish army troops rioted because their pay and rations were delayed. The army vent its vengeance by sacking the city of Antwerp in 1576. Antwerp never recovered from this blow as those who were involved in making the city Europe's commerce center fled to Amsterdam.

Charlemagne, in creating his empire in the ninth century, brought all Europe under Christianity. At that time, except for the Eastern Orthodox Church, all Christians accepted the authority of the Pope and the church of Rome. With Martin Luther's successful revolt against the Church of Rome in 1521, Christianity in Europe was split into many sects as theologians interpreted Holy Scripture in different ways. The Dutch Reformed Church, to which most Dutch Protestants belonged towards the end of the sixteenth century, followed the theology of Calvin. Phillip II of Spain, was alarmed by the spread of Protestantism in the Spanish Netherlands. As a Catholic Hapsburg king, he championed the authority of the Pope. This brings us to the great religious and political war between Spain and the Spanish Netherlands in the struggle for Dutch independence.

Phillip sent his best general, the Duke of Avila, to stamp out disloyalty. A great leader, William of Orange, arose to lead the Dutch resistance. Although the puny Dutch forces fared poorly against the forces of the Duke of Avila at the outset, in 1569 the Dutch began the outfitting of privateers to attack Spanish shipping. With the tremendous loot captured by these privateers, the Dutch were able to mount strong resistance. Under the leadership of William of Orange, they were victorious over the Duke of Avila, and he was recalled to Spain.

In 1576, The Pacification of Ghent was signed by all parties. This was the Dutch declaration of independence. Under this agreement, both Protestants and Catholics would be permitted the unopposed practice of their religions. The provinces agreed to recognize Phillip II as king but William of Orange was actually to head the government.

In 1579, the Southern Netherlands, now known as Belgium, split from the Northern Netherlands, known as Holland, and agreed to reconcile with Phillip II of Spain. The Northern Provinces, Holland, stated they would fight on until complete freedom was achieved. In 1609 a truce was declared by both sides, and in 1648, complete independence was given to the Dutch Netherlands.

In 1580, Spain annexed Portugal upon the death of the king of Portugal because Phillip II of Spain was the heir apparent to Portugal's throne. Thereupon, he excluded Dutch ships from Portugal's ports. Thus cut off from trade with Portugal's far flung empire, the Dutch invaded Spain's trade routes by sending fleets of their ships around the Cape of Good Hope to the Spanish Spice Islands and the far east. Any Portuguese or Spanish ships encountered along the way were considered enemy ships and their cargoes were confiscated. Dutch ships were more maneuverable and, thus, superior to the heavy Spanish galleons.

As the fleet of Dutch ships grew, Dutch naval forces surpassed those of the Spanish who never recovered from the defeat of the Invincible Armada in 1588 by a terrible storm off the Irish coast and the English fleet under command of Sir Francis Drake.

PART I

THE FIRST SEVEN GENERATIONS

CHAPTER 1

A LONG, LONG TIME AGO, IN A LAND FAR, FAR AWAY. FRIESLAND, THE NORTHERN PROVENCE OF HOLLAND.

Our story begins a long, long time ago, in a land far, far away called Friesland. It lies at the mouth of the great Rhine River which flows from Switzerland to the North Sea. The main course of the River ends at the Zyder Zee at Amsterdam but over eons it built up such an estuary of silt that it split into two at the beginning of this estuary and the lesser mouth of the Rhine flowed north of the Zyder Zee through Friesland. This branch of the Rhine built its estuary of silt out into the North Sea.

Thus, most of Friesland is at or below sea level. It is a very marshy area where the ancient inhabitants built up mounds on which they lived in order to be above the wet marsh lands. In the days when Rome conquered and controlled this area, the Romans started building dikes to drain and reclaim low areas from the seas. After the days of Rome the Frieslanders continued building and maintaining the Roman dikes. In addition, they constructed new dikes until the area of Friesland, where our story begins, held the sea back with a dike forty feet high.

The land was called Friesland because after the decline of Rome no one ever conquered and occupied it. Because the language of the Frieslanders is different from the Dutch and German tongue and is the closest language to the English language, it is easy for

English speaking people to interpret what Friesland means, for just as it sounds, it means Free land. Historians have said, tongue in cheek, that the climate and land were so disagreeable that no one else was dumb enough to want to live there and therefore never bothered to occupy it. Be that as it may, the Frieslanders cherished their freedom and were fully in favor of freeing the low lands from Spanish domination.

After William of Orange freed Holland from Spanish domination, the state church was the Low Dutch Reformed Church which was Calvinist in doctrine. Low, as used in the name of the church was used to define it as the church of the low countries of the Netherlands.

Off the shores of Friesland in the North Atlantic were the Frieslandic Islands. These islands reduced some of the mighty forces of the storms that blew into Friesland from the North Sea. Even with them as barriers to the open sea, it was a constant struggle to maintain the dikes that sheltered the low lands from the Atlantic ocean. Every school child has read the story of the little Dutch boy who saved his village but lost his life by holding his finger in a hole in the dike. It was a constant struggle by all the people of Friesland to maintain the integrity of the dikes that protected the farm land from the ocean.

Behind the dikes, windmills pumped water from the fields into the canals that carried it back to the seas. The farm land was so damp and wet that all the Dutch people wore wooden shoes (klompen)when working in the fields or walking along the roads. Though the land and the climate were disagreeable, the silt that formed the delta of the Rhine River was so rich that crops grew in luxurious abundance during the warmer portion of the year. When the Frieslanders entered their houses, they removed the wooden shoes and put on woolen slippers.

The Frieslanders were a handsome race, taller than other Dutchmen who lived in the south. They were blond or had reddish hair and generally had a florid complexion. The traditional dress for women was very impressive: a full apron, wide lace collar and on her head she wore an "oorkjker" which was a close fitting head band from which dangled precious stones. In the middle 1600s Dutch women were not seen in public without a covered head. Thus when women gathered in public, the glittering helmets were a dazzling sight. Over this helmet they often wore a straw bonnet.

The men wore ballooning Dutch pantaloons, and white full sleeved shirts. When they went out of their house, they wore a black coat with ruffled collar. Square toed black shoes with silver buckles and a flat topped tapering round Dutch hat with a wide brim completed their outfit.

Each farmer's home was built so that it encompassed the barn where the cows were kept. Holland, even in the fifteen hundreds, when our story begins, was well known for its fine dairy products and cheeses. Having the cow shed attached to the house made it easy for the farmer to feed and milk the cows in the cold harsh winters. Each cow's stall was fitted to a window. The cow was in its stall facing the window so it could have light and look out on the countryside. Because the cow's udder was facing inward, it was easy for the milkmaid to milk the cows. Each cow's window was fitted with window curtains, just as were the windows inside the living area.

Whether the house was a farm house with stalls for the cows or a town house in the many little towns that were placed at intervals along the canals, the center of activity in the main living area was the great fire place which covered one wall of the living room and which also contained a bed. The Dutch did not build their fire-places outside and attach them to the house as did the English. Instead, the Dutch fireplace was one full wall with the chimney extending up from the wall and over part of the roof. To this wall were attached iron mountings on which large iron kettles were hung and into this wall the brick oven was installed.

The Frieslanders, as did all of the Dutch, kept their houses spotless. Everything in the house was scrubbed and washed daily till it shown like the sun. The front stoop was also scrubbed daily as was the walk. Cleanliness was next to godliness to the Frieslanders, and they practiced it fastidiously.

Being the delta of the great Rhine River, the land was very flat and crisscrossed with dikes and canals which served the purpose of carrying the excess water from the fields to the ocean. Windmills dotted the countryside as they were used for both pumping the water from the fields into the canals and to turn the mills that ground grain into flour. Trimmed trees were used for decorative purposes. Few were over twenty feet tall because the giant storms that blew in from the North Sea uprooted taller trees.

Each town lay on the banks of a canal and was composed of a church (Groote Kerk), city hall, and brick buildings dating back to the 12th century. The homes in the town were built in the traditional way described earlier, with the center of activity being the full wall hearth. Most had a second story loft and the roofs were thatched. Everything in the town , including the streets, was kept spotless by the efforts of the town's housewives. Thus, the countryside was a thing of beauty with little villages, dikes, canals and green fields. Many of the fields were dotted with black and white cows. To this add the many windmills for an additional bit of charm. This was Friesland as our story begins.

The canals were used to get from one town to the other. Canal boats were very popular. These were propelled by a long pole which the boater pushed against the bottom of the canal. In the winter the canals froze solid and the means of going from one place to another was by ice skating. Every man, woman and child was an expert skater. It was the principal form of recreation during the long winter months. Ice skate racing and games played on the ice in the canals was the favorite sport of the Frieslanders.

In the 1500s, the Spanish Netherlands was attempting to break away from Spanish rule. We begin our story with the birth of Epke Luuese, born in 1569. He married Sil Cornelisda at around the turn of the century and lived his entire life in Minnertsga with his family estate, Jelgeroma, nearby. Because he owned land, he had the hereditary right to vote in the Landdag which was established in approximately 1588 as the legislative assembly of the new Dutch republic.

Surnames were not used in Friesland at this time. Instead it was common to use the name of the father followed by s, se, sen or son, which meant "son of" as a second name to differentiate between those with the same first name. Epke Luuese therefore meant Epke, son of Luue.

Epke Luuese and his wife Sil had five sons. His youngest son, Jacob Epkese, whom we will follow in this story, sold his inheritance as did his three other brothers to the second oldest child, Cornelius. Though Jacob was un-landed from the inheritance from his father, he solved this political problem by marrying a landed wife, Reytske Sickedr, who acquired property at the plantation at Bonte through her own family inheritance. Jacob Epkese signed his name "Jacob Epkese te Bonte," which means Jacob Epkese at Bonte. Because of his marriage he was landed and entitled to vote in the Landdag.

Jacob and Reytske had only one son, Epke. When Reytske died sometime prior to 1652, her estate was sold to her family and she left her cash estate to her husband Jacob and her son Epke. Epke's share was held in trust as late as February, 1656.

Epke Jacobse was born in 1619 and married Sitske Dircksda in 1650. Because Epke was not landed, as his mother's estate had been sold back to her family, he became a miller in Minnertsga as his trade to support his family. The couple had five sons in the next seven years. In order to support this large family without his inheritance, which was still held in trust by his father, he was forced to go deeply into debt.

Epke had also become embroiled with the law for an offense that we today would find hard to believe in a country that professed religious freedom. He was arrested and fined for having a papist priest in his house to baptize his third son, Hendrick. Though the country permitted religious freedom, the war with the Catholic King Phillip of Spain was still fresh in the memory of the Dutch nation. Since the end of the war with Spain, Catholic

France had driven the Calvinist Huguenots from its borders into Holland, fanning the flames of religious bigotry.

Thus when his inheritance was released from trust in 1657, Epke had been in trouble with the law for having a Papist priest baptize his child and was deeply in debt. He was ripe to look westward for a new start in the Dutch West Indies Company's colony on the North American continent.

One day at the local inn, the center of the social life for the little town of Minnertsga, Epke found the men in a discussion about the new colony of New Netherland being established by the Dutch West Indies Company. One of the men had brought a brochure advertizing for colonists for this new colony.

New Netherland was not a colony of Holland. It was the product of a stock company established by the Estates General of the Netherlands. Its purpose was to produce a profit for its stockholders. While it was chartered by the Estates General, the Dutch legislative body which was subject to their High Mightinesses, the King and Queen of Orange, the company administered the colony with all the authority of a monarch. Its colonists did not enjoy all the civil liberties of citizens in Holland, who at that time in history, led the world in freedom of the individual.

In the New Netherland, there was no representative government as there was in Holland. The company appointed the governor and vice governor. The governor was answerable only to the Dutch West Indies Company

The facts that the citizens of Holland had ample employment available and that their enlightened rights such as freedom of religion were guaranteed, resulted in slow growth for the colony. There was little reason for the people of Holland to undertake the long and hazardous sea voyage and the rigorous life of a colonist.

At the beginning of its existence, the company offered large land holdings to stockholders who agreed to colonize their holdings. These large land holders were called Patroons. They intended to work the land with indentured laborers. The indentured workers were like vassals under the feudal system that was dying out in

Europe, except that they would be freed from their indenture in a set number of years. Then they could obtain their own land and work for themselves.

This plan failed, of course, as very few could be recruited to work for the Patroon to make him rich. For this reason, after consulting with the Estates General, the company in September, 1638, issued a proclamation which marked the beginning of a new era. The right to hold land in free allodial proprietorship was thrown open to all potential colonists. The company offered the land at very attractive terms, with other inducements such as free transportation, and a house and a barn. Under this arrangement the colony began to grow and prosper.

The Netherlands claim to the colony was solid and rested upon the voyage of Henry Hudson, chartered and paid for by the Dutch East Indies Company in their search for a northern passage to the Far East. On this voyage, he sailed up the river subsequently named the Hudson river in his honor. He thought it might be the sought after northwest passage to the far East. When he arrived at fresh water he realized this was not the passage but the mouth of a large river. He, thereupon, claimed this newly discovered land for their High Mightinesses, the King and Queen of the Netherlands.

The English had two colonies on the North American continent, Virginia and New England. They had claimed the entire coast of North America but insisted that these two colonies maintain one hundred mile separation between themselves. In this one hundred mile coastal area, the Dutch West Indies Company established its colony, New Netherland. This was to lead to later disputes between the English and the Dutch.

Henry Hudson discovered the Hudson river in 1609. By 1623 the Company had delivered the first colonists to the new colony. There were but eighty colonists in this group who arrived on the Dutch ship **Goede Vrouw** (Pleasant Wife) in 1623. It took this small craft, whose keel length was but one-hundred feet, over seven weeks to make the journey across the Atlantic ocean. Since that time, the company tried hard to induce new colonists to New

Netherland, including distributing brochures such as the one Epke and his fellow villagers were discussing.

As the discussion progressed, Epke found himself thinking that this could be the answer to the dilemma of being in debt and the debt growing larger as he raised a growing family on a miller's wages. There was no possibility for him to become landed in Friesland as land was inherited and very expensive if bought outside of a family.

After he left the inn and went home, the matter was still on his mind so he broached the idea with his wife Sitske.

"Sitske," he said, "I love Friesland. I love the people with whom we have grown up. I love all the towns and cities and the beautiful countryside. This is my country and I am proud of it, but we have little chance for ourselves and our family of five children. My inheritance has just been released but it has been released too late. It will all go to satisfy my debtors. If one is un-landed here, there is no way to correct this defect. We as a family are simply nothing. I can't stand to think of raising my family under such conditions. My ancestors have always been landed and voted in the Landdag. I believe there is only one way out of this dilemma and that is to immigrate to the Dutch West Indies colony, New Netherland, on the North American continent. This would be a harsh and dangerous plan but I believe it is our only hope."

"There will be nothing lost in your making an inquiry," Sistke responded. "Why don't you go to Amsterdam and visit the company to find out what sort of terms they are offering to attract new colonists?"

Epke and Sistke prepared for his journey from Minnertsga to Amsterdam to talk to the officials of the Dutch West Indies Company so as to determine what they might be offered. He and Sistke immediately started making arrangements for this trip to Amsterdam which he would undertake in November of 1657.

When the time for the trip arrived, he bid goodby to Sitske and their five boys and took a canal boat to the port of Harlingen on the coast of Friesland from whence he boarded a ship to take him to the port of Amsterdam. Epke had been to the City of Amsterdam before but he was still amazed at how large the city was. He asked directions to the offices of the Dutch West Indies Company and found them with minimal effort.

Once inside the offices, he was directed to an area where several other men were seeking information about migrating to the New Netherland colony. The number was small, however, indicating that such a future was not sought after by many Dutchmen. In time he was granted an interview with one of the company officials.

The official was dressed as all Amsterdam businessmen dressed, with black knee britches, white stockings and black square toed shoes with large silver buckles. He wore a black suit coat over his ruffled shirt and had great powdered sideburns surrounding his ruddy Dutch face. He was smoking one of the long Dutch white clay pipes, puffing furiously on it and enveloping himself with the smoke.

"My family and I are interested in going to the New World," Epke said to the official.

"Beside you and your wife, how many are in your family? What are their ages and sexes?" The official asked.

"I have five boys," replied Epke. "Their ages range from five months old for the youngest to six years for the oldest."

"They are very young for the New World," the official said. "It would be far better if they were old enough to help you. You will need help in building your new life if you decide to go to the new colony and if we accept. Little boys, such as they, will take time from you and your wife and will be able to create nothing."

"Then you would advise against our going?"Epke responded.

New colonists were hard to find but the official knew he dare not impart this image to this new prospect. He must make his sale by not acting to eager and by making Epke want whatever offer he made him.

"Let's see what is available and where you might fit in," the official said rubbing his chin.

With this he went over to a table on which a large book lay. He opened the book and ran his finger down the pages as if looking for something. There were not many in Holland who wanted to go to this savage frontier and he had an interested one here. He wanted to recruit Epke and his family as colonists if he could find a place and a living for them. Suddenly his eyes brightened and he uttered an, "A-haa." His face broke out in a broad smile.

"How would you and your wife like to be inn keepers? We have an inn already built in Vlissingen (Flushing) which is in Queens County on Long Island. The present proprietor does not get along well with Governor Stuyvesant, the present company administrator of the colony. The Governor has made an offer to buy the proprietor's interest and the owner has agreed to sell. The Governor has asked for a staunch Frieslander to take over the operation of the inn. Long Island is just across the East River from New Amsterdam, the capital of our colony, New Netherland. It would be better if you had daughters over seven for this type of work but we have been using African slaves in the colony to help a family such as yours. Your wife and two African slaves would be able to operate the inn with no difficulties. What do you think?" the official queried.

"We would have no problem running an inn but I am a miller and was hoping that you might have need for one in my profession," Epke said. "I don't know about using slaves to operate an inn. I wouldn't feel proper about owning slaves."

"The company feels it is necessary to use slaves if we are to prosper in our attempt to colonize a new world," responded the official. "You will not own the slaves. The company will own them and we will loan them to you. Your wife could not handle all the duties without daughters old enough to do the chores. We do not need a miller. Our need is for an inn keeper. This is a prize offer. It will be snapped up quickly. If you are truly interested in starting a new life in the new world, take this opportunity now or it will be gone."

Epke's house in Minertsga

Epke put his hand to his chin and rubbed it in intense thought. This would be far better than to accept land and then clear it and till it by himself. He was not a farmer and he would receive no help from his children for many years.

"What are the terms if I accept this offer?" he asked.

"You must agree to operate the inn in Vlissingen for six years," the official answered. "After that you may leave to do what you like. You must remain a true Calvinist, as a member of the Dutch Reformed church. These are our primary conditions. You will operate the inn as your own business and be its proprietor. Our terms are that you will pay us 20% of our cost for the inn each year for the first six years then the inn will be yours. The business will be yours after you make the payments over the first six years."

Epke decided to say nothing about his run-in with the local authorities over his leanings towards the Catholic church. This sounded like an offer too good to refuse. He would start a new life with an inn waiting for him to run it in Vlissingen in the new Netherland.

"If I accept, when would we have to be ready to leave?" he asked.

"If you accept our offer, you and your family will board the Dutch ship "De Trouw" (The Faith) in Amsterdam on February 13, 1659, which is three months from now."

"I accept," Epke said.

Then, shall I have the documents prepared for our signatures?" inquired the official.

"Yes," said Epke, "and I will sign them."

After Epke signed the documents, the official kept one set and gave the other to him along with explicit instructions concerning his families boarding of the De Trouw on February 13.

"I am also giving you a letter of introduction to Governor Stuyvesant," said the company official. "He would like a good Dutchman operating the inn located there. When you get to New Amsterdam, contact him."

"It will be my pleasure," replied Epke. "He is also from Friesland and I greatly admire him."

Epke spent the night at an inn in Amsterdam.

After Epke had boarded the canal boat on his return trip home the next day, which would take him from the port of Harlingen to his home town of Minnertsga, buyer's remorse set in. Had he been sold a bill of goods by the company official? Why had he been so eager to agree to be the proprietor of an inn in a place he had never heard of? Was it because the official of the company had tricked him by telling him someone else would snap up the offer if he didn't take it immediately?

Sitske had merely agreed to have him look at the opportunities in the New Netherland. Now, he had to tell her he had committed her and the boys to six years of running an inn in some god-forsaken spot on some island off the coast of North America. How would she react to such news? Up ahead, he could see the steeple of the church in Minnerstsga in the distance. Soon he would be there.

Now he found himself disembarking the canal boat and walking to his front door. He opened it and there was Sitske in front of the great Dutch hearth, standing on the floor she had scrubbed til it shown like sun. The boys were playing except for five month old Wiert who was in his crib. Now he had to tell her.

"Sitske, I think I have made a mistake that will ruin our whole life," he blurted out. " I have committed us to going to the Dutch West Indies Company's colony of New Netherland. I have signed-up our family as proprietors of an inn in the town of Vlissingen on an island of the coast of North America called Long Island. I put my signature on the document. There is no honorable way out of what I have done." He then showed Siske the copy of the documents he had signed, the boarding instructions and the letter of introduction· to Governor Stuyvesant.

Epke's windmill has been moved from Minertsga and restored

Sitske's face turned white and she put her hand against the hearth to brace herself. She had not expected this. She had been merely toying with the matter and had thought of it only as a romantic daydream.

"Papa, tell me what happened in detail. What is this you are telling me?" Sitske pleaded.

Epke related the story of his meeting with the company official and every detail of what had happened. Sitske sat down at the table and motioned for Epke to pull up a chair and sit down also. Then they began to analyze the deal he had made with the Dutch West Indies Company with all its pros and cons. They discussed it during dinner and as they put the boys to bed. They discussed the matter well into the night. As the discussion went on, both became less frightened and more enthusiastic about running an inn in this town named Vlissingen on this island named Long Island.

Finally, Sitske said, "I think you have made a prudent deal. This is far better than attempting to start our own bowery (farm) in the new country. That would have been impossible all by yourself. Yes, this makes sense. We will take over operation of the inn and we will have two Africans to help us run it. It is done and we will make it work. You say that the ship will leave Amsterdam on the 13th of February. We have much to do to get ready."

The next three months sped by. The canals froze over and ice skating became the means of transportation and recreation. Epke continued his work as miller but dreams of his life in the new world took over his mind and he thought of little else. Other friends admired Epke and Sitske's courage but questioned their judgement to go to such a godforsaken place as the colony of New Netherland.

Their days were spent preparing for the long ocean voyage and packing all their precious belongings that they had acquired in the seven years of their marriage. The clothing, linen, blankets and other software were packed in great trunks between the breakable things which were carefully wrapped. The heavy kitchen pots and utensils were kept away from the breakables. They carefully wrapped the silver, china, pewter dishes, bowls and other precious items so that they would be as safe as possible during their lengthy journey. When the packing was completed, they had four great trunks with all their earthly belongings that they would transport to their new home in the wilderness. They expected that these things would be hard to come by on the frontier of a new continent.

As the departure date drew near, Epke made arrangements to hire a driver with a freight sled and two horses to carry his family and their goods to the Friesland port of Harlingen. It had a large flat bed to carry his family, the four great trunks and the furniture they were to take with them. From Harlingen they would take a ship to Amsterdam to board the ship "De Trouw" (The Faith) for their voyage across the Atlantic Ocean to the colony of New Netherland.

As the time passed before their departure, Epke found himself absorbing in vivid detail the countryside he knew so well. This was his home and had been the home of his father and grandfather. It had been the home of numberless generations before them though he did not know their names. All had grown and lived in an area within one days walking distance. He had never thought of living anywhere else and thought his boys would grow up where their family had existed for many centuries.

His eyes drank in every detail and his soul memorized them so that he could remember the land of his birth to the day he died. His little boys would not remember but he would tell them about the land of their birth so that they would know this wonderful land of beautiful spring days and terrible winter storms and how it looked in each season of the year. He would tell them of the great dikes, the canals that drained the land and carried the water to the ocean, about the beautiful little towns that dotted the countryside always alongside a canal, the windmills, the canal boats, the green fields in spring with the black and white cows in the pastures eating the spring grass, the great fun in winter ice skating to where ever you wanted to go and all the winter fun playing games on the frozen canals with all his friends. He tried to cement in his mind all the things that he loved so much about this land so that he could vividly recall them for his own thoughts and to tell his sons about the land of their birth.

Most of all he thought of Siske's and his many lifelong friends that they would be leaving behind. As the number of days to departure shortened in number, these lifelong friendships became more precious and the thought of leaving them behind became harder to bear. There were many parties and much visiting always with the discussion of their great journey the foremost topic of conversation. The other men envied him and his great adventure that lay ahead. It was something that they would daydream about but Epke and his family were actually going to do it.

The day of departure arrived and the sled driver had his sled at their front door before dawn at six in the morning. The date was February 12, 1659 and their ship from Amsterdam to the new world left at one in the afternoon the following day. It was a typical winter's day in Friesland. The wind was blustery and the snow was lightly falling.

Sitske and he had been up late the night before making last minute preparations. Now they and the driver loaded all their earthly belongings that they were to take to the new country on the sled. Their neighbors arose early to help them and to wish them God's help for a safe voyage across the great Atlantic Ocean.

As the light of dawn shown through the storm clouds, the driver slapped the horses flanks with the reins. The sled moved ahead and Epke and his family moved away from Minnerstga forever as they began their great adventure heading for Vlissingen, on Long Island in the New world.

The journey from Minnerstga to the port of Harlingen, where they loaded their possessions onto a ship to cross the Zyder Zee to Amsterdam, was cold with snow covering the blankets of Epke, Sistke and the five boys by the time they reached Harlingen but otherwise was uneventful. The voyage from Harlingen to Amsterdam was their first day of sailing, something that would fill all their days for the next seven weeks.

They arrived in Amsterdam in the early afternoon and had their belongings transferred to the dock where the ship "De Trouw" lay at anchor. Epke, Sistke and the boys went to an inn close to the dock to spend the night. The official of the Dutch West Indies Company had instructed Epke to be at the dock by seven in the morning of February 13, with his family to have his belongings loaded aboard the sailing ship. At nine, they and the other passengers would be lined up and read the provisional orders of the Dutch West Indies Company. Then they would board the ship and find their bunks. The ship would weigh anchor and be under way at two o'clock in the afternoon.

When they arrived at the dock the following morning, Epke's whole family looked with awe upon the ship that would be their home for the next six to eight weeks. It was the largest ship they had ever seen. 170 feet in length, it had a 49 foot beam, two decks, a high stern and low bow. It had three masts and a long bow sprint to take the greatest advantage of the winds. They were told that their captain would be Captain Jan Bestever. The passage cost Epke 159 Florins for his wife, five sons and himself.

Events of the day of departure went just as the official who had induced Epke to sign up had described. As they lined up on the dock to be read the provisional orders, they fell into discussions with many of their fellow passengers with whom they were going to spend the next seven weeks in very crowded quarters. There were many children among the group of emigrants.

Epke found that the men were of every occupation and from every area of Holland with some from Denmark. He met a baker, a tailor, a glazier, a shoemaker, a mason and farmers and laborers. Every occupation a new colony needed seemed to be among the group. Many men had their wives and children with them while some women were traveling with their children to meet their husbands who were already in the New Netherland. The company was doing a good job in recruiting trades essential to a new colony in a primitive land, Epke thought.

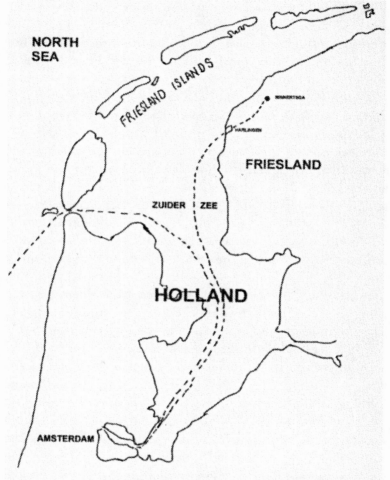

NORTH SEA

FRIESLAND ISLANDS

FRIESLAND

ZUIDER ZEE

HOLLAND

AMSTERDAM

THE JACOBSE FAMILY LEAVES FRIESLAND, FEBRUARY, 1659

As they found their bunks and did their best to make their crowded quarters livable with the few things they carried aboard with them, they could see the sailors busy getting the sailing ship ready to weigh anchor. At exactly two in the afternoon, the sailing ship moved from its moorings and started its treacherous winter's voyage across the Atlantic ocean.

The ship would take a southerly course to avoid the worst weather. Its first stop would be the Canary Islands. The first day out and under sail was through the southern part of the North Sea and the ocean swells were very heavy. All but a few on board were so sea-sick that they feared that they would never live to see the Canary Islands. But sea sickness never kills. It just makes persons feel that dying would be a relief to get them out of their misery. So they lived on and as the ship moved southerly through the English Channel the seas quieted and all but a few recovered their health. Soon most were out of their bunks and on the deck even though it was cold and raining.

The Canary Island port of call was a welcome relief from the crowded quarters on the De Trouw. Almost everyone left the ship to stretch their legs and they found that the land seemed to be rocking for they still had their sea legs. The stop at the Canary Islands was a short one and soon they were on the second and longest leg of the trip.

From the Canary Islands, the De Trouw sailed across the great Atlantic to the West Indies. The days seemed endless in such cramped quarters. The perishable food in the hold of the ship had to be eaten first so that their diet became more monotonous as the voyage progressed. As the days went by, Epke and Siske were strained by the sameness of each day while the boys seemed to enjoy it immensely. They loved to watch the sailors as they went about their work raising and lowering the sails on the three masts, climbing the rigging and a myriad of other exciting tasks.

It took almost four weeks to cross the Atlantic to the West Indies. After a short stop at one of the islands to replenish the water supply, the De Trouw steered a course toward the mainland of Virginia and then northward to the port of New Amsterdam, the capital of the Dutch West Indies Company colony of New Netherland.

As the ship sailed up the Hudson River between Staten Island

and Long Island the passengers caught sight of the tip of Manhattan Island and New Amsterdam. They could see the fort and inside the fort the church, a giant windmill and houses mostly built of wood but some of brick. One built of brick appeared to be three stories high. Beyond the city lay green fields just sprouting in the early spring with wooded hills and dales. The fort lay where the two rivers converged at the tip of Manhattan Island. As soon as the people in the fort saw the De Trouw, a flag was raised on the fort's tall flagstaff. The passengers offered up a fervent prayer, thanking God they had completed a safe voyage, avoiding calm, contrary winds, serious storms and capture by Barbary pirates.

Everyone on board was on deck to see the very small city. As small as it was, the sight of the church tower and the giant windmill plus the houses that looked just like the ones in Holland except that they were mainly made of wood buoyed the spirits of all on board. They had arrived at their new home in the New Netherland.

Epke's oldest son, Cornelius, was six years old, while Seba, next oldest, was five. Of the five boys, they alone would remembered their life in Friesland and their trip across the Atlantic to their new home on Long Island. Hendrick, who was four, later couldn't quite recall whether he remembered the voyage or only thought he remember it because of the many times the story was retold by Epke in the new world. Dirk, who was two, remembered nothing of the old world or the voyage. Wiert was only nine months old.

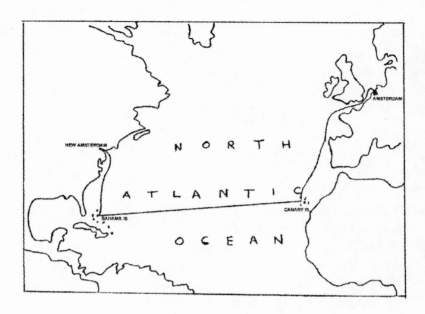

VOYAGE OF THE "DE TROUW,"
FEBRUARY - APRIL, 1659

CHAPTER 2

THE NEW WORLD

Thus begins the portion of this historical novel dedicated to the individuals of the frontier. They are the central characters with their lives and their efforts woven around the great events of history. This is the story of one line of one family who lived and died through ten generations, nine of which were always on the frontier and moving ever westward as the frontier moved westward. It is the story of what motivated this line of this family in search of an ever elusive goal. A goal they felt was more important than the safety offered in a established community. Generation after generation, they choose the dangers of a new frontier over the peace and security of their established home towns.

Our first hero is Epke Jacobse, who left his home in Minertsga, Friesland, and arrived in New Netherland in April of 1659, with his wife and five boys, all under six years of age. He and his sons were the progenitors of one of the largest Holland Dutch families in the United States.

While we will follow but one family line of Epke's progeny in our story, there could be more than seventy thousand variations of this story, as there are now more than that number of descendants of Epke Jacobs, male and female. Later, his sons adopted the name Banta as their surname in honor of their grandfather who signed his name Jacob Epkese te Bonte.

Our story restricts itself to one line from this family that sailed from the cold and storm-swept estuary of the Rhine River in Holland to land in New Amsterdam in April 1659. Through eight generations they pushed ever forward beyond the western frontier until T. P. Banta, of the eighth generation, and his family became one of the first four families to settle in the arid Colorado Desert, sixty miles from the Pacific Ocean in the year 1901. This was the estuary of the mighty Colorado River and contrary to the estuary of the Rhine, was the most God-forsaken desolate desert imaginable. Through many trials and tribulations, T. P. and his family worked and watched as this desolate desert grew into the fabulously productive Imperial Valley, the last frontier in the contiguous United States

T. P. and his family arrived at the very hot and dry Colorado Desert in what was then San Diego County bordering the mighty Pacific ocean, in 1901. This was two-hundred and forty four years after Epke Jacobse migrated from the cold and damp estuary of the Rhine River in Holland. This is the story of one family's journey across a new continent over those two hundred and forty-two years. Always on the frontier, they had participated in conquering the continent over nine generations.

CHAPTER 3

NEW AMSTERDAM

When Epke, and his family, arrived in the New Netherland at the port of New Amsterdam in April, 1659, the city's population was approximately twelve hundred colonists, while the entire population of New Netherland was less than eight thousand.

The ship arrived on a Monday in the early morning and it was a beautiful but chilly spring day. The weather was perfect. The sun shone brightly and made the river and city sparkle. Epke had his family dressed in their finest clothes in anticipation of meeting Governor Stuyvesant. They were not allowed to go on shore until all passengers' goods were transported to a public warehouse for inspection. This was done at the leisure of the officious inspectors. The family had packed and transported their valuable as well as necessary worldly goods in four large trunks and had also brought pieces of furniture. After a period of time an inspector examined their traveling chests and furniture and informed Epke the amount of the duties, which he paid.

The entire Capital of New Amsterdam lay between what is now Wall Street and the tip of Manhattan Island which was a distance of less than one half mile. Wall Street was a fortified revetment composed of logs standing on end across the width of the southern tip of Manhattan Island. This wall formed a defense for the small village from the Indian menace. The wall contained two gates through which those outside the wall could enter behind the safety it provided when those intermittent squalls with the native Americans made such action prudent.

Epke had all his goods transported from the West Indies Company warehouse to Egbert Van Borsum's inn where he made arrangements for his family to spend the night. The inn's owner operated the ferry across the East river to Long Island. Egbert had his inn constructed over his ferry boat slip in 1655. The carpenters who had constructed his inn were the same ones who had constructed the inn that Epke was to operate. The inn had cost Egbert 550 guilders, "one third in beavers, one third in good merchantable wampum (Indian money which consisted of small beads made by hand by the Indians on the coast of Long Island from oyster shells and was accepted as money by all in New Netherland.), one third in good silver coin, and free passage over the ferry so long as work continues, and small beer to be drunk during work." This gave Epke an idea of what the inn in Vlissingen must have cost the company and what he would have to repay in the next six years.

The Jacobse family finished with the customs officer late Monday morning and Epke's first desire was to go to the governor's palace and present his letter of introduction to Governor Stuyvesant. The city's main structure was the earthen fort. Inside the fort and on the outermost wall towards the river stood a giant windmill. The city's population could tell the coming weather by the sails of the windmill. If they were unfurled, the weather would be pleasant. If they were taken in, a storm could be expected.

Next to the windmill was the very high flagstaff on which the flag was raised when a ship was sighted coming up the river from the ocean. The church had been built within the fort with a double gabled roof between which stood the square church steeple. On the river side were the gallows and whipping-post. On the other side of the church stood the Governor's house. A very attractive tavern stood on the farthest point. A row of well-built dwelling houses were between the fort and the tavern. The warehouses of the West Indies Company stood out clearly among these houses. The customs house was in these warehouses.

Within the walls of the city, between Wall Street and the fort, were the houses built by many of the city's inhabitants. Only one street was paved and it, as well as the unpaved streets, was filthy with refuse thrown out by the housewives. The houses themselves and their stoops were kept immaculate but the streets were filthy.

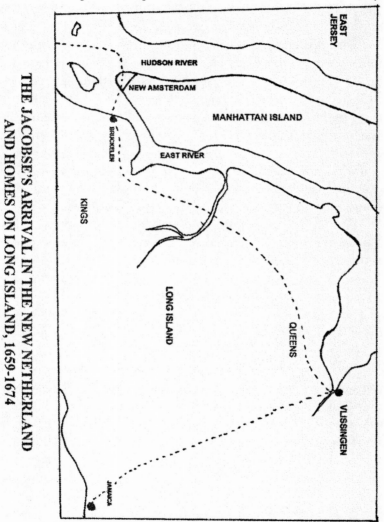

THE JACOBSE'S ARRIVAL IN THE NEW NETHERLAND AND HOMES ON LONG ISLAND, 1659-1674

Epke and his family walked from the custom house to the Governor's house but were told that the Governor didn't care for that house and had built himself a lovely stone house outside the fort which he named "Whitehall." Whitehall was a great stone house on the edge of the river where the governor had constructed a wharf of wood with a wall above to keep his property safe from the river. On the river he had a dock built where he kept his barge of state. His home was surrounded by lovely gardens full of shrubs and beds where flowers would grow as spring progressed.

Epke led his family up the path toward the double-layered Dutch front door. He immediately recognized Governor Stuyvesant sitting on his typical Dutch front porch smoking his long clay pipe. Even if he had not seen his famous wooden leg encased in silver, he would have known him for he was both elegant and fierce at the same moment. Epke could see the strength of his character just by his size and the way he held himself. He was a magnificent model of a Frieslander. His shoulders were so broad that it appeared he could pick up a bull by the horns and hold him straight over his head.

He was dressed elegantly in the traditional dress of the Dutch gentleman. He wore a magnificent Dutch coat, while around his large neck he wore a white ruffled collar which stood straight out. Over his shoulder was a wide belt which hung down to his side like a sash and to which his scabbard and sword were attached. One leg of his wide pantaloons went down to his knee and there entered a red stocking that descended to a black square-toed Dutch shoe with a magnificent square silver buckle. The left leg of his pantaloons reached down to his silver encased wooden leg. He had lost his leg on the battlefield and the wooden leg only added to his mystique.

As Epke and his family approached the governor, he took the long pipe from his mouth and bellowed, "Who is this coming up my path to my door!"

His voice sounded as if it were coming from the bottom of a barrel and frightened the boys to such an extent that Cornelius, Seba, Hendrick and Dirck all hid behind their parents' clothing, hiding their faces in their mother's dress and their father's pantaloons. Even little Wiert stiffened in his mother's arms.

"I am Epke Jacobse and this is my wife Siske. These are my five sons. I am a fellow Frieslander and have a letter of introduction from the Dutch West Indies Company," Epke replied. With this he handed the letter of introduction to Governor Stuyvesant.

With the mention of the company's letter and his native land, Peter's face softened and his voice though still loud became friendly. The governor read the letter and then said, "Tell me about my homeland. How I miss my friends and country. I have been governor here for twelve years and miss the canals, dikes and fields and my old friends."

Epke and the governor established a bond as they discussed their homeland. Peter acknowledged Sitske and welcomed the boys who by now were greatly intrigued by this larger than life, tough, lionhearted governor. His friendliness with the boys showed them that he was kindly as well as tough and weatherbeaten.

After their conversation about home the governor said to Epke, "Come into my fore room and have a bit of lunch while I tell you why I asked to have a good Dutchman sent over here to take over the inn at Vlissengen."

Epke, Sitske and the boys followed the Director General into the "voorhuis" or fore room of his fine home. His fore room was very elegant and elaborate. Clean white sand was swirled on the bleached wood floor in the manner of the Dutch. The room was beautifully appointed with a large walnut table and matching low backed chairs except for the chair at the head of the table which was high backed with arms. The seat of each chair was upholstered with red plush. In addition there were six high and low-backed chairs whose seats were covered with green plush appropriately placed around the room accompanied by two smaller tables, one of cherry wood and the other, Java mahogany. Along the wall were two great wardrobes and two Dutch china cabinets, one filled with porcelain and another displaying objects of silver. On the walls were several picture-sized frames containing the Governor's appointment as Director General of the New Netherland, his family's coat of arms and other honors he had received from their High Mightynesses, the King and Queen of Orange and the Estates

General. On the wall behind the great table was a large mirror framed by crystal borders. Three tall but slim leaded glass windows allowed light into the room. On these windows were beautiful white lace curtains.

Epke was thrilled by the magnificence of these furnishings that made this a room fit for the Director General of the New Netherland. He was deeply honored to be having lunch with the Director General and was happy he had insisted that all his family be dressed in their best clothes.

The Governor summoned his African housekeeper to prepare a table laden with pastries of pork and capon along with salads and all the baked goods loved by the Dutch. He then asked her to mind and feed the boys while he talked to Epke and Sitske. All three sat down at the table and filled their plates with delectables of their choice.

"Vlissingen," Governor Stuyvesant continued as they sat around the table, "is about ten miles beyond the East River on Long Island in what we refer to as Queens County. Queens County is almost completely inhabited by towns made up of English colonists. Many of them have come here to escape religious problems in England and in the New England colony. Even though we have had a great deal of controversy with the Governor of Connecticut over sovereignty of Long Island, I feel we will hold the loyalty of our English colonists because they despise the government of the New England colonies more than they dislike being under the laws of the New Netherland.

"Connecticut claimed sovereignty over Long Island but through compromise, we signed a treaty at Hartford. Connecticut has sovereignty over the eastern part of Long Island beyond a dividing line going south from Oyster Bay. The Dutch West Indies Company has sovereignty over the part that lies west of Oyster Bay. This bay is twenty miles further east than Vlissingen. The Indians are friendly but we have had some mischief from Connecticut renegades and the inhabitants of our own English villages. I do not trust the English.

"One year before my coming here as Governor, my predecessor, Governor Kieft chartered the City of Vlissingen to a group of English who had lived in Holland before coming here. They have sworn allegiance to their High Mightynesses, the King and Queen of Orange. However, by race the people of Vlissingen are English and, of late, things have been happening that make me suspicious of their loyalty. Recently a sect of English called Quakers have infiltrated the settlement. The Quakers came from the English colony of New England where the Puritans had driven them out. I do not trust these Quakers as their religion is heretical, they take no allegiance and are pacifists. Here on a new continent with both the Indians and the English threatening, I need courageous men who will stand behind our government and organized Christian religions with ordained ministers. These Quakers treat with contempt all political and ecclesiastic authority and undermine the foundations of all government and religion. They are an abominable sect who vilify both political magistrates and ministers of God."

"If these Quakers have been driven out by the English, how do they represent a political danger to the New Netherland?" Epke asked. "They would surely choose Holland over the English."

Governor Stuyvesant pounded his fist heavily on the table as his wooden leg stamped on the floor. "They are a heretical and lawless sect that accepts neither the authority of church or government and can bring nothing but God's wrath on our state," thundered the Governor.

Epke realized that he must avoid this subject for this was not a matter that one could discuss with the governor in a civil manner.

"Let me tell you the trouble that has just last year taken place in the village of Vlissingen and why I need a loyal Dutchman to be proprietor of the only inn in Queens County," continued the governor. "I issued an order which was posted in all the towns inhabited by English colonists in Queens County that everyone must cease from giving continence to Quakers and that the names of those who profess or preach doctrines of the heretical sect be sent to me.

"Upon the posting of this order, I received information that a Henry Townsend was holding secret Quaker conventicles in Vlissingen. He was arrested and fined eight pounds. In answer to this, a remonstrance was drafted by Vlissingen's elected clerk, Edward Clark, delivered to me by Tobias Feeks, elected sheriff, and which had been signed by thirty principal inhabitants of Vlissingen including two elected magistrates, Edward Farrington and William Noble. This remonstrance was seditious in that it called into question the Governor's authority to protect the Colony from this trouble-making sect. It is my belief that all thirty of the signatories are members of the sect and that all their secret meetings and conventicles are seditious.

"I have tried in every way to provide them with an ordained minister of their own protestant belief but they refuse to pay his salary and so he won't stay. In the absence of a good shepherd, they have fallen into the grasp of this heretical sect. After they were found guilty of writing and delivering this seditious remonstrance and I talked individually to the sheriff, clerk and magistrates, all humbly apologized for their impertinence. None the less, I humbled the town by adding seven tribunes to the municipal authority who must agree with all town actions before they are acted upon.

"This is why I asked that you be sent to Vlissingen as a true patriot of Holland to take over as inn keeper. As you know, the inn is the most important institution in a small village like Vlissingen. It is where the civic government holds its meetings and the most respectable members of the town, including its officials spend much of their time in friendly discussion. Its previous proprietor was English. You will be the company's eyes and ears for any seditious talk. As you know, the inn is the center of social life in such a village."

Suddenly, Epke realized why he was being given such a fine welcome by the Director General. "You mean that I and my fam-

ily are to be spies?" Epke said in alarm. "I am to be the lone Dutchman in an English settlement! This is not at all what we expected."

"No." said the Governor. "You misunderstood what I have
said. I do not expect you to spy. The inn is the center of social life
and all I ask is that you keep your ears open for any seditious talk
or the harboring of Quakers by the townspeople. We have promised them that they will be allowed freedom of Christian religion.
By that we mean established religions not heretical sects.

"Because this is an English village, the closest Low Dutch Reformed Church is by the ferry landing in Bruckelen. There are
some Dutchmen living in Vlissingen and many Dutch boweries
on the road outside the town, plus the New Netherland poor bowery
is just west of Vlissingen Creek, the town's west boundary. All of
Queens County for the most part is settled by people of the English race while Kings County to the west is settled mainly by our
own countrymen. We have need for a good Dutchman to run the
inn and tavern in Vlissingen."

Epke was taken aback. He knew that the West Indies Company was recruiting colonists of other nationalities but he had no
idea he would be living in an English speaking town as what he
considered being a spy for the company. In addition, he didn't
speak or understand one word of English.

"Your honor," he responded, "I had no idea that we were being placed in an English-speaking town with English traditions.
This is a shock to me and my family. We are Dutchmen and love
the Dutch ways."

"Don't worry," said the governor, "Our Friesland language is
the closest language to English. That is why I asked the company
to send me a Frieslander. You will quickly learn English. There are
ample Dutchmen in the area and the tavern will have Dutch customs for you will be running it and you will set the traditions. The
inn and tavern is the center of social life and I need you and your
wife as the inn keepers. The inn is already in operation and two
African women are already working at the inn. They both speak
English and a little Dutch."

Epke and Siske left their meeting with the governor shaken with queasy feelings in their stomachs. They were in a new land and had nowhere else to turn. They had no alternative but to continue on to Vlissingen with their five boys. Epke and his family walked around the small town of New Amsterdam thinking thoughts to themselves but saying nothing so as not to disturb the boys.

Nighttime came early in April in New Amsterdam and soon it was time to go to the inn over the ferry boat dock. They needed a good night's sleep because tomorrow they would start their journey to Vlissingen.

When the boys were asleep, Epke whispered to Sitske, "We must get along with our English neighbors. If they are to be our customers we can not spy on them and report their activities to Governor Stuyvesant. What we hear must go in one ear and out the other."

"You are correct," Sitske responded. "We will run the inn and not be informers. We must remain Dutch and not let our boys turn into little Englishmen but the English inhabitants have their rights to feel secure in their own town. What I heard from Governor Stuyvesant did not sound seditious but simply a difference in religious conscience. Let's get to sleep for we have much to do tomorrow."

CHAPTER 4

VLISSINGEN (Flushing), LONG ISLAND

Epke assembled his family the next morning to cross the East river for his destination of the small settlement of Vlissingen on Long Island. After breakfast, the family went to the shore of the East river and boarded, along with their belongings, a row boat which served as the ferry boat that carried a sail for good weather and tide. They had been told by New Amsterdam residents that it was possible to travel by water to Vlissingen but that only one boatsman would make the trip and that in a canoe barely large enough for three passengers. Few traveled by water because the water route passed through an area called "Hells Gate" where the tides and the river caused the ocean to be so rough that the crashing of the waves made a monestrous roar and most felt the currents were far too dangerous. For this reason, most travelers took the ferry to Bruckelen and from there traveled by land to the village.

After crossing the East River they arrived in the village of Bruckelen and upon paying the boatman, they rented two wagons to carry them and their goods to the settlement of Vlissingen. There were three wagon trails leading from Bruckelen onto Long Island and the northern trail was the one they took for it led to the village.

Long Island is a long flat island 1and 1/2 mile wide at its widest point and 18 miles long at its longest. Bluffs along its rugged north shore rise to hills several hundred feet high in its center and then gently slope down to broad sandy beaches on its south side. In 1659, most of the island was covered with forests containing many native trees. It was Spring time and the trees and underbrush were leafing out after the cold winter days. The boys were enchanted to see wild turkeys, deer, moose and elk running or flying through the half naked woods that were just starting to sprout their new spring leaves as the cart startled them for these native animals were numerous on the island.

Vlissingen was a pretty little village on the north side of Long Island about eleven miles from New Amsterdam. Vlissingen itself was laid out in a large meadow on which new spring grass had just erupted from the soil after the snow that covered it during the winter months had melted. The people of Vlissingen were justly proud of the ancient oaks that grew in the meadow and in the forests surrounding the city. These were the most prominent natural phenomenon a traveler saw as one entered the village. Two giant oaks whose trunks, four feet above the ground, had a circumference of over eighteen feet, stood in the pasture just behind the village

As the wagon carrying Epke, Sitske and the boys crossed Vlissingen Creek, the western boundary of the village, they saw these giant oaks on the inland side of the town and the Long Island Sound on its northern side. In between, about forty one-story homes had been built, all in the Dutch custom, with the fireplace chimney arising through the roof at one end and a wall of stone on that same end of the house with the large brick oven covered with plaster protruding from it. At the very western most point of the town, stood a large two story building that they knew must be the inn and tavern of which they were going to to be the proprietors.

The driver of the cart delivered Epke, Sitske and the boys to the front door of the inn and helped them carry their belongings from the cart into the tavern. The two African women were inside the inn and had everything in perfect order. Everything had been scrubbed and polished. There were quite a few of the townspeople at the tables waiting to greet the new owners. The shoute (sheriff),who was standing with the two African women, introduced

Epke and Sitske to himself and the two Africans, speaking in English. When Epke told him in Dutch that he did not understand English, the shoute immediately spoke to him in Dutch.

"There is no problem if you do not speak English. Many of us lived in Holland before we came here and learned Dutch while we were there. Since this is a Dutch colony, all of us speak enough Dutch to get by." The sheriff responded. "What I said in English was that I am John Mastine, Vlissingen's sheriff and have been looking after the inn in your absence along with your two African servants. This is Maria on my right and Liza on my left. With their aid, I have been operating the inn until you arrived. As you can see, they are well trained and have kept the inn spotless. All the town knows them and with their help you will have no trouble stepping in as Vlissingen's inn keepers."

"Let me introduce you to those present," the schout continued. "Most of us are English but some are your fellow Dutchmen and a few of us are French Huguenots. Though our personal social lives may differ, we all come to the inn for entertainment." He then introduced Epke and Sitske to the dozen or more men who were present. "You will get to know all of us in short order for almost all villagers and the farmers from the bowries surrounding Vlissingen come here regularly."

As he was saying this, the other townspeople began entering the inn to meet the new proprietors. Three men entered together and the sheriff stopped introductions of those present to introduce these three newcomers. "These," said the sheriff, "are our distinguished magistrates, William Nobel, William Lawrence and Edward Farrington." As Epke shook hands and passed pleasantries with the three men, he recognized that William Lawrence and Edward Farrington were the two magistrates who had signed the remonstrance that had so angered Governor Stuyvesant.

"It looks like the sheriff has been replaced," he thought, "but these two are still in the Governor's good graces. I wonder how the town clerk, Edward Hart, fared." As he was thinking this another man hurried into the inn. John promptly introduced him to Epke.

"This is our town clerk, Edward Hart," he continued. "Now you have met all of our town's officials."

"I guess he also made it," he thought as he visited with Edward.

The day and evening turned into a work day for Epke and Sitske as everyone in town was interested in getting acquainted with the new innkeepers. Their things remained packed until the inn closed for the night. Sitske spent most of the time looking after the boys and preparing their beds for they needed rest after the arduous day's journey and the excitement that surrounded them in their new living quarters.

After all the guests had left at 9:00 P. M. and the travelers who were staying for the night retired, Maria and Liza did the chores of cleaning up while Epke and Sitske unpacked the three trunks, placing their soft goods in a large oak cabinet and their precious china and pewter along the shelf which surrounded the great tavern room. They moved their furniture into their quarters. They were so excited with their new village, neighbors, Liza and Maria and the inn that they knew they wouldn't be able to sleep, so they stayed up until three in the morning fussing with unpacking. Lisa and Maria said they would get up early and get the travelers' breakfast ready in time for their departure. They knew the hardest day is the first day in any new endeavor. It was now over and they fell asleep as soon as they climbed into bed and slept soundly in the inn and village where they planned to spend the rest of their lives.

During the spring, as the soil warmed up and could be tilled, the farmers sowed the fields with wheat and other grains. As spring turned into summer, the trees and bushes became a gorgeous green forest and the fields filled with crops while all the villagers sweated in the hot humid weather. They visited the inn for liquid refreshment to enjoy themselves after a hard day's work. The city officials met at the inn for their business meetings every two weeks and Epke and Sitske became well acquainted with them. All the villagers became their friends and customers. They developed a close personal relationship with the small group of Dutch and

Huguenot families who usually sat at the same tables and formed their own small social group.

They realized how blessed they were to have such fine helpers as Maria and Liza. They both had become part of the family, eating at the table with the family and becoming second mothers to the boys. The inn was flourishing and was the center of entertainment for the village and surrounding areas.

In Fall a new concern faced Epke and Sitske. Cornelius was seven and should be starting school but there was no Dutch school available. They realized that going to an English school would destroy their Dutch ethnicity and customs leaving them between two cultures. They had come to the New Netherland because it was a Dutch colony and found themselves in an English community because of circumstances beyond their control. They checked with the other Dutch families in the area and were told that none were sending their children to the English school. They decided they would let the matter slide and worry about the boys education at a later time. Cornelius stayed at home and helped around the inn.

The Dutch and the French Huguenots felt that they had the superior culture while the English felt just as strongly that theirs was best. Both groups had warm feelings towards the other and they got along just fine but there was little socializing between families of the two groups. Because Vlissingen was in the colony of the New Netherland, both groups realized that the English were foreigners in a Dutch colony while the Dutch were at home.

In order to keep their Dutchness, Epke and Sitske took the boys to church in Bruckelen as often as they could. The closest Low Dutch Reformed Church was there and it was seventeen miles from Vlissengen. The road while maintained was often in such poor condition due to rain and snow that they could attend only occasionally and did not belong as regular members. They tried to make up to the boys for this by having Epke read daily to his family from the bible.

Fall was also harvest time and the farmers were busy harvesting their crops and threshing the wheat. Another yearly custom of the Indians was also taking place called brush burning. When the leaves had fallen from the trees and the underbrush was dead or dying, the Indians would set fire to the brush to burn away the undergrowth. They did this for three reasons. First, It made hunting easier and eliminated their stepping on the dead brush which caused cracking sounds that scared away the wild game. Second, it cleared away the dead brush so that the underbrush would grow better the next year. Third, The fires circled the game, which was then easier taken and the game that was not taken during the fires was easier to track over the ashes.

During this brush burning, the fires would light up the night sky until you could see easily by the light and it was a spectacular sight which thrilled the Jacobse family new to such an experience. After the brush burning, the Indians offered quarters of moose, elk and deer to the settlers for ridiculously low prices. Epke stocked up for the table of the inn with as much meat as he could keep before it would spoil

As the boys learned the new customs of the Indians and the English, Epke and Sitske made sure that they also remembered the traditions of their Dutch culture. Each night before they went to sleep, they told them stories of what it was like in Friesland. They described the fields, canals, the windmills, the little villages, the various seasons of the year, the ice skating in winter on the canals and everything else about the old country until all five of the boys believed they remembered Holland from their own memories, even little Weart who was less than a year old when they came to New Netherland. They also enjoyed visiting with the small group of Dutch families in the area so that the boys could get a feeling for a Dutch family living in a Dutch home. Because the boys were being raised in an inn, without these visits they would have no way to know what the life of a Dutch family was like in its own private home.

In addition, as the seasons rolled by, they kept each of the festivals and traditional holidays that were part of Dutch life.

December fifth was the feast day of Saint Nicholas and the boys put their shoes out by the great hearth so that the good saint could fill them with goodies and small toys.

As winter came, the farmers had much to do in repairing equipment, making saddles and halters, shoes for their families and a myriad of other frontier family chores. Nonetheless they had much more leisure time to spend at the inn. Even though a fire was constantly roaring in the great hearth, the inn was very cold and everyone bundled up as they visited their friends and played the games common to Dutch and English inns. During the winter months, Epke , Sitske, Maria and Liza were kept busier than during the other three seasons.

Christmas and the New Year were celebrated at the inn in the the Dutch tradition which was fine with the Englishmen since they had become accustomed to the Dutch way of keeping these holidays when they were living in Holland.

When Spring finally arrived, the Jacobses invited the town to help them celebrate their first anniversary as proprietors of the Vlissingen Inn. By now, they were no longer new to the job or the village. They had been accepted by the townspeople and they had grown to love the village. As the family moved into the year 1660, Epke and Sitske knew they had made a good choice. The English, having lived in Holland before coming to Vlissingen, had acquired many of the Dutch customs, and though the Jacobses would have preferred to live in a Dutch town, they found their neighbors to be both friendly and accepting.

At Easter they continued the Dutch custom of exchanging colored eggs, a custom the English had brought from Holland when they came to the New Netherland. In May, the May Day festivities with the May pole and other activities were similar in Holland and England and were celebrated with much eating and drinking and a myriad of games. All these holidays were excellent for the business at the inn.

As the Spring of 1660 turned into Summer, Summer into Fall and Fall into Winter, Epke and Sitske knew that they had made the right choice in coming to the New Netherland. The inn had become a very prosperous and popular enterprise and though the work was hard and the hours long, these were the happiest days of their lives.

In April, Sitske became pregnant with their sixth child. All the family hoped the new baby would be a girl to bring a feminine touch among the children as they grew up. In January, the time for the birth had come and when Sitske began having contractions, the village mid-wife was called to assist in the birth. The birth was breach and though the mid-wife tried every technique she knew to realign the baby in Sitske's womb nothing could be done. The birth was long and agonizing. When the baby was finally delivered, it was a little girl and she was stillborn. Sitske was terribly spent and cried herself to sleep while Epke held her in his arms comforting her.

She had lost a great deal of blood and in a short while was burning up with fever and slipped into a coma. Epke, the boys, Maria and Liza surrounded her bed while they tried to reduce her fever with wet cloths. Sitske opened her eyes and for a moment her mind cleared. She motioned for Epke to come close so that he could hear her soft voice through her heavy breathing. Epke did as he was bid while telling her how much he and the boys loved and needed her.

"Hush, Epke," Sitske said. "I know that I'm dying and I have something that is of the greatest importance to me that I must tell you. It's about the boys. You know that we came here to find a new life in a new land but we are Dutch and we thought that we would be in a Dutch community. I want you to promise me that you will raise our boys to be fine Dutchmen. It would be so easy for them to become little Englishmen being raised as they will be in an English town without the guidance of a Dutch mother. Give me your word that you will keep them Dutch in language, religion and customs. They and you are in my last thoughts and their future is my greatest distress."

"Sitske, my beloved wife, I promise you that your wish will be fulfilled for that is also my desire. They will be raised in the Dutch ways."

With this promise in her ears, Sitske drifted back into a coma and within a few minutes ceased breathing. All eyes were filled with tears. Even little Weart who was only two years old understood the sadness and finality of the moment. Epke was inconsolable. Breaking into sobs, he leaned over and held his dead wife in his arms.

Maria, standing behind him said with a voice full of emotion, "Don't worry Mr. Epke, Liza and I will help you raise the boys. We love them as if they were our own. We can run the inn and be like second mothers to them. There's no way Mrs. Sitske can be brought back or replaced but we'll do our best to raise the boys as little Dutch gentlemen as she wanted."

These words were a great comfort to Epke, who in addition to the terrible tragedy of losing his life partner, was a widower with five small sons aged two to eight with the incredible task of raising them as good Dutchmen while running an inn in an English village. From that day forward, Maria and Liza not only helped Epke in the tasks of running the inn but also helped raise the five boys. Their close friends among the few Dutch families in the area became even closer to Epke and the boys.

Epke buried Sitske and his baby daughter under one of the great oaks that stood on his property.

After the death of Sitske, the life at the inn and in the village of Vlissingen continued in its same pattern but the lives of Epke and the boys were forever changed. Epke had no partner with whom he could share his successes and failures. The boys had lost an important part of their lives, for most learning about ethnic roots and customs occurs in a mother's lap or at her knees. Epke quite successfully played both the role of father and mother to his five sons and both Maria and Liza showered them with love and attention but life changed for all of them. No one can say how this family's life would have been altered if she had lived. We only can relate how their lives unfolded in a motherless family.

In 1661, John Bowne, a local farmer, constructed a new house in the village for his wife and family. John was a sturdy Englishman with great strength of character. The village looked up to him as a man who would battle for his convictions. Epke came to know John and his family well and considered them good friends and customers of the inn.

Because of Governor Stuyvesant's distrust and hatred of the Quakers, posters had been placed throughout Queens County which forbade anyone from harboring a Quaker in their house or permitting their house to be used as a meeting place for Quaker services. For this reason, Quaker meetings were held secretly in the woods. John's wife had joined the Society of Friends and, out of curiosity, John started attending these meetings. He felt strongly that a person must follow his conscience and that the order by Governor Stuyvesant was improper and immoral. Therefore, he invited the Quakers to meet in his house.

The town of Vlissingen closed its eyes to this breach of the Governor's orders for the villagers secretly agreed with John. Epke discreetly ignored his knowledge of what was going on in John Bowne's house. He knew that many inhabitants of Vlissingen were Quakers and he knew them to be honest God fearing people. However, the magistrates of Jamaica, the English town just south of Vlissingen in Queens County, learned that John's house had become a conventicle for Quakers of all the surrounding villages in Queens County. They reported this information to the Governor.

Director General Stuyvesant immediately sent his sheriff to John's house to arrest him and to bring him back to New Amsterdam for trial. When the sheriff arrived at the Bowne house, he found John at home caring for his wife and two children who had taken sick and were confined to bed. He informed John that he must accompany him back to New Amsterdam on orders of the Governor.

"My wife and children are sick," he told the sheriff. "How much time will you allow me to prepare for the journey?"

"You've as much time," the sheriff replied, "as it takes me to go over to the inn and drink a couple of beers."

With this, the sheriff walked over to the inn, identified himself and asked Epke to pour him a beer.

"What brings you to our village?" Epke asked.

"I'm here," the sheriff replied, "to take John Bowne To New Amsterdam to stand trial for having Quaker meetings in his house."

"That's strange," Epke said, "I knew nothing about such goings on. How did you hear of it?"

"The magistrates from Jamaica reported it to Director General Stuyvesant," the sheriff answered. "What the Governor can't understand is why he didn't hear of it from you. This occurred right in your village almost next door to the inn. How could you not have known about it?"

"I'm a Dutchman in an English village," Epke answered. "My relationship with the English villagers is a business relationship. My boys don't go to their schools so they would hear nothing of such things. I have no idea of what is happening in the homes of the English for all my relationships outside the inn are with Dutch and Huguenot families. This is their place of entertainment and we have very cordial relationships but we are not involved in their personal lives. The Governor must understand this for he told me I was not to be a spy but simply keep my ears open to what takes place in the inn."

"I will report your answer to the Director General," the sheriff said. "Bring me another beer and then I must be on my way."

After drinking the second beer, the sheriff returned to the Bowne house where John was packed and ready to be escorted to New Amsterdam. John saddled his horse, mounted it, and the two rode off together across the bridge which took them over Vlissingen Creek on the road to Bruckelen.

John Bowne's house still stands in Flushing, Long Island

The arrest of John Bowne was the talk of the village and a constant topic of conversation in the inn. Sheriff Mastine and magistrates Nobell and Hallet went regularly to New Amsterdam and returned with news of how Bowne was faring. First, they reported that John had been fined twenty five pounds, Flemish, and threatened with banishment. That, it seemed would be his punishment and the end of it. Within days they were reporting that he had refused to pay the fine and was being imprisoned until he did.

As the weeks went by, it was apparent that John had no intention of paying the fine, and it became an embarrassment to the Governor. After three months of this standoff, the sheriff reported that the Director General informed him that "for the welfare of the community" Bowne would be transported "in the first ship to ready to sail" if he continued to show contempt for the court's orders. Bowne was not about to give in and, therefore he was sent to Holland on the Gilded Fox on the ninth of February, 1663.

It was obvious from the conversations in the inn that almost all the villagers sided with John. Epke was careful not to express himself either way but secretly admired and agreed with John for standing up for freedom of conscience. The English in New England, he thought, showed a complete lack of religious freedom and drove these Quakers to Vlissingen, but an Englishmen in Vlissingen was teaching the good Governor a lesson in tolerance.

While this test of wills was being conducted between John Bowne and Governor Stuyvesant, matters of great consequence were facing the New Netherland from New England. The English colony was disavowing the Treaty of Hartford under which the dispute of land on Long Island was put aside "until a full and final determination be agreed upon in Europe, by the mutual consent of the two states of England and Holland." Holland advised the Director General that there was no hope of resolving the dispute in Europe.

Governor Stuyvesant was in a very weak condition as compared to the might of the New England colonies. Therefore , they continued to send agents to the English towns in Queens in order to stir things up and cause a rebellion by the English against the New Netherland. The Director General went to Connecticut to see if he could defuse the dispute. Because he held a weak hand and the English colonies knew this, they insisted that Long Island was English territory and that the Dutch had invaded it and had no claim. The Governor returned to New Amsterdam dejected, with nothing accomplished.

Meanwhile, Epke could see from the conversations in the inn that the agents from Connecticut were accomplishing their goal and that some English in Queens County were becoming disturbed and leaning towards the their arguments. A petition was passed among the English inhabitants of the villages of Jamaica, Middleburgh and Hemstead in Queens County and signed by some of those who lived there "To cast over us scurts of your government and protection." This petition was sent to Hartford. From the conversations he heard in the inn he could tell that the Englishmen who signed the petition were a small minority of all Englishmen in Queens County. Most preferred the autocratic

Dutch government to the even more intolerant Connecticut government.

Peter Stuyvesant sent a delegation to Hartford in a last ditch effort to save Queens County for New Netherland. The Connecticut government gave Peter an ultimatum that New Netherland must give up Westchester and give the English towns of Queens County quasi-independence. Under the ultimatum, Connecticut would exercise no authority over them if Stuyvesant refrained from coercing them.

Disorders in the English villages forced the Director General to accept the ultimatum. Epke was shocked at the Governors action. He was unaware of the weakness of the Governor's position. It was either that he must accept what was offered or lose all authority over Queens County to Connecticut.

In addition to all his political and military problems, Peter received a severe rebuke from the West Indies Company concerning the John Bowne affair. John Bowne had stated his case to its directors and they released him and sent Peter a letter censuring him for the actions he took in that matter. This stung the old patriot who thought he was following their wishes to the letter. Their letter stated in part;

Although it is our cordial desire that similar and other sectarians may not be found there, yet as the contrary seems to be the fact, we doubt very much whether vigorous proceedings against them ought not to be discontinued; unless, indeed, you intend to check and destroy your population, which in the youth of its existence, ought rather to be encouraged by all possible means . . . The conscience of men ought to remain free and unshackled. Let everyone remain free, as long as he is modest, moderate, his political conduct remains irreproachable, and as long as he does not offend others or oppose the government.

The contents of this letter was soon spread among the English in Queens County much to the embarrassment of Peter. Epke thought it would do much to defuse the antagonism against the Dutch government that had been induced by the arrest of John

Bowne. Much to his distress, he discovered by listening to the conversations in the inn that it only made the English more discontented from having no representation in the government. After all, they argued, the colony was a company and companies are completely autocratic and have to answer to no one but their directors. This rebuke to the Governor while resolving the Bowne matter brought to the forefront the fact that inhabitants of the colony had no representation in the government. This became the hot political issue.

Two Englishmen, Anthony Waters of Hempstead and John Coe, A miller at Middleburgh, came to Vlissingen and other English town in Queens County with a force of one hundred men. Here, they declared the county belonged to the King of England, removed the elected magistrates and appointed their own. They even renamed the towns. As an example Vlissingen became Newarke. Thus the villages in Queens were in a quasi independent position. Many of these villagers were opposed to English control and hastened to form a "combination" of free villages.

Epke was astonished by what was happening and realized that all Dutchness was about to exit his village.

A new English adventurer named John Scott came upon the scene with a letter from the King's Committee on Foreign Plantations which recommended him to the protection of the New England governors. Connecticut sent him to Long Island to bring the Queens County towns under its authority. Most of the Englishmen there had fled New England and dreaded this resolution of the situation. For them, it was out of the frying pan into the fire. Adventurer John Scott recognized they preferred independence under their "combination." He assisted them in forming the "combination" and was elected as its President "until his Royal Highness the Duke of York, or his Majesty, should establish a government among them." The English towns tried without success to get the Dutch towns in Kings County to join them.

Governor Stuyvesant rushed a delegation to Vlissingen, now

renamed Newarke, to confer with Scott and it was agreed to let the old order continue for the present. Peter Stuyvesant went personally to Vlissingen in March with a military escort to meet with John Scott and the town's new delegates elected under the "combination." They met in the inn for these discussions and Epke was amazed at the ability of the old Director General in his debate with those who held four aces in their hands while he didn't even have a pair in his. The final agreement was that the English towns should stay under English rule for twelve months or until the matter was resolved in Europe while the Dutch towns should remain under their High Mightinesses, the King and Queen of Orange.

Connecticut was furious with Scott for they realized he had used them to feather his own nest. In their eyes he was a traitor. Therefore in June, Epke's inn had as distinguished guests, John Winthop Jr., Governor of Connecticut, along with his deputies. He summarily replaced the magistrates appointed by Scott with his own, retaining William Hallet and William Nobel but replacing John Townsend with one of his own choosing.

Epke and his inn were in the very center of exciting events that bothered him greatly. He had always felt that his English neighbors would be true to there oaths to their high Mightinesses. Now he found himself surrounded by a group of men he considered traitors. This, ever after, caused him to chaff under English authority. He had never considered being a subject of an English colony and now the Governor of Connecticut was appointing the magistrates of his town. His mind went to the last wish of Sitske that the boys be raised as little Dutchmen. She never could have foreseen the developing situation.

Then Peter Stuyvesant along with a retinue including Secretary Van Ruyven and Burgomaster Courtlandt came to the village and held a meeting at the inn "to protest against such irregularity." Epke had never seen the Governor so upset. He shouted and slammed the table saying he would be guiltless of the bloodshed that would surely follow. He predicted great problems for the villages involved. His protest was to no avail and the villages continued their course. Epke was horrified at what he felt would be certain retaliation by New Netherland. He was distraught at the actions of those who had suckled at the teats of the West Indies colony under which they had grown fat and prosperous only to desert it at the first opportunity. These thoughts he had to keep to himself for the English villagers were still his customers.

Connecticut was furious with John Scott who they accused of "sedition, forgery and violation of solemn oath" and "sundry hainous crimes and practices." All civil authorities were admonished to arrest him. He was arrested and taken to the capitol of Connecticut where he stood trial. Vlissingen stood solidly behind him and a petition was circulated in the village and was sent to Hartford signed by one hundred and forty-four of its prominent villagers. This petition called attention of the court to the fact that Scott had acted with the backing of the village's citizens. Scott also sent "A humble petition to the court at Hartford." In this petition he was most contrite and pleaded with the court for mercy. Taking these petitions into account and desiring not to offend the citizens of Vlissingen, whom they were cultivating, the court released Scott.

Epke had been the innkeeper in Vlissingen for five years when Connecticut assumed authority from New Netherland. He felt sure this would only be temporary. He had heard Governor Stuyvasant assure that bloodshed would follow and he was torn between his country and his friends in the village. While he was caught in the middle of the two factions, new happenings in Europe were occurring that would eliminate the contentious atmosphere between Connecticut and New Netherland. On the 22nd of March, 1664, the English King awarded a patent for Long Island and most of the New Netherland to his brother, James, the Duke of York.

The Duke appointed Colonel Richard Nicholls governor of his province. He was also appointed commander of a fleet the English would dispatch to conquer the New Netherland from the Dutch. The English fleet surrounded New Amsterdam on the Eighth of September, 1664. Peter Stuyvesant had no army to compete with the fleet and, his next door neighbors, the New England colonies. While the lion-hearted Governor insisted that they should resist the English until all powder and shot was spent, his council could see no advantage in such a useless and costly venture. Twenty-five hard years had been spent building New Amsterdam and the English fleet could easily destroy much of it in hours and would ultimately capture the destroyed village. When his council refused to agree to firing on the English fleet, the old soldier fumed and raged, but the council held its ground. Without the agreement of his council to engage the English fleet, Peter had to capitulate without a shot being fired.

When Epke heard the news that New Netherland had fallen to the English and that he was now under the English flag, he was devastated. Now he was a foreigner in his own land. Now the English ways were the standard and he and the other Dutch families were aliens in an English colony. Surely Holland would send a fleet to liberate the colony from these foreigners. He was certain that if he were patient this terrible wrong would be righted.

The news was received by the English townsmen with rejoicing. This was the best of all outcomes they thought. They would not be under Connecticut nor New Netherland. They would be under a new government headed by James, the Duke of York. Peter Stuyvesant was out and had sailed for Holland to give an account to the Dutch West Indies Company as to what had transpired. The name Newarke was dropped and Vlissingen became Flushing. Flushing was now in the county of Yorkshire and the North Riding of Yorkshire County. Royalist Richard Nicholls was the new governor of New York and all awaited the new laws under which the colony would function.

In the agreement of capitulation signed by both Peter Stuyvesant and Richard Nicholls, the Duke of York agreed that under the new laws all titles to real estate held under the West Indies Company would be binding as well as all previous decisions of the Dutch courts. Thus, no one would be the worse for the change.

Governor Nicholls called an assembly of delegates from the villages consisting of its magistrates to meet in Hempstead in early 1665. Here a new code of laws known as the Dukes Laws was presented to the delegates. A new series of courts was set up. The governor would appoint the high sheriff over Yorkshire, the undersheriffs and justices of the peace. Each town would elect a constable and eight overseers for trial of cases not over five pounds. The Dukes Law did not establish the Church of England but each town was required to build a church and the minister must have received ordination from "either some Protestant Bishop or minister." under his Majesty or a king of a country whose church was of the Reformed Religion.

The delegates from the towns were delighted with the new laws and cordially agreed to them. When they returned to their villages, the townspeople were furious that they had made no protest to laws the people felt were unacceptable. Quakers would now be worse off than they would have been under the director's letter to Peter Stuyvesant and worst of all the new laws made no provisions for representative government. In this respect they were inferior to the laws of the West Indies Company which they were replacing.

With the return of the delegates from the assembly, the conversation in the inn turned against the new government and agreed that the laws of the West Indies Company were better than those they were now under. Epke realized that the English weren't opposed to Dutch rule but were truly for freedom of conscience and representative government. He listened to how the villagers criticized their own delegates and stood firmly behind their convictions.

July 3, 1667, Governor Nicholls came to Flushing with Captain Betts to inspect the local militia. The militiamen were assembled in the green in front of the inn. The Governor addressed the assembled troops and told them that he would furnish them with powder and would be content to receive firewood in exchange for it.

After this comment, Captain Betts heard a villager named William Bishop exclaim, "That there was another cunning trick." Captain Betts told Bishop that if he had something to say, he should say it to the Governor rather than muttering it to the crowd.

William Bishop then replied, "It is very like that he hath sent you here to harken to what we say, that you may tell him." To which Captain Betts replied, "It is not so, but since you think it so, I shall take further notice to what you said."

William then answered, "What have I said? I have said nothing but 'there is another cunning trick.'"

Epke shuddered when he heard his fellow villager's answer to a powerful officer such as Captain Betts in a similar manner to what was being said nightly in the inn. And he had reason to shudder for William Bishop was tried and sentenced in New York "to be made fast to the whipping post, there to stand, with rods fastened to his back, during the sitting of the court of the mayor and aldermen, and thence to be conveyed to the Common Goale [jail] till further order."

Other cases of disloyal speech or actions must have also been called to the Governor's attention for he ordered that a town meeting be assembled and required the following letter to be read at that meeting. The meeting was held on the village green. Epke listened intently to what the Governor had written which is quoted in part:

> I did very much wonder, and am not less troubled at your absurd returns which have given me just cause to call back my former favors to you and not to qualify you hereafter to receive from mee the civilityes truly intended. Now, because you have given me just reason to suspect your fidelities and your courage, at a season when a true Englishman is most zealous, and seeks the first occasion to serve the king and country. You are to expect all the scorne and disdain that lyes in my power against such mean spirited fellows.

He then listed the following orders which were to be enforced
by the local officials:

- Commissioned and non-commissioned officers were to be
  suspended.
- The colors presented to the company had to be returned.
- Twelve Matchlocks had to be returned to his Majesty's store
  at the fort.
- No one in the company could carry arms without a special
  permit from the governor.
- "None of the company which I saw stand in arms under his
  Majesty's colors (whose names are enclosed) shall presume,
  upon any private occasion, to resort to New York for three
  months, under penalty of being arrested as a spy, unless he
  first report to the officer of the guard in the fort, state his
  business, and the length of time he desires to stay."

The Governor had insulted and disgraced the entire village for
some of its inhabitants speaking their minds freely. Epke recognized that these men living on the frontier were like unbroken
horses never brought to saddle or halter. He had admired them for
standing up to Peter Stuyvesant when he had stepped on freedom
of conscience. At the time, he thought it was because they disliked
the Dutch government. Now he saw them stand up to Governor
Nicholls for what they believed. These Englishmen in Flushing
were a breed apart. They were unlike any other men he had ever
met. When they believed in something, they stood behind it. He
admired them but questioned their sanity.

They too must have wondered if they had gone to far for fourteen men whose name was on the list, sent a letter to the governor
stating that they were "ready to serve him on all occasions." One of
these was William Bishop. They must have realized that there were
no company directors to turn to and that it would be futile to
appeal to the Duke of York. The governor relented his orders to
the town and brought it back into his good graces since he said the
villagers had become "sensible of their late error." From this, Epke
was reminded that even wild horses could be broken.

In August, Governor Nicholls was relieved of his duties as governor and Colonel Francis Lovelace was appointed to the office. With the new governor, the villagers of Flushing again broached the subject of a representative form of government. This was foremost on their minds and agenda. Perhaps, they thought, Governor Lovelace would be less rigid and authoritarian than Nicholls. They presented a petition at the November Court of Assizes asking for privileges similar to those given his Majesty's subjects in other English colonies on the North American continent, "which privileges consist in advising about the approving of all such laws, with the Governor and his Council, as may be for the good and benefit of the commonwealth by such deputies as shall be yearly chosen by the freeholders of every town or parish." Lovelace did nothing about the petition or others sent by various Long Island villages.

In spite of the fact that the village had lost even the right to elect their own town officials and all request for any form of representative government was ignored, economic conditions in the town continued to improve and with prosperity came a certain dissatisfied contentment. Epke's inn flourished as the town grew. As year after year went by, Epke still hoped that Holland would again recapture the colony. His boys grew to be young men. They learned the Dutch ways from the Dutch families in the area but their education had been sadly restricted to a minimum because Epke refused to let them attend English schools. He believed that such an education would have been against Sitske's last wish and would have turned them into little Englishmen. Instead of school, they worked at the inn under the direction of Epke, Maria and Liza. They were good boys and tried very hard to please. Epke, Maria and Liza raised the boys in a home full of love and respect and they grew to be righteous and moral young men of whom Epke was justly proud.

As the decade of the 1660s closed and the decade of the 1670s emerged, Epke found himself wondering about his boys' future. They had no education and all they knew was how to operate an inn. What could he do to help them find trades by which they could support themselves and their future families? The inn was very prosperous but there was no way it could support five families. Many of the tasks they did around the inn each day were tasks that were normally done by women. He felt he had to help them find masculine trades or he would not be preforming the principal duty of a father. While in this mode of conjecture, he thought back to his days in Friesland when he had been a miller. Being a miller was a masculine trade and all the jobs around a mill were held by men. Perhaps, he thought, he should sell the inn and return to his former trade as a miller.

The matter of the children's future was a main topic of conversation among his Dutch neighbors. With the English conquest of the New Netherland, all the parents recognized that they were in a far different position. This was not part of their native land and theirs was not the native culture. Now they found themselves with uneducated children while the English had educated their children. Now the English ruled and their culture was taking over. Many fathers thought that the only answer was to go to the new frontier in New Jersey where land was available at reasonable costs.

The Duke of York had released the portion of New Netherland known as East Jersey to two lords, Lord Berkley and Lord Carteret, who had appointed their own governor, Phillip Carteret, brother of Lord Carteret. Thus, they would not be under Governor Nicholls and The Duke's law. In addition, these two lords had signed a document known as the "Concessions and Agreements" which gave guarantees of civil and religious liberties. It became known as the "Magna Charta" of New Jersey.

The Dutch families in Queens County had become quite wealthy and could sell their boweries or businesses at a handsome price. To many, the frontier held the best possibilities for there they could get out of this land of English villages and form Dutch communities away from the Duke's Laws. They argued with Epke about the futility of continuing in business in Queens County. Epke argued that the Dutch would not let the colony go without raising a hand. He felt certain that even with the time that had passed Holland had not given up on recapturing the colony. If he was wrong he could sell a mill and still move to land on the new frontier.

In purchasing flour and other ground cereals for the inn's supplies, Epke had met members of the Coe family who ran several mills in Queens County. He decided he would talk to them about purchasing one of their mills. He had told them many times about his being a miller in Holland. When Benjamine Coe heard of his interest in returning to being a miller, he suggested Epke look at his tidal mill alongside a mill pond and a stream just off a beach on the south side of the island. The mill was located in Jamaica and it had been built by the town of Jamaica with the agreement that Coe would grind all the town's cereals for the farmers in the surrounding area. A tidal mill takes a good bit of maintenance which had been neglected badly. He said he would sell his contract with the town to Epke at a very low price if Epke agreed to repair the mill and carry out his contract with the town.

Epke went to look at the mill taking his five sons with him. This was in December, 1671, and Epke was now fifty-two while Cornelius was eighteen, Seba seventeen, Hendrick sixteen, Dirk fourteen and Wiert thirteen. When they arrived at the mill they could see that much had to be done in repairs. The boys had grown to be tall, husky young men and they had much training in carpentry around the inn. Though the repairs to the machinery of the mill was different from any they had done before, it mainly consisted of carpentry work. Epke and his boys agreed that they could do the repair work themselves and that it would be good training in how a tidal mill operated. With this consensus, Epke worked out the details of the purchase with the town and Benjamin Coe.

The boys were excited about starting a new life in Jamaica rebuilding a tidal mill and becoming millers. Only Cornelius was concerned about leaving Vlissingen for at eighteen he was at an age where he was attracted to the young ladies of the village. Recently he had become romantically smitten by one young lady in particular, Jannettie de Pre, who was the daughter of a French Huguenot couple that were close friends of Epke's. Seba, Hendrick, Dirk and Wiert had no romantic ties and though they loved their village of Vlissingen, were anxious to go on this new adventure to Jamaica.

There was no problem selling the inn for the town had grown and the inn had prospered. The question from the potential buyer was whether he would retain the services of Maria and Liza since they knew all the arts of running a successful inn. This was an impossible decision for Epke. The boys had been raised by these two women in a loving and caring way. Epke decided the decision should be made by Maria and Lisa. They had always been a part of the business and of the family. Maria and Liza had heard the family talking about the boys' future and had talked the matter over between themselves. Epke asked the two women to sit down and discuss a matter that required their decision. He then explained that the new owner wanted them to stay and work at the inn. The boys would miss the two women that had raised them but they were now growing into men.

"Mr. Epke," Maria said, "we've been talking this over between ourselves and recognize there is little around a mill for us to do. We could keep your house but the boys will soon be off marrying. We know the work of the inn and would like to stay though we will miss the family terribly."

Epke accepted their decision though it pained him to part with what had become two members of his family. He completed the papers to free them and the new owner was delighted to hire them as free persons who were experts at inn keeping.

When the day arrived for departure of the family from the inn, Maria and Liza kissed the boys goodby as tears flowed from every eye. They hugged these young men who they had raised from babies and the parting couldn't have been more emotional between the boys and these two women if they had been their birth mothers.

"Remember," Epke said as he mounted one of the three wagons filled with the family's earthly goods, "If you are discontent for any reason, let me know for we are only five miles away and we will come and get you. We are close enough that we will be in constant touch."

The family's many friends in the village flocked around the wagons to bid goodbye to the family that had run their inn for the last twelve years and had become such an intimate part of Vlissingen's life. Among those bidding the family goodbye was Jannettie de Pre, the holder of Cornelius's heart strings. She came to the cart and reached up her petite hand to hold his as the two sweethearts bid good bye.

"Don't fret, Jannette," Cornelius said, "I'll be back to visit you every chance I get."

With this, the small wagon train set out on its journey to the tidal mill.

CHAPTER 5

JAMAICA, LONG ISLAND

Epke and the boys arrived in Jamaica in January, 1672, and moved into a house on the ten acres of salt meadows that the town had given Benjamin Coe along with the good dam they had built for the mill. It was a rather small house built for the miller employed by Coe but amply large for the six Bantas as they undertook the repair of the mill.

This was a time when the boys became men in Epke's eyes. They shouldered their responsibilities as equals and made a wonderful team. This was a time of family growth and solidarity. The mill was soon repaired and the house enlarged. The winter was the perfect time to repair the mill for next year's harvest without inconveniencing the local farmers.

Even with the harsh winter weather, Cornelius was regularly riding his horse to Vlissingen to visit Jannettie. The distance between their villages only made their meetings the sweeter. Everyone could see that Cornelius was seriously in love. Epke expected that in the Dutch custom Cornelius would soon be asking his permission to marry the lovely young lady.

As things settled down, the family felt at home in the house in Jamaica. They loved the privacy of a home after spending twelve years of family living in their private quarters which were part of a public inn. The six men became especially close by living together with the common object of repairing the mill and making it prosperous.

Other people in Jamaica were astonished that Epke had raised his five sons as a widower. On the frontier, it seemed economially essential for widows or widowers to remarry. The husband provided the living for the family while the wife worked from when she arose in the morning till she went to bed at night spinning, weaving and dying the cloth used for clothing, bedding and all other places where yardage was used, baking in the brick oven and cooking on the great hearth, spotlessly cleaning the house, gardening and feeding the livestock plus the myriad of other chores a frontier woman was obliged to endure. The people in Jamaica became entranced by this family of six men living without the aid and comfort of a sister, wife or mother.

Jamaica, as was Vlissingen, was a village primarily populated by the English. Epke had made many friends in Jamaica in his business dealings prior to moving his family there. Most of them were Dutch. Again, his family joined with his Dutch and Huguenot neighbors in social events. Most of these families were involved in organizing a Low Dutch Reformed church in the small village of New Utrecht near Bruckelen and attended meetings there regularly though the church building would not be built until 1677. Currently they met in a barn that had been converted into their place of worship. Epke felt that being so far from a Dutch Reformed church had impeded his boys religious training; therefore, he joined with his friends in Jamaica in making every effort to take the boys to church meetings every Sunday without exception.

This was not easy nor comfortable during the winter months for the distance was over seven miles often through the snow and the building was unheated. If it was below freezing outside the church, it was below freezing inside the church. Women brought live coals in footwarmers which were wooden boxes lined with a metal container. These boxes the size of a bread box had holes the size of a silver dollar cut into their tops which supplied enough oxygen to keep the coals burning and allowed heat to escape in an upward direction. The ladies placed their feet on these boxes and then placed their long skirts around the boxes forming a tent to warm their legs and buttoxes. The men dressed as warmly as possible and boldly suffered the cold while singing psalms as they followed the sexton's lining and listening to the minister preach in Dutch for several hours. The church and the Jacobse's social life now became one. The boys, as if starved of religious experience, became devoutly religious and closely involved in organizing the new church.

By July 1672, they had completed most of the work on repairing the mill and had added an extra suite onto the house. Epke said he was adding the suite so that he could have some privacy but his real reason was to have a place for Cornelius and Jannettie when Cornelius asked his permission to marry. Epke couldn't imagine the family breaking up and hoped that Jannettie would agree to such a arrangement. The mill was doing some grinding of last years crops for the local farmers and would be ready for the new crops coming in the fall.

It had been almost eight years since the English had demanded the surrender of New Netherland and old Peter Stuyvesant had been obliged to comply. Epke Still believed that the their High Mightinesses and the Estates General of Holland would retake the colony and the dreaded Duke's Laws would be replaced by the Dutch government. Most other Dutchmen had given up this belief and Epke's was beginning to waver. Holland and England were now at war, and he felt that if it were to ever happen it would be during the war.

July 28, 1672, twelve Dutch men of war sailed into New York bay and demanded the surrender of the colony. English Governor Lovelace, who had taken over from Governor Nicholls, found himself in the same position Peter had been in eight years earlier. He and his troops could not stand up to such a force and to do so would cripple the city and the colony; therefore just as Peter had done, he surrendered New York back to the Dutch. The news traveled to Jamaica within hours.

More news quickly followed that Holland had taken over the colony under the Estates General and that the Dutch West Indies Company no longer controlled its future. The colony's new name was New Orange and its new governor was Governor Cove, a

Dutchman. The Duke's Law was out and new Dutch laws were established. As when the English assumed power, all rights to property were undisturbed by the change in government. Everyone was ecstatic, even the English for they also chaffed under The Duke's Law. Epke felt vindicated in his continued belief in his native land and the family went about the business of milling the local farmers crops with new enthusiasm.

During 1673, the Jacobses cheerfully worked at their trade as millers and the boys learned their jobs quickly under their father's tutelage. Epke had made the right choice by staying on Long Island, he thought, for it was now under the King and Queen of Orange. Though he lived in an English village, the colony was again under the rule of his own country and he was not a foreigner obliged to live under the English Duke's Laws.

His euphoria was short-lived, for word reached the colony in early 1674 that the Dutch Estates General had traded the colony of New Orange with England in exchange for certain concessions in the East Indies under the treaty ending the Dutch English war. The treaty had been signed February 19, 1674.

Epke and the boys were furious and felt they had been betrayed by their homeland. How could they induce Dutchmen to come to this frontier and build a new country and then when it was built trade it to the English for favors in other parts of the world? The homeland looked at it strictly from a business viewpoint. The colony was not as valuable an asset as the concessions they received in the East Indies which was their primary profit center. The English, on the other hand, had invested much in North America and the acquisition of this middle colony completed their plan for controlling the entire coast of North America to the southern boundary of their Virginia colony. The trade was advantageous to both countries and under such conditions in this age of commerce, business was business.

The die was cast and England had won Epke's colony. The Duke's Laws were again in effect and there was no representation of the colonists in the Duke's government. Epke and his Dutch friends could talk of nothing else than how to get out of New York and once again become part of a Dutch community. The only way they could see was to move to New Jersey where Lord Proprietors Berkeley and Carteret were again in control of the colony and their Concessions and Agreements that guaranteed civil and religious liberties under republican principles were still in effect. They had appointed Sir Edmund Andros as the new governor and he was encouraging Dutch settlers to come to New Jersey. Epke, along with many other Dutch and Huguenot families, was strongly considering doing just that.

Epke's spirits were low as he recognized that he would be obliged to once again move his family if he was to keep his promise to Sitske to raise the boys as Dutchmen. At this low point in his life, his spirits were buoyed by Cornelius's romance with Jannettie blossoming into a commitment to marry. Epke was elated when Cornelius came to him and asked his permission to marry. When Epke enthusiastically agreed to the marriage, Cornelius left immediately to ask Jannettie's parents for her hand. When they also agreed, preparations for the wedding began immediately. Jannettie's family also were involved in the organizing of the Low Dutch Reformed Church in New Utretch and the Du Pre's decided that this is where the wedding would take place.

After the marriage, Epke carefully approached the subject of the couple's moving into the new suite he had added onto the house. He was delighted when they agreed that this would be an ideal situation for the short term. Jannettie was not apprehensive of the fact that she would be the only female in a house full of men; for she recognized that they had taken care of the household by themselves for almost two years since they had left Vlissingen, and she found the house in spotless condition.

The wedding with all the Dutch customs and trappings took place in the fall of the year and the new couple set up housekeeping in the new suite Epke had added on to the house. Jannettie fit in with the family beautifully, and the village thought of the Jacobse family as including her. Though they had been amazed at this family of six men functioning as a family unit, they were delighted to see the touch of a woman in the house.

Epke started seriously looking at the advantages of moving to New Jersey. There, he thought, the boys could become landed gentlemen because .land was available at such reasonable costs on this new frontier. This would be even better than having his boys follow a trade. He had noticed that those pioneers who had acquired land on Long Island fared far better than those who had been tradesmen. He sent Cornelius over to the New Jersey village of Bergen which was an entirely Dutch and French Huguenot community. It had been established by Peter Stuyvesant in 1660 just inland from the coast of New Jersey which lay directly across from New York. Cornelius returned with a glowing report.

His oldest son, Cornelius, was now twenty-two and married to Jannettie, while Seba was twenty, Hendrick was nineteen, Derick was eighteen and Weart was seventeen.

CHAPTER 6

NEW JERSEY

How The Village of Bergen Came into Being

During the period of time that the area west of the Hudson River, now know as New Jersey, had been under the Dutch West Indies Company, its primary settlement was by patroonship. Large tracts of land had been given to patroons who had made promises to the company to populate these tracts with colonists. Because profits would enure to the patroon rather than the colonist, the patroons found it difficult to fulfill their quotas of colonists. Nonetheless, large areas along New Jerseys waterways were populated under the grants to patroons. Colonization of the area was proceeding at a slow but a steady pace.

The Indians in the area, who were from the Lenni-Lenape nation, were peaceful and saw the advantage of trading with the European colonists. They sold their land to the Dutch for trinkets but both sides were content with the arrangement. Under the Dutch West Indies Company, it was a standard procedure to purchase land from the Sachem or Chief in the area who in this area was Chief Oratam. (1577-1667) These were the same Indians who occupied Manhattan and sold it to Peter Minuet. With a few isolated incidents, the Indians and colonists existed side by side in peace though the two cultures were vastly different in customs and in the way they settled differences. The white man's law was an enigma to the Indians who were far less organized in such matters and who punished wrongdoing by their own customs. Thus, under the reign of Governor Kieft, who immediately preceded Peter Stuyvesant, a matter arose that put the two systems of justice at odds with each other.

The incident that started the Dutch-Indian war in the area west of the Hudson River is related in an excerpt from the diary of Captain David DeVries who had established two plantations between the Hudson and Hackensack Rivers in 1640.

> In passing through the woods toward Ackensack I met an Indian who said the whites had sold him brandy mixed with water and stolen his beaverskin coat. He said he was going home for his bow and arrows and would shoot the roguish Swanekins (Dutchmen). He shot Garret Jansen Van Vorst who was roofing a house at Achter Kul (Newark). The chiefs offered to pay Van Vorst's widow two hundred fathoms of wampum to purchase peace, but Kieft would accept nothing but the surrender of the murderer. The chiefs would not agree to that, since the Indian was the son of a chief.

Kieft's demands on Chief Oratam of the Lenni-Lenape nation to turn the young brave over to the colony to be tried under Dutch law was thus refused. The chief offered to pay reparation to keep the peace but refused to turn the brave over to Kieft. Prior to this event, Kieft had ordered the Lenni-Lenape to pay a tax to the Dutch West Indies Company which they had refused to do. At the same time the Lenni-Lenape were paying a tribute to the Mohawk nation for protection, as the Lenni-Lenape greatly feared the fierce Mohawk.

These two events caused Governor Kieft to do an unthinkable thing. He reasoned that the Lenni-Lenape must fear the Dutch just as they feared the Mohawk. He, therefore, sent his troops across to the western side of the Hudson River to where New Jersey now lies. These troops fell upon three sleeping and unsuspecting Indian villages and killed every man, woman and child in each village. The Indians became so incensed that they in turn fell upon the colonists' plantations along the waterways of what is now New

Jersey where they killed all the men who could not escape and took their women and children captive. Kieft's cruel action caused all colonists who could escape to the east side of the Hudson River to flee to New Amsterdam and all colonization ended on the west side of the Hudson River.

Governor Kieft had many failings but this terrible act caused the colonists of New Netherland to write to the directors of the Dutch West Indies Company and demand the replacement of Kieft. Governor Stuyvesant, Kieft's replacement, through thoughtful negotiations with Chief Oratam, reestablished relations with the Lenni-Lenape and ended the war. It was a tenuous peace, however, and when the colonists wanted to go back to their farms and homes on the west bank of the Hudson and new colonists wanted to go there also, Peter permitted them to do so but under very cautious terms.

Peter was extremely paternal in his administration of the colony and insisted that the colonists not live on farms separated from each other. Instead they must live in a village protected by a wooden palisade of logs standing on end like the one that protected the village of New Amsterdam. Because the village they would occupy would not be on the tip of an island as was New Amsterdam, the wall would surround the village on all four sides and have four gates, one on each side, for entrance and egress. All villagers would live within or just outside these walls and tend their fields surrounding the village during the day while returning to their protected homes at night. They were to enter inside the barred gates when squalls with the Indians seemed imminent. Under these conditions, he granted 11,500 acres of land in Bergen Neck to freeholders of lots in this secured village and he would only permit the re-colonization of the west side of the Hudson river under this restriction.

In 1660, he established the village of Bergen for this protection from the Indian menace. The village was located in the center of what is now Jersey City, between the Hudson River and the Hackensack River. He hired Jacques Cortelyou of New Utrech, the

Company's leading surveyor, to lay out the village in an area that would be easy to defend from hostile Indians. Cortelyou picked a site on the neck of land between the Hudson River and Newark Bay. This triangle of land had Newark bay on its west side and the Hudson river on its east side. The tip of the triangle where the Kill Van Kull ran between Newark Bay and the Hudson River, separating Staten Island from this neck of the mainland, was about five miles south. He chose to place the village on a hill two miles north of Paulus Hook and midway between the two rivers. The township, however, was to cover all the land in this triangle which was known as Bergen Hook.

The village he laid out within the township was eight hundred feet square divided by two roads at right angles to each other which intersected in the center of the village. He named the north-south road Bergen Avenue and the east-west street Academy street. At the intersection of these two roads, he placed the town square which was one hundred and sixty feet deep by two hundred and twenty-five feet wide. Thus, the village was divided into four blocks with a commons square in the center. He surrounded these four blocks with a heavy log palisade. A barred gate was built where the roads entered the village on each of its four sides. Each of the four blocks was divided into eight irregularly shaped lots.

A well was dug in the town square with a long sweep pole to raise the water bucket. It was essential to have water inside the walls for the villagers and their livestock in case of an attack by the Indians. A corner lot by the square was reserved for a school. An additional twenty-seven lots were surveyed outside the palisade where houses could be built with the intention that these colonists would retreat inside the gates if danger was imminent. There was a total of fifty-nine lots counting those both inside and outside the palisade. These lots were awarded by lot and without cost to those who wished to settle the township of Bergen. All lots were quickly claimed. A lot was reserved on a rise just outside and south of the palisade for a church to be built when the population had grown to a point where the villagers could support it.

The area surrounding the village was virgin forest and would be cleared by the new colonists. As it was cleared, the land for individual farms would be fenced off for individual farms but a larger part was common land kept in open meadows where all could raise cattle and sheep. These animals would be marked so that each farmer could keep track of his own animals. This common land caused many disputes in latter years as to who owned what land. The arrangement was a communal agreement for mutual protection.

All the land in the Bergen Hook triangle had been granted to the villagers by Peter Steyvesant by certificate October 26, 1661 and confirmed by charter granted by Carteret as a "Towne and Corporation." This Charter by Carteret set the same limits as were set by Stuyvesant but listed the town's immunities and privileges in eight articles which gave the town and corporation much power to appoint its own officials. It also authorized Bergen to "errect and ordaine a Court of Judicature within their own jurisdiction." The township was a corporate entity much in charge of its own destiny but subject to the laws of New Jersey. The freeholders and inhabitants of Bergen were required to pay quit rents to New Jersey but controlled the township and corporation.

Epke and the Village of Bergen

The village of Bergen received much attention in Jamacia because Cortelyou, its surveyor, was a prominent citizen in New Utrecht where the Dutch were organizing their new church. It was from talk with fellow church members that Epke became enchanted with the story of Bergen village which in 1675 was fifteen years old. The village was almost entirely populated by Dutchmen and French Huguenots whose culture and religion were his own. Here he would again be surrounded by Dutch ways and customs for the first time since he had left Friesland.

With Cornelius' enthusiastic report firing Epke's impression of Bergen, he seriously discussed with his family their moving to this Dutch sanctuary away from the Duke's Laws. The New Jersey government under Governor Carteret offered the "Concessions and Agreements" guaranteeing civil and religious liberties under republican principles and the township and corporation of Bergen controlled its own destiny. The five boys and Jannettie were solidly behind this movement of the family for they could see the possibilities of becoming large land owners in this new territory while all the good land on Long Island had already been claimed and was too expensive.

It was apparent not only to Epke, but to the entire family that those who had become very wealthy on Long Island were the land owners not the tradesmen. Now that Epke had five strong young men to help him settle land, they all felt that acquiring land made more sense than learning a trade. For this reason, Epke took all five boys over to investigate the possibilities of acquiring land in Bergen village as the first step towards more extensive land holdings on this new frontier. The family would have more than ample assets from the sale of the inn and the prospective sale of the mill which had become very profitable.

The boys fell in love with this new village. They could not remember living in a village with all Dutch customs and longed for the type of life Epke had told them about nightly in his descriptions of Friesland. The fields surrounding the village had been cleared early after the village was laid out in 1660 and now were covered with mature orchards, vineyards and fields of grain. Beyond these cultivated fields were the meadows divided by streams where the livestock grazed and waterfoul fed. The streams were full of fish for the taking. It was an idyllic garden spot in an ethnic community populated by fellow Dutchmen. There was no uncertainty in any of their minds that this was the land of their dreams.

They began to search for someone who would sell them a lot in Bergen. The owner of lot #95, just outside the palisade on the west side of the village, was leaving to settle land further north along the Hudson River and had his lot and the house he had built on it up for sale. With the lot went the land he was farming and one-half of his livestock which grazed on the common meadow land. Epke and the owner haggled back and forth as to the price till Epke made an offer the owner accepted. This was in the Spring of 1675, and all differences with the Lenni-Lenape Indians had been resolved years ago.

They returned to Jamaica to tell Jannettie what they had done. She was both pleased and excited at the prospect of their new home in the beautiful surroundings they described to her. She was pleased that they were moving into a house that was already built, though she knew the boys could have quickly built a new home if such had been required. Epke immediately put his mill up for sale. Since it had become quite profitable with the new repairs, he quickly received a fair offer from a responsible party whom the town of Jamaica approved as the mills new owner.

For the third time in Epke and the boy's life, the family packed its earthly belongings and headed for a new frontier. Their household belongings were packed into trunks and taken in their wagons to the wharf in Bruckelen where they were loaded onto flat boats along with the family and horses and ferried to New York. They traveled by land across Manhattan Island and then reloaded everything onto flat boats to cross the Hudson River to the village of Cumminipa which lay on the west bank of the river on the New Jersey shore.

Cumminipa was the port that transported the produce from Bergen to New York City. It was composed of a wharf and about twenty houses for the families that lived there. From here, they again hitched their horses to the wagons, loaded the trunks on them, and proceeded to their new home two mile inland at the village of Bergen.

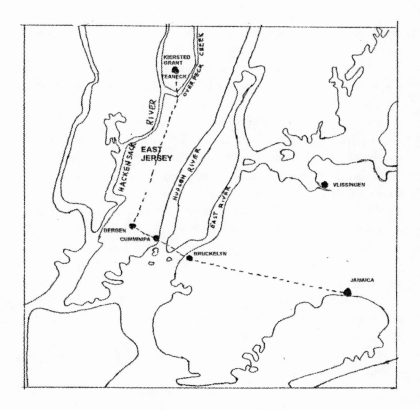

THE BANTAS IN EAST JERSEY
1674 - 1752

When Jannettie saw the village in its beautiful setting of farm lands surrounded by meadows with cattle and sheep grazing, she was so delighted and pleased that tears filled her eyes. Cornelius saw how pleased she was and was proud that he had found this Garden of Eden for the woman he loved. Jannettie was pregnant with their first child and that child would be raised in this beautiful place with a Dutch school to teach it how to read and write, abilities that he sorely missed. He would take up the organization of a church from where he had left off in New Utrecht so that his child would be raised with a religious background from its earliest days.

When the Jacobse family arrived at the village, "the town and corporation of Bergen," under Governor Carteret's charter covered an area of eleven-thousand five-hundred acres. About four thousand of these acres had been patented to the villagers and about seventy-five hundred acres were held in common as meadow lands for their livestock herds. The villagers also used much of their equipment in common and worked in common to erect the houses and barns of their neighbors and complete many farm tasks. The Jacobse's loved this arrangement among the Dutch of turning work into a party. The women also followed this social pattern and got together for spinning bees, sewing bees, quilting bees and other bees which included their required daily work. In addition when the men got together to slaughter farm animals, build a barn or any community task, the women would meet after the days work and together cook a meal which would result in a party with much celebrating including drinking and dancing. Epke, the boys and Jannettie loved this method of turning a hard day's work into a playful evening.

They had known some of the villagers on Long Island before they had moved to Bergen. In no time they were heavily involved in the town's social life. The school had been organized but the church was in its very earliest days of organization. All the Jacobses made the organization and building of a Low Dutch Reformed Church a top priority. When Cornelius and Jannettie's baby girl was born in 1676, they waited until the church they had been building in New Utrecht was completed in 1677 and then took the baby back there to have her baptized. They named the little girl Jannettie after her mother. This was Epke's first grandchild, the first of a new generation and the first live birth in the family on the North American continent. With the arrival of little Jannettie, Epke bought Cornelius and Jannettie their own house and lot #16, inside the gates of the village and here they set up housekeeping as a family. The lot was a large one, L shaped around a smaller lot which it abutted on two sides, at the southwest corner of the town square. One end of the L shaped lot fronted on Academy street while the other fronted Bergen Avenue. It had ample room for more than one house for Epke knew that he soon must supply homes for his other sons who were now of marriageable age.

It was becoming the custom of other Dutch families to adopt a surname based on where they had come from or what they had done as a trade in the old world. With the new generation, the boys decided that changing the family name each generation by adding "son" to the father's name was confusing and old fashioned. Recalling from the stories that Epke told them each night as children that his father had signed his name "Jacob Epkese te Bonte" after his wife's property at Bonte, they decided to take that name. However the Dutch were very careless in writing; and with the boys being unable to write, they had to depend on Epke for the spelling. Though they pronounced their name Bonte, he told them the proper spelling of it was Banta. The southern provinces of Holland always put "van," meaning from, in front of the town or area name. Thus, if a family was from the town of Buren, they would take the name van Buren. This was not the custom of those families from the northern province of Friesland so the Bantas did not put "van" in front of the area from which they had come. Jannettie was christened Jannettie Banta and was the first to be baptized with the Banta surname as a maiden name. From this point on, the families of the five boys bore the name Banta as a sur-name.

As the Village grew, tradesmen set up their shops and the villagers, who out of necessity had relied on themselves and their families for all the essentials of civilized life, purchased them at the town's shops. Shoes were made by the cobbler who obtained hides from the tanner. Pottery was purchased from the potter, while furniture was made by the joiner and carpenter. Living in Bergen was not much different from living on Long Island.

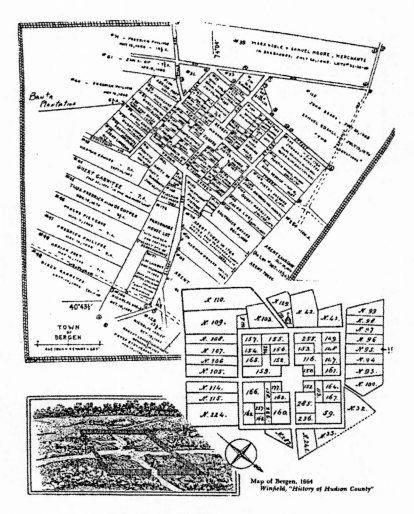

Map of Bergen, 1664
Winfield, "History of Hudson County"

FROM "BANTA PIONEERS," ELSA BANTA

School was taught in a log schoolhouse facing the town square. It was eighteen feet square with slab seats on three sides in front of which were small tables for desks. The teacher was James Christie who taught the three R's to the tune of a hickory stick. He loved to knit and sat knitting as the youngsters went about their studies.

Being a farm community, the school year was of necessity short as the children were obliged to perform their farm tasks in order to survive. However, the school day was long making up for the short school year and discipline was harsh. When the Banta family first came to Bergen this log school house was used as the church on Sunday.

With the new lot purchased by Epke for Cornelius came the farm land owned by the previous owner. The Banta family quickly learned the trade of farming which was completely foreign to all of them prior to coming to Bergen. As full working members of the village corporation, they quickly became totally enmeshed in the villages social and political life. A top priority of the family was to organize the building of a proper church and they quickly became leaders in this endeavor.

Both Seba and Hendrick had been hit by cupid's arrow. Seba had fallen in love with Mary Sip, whose father had lived in Bergen for some time as a farmer. Since there was no church in the village, they were married November 6, 1678, "in the presence of the court." Two weeks later, November 17, Hendrick married his sweetheart Maritje Westervelt also "in the presence of the court." The Bantas had known the Westervelts from their activities in organizing the church in New Utrecht and the families had moved to Bergen in the same year. The Westervelt family, through friendship, inter-marriage, and sharing future frontiers became one of four families whose history was intertwined with the Bantas over the next one hundred years.

These two marriages of brothers within two weeks of each other were the social events of the year. The Dutch loved celebrating and these two events rose to the level of Christmas or Easter in joyous reveling.

Seba and Maritje built their house and set up house keeping on the other side of the L shaped lot from Cornelius and Jannettie's house while Hendrich and Maritje built their house next to Epke's on the lot outside the gates. With three of his sons married, Epke's grand children began to increase and multiply. Hendrick and

Maritje's first child, Jacob, named after his great grand father, arrived in 1679 while Seba and Mary's first child, Antie, was born in
1680. With three families now living in Bergen, the Bantas were
becoming an important part of the community as was displayed
by Epke's being appointed a Magistrate of the Bergen court in
1680, the same year the church was completed.

The fact that both marriages were performed in the presence
of the court rather than in a dedicated church, brought the importance of a church building forcefully before the village's attention.
With the village's enthusiastic support, an octagonal church was
erected and dedicated on a hill just outside the south gate on
Bergen ave. The octagonal shaped church with eight equal sides
formed a structure that was essentially round. The parishioners sat
against the walls all around the preacher while his pulpit hung
from the center of a cone-shaped roof. He was required to ascend
the pulpit by a ladder. Below the pulpit sat the sexton who did the
lining of the hymns and communicated with the Dominie by placing written messages on a forked stick and then holding the top of
the stick up where the Reverend could reach the note. As in New
Utrecht, there was no way of heating the church and whatever the
temperature was outside the building was the same as the temperature inside. In winter, when it was often well below freezing,
here too the women brought foot-warmers while the men toughed
it out during the three hour services.

The very first weddings in the new church involved Epke's
two youngest sons. On October 3, 1681, Dirck married Ethel
Dedrick and Wiert married Geertje Mandiville in a double ceremony. Ethel Dedrick was the daughter of a Bergen farmer and
Geertje Mandiville's father was the innkeeper of the second inn
built in Bergen. Mr. Mandiville said he was not losing a daughter
he was gaining a trained innkeeper son-in-law. When they were
first married Wiert did help out at the inn and the couple lived at
the inn, until Epke bought another lot and the farm land that
went with it for the newlyweds. Epke built a house for Dirck and
Ethel next to his and Hendrick's house.

The first marriage in the church would have been a major celebration in any event, but the double ceremony of the two Banta brothers caused a three day long festival. Epke's house, the house of the Sip family and Mr. Mandiville's inn were open all three days with laden tables filled with Dutch meats, cakes and other baked goods while the beverages included beer, wine, cider and other hard and soft drinks. Each night the local musicians played at the inn and the villagers danced til early morning. The Dutch loved revelry and the double wedding of these two well loved boys and their wives brought the towns people happily together to wish the two couples happiness and many children.

Bergen Square is now a parking lot in Jersey City

**THE OCTAGONAL LOW DUTCH REFORMED CHURCH
IN BERGEN**
Adapted from a drawing in "Banta Pioneers," by Elsa M. Banta

Doug Sullivan, sexton of the current Low Dutch
Reformed Church, shows the author the hillock in the old
Bergen graveyard where the octagonal church stood. They
are standing where the pulpit hung from the ceiling.

The year 1682 brought Epke three more grandchildren.
Seba and Maritje had their second child, Antie. Hendrick and
Maritje also had their second child, Angenitie. While Dirck
and Ester's first child, Margriete, was born. In 1683, Epke's
list of grandchildren increased by an additional two. After this,
each year saw the number grow by one, two and occasionally
three. The newly named Banta family in America was growing
by leaps and bounds.

The Banta family now owned three lots and eighty acres of
land in Bergen township. Even before they had left Jamaica,
Epke and the boys knew that their financial future lay not in
land in Bergen township which was already developed, but in
going to the new frontier north of Bergen township in northern
New Jersey. Above the line defining the limits of Bergen

township lay the township of Hackensack. To reach Hackensack township was as easy as sailing up the Hudson or Hackensack rivers or riding one's horse over the Indian traces many of which had been turned into wagon trails.

CHAPTER 7

HACKENSACK TOWNSHIP

The area north of Bergen township between the Hudson river and the Hackensack River had not been opened to settlement after the Dutch-Indian war. While the Indian menace was still of concern, Peter Stuyvesant only permitted settling of the west side of the Hudson river by colonists living within the protection of Bergen village. By 1680, the Indian menace had subsided and a protected village was not a necessity. People who wanted land on the frontier could settle anywhere they could obtain land. This could either be by grant from the Dutch government or, after the English take over, from the Lord Proprietors or government of New Jersey. In addition, land could be purchased from those who had such grants.

North of the township of Bergen lay a hook of land between the Hackensack River and the Overpeck Creek known as Hackensack Neck. Overpeck Creek was a tributary of the Hackensack River and since both flowed north to south at an angle to each other, the land north of where their waters merged formed a triangle or hook of land between the two streams of water. This land had been granted to Sarah Kiersted by Chief Oratam when he was a very old man in his nineties. Sarah had acted as interpreter for the chief in his negotiations with the Dutch. How she had learned the language of the Lenni-Lenape nation was not known, but she had learned it as a little girl. The chief had granted her about twenty-one hundred and twenty acres in this hook of land known as Hackensack Neck in appreciation for her years of service as his interpreter. Sarah's land grant had been confirmed by Sir George Carteret and Lord John Berkley in 1669.

Epke sought out Sarah and found she would be willing to sell him land just east of the Hackensack River about a mile north of where the two streams of water merged. This was about seven miles north of the Village of Bergen and just across the river from the very small village of New Barbadoes, now Hackensack. It lay in what is now the city of Teaneck. He, along with other Dutchmen and French Huguenots from Bergen, visited this land and found it a beautiful area covered by willows and other native trees. The soil was a red sandy loam that was very rich as it had been flooded many times in the past and was composed of silt from the two rivers. It also had the advantage of being located alongside the Hackensack River where it would be easy to ship a farm's produce to market.

The land lay in virgin forests which would have to be cleared in order to make it ready for the plow. This was just what Epke had been looking for. The land could be purchased cheaply and when improved would become very valuable. It would be backbreaking work but he and his five sons could do it. When he had been running the inn in Vlissingen, he had wished that God had sent him daughters to do the work around the inn. Now, he saw God's plan for turning a frontier forest into farm lands. In 1683, he agree to purchase about three hundred and sixty acres bordering the Hackensack River from Sarah at a very attractive price.

Several other Dutchmen purchased land from Mrs. Kiersted about the same time. These families formed a small Dutch settlement on the new frontier. Among the other families was the Vanderlinda family whose land adjoined the Banta land and who were also in the process of developing their property.

This new venture caused Epke and his five sons to leave Bergen and their wives while they constructed primitive log cabins for their families on this land. This was the first time in the twenty-two years they had been on this continent that they were living as true frontiersmen. The six men constructed four cabins. Epke, Cornelius and his family would occupy one, while Hendrick, Dirck, Wiert and their families would occupy the other three. Seba and his family would stay in Bergen to manage the family's property there.

Epke was sixty-two when he started this new undertaking with the intention of making his boys wealthy landed Dutchmen as their families grew to maturity. Being landed would make up for his neglect of their early schooling. He felt guilty that he had not made arrangements for their education. Land for his boys was what had brought him to the new frontier in Hackensack township.

By the winter of 1683, the cabins were completed and some ground had been cleared. It had been backbreaking work for the five strong backs but they learned as they progressed. As the learning curve took over, things that had taken them a week to accomplish were accomplished in hours. Their muscles developed into steel bands and they became a professional frontier team. Much of the work was dangerous and accidents that could have been disastrous but luckily resulted in minor injuries occurred often as they learned the proper ways to build log cabins, fell large trees and clear the underbrush. These things had to be done before they could bring their families to the cabins and farm this new land the next spring.

With the onset of winter, the Bantas returned to their families, friends and their comfortable homes in Bergen. They stayed in the village until the winter was over and the spring of 1684 had thawed the soil to the point where it could be plowed. In early Spring, Cornelius, Hendrick, Dirck and Wiert moved their families and their belongings to the frontier and set up permanent housekeeping in the crude log cabins.

Jannetie, Maritje, Ester, and Gerritje teased Mary about how lucky she was to stay in her nice house with Seba and her children while they had to live in primitive log cabins on the frontier. She insisted that she also wanted to go with them. They knew she meant what she said for not one of them would have changed places with her. The five sisters-in-law had grown very close and all wished Mary could have joined them on this fantastic adventure, but they recognized that the family property in Bergen had to be looked after.

At the time they moved to the frontier alongside the Hackensack river, Cornelius and Jannettie had one child, little Jannetie, who was now seven. Hendrick and Maritje (Maria) had three children, Jacob, age 4, Angenitie, age two and Roelof, six months. Dirck and Ester had one child, Margriete, age one. And Wiert and Gerritje had one child, nine months old.

The Bantas building a log cabin in the Kiersted Grant.
From "Banta Pioneers," by Elsa M. Banta

The four sister-in laws and their children became as close to each other as if they were blood sisters. Other families were also moving onto the Kiersted grant in the same area which they now called Teaneck. The new families were mainly Dutch or French Huguenot and formed a close Dutch community on the new frontier. The four Banta families and cabins formed a large part of this new community. The ladies' days were completely filled with the duties of a housewife in the late 1600s but were made many times more difficult on New Jersey's frontier. The Dutch custom of getting together to do work in bees at one or the other's cabin removed some of the loneliness, isolation and drudgery of frontier living and it added a social life to raising their families on the very edge of civilization.

The men's day started at daybreak and didn't end til dusk. It was wonderful for the Bantas to have a team of five men rather than like other families who had only one man and what ever lads were in the family. All the families worked together on heavy tasks and the Banta families were always ready to help their neighbors when muscle power and strong backs were needed. With the new families in Teaneck building, clearing land and raising their first crops, the community began to take shape. By the end of 1684, the first crops had been harvested though, due to the land's being so fertile, most grains grew so lushly that they grew to straw and didn't form heads. These crops were harvested and tied into small bundles for the thatched roofs of their new buildings. They knew from the growth of the first year's crop that the next year would produce a bumper yield of grain.

The woods were filled with game and the river and creek with fish so that the families ate well on the bounty of the forests and streams. Livestock was introduced to the new community and cattle and sheep fed in the meadows as they grew fat and ready for market. Milk cows were kept in barns attached to new permanent houses that were being built of stone or of finished lumber so that milk was always available to the new village. Since Teaneck was only six miles from Bergen, it was possible to bring in many finished items for building their new permanent homes. Also, a lumber mill was built along the creek so that milled lumber was readily available. Permanent homes comparative to those in Bergen began to rise throughout the new community with the familiar American Dutch architecture with its double slope in the roofs eves, double Dutch doors and the giant hearth and brick oven stretching across one wall of the great room where the two spinning wheels stood in the light of the great fire.

Cornelius, whose daughter was eight, began along with other settlers to make arrangements for a schoolmaster to conduct school lessons in Dutch. They built a typical one room school for this purpose and hired a teacher. There were many other small villages springing up in Hackensack township and the school was centrally located to take care of the children in nearby villages. Cornelius had been handicapped by lack of formal grammar school and he and his brothers wanted to avoid this with their new families. The Bantas along with the other Dutch families began organizing a Low Dutch Reformed Church in the new village.

By the spring of 1685, The Bantas' plantation had been well cleared and Cornelius and Epke had built a fine new house while Hendrick had also finished his. Dirk's and Wiert's families were living in their new houses while they were being completed. Their farm was beginning to flourish and was getting attention from prospective settlers. Epke had an offer from Hendrick Joris Brinkerhoff for some of the Banta farm. Epke had been looking at some fertile land in the beautiful Spring Valley area which was about two miles northwest of Teaneck. It abutted the Albert Zabriske grant and he could receive a land grant of two hundred and forty acres from the province's Lord Proprietors and the present Governor, Gawen Lawrie, at a favorable price. Others he knew were buying up this property including Albert Zabriskie, David Demarest, and John Duryea. He could use the money from Brinkerhoff to help finance this new land. He therefore sold part of his land in Teaneck to him in June of 1685. Epke took the money from the sale and purchased two hundred and forty acres of land in fertile, beautiful Spring Valley which he added to his remaining acreage in Teanek. The families land holdings were spreading out from the original one in the Kiersted grant.

The Brinkerhoffs, who were now the Bantas neighbors, became one of the four families whose histories and friendship merged through intermarriage and sharing the rigors of future frontiers for over a hundred years.

Again the strong Banta backs were put to a task with which they had become familiar. By now they were true professional frontiersmen. They had given up their formal Dutch clothing for the clothing of the frontier which was mainly made by their wives of leather for it alone could withstand the snags and tears of clearing the forests and underbrush. The normal Dutch clothing was kept for when they went to Bergen, Sundays and social gatherings. Although Teaneck was but six miles from Bergen, there was a vast change in their mode of living from that of the village of Bergen to that of the frontier.

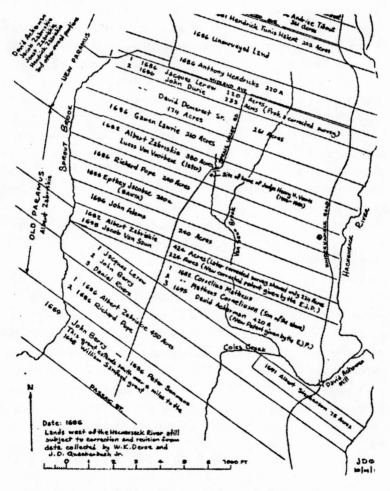

EPKE JACOBSE BANTA'S FARM IN SPRING VALLEY

The old Spring Valley cemetery where many early Bantas
are buried

In 1686, John Berry, a neighbor in Teaneck and in Spring
Valley, donated a tract of land across the Hackensack River from
Teaneck in New Barbadeos, now the City of Hackensack, for the
erection of a Low Dutch Reformed church building. There, the
first church was organized and and the building constructed of
rough lumber as it would be a few years before the permanent
church could be built. Around the church, they laid out the cemetery which was kept carefully tended. The church was named
The Church on the Green. Organization of the congregation began in earnest with the erection of the crude church building on
the land John Berry had donated. Hendrick was chosen as one of
the church's first deacons and installed into office July 25, 1686.

Now that the settlers had opened land in Hackensack township,
the province of New Jersey was anxious to collect quit rents on the
land. All the villagers were discontent with this arrangement as
the Provence had done nothing to help the settlers. Even in Bergen,
the villagers received nothing for the money they paid the Lord
Proprietors in quit rents while they were still responsible for all

expenses from upkeep of the roads to the offices of sheriff, magistrates of the court and all other costs of government. They received nothing in return for this tax. The quit rent was a tax to reward the Lord Proprietors strictly for the use of the land.

On the frontier this tax was even more resented, for the frontiersmen had hacked their villages out of wild forests without any help from anyone but themselves. They were creating an economic base that brought in and shipped out trade items that were taxed by the province. Why should they pay for creating this base with their own labor and then pay quit rents on what they had created?

The villagers resisted paying the tax collectors in a defiant shouting match led by Epke, Dirck and Wiert. Cornelius and Hendrick would have joined in this display but they were away from Teaneck at the time. Epke, Dirck and Wiert were arrested and jailed for "contempt of the laws of the province and rioting." Epke was sixty-seven but still a big, strong feisty Dutchman when he suffered this indignity. He could see that there was no way he could win this battle with the Lord Proprietors and, at his age, he had no desire to remain in jail as had John Bowne in Vlissingen. The Dutch, he reasoned, were realists while the Englishman, John Bowne, was an idealist. Therefore, he reached an amicable resolution of the matter with the province and was released. His amicable resolution consisted of paying the quit rents.

In 1685, two more cousins were added to the Banta family. The Dirk Bantas added a son, Hendrick, bringing their family to three children, and the Weart Bantas had a daughter, Antie, their second child, bringing the total number of cousins to fifteen. Childbirth was dangerous in the mid 1600s and even more so on the frontier. The five boys had been very fortunate to have had this number of children with no stillbirths and no casualties among their beloved wives.

In 1686, Hendrick's wife Maritje was delivering their fourth child when complications set in and luck ran out. The baby daughter was born a healthy child but Maritje died a few days after the birth from the complications of childbirth. She was thirty-two years old and her eldest son was seven. Hendrick was a widower with four children, one but a few days old. The tragic death of this young mother overwhelmed the close Banta family. None of the five boys had named a baby girl after their mother, Sitske. Now, Epke asked Hendrick to name the baby girl Sitske after his wife who had died giving birth to their sixth child in Vlissengen. The baby girl was baptized with that name. Maritje was buried on the land John Berry had donated for the church and cemetery across the river in New Barbadoes. She was one of the first burials in the new cemetery.

Epke, who had lived the life of a widower since Sitske's death, went into a deep depression realizing his son had suffered the same fate he had and now had four babies to raise as a widower. He and the rest of the family surrounded Hendrick and his children with love. While Epke had mourned his wife's death with no extended family around him in an English village on a strange new continent, Hendrick had Epke and the families of his four brothers to help him through this sorrowful period of his life. His sister-in-laws minded the children while Hendrick continued working with his father and three brothers clearing the land in Spring Valley. The village of Teaneck and his church also provided him with solace and consolation.

During the latter years of the 1680s, the family grew in both the number of cousins and in wealth. As the family grew so did Teaneck and the surrounding villages for Hackensack township was drawing hundreds of new settlers to the various land grants. Many of these grants were contested by several parties who claimed to have grants or deeds to the same land. The Demarest family, who were good friends of the Bantas, purchased a large amount of land in 1677 from the Indians in the area known as Schraalenburgh (which meant gravel land) and sometimes as "Old Hackensack." They repurchased it two more times from others who claimed title to the same land before their title was secure. Schraalenburgh lay a little north of Teaneck and a new village developed there on the Demarest grant. The Demarest family became one of the four fami-

lies that through inter-marriage and friendship shared the next
century on the frontiers of America with the Banta family.

Tragedy suddenly struck the Banta family again in the summer of 1690, when Wiert Banta, the youngest of Epke's five boys,
was killed in an accident while clearing land. Wiert was thirty-two
when the accident occurred and left his wife, Geritje, a widow
with four children, the oldest seven and the youngest a new born.
Again, Epke was thrown into a deep depression and the four Banta
families surrounded Geritje with their love and caring. Wiert was
buried in the cemetery of the Church on the Green across the river
in New Barbardeos next to Maritje. Within four years the Banta
family had sadly acquired a widower with four children and a widow
with a like number.

Losing his daughter-in-law, Maritje, was a blow to Epke but
losing his youngest son tore his heart out. There is no grief to be
compared with the loss of a child. Epke had raised his five sons by
himself and was justly proud of the fine Dutchmen and family
men they had become. His youngest always seemed the most vul-
nerable and the most in need of his guidance and protection. Why
had he not sheltered Wiert from the dangers he knew existed
on the frontier? This question haunted him daily after Wiert's
death.

Epke was now seventy-one but he was as strong and as supple
as a man of fifty from living on the frontier. With the death of
Wiert, he changed before the eyes of his family and friends into an
old man within a matter of weeks. The confidence and authority
had left his physical bearing. He continued working with the boys
improving and supervising his land holdings but his body was
spent. One evening in the fall of 1690, he complained to Cornelius
of a bad case of indigestion and retired to his bed. In the morning
he failed to arise and Cornelius went to his room to awaken him.
He found his father had passed quietly from this world in his
sleep. The doctor was summoned and diagnosed the cause as acute
indigestion.

Epke Jacobse Banta had come to this continent in 1659 with

no family but his wife, Sitske, and his five sons. He owned nothing and had agreed to pay the Dutch West Indies Company for an inn in a town he had neither seen nor heard of. With his passing from this world, he left four living sons and daughter-in-laws with twenty three grandchildren, the beginning of one of the largest Freisian families in today's United States of America. He had acquired, for his family, about one thousand acres of fertile land in a garden spot named New Jersey. He was and is the father of all Bantas across our nation.

The law of Progenitor, used in English law of that period, was not practiced by the Dutch. The law of Progenitor left all of a family's estate to the oldest son. All other children held no interest in the parent's estate upon their parent's death. This was to avoid dilution of a family's property to the point where there would be so many owners that the property would have to be sold and the proceeds divided among the inheritors thereby having the title to the property pass out of the family name. Epke, in the Dutch manner, left his estate to his sons as equally as he could divide it. Cornelius inherited the farm in Spring Valley while the property in Teaneck was divided between Hendrick and Wiert. The property in Bergen village was left to Seba who had been living in Bergen and caring for that land while his brothers went with Epke to Teaneck.

Epke funeral was conducted with the Dutch customs of the time and the entire village shared in the families grief. He was buried in the Banta plot in the new cemetery of the Church on the Green next to his son, Wiert, and his daughter-in-law, Maritje.

While the progenitor and center of this new American family could no longer lead its destiny, the families continued to grow and prosper as a well respected, close knit group in their church and community. Each brother continued to help the others as each of them continued to add additional acreage to what they already owned. In 1693, seven years after Maritje's death, Hendrick remained a widower but with his families' help in raising his four children, he was able to purchase and clear one hundred acres of land he had purchased along side the Hudson River almost directly east of Teaneck and just north of Fort Lee.

Two years later, Hendrick, a successful land owner and a deeply religious man, fell in love with a young beauty who belonged to the church. Her name was Angenitie Hendrickse and she was nineteen years his junior. She returned his love and they were married in 1695. She took over the task of running a full household for she became the step-mother of his four children of whom Jacob, now being sixteen, was the oldest. Angenitie was up to the task and her step-children loved her for they had known her all their lives. Her family and the Bantas became very close. So close that a few years later Angenitie's sister, Diever, married Hendrick's oldest son, Jacob, causing the odd situation of Angenitie's becoming her own sister's mother-in-law.

This was a year in which the Bantas added substantially to their already large land holdings. Hendrick purchased about one hundred acres of land along side the Hudson River at Edgewater just north of Bergen Township. This was a mile or two south of his land on the Hudson north of Fort Lee. Here he built a home along side the river for his new wife Angenitie's and his children's use during the hot summer months.

In 1695, about three thousand acres of land along the Hudson River was bought by Cornelius, Seba, Hendrick and Dirck, the four living sons of Epke, in union with Lubberts Westervelt, brother of Hendricks first wife, Maritje. Her brother-in-law, John Loots, owned the property just north of it. The combined property of the Bantas, Loots and Westervelts encompassed the area from the Hudson River west to Overpeck Creek and from Englewood on the south to Tenafly on the north. It lay about two miles north of Hendrick's land above Fort Lee. The Bantas, with Teaneck as their center, held property in Spring Valley just to the north west of Teaneck, along with parcels to the east along the Hudson River and to the south in the village of Bergen. Since the death of father Epke, some of the property was owned by individual families while some was jointly owned by all four.

In 1696, Hendrick's new wife, Angenitie, bore their first child who they named Hendrick after the baby boy's father and had him baptized in the Church on the Green. This was Angenitie's first but Hendrick's fifth child. He was born when his father had become prosperous, was the pillar of the church and well respected in the township of Hackensack. Teaneck was no longer the frontier for it had been thirteen years since Epke and his four sons had cleared land along with the other settlers for their new farms. The village was now established with a school, the Church on the Green across the river, all the trades, and an inn. The roads were improved and local government established. Hendrick's brother's families had also grown; Cornelius and Jannetiee had five children. Seba and Mary had four. Dirck and Ester had six and Weart and Gerritije had four children before his death. Altogether, there were twenty-three cousins in the Banta family.

As our story progresses and the cast of characters making up the Banta family increases almost exponentially, it becomes impossible to focus on the dozens of newcomers involved. Therefore, from this point on, the story focuses on the linage of one of Epke's five sons. That son is his middle son, Hendrick Epkese Banta who will be called Hendrick Epkese in the telling of the story because there will be three Hendricks whom we will follow in the course of the next three generations. It will concentrate on one son from his family line in each new generation. The remainder of our story, therefore, will carry the reader a generation at a time across the frontiers of our great country following the line of Epke Jacobse through his middle son, Hendrick Epkese Banta. Then we will follow his son, Hendrick, who in our story has just been born and whom we will call Hendrick II. From there we will follow this new baby boy's future family through his first son also named Hendrick for whom our story will use the name Hendrick III. Hendrick Epkese Banta's brother's families and their offspring will become peripheral to these three Hendricks who will be the central characters in this historical novel for the current and following two generations.

Little Hendrick II was born on the frontier but only after it had been tamed. He never remembered log cabins or virgin forests filled with game and rivers filled with fish. The village had been established thirteen years prior to his birth and his remembrance of the frontier was one of a thriving small but new community. Certainly, his frontier was different in life style from the bustling city life in New York at the turn of the eighteenth century but he had not witnessed the hardships of being the first pioneers on a brand new frontier as had his older brothers and sisters.

One of his first remembrances was the funeral in 1698 of his Aunt Jannettie, his Uncle Cornelius's wife. Though he was only two, he remembered the sadness of the family and the journey to the grave yard for her burial in the Banta plot. His next recollection, at the turn of the century in 1700, was of the birth of his baby sister, Margarite, who was the last child born to Hendrick and Angenitie. About the same time as Margarite was born, he remembered going to the marriage of his Uncle Cornelius to his second wife, Magdalena Demarest. This was the first inter-marriage between these close families.

His father, Hendrick Epkese, had worked hard in organizing the congregation to erect an octagonal church of stone, similar to the church in Bergen, on the land John Berry had donated. This church was dedicated in 1696 and stones with the names or initials of all the deacons and elders of the church that year were included as building blocks. Hendrick was proud to have a stone with the initials H E B for himself and A H H for his wife in the front of the church by the door. Though the octagonal church has since been torn down and twice replaced by new stone churches, this stone has been saved and placed just around the right corner of the current Church on the Green in Hackensack. If you are ever in that city, look for this stone and you will find it.

In 1705, Hendrick Epkese was honored by being elected as an elder of the church. Two years later, his brother, Dirck, was elected church warden. The following year Dirck and Joost Debaum erected the belfry on the church and this was recorded in their praise. The

Bantas were pillars of the church and the Church on the Green was the center of the life of villagers in the villages that surrounded it.

Hendrick Epkese's second son, Roelof, died as a youth. For his two living sons, Jacob and Hendrick, he made careful plans for their futures. He planned to will his property to Jacob, therefore, he decided that he must find a trade for Hendrick so that he could support his future family. He decided to enter Hendrick at age thirteen under apprenticeship to the finest blacksmith in Bergen. The members of the Banta family, both males still carrying the name and females who had married into other land-owning substantial families, were spread throughout the local villages and would become his clients when he opened his own blacksmith shop. With this trade he could support his future family in a substantial if not luxurious style.

Hendrick Epke Banta's will required that his estate be sold to his oldest son, Jacob, and the money be divided amoung his other five living children. Hendrick II was not landed but inherited a substantial amount of money. When Hendrick II finished his apprenticeship, Hendrick Epkese loaned him the money to purchase land in Schraalemburg and to open his own blacksmith shop there. This land was mid-way between the Dutch communities of Hackensack and Tappan to the north.

Opening a blacksmith shop in those days meant an enormous amount of work for Hendrick II; he had to build his shop which he attached to a house large enough for his future family. In addition, he had to mold bricks for, and build, the forge. He was required to construct his own bellows. The anvil was not made on this continent but was imported from Europe at considerable expense. He then had to make his own tongs, tubs for holding the water for cooling the red hot metal and a myriad of other tools necessary to his trade.

The advantage of being from a large family and a close knit Dutch community was that he had help available in accomplishing these tasks. When the work was finished it was a Dutch community achievement as well as his own for the towns needed a good blacksmith as much as he needed their business. Without the blacksmith in those days, there would be no axes so necessary to felling the trees on the frontier, nor latches or hinges for their doors, no saws nor the iron hardware attached to the walls of the Dutch hearths without which the women would not be able to hang their kettles over the fire. In addition, though most farmers had a forge in their barns for shoeing their horses, only the blacksmith could shoe the cleft hoofs of the oxen. All iron work for a wagon, from that which attached the tongue to the axle to the iron rims that held the wagon wheels together were work of the blacksmith. Nails, bolts, hammers, everything made of iron needed by the community came from his forge.

The author finds Hendrick Epkese Banta's stone with his
initials and those of his wife's, Angenitie Hendrick
Hendrickse, in the current Church on the Green,
Hackensack, New Jersey

In 1717 Hendrick II met, Geetury, a lovely young lady whose family lived in Schraalenburg. They were both immediately attracted to each other and after a few months of courting her, he asked his father if he might ask her to marry him. With Hendrick Epkese's enthusiastic permission, Hendrick II asked Geertury to marry him and she agreed. They had a family of four children. Their oldest son, Hendrick III, was destined to be a truly unique person and a man of destiny.

His second child, Wyntie, born in 1721, married Samuel Duryea in 1744 and their lives became closely intertwined with her older brother, as Sam and Hendrick had been best friends even before the wedding. The Banta and Duryea families had always admired each other and now through inter-marriage the two families became even closer. The Duryea family became one of the four families who as neighbors, and through intermarriage and sharing mutual future frontiers combined their history with the Banta family over the next century

Their third child Anginitie died as a child. Their fourth child, Albert, born in 1728, married Lena Van Voorhees and became the third leg of the triangle of two brothers and a sister who helped conquer the wild west. These three, with Wyntie's husband, Samuel Duryea, played a unique part in the development of our great nation.

Hendrick II arose at sunrise and worked six days a week till sunset keeping up with the needs of his neighbors. He was a tall man with a large frame which was the build necessary for the profession of being a blacksmith. He developed muscles of steel from the hard labor of being a smithy. At age 13, his oldest son, Hendrick III, became an apprentice to his father and the two operated the blacksmith shop.

The blacksmith shop of a small village was the place where the men of the area would congregate to visit and pass on gossip and information about the community. Politics was a major topic of conversation. Thus, Hendrick II and Hendrick III were both heavily involved in discussing politics about Hackensack township,

Bergen County, the Low Dutch Reformed Church and the province.

Hendrick Epkese Banta lived only a short distance from his son and the two kept in close touch with each other. Hendrick II and his family also met daily with his brother and three sisters and their families.

In 1740 Hendrick Epkese Banta passed away at the age of eighty-five. He was the last survivor of Epke's five sons. His oldest son, Jacob, was heir to Hendrick's property but as instructed in the will, he paid his sisters and brother for their share of the land at a fair price. By this means, Hendrick II became well-to-do in his own right as well as being a successful blacksmith.

Hendrick Epkese Banta's nieces and nephews, grandchildren of Epke, now numbered thirty-five and the older ones had married and had children of their own. The Church on the Green was not large enough to hold all the mourners at Hendrick's funeral and many had to stand outside during the burial service of the last remaining of Epke's five sons. Hendrick Epkese Banta was laid to rest in the Banta Plot of the cemetery surrounding the Church on the Green as had been Epke, his four other sons, their wives and the cousins who had died as infants or as youngsters. The older generation had all gone to their heavenly reward, and now Hendrick II's generation took up that position in the circle of life where their children considered them to be the older generation.

In 1738, Hendrick III married Rachel Brower at the Church in Schraalenburgh, which was her church, though he continued as a member of the Banta family's Church on the Green in Hackensack. Rachel Brower's mother's maiden name had been Demarest. Thus she was one-half Demarest though she carried her father's name. This was the second inter-marriage between the Demarest and Banta families.

In the Dutch fashion, he and Rachel started a large family. Their first son, Hendrick IV, was born in July of 1740. Then followed Abraham in 1742 who died in infancy, and his first daughter, Leah, in 1744.

Hendrick II and his son made a wonderful team. Both of them were tall men with excellent physiques. The heavy lifting and the work a blacksmith does all day long had made them both as strong as bulls. They were a handsome team in their leather aprons with biceps as large around as ham butts from working together at the forge, bellows and anvil. They worked side by side for thirteen years. Then, in 1744 Hendrick II died an untimely death at age of 48 from a kick in the head by an unruly horse just four years after the death of his father. Hendrick II had been born and spent his entire life in Hackensack township except for his apprenticeship in Bergen. He was baptized, married and buried in the Church on the Green. When he was a little boy, he could remember that only Dutch was spoken in his village whether in conversation or business. The schoolhouse taught all classes in Dutch. All the Dutch holidays were celebrated in the Dutch tradition. As he grew older, all these things changed and now English was spoken everywhere but in the home and the sermons at the church. He spoke often to his children about how wonderful it was when the village was Dutch and how the English language and customs made him feel like a stranger in his own town. During the course of his forty-eight years, he had seen a remarkable transition in the culture of his village. He is a unique character in our saga of nine generations for he was the only one who was content to live his entire life in the area where he was born.

Hendrick III at age twenty-six along with his brother and sister became the support of their mother, Geetury. Without his father, he took on an apprentice and continued to operate his father's shop. The talk in the shop by the kibitzers who dropped by regularly and sometimes stayed all day was a familiar one but new to this generation. The men complained of how the Dutch community had become overrun by Yankees and how the old Dutch ways and religion were being taken over by English ways and traditions. All agreed that they were losing their ethnicity and were being Anglicized. Talk always came around to the fertile land on the western frontiers that was there for very low prices if one was willing to live in a log cabin and clear the virgin forests that in many cases had not even a trace to follow if a person wanted to get to them.

Many Dutch from Long Island, New York, and Hudson and Bergen counties, New Jersey, had left for new frontiers where they were setting up new Dutch settlements to preserve their Dutch cultural roots and avoid being Anglicized. "After all," they said as if they were saying it for the first time, "we were here first. Why should we adopt a culture that is not ours? That is not why our parents came to this new continent. This was our colony and now they insist we be absorbed into their ways rather than them adopting ours." The Dutch community was still firmly convinced that their culture was the superior culture.

Some of the Dutch families were leaving New York and New Jersey and following a trace called the Old Dutch Trail which led out into eastern New Jersey. These Dutchmen were escaping from the incursion of English culture and traditions and were settling in Dutch colonies on the frontier. In their traditional practical manner they were leaving nothing to chance and were organizing so that all necessary trades would be represented. Together they built their cabins and cleared the land. These colonies were intended to be like a Dutch nation as they had been many years before under Peter Stuyvesant. This way they would not have their culture absorbed and eliminated by the English society that was overwhelming such a small group as the Dutch.

This was a very appealing picture to Hendrick III and his brother and sister. They recalled their father and grandfather telling them stories of their culture and heritage and how great-grandfather Epke had come to this continent to build a new Dutch nation. They remembered being told how the family moved to New Jersey to preserve their heritage. While they knew that their mother depended on them and they could not leave her alone, they talked late into many a night imagining that they had become pioneers with the other Dutch families who had emigrated to the new frontier. In these daydreams, they were vicariously farming their own fertile land in a Dutch community with Dutch customs and traditions.

Hendrick and Rachel continued to increase their family at the rate of a child every eighteen months. Their son, Abraham, was born in 1745, Albert in 1747 and Geertruid in 1749. Then, great sadness overtook Hendrick's family when Rachel Brower Banta, tragically died from complications following child-birth of their sixth child, Geertruid. Hendrick III was heartbroken and had six small children from age nine to a few months old to whom he must be both father and mother. Hendrick IV, his oldest son had to assume all the responsibility of rearing his five siblings and tending the house while his father worked from dawn to dusk at the blacksmith shop to supply them a living.

Through the Banta's close relationship with the Demarest's, Hendrick III met and married a wonderful woman, unequaled by any other in this four hundred year saga. She was to step in and become a mother to his children and the ideal partner to accompany and assist him in a magnificent dream that would shortly envelope the rest of their lives. Her name was Anna Demarest and she was the cousin of Rachel Brower. They fell in love and were married in 1750. This was the third inter-marriage between the two families. Since Hendrick III's children had known and loved her all their lives the children unconditionally welcomed her as their mother though they never ceased mourning over the death of their birth mother, Rachel. In 1751, Hendrick III and Anna had their first child, Rachel, so that he then had a family of six living children.

In 1750, the same year he had married Anna, his mother, Geertruy, passed away and the duty to stay in Bergen County and take care of her no longer held him there. Now the dreams of the frontier which he, his sister and brother had so often discussed into the small hours in the morning could turn to reality. They had to face the fact that he and his sister were now married and had family responsibilities. Hendrick had six children while his sister, Wyntie and her husband Sam Duryea, had three. His brother Albert was still unmarried

The latest news being told in his blacksmith shop was that a new group of Dutch families was preparing to migrate further west in New Jersey, somewhere in Somerset County. Many Dutch families in Bergen County were already in touch by family ties with Dutch settlements that had already been established there. Land was cheap and very fertile when the forests were cleared and the fields made ready for the plow. Hendrick broached the matter with Anna of selling the blacksmith shop and moving with the new colony to the new frontier. He told her that he longed to be a farmer in a Dutch village and that this was their chance to acquire land and live in a Dutch community where they could raise their children in the Dutch manner and customs. The community, he said, would need a good blacksmith and he would work at his trade in addition to farming.

Anna immediately agreed. She, too, saw English ways taking over and though her parents were French Huguenots they had lived among the Dutch so long that they were as Dutch as were the Bantas. "But," she said, "With six children, it will be most difficult to move to a new frontier and construct a cabin, even with the help of the Dutch community"

"It will not be so bad." said Hendrick. "I will build us strong Jersey wagons and though the trip will be arduous and exhausting it will serve us well as sleeping quarters until we construct our cabin. We can live in it until the cabin is completed. We will have the money from the sale of the shop to carry us over until our first crop comes in. I will also take my tools with me and build a new shop in the new community. The new settlement will have great need for the abilities of a well trained blacksmith."

"How many days do men who have already made the trip say it will take?" Anna asked.

"They say it takes about five days," Hendrick replied. "It will take only one day from here to the wharf west of Bergen for we will follow a good road all the way. Then we will load our families, animals and wagons on flat boats to be ferried across Newark Bay to Elizabethtown. From there we will take the Old Dutch Trail which is a wilderness trail westward to the Raritan River at Bound Brook. From there we will follow an Indian trace to a township called Bedminister through which flows the North Branch of the Raritan river. There is nothing there now but with our colony we will create a new Dutch farming community.

"It is a little over twenty miles to Elizabethtown," He continued, "and another twenty some miles to Bound Brook on the Raritan River. From there the Bedminister township is perhaps another fifteen miles. The total journey is estimated to cover about fifty-five miles. With good luck we will be able to traverse the entire journey in five days."

"It could be worse," Anna said. "Many Dutch families are going to Pennsylvania which is over twice as far as we are going. How many families are in the migration?"

"The number changes but we are certain of twenty families," Hendrick answered.

Anna agreed that this plan would work and they both announced to the community that was preparing to leave for the new frontier that they wished to join them. The other colonists planning to migrate were delighted to hear a trained blacksmith would be with their wagon train. They met daily in his shop to discuss their migration to the new frontier

Hendrick sold his blacksmith shop to the young man he had apprenticed nine years earlier. The boy was now twenty-three and all the shop's customers knew and trusted him. The young man came from a comfortable family who were delighted for him to take over a well established business and gladly paid the fair price Hendrick was asking.

Hendrick and Anna went to visit Sam and Wyntie Duryea. Hendrick and Sam often visited and while smoking their long Dutch clay pipes would talk of the absorption of the Dutch culture into the English culture. Both were in agreement that this was very unfortunate for their children. When Hendrick told his brother-in-law and his sister that his family was definitely going to Somerset county, New Jersey, where a new Dutch colony was being formed, they immediately found a buyer for their farm and with their three children decided to join the wagon train to the new frontier. Hendrick and Samuel together built four wagons for the journey. Each family would take two wagons to carry the goods they were taking to the new frontier. Hendrick's younger brother, who was not yet married, felt an attachment to Bergen county and his many relatives who lived there and decided not to leave at this time.

In the early Spring of 1752, The Dutch emigrants assembled at daybreak for the trip. Each family had at least one Jersey wagon which was the principal means of transportation at that time. These wagons were constructed of oak. Over the bed of the wagon, six hoops were spaced evenly . The hoops at each end of the bed were higher than those in the middle. Over these hoops was stretched a canvass cover. There were no springs and the ride on the floor inside the wagon was teeth jarring. All who could walk beside the wagon did so without urging. The axles had wooden boxes for bearings which had to be constantly greased with a pot of grease that hung beneath the wagon.

The wheels were held in place by linchpins which had a bad habit of vibrating out of their sockets at the most inappropriate times causing the wheel to come off which dropped the axle to the ground with a terrible thump. Each wagon was piled to the canvas roof with the family's precious belongings that had been acquired over generations. Though breakable items were packed with care in straw and old cloth, no one expected to arrive at Bedminister without loss of some of their most precious belongings.

Each wagon, depending on its size and the weight of cargo it carried, was pulled by two or four oxen. Hendrick needed all of two wagons built by him and Samuel to carry his family's belongings including a full set of his heavy blacksmith tools. He drove one wagon while twelve year old Hendrick Jr. drove the other. On the frontier a twelve-year old boy was considered a man. Samuel and Wyntie Durea had their two wagons immediately behind those of Hendrick III so that the two families could look after each other.

There were more than twenty families in the wagon train. Following each wagon were the members of the family whose belongings it carried. The father and mother accompanied by their children and often by their aging parents trudged behind their wagon driving the live stock they were taking with them to Bedminister.

Just as their forefathers had done before them, they were leaving the comforts of a well-established community. They were trading security for their hopes and aspirations of a better life for themselves and their children in a new Dutch settlement on land available to those who were willing to accept the rigorous and dangerous work of clearing and settling the forests of a new frontier.

First, the wagon train, with close to two hundred Dutch men, women and children, traveled south parallel to Newark Bay till they reached the wharf opposite Elizabethtown and crossed the water on flat boats. At Elizibethtown they met the Old Dutch Trail that connected New York with Philadelphia. Here they turned west along the trail which had been worn into wagon wheel ruts by countless wagons bringing Dutch families from Long Island. All good land had been settled on Long Island and those who wanted new land had to migrate to the western frontier where fertile land awaited those willing to clear the trees and underbrush from the virgin forests and prepare the fields for the plow and cultivation.

This trail, not many years before, had been an Indian trace untouched by any human contact other than Indian moccasins which softly tread on the matted tree leaves that had fallen on the pathway over hundreds of years. The Dutch found the Indian trace to be the best path across New Jersey to the Delaware River beyond which lay Pennsylvania. At first it carried only Dutchmen on horseback but, with an increase in traffic, the vines and underbrush was cleared until carts began to travel the trail, their hubs scarring the trees on both sides until those trees too were removed.

The Old Dutch Trail was a trail, not a road. It received no maintenance except for that done by those who traveled it. The trail was in a miserable condition with tree stumps alternating with mud holes big enough to bury a wheel up to the bed of the wagon. Much time and energy were spent by the men getting behind the unstuck wheels and the rear wagon bed and heaving with all their might to get a mired wagon free from being imprisoned in the mud. The spring rains and storms soaked the families as they muddled through the awful conditions encountered on their migration.

As they left Elizabethville, the trail was cleared on both sides for much of the first miles by Dutch families who decided they need not go farther as the land they were passing would be excellent when the underbrush and trees were removed. Here, handsome farms bordered the trail; farms where the families were beyond the log cabin stage and where they had built substantial homes and barns. These farms along the trail were interlaced with forests where the large Oaks, Hickories, Hazel Nut and other giant virgin forest trees sheltered the wagon train from the sun if it were shining, and the vines and underbrush encroached into the trail.

When the wagon train came to a river or stream there was no bridge on which to cross. The horses with the help of every able-bodied man had to pull the wagons across the flowing water where the river or stream was wide and shallow. Fording these streams took much time and everyone had to help each other. Many times only one wagon was allowed to cross at a time with everyone helping to get it across before the next wagon was allowed to enter the stream. If a river or stream was too high because of a recent rain storm the wagon train had to wait for the water to subside before continuing.

The farther the wagon-train moved westward from Elizabeth, the fewer farms were located along the trail and the worse the trail became. The families infrequently traveled through hamlets where there were several pioneer homes and occasionally an inn but for miles they would travel with only the forest's great trees for a canopy. After a day and a half on the trail they began to see fields that were cleared to the stumps and had already met the plow. They had reached the outskirts of Bound Brook in the Raritan Valley through which flowed the Raritan River. Bedminister Township, for which they were heading, was in the valley formed by the north branch of the Raritan.

The Raritan Valley from Newark Bay to Bound Brook had been found and settled by the earliest pioneers when they came to New Jersey seeking land to farm. They had found the mouth of the river as it entered Newark Bay where Perth Amboy now stands. They discovered they could take their sloops up the tidal basin as far as to where New Brunswick is now located. From here they had settled both sides of the river far up the Raritan valley to the area where the wagon train now stood. These early pioneers had been induced to travel northwest along the Raritan valley floor by the finding of cleared meadows ready for the plow. These meadows had been cleared by the Indians who had discovered the fertility of the land once cleared produced bounteous crops of pumpkins, corn, beans and other fruits. The early settlers found this land to be ready for raising grain and rearing all description of farm animals.

As was the habit of the Dutch, they had purchased this meadow land from the Indians who still had their cabins under the bordering trees at the time when the immigrants wagon train reached Bound Brook. The valley of the Raritan was beautiful beyond description with the grasses of these broad meadows surrounded by the forests while through its center flowed this handsome river. Bound Brook was situated in this beautiful valley about three miles east of the fork that split the river into its North and South branches. The north branch of the Raritan ran through Bedminister Township ten miles northeast of Bound Brook.

In Bound Brook, the migrants met with Dutchmen from the nearby Somerset County communities of New Brunswick and Millstone. These Dutch villagers would assist the immigrants in establishing their new settlement at Bedminister by making available many things that would have otherwise been unavailable on a frontier. These villages and the Dutch who lived in the Raritan

Valley had become a close-knit Dutch community. Soon the immigrant's new village to be erected in Bedminister would join them.

The Dutch settlers in the spring of 1752 found the village of Bound Brook to be made up of about twenty houses, all of one story. To the south of the town stood the church while to the north stood William Harris's Tavern and Inn. The town also had a store which had been built by Tobias Van Norden but three years prior. It was a long one story building with a gambrel roof containing two dormer windows. This would be the closest store and church to the land they planned to settle.

The group of Dutch immigrants stopped for the rest of the day and overnight in the town to get acquainted with its inhabitants and purchase a few needed items from the Dutch storekeeper. Then they started the last leg of their journey leaving the Old Dutch Trail and following an Indian trace that would take them to the north fork of the Raritan River and to the Township of Bedminister.

The Indian Trace was little more than a trail barely wide enough for the wagons. It passed through the giant trees of the forest and their underbrush through which wild honeysuckles and blossoming grape-vines had stung themselves filling the air with their aromatic delights. Through this foliage, the men were often forced to cut their way to enlarge the trace to accept the breadth of the wagon's axles which often brushed the trees on each side of the path. As they slowly moved along the trace they would see frightened woodland animals flee in fear. It thrilled the children to see a graceful deer suddenly bound up the trail in front of them. It frightened them when the men came upon a mother bear and her cub though the bear was even more frightened and ran off into the brush to escape the noise and clatter of the men, their domestic animals and their carts.

As they moved through this arch of green, the road came upon a clearing as the road met the North Raritin River. This clearing had about a dozen little houses and a tavern owned by a Dutchman named Jacob Eoff. This was the village of Pluckemin, they were told by Jacob. He said he had built the inn less than two years ago. His inn was the only place of entertainment in the entire Township of Bedminister. He had purchased five hundred acres of land from the heirs of a John Johnstone which included the site where he had established Pluckemin. Hendrick asked Jacob whether Pluckemin was an Indian name he had taken for his village.

"No," Jacob laughed, "There are so few travelers who pass by here that when a horseman or wagon pass by I 'pluck em in' and don't let them get away." Hendrick and the other Dutchmen laughed heartily at his joke but weren't quite sure whether that was the real way the town got its name.

The men saw there was no bridge to cross the river at this point. The road went to the river bank on one side, disappeared, and then reappeared on the other side of the river. The river was quite high from the spring rains and was too deep and fast to ford. They asked Jacob what others did to get across the river.

"You have two choices,"he told them. You can either put up here til the river recedes or you can travel on this side of the river til you get to where Peapack Brook joins the Raritan and cross there. The river is almost always fordable at that point. It may be some time before the river recedes because of the Spring rains."

The men talked it over and decided to continue on the east side of the river to Peapack Creek. This part of the journey along a faint Indian trace across an unbroken frontier was the most difficult of all they had endured. Finally, in the early afternoon of the fifth day, the men hacked their way through the last part of the Indian trace and the colony reached the shore of the North Raritan River where Peapack Creek flowed into it. They forded the river at this point and then stopped along the west side of the river at the spot where now lies the village of Bedminister.

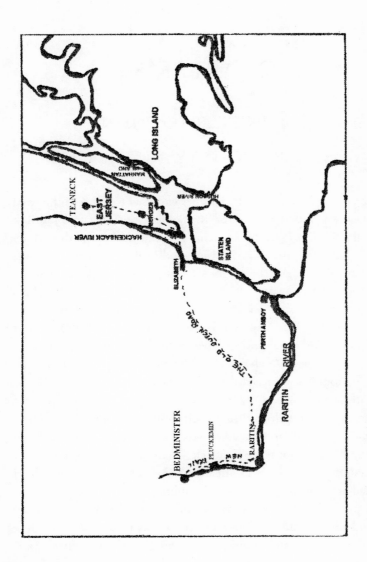

MIGRATION OF LOW DUTCH COLONY FROM TEANECK TO BEDMISTER

CHAPTER 8

BEDMINISTER TOWNSHIP,

SOMERSET COUNTY, NEW JERSEY.

After crossing the river, all the families gathered together and bowed their heads as Hendrick offered thanks to God for a safe journey. There had been no serious accidents and all members of the colony and all the farm animals arrived in good health. That evening was a time to rejoice. All the wagons arranged themselves in a semicircle with the river as their background and the women collectively prepared a frontier feast. Spirits were brought out for the first time since they had left Teaneck. The men took out their Dutch long clay pipes and lit them to enjoy a leisurely smoke. It was a party in true Dutch custom. The party went on well into the night for tomorrow the hard work would begin.

Early next morning the women arose with the men to prepare breakfast prior to their starting the clearing of the land. They found they were not alone in this wilderness for a German, who had been building a stone house on Peapack Creek, came on horseback to bid them welcome. He had already cleared a large part of his land and had it ready for the plow. He offered them any assistance he could provide. The Dutchmen thanked him for his hospitality and said they would visit his farm as soon as they could take time from their immediate essentials of building roofs over their families heads. The German bid them good day, mounted his horse and road back to his farm.

The men that day began the communal work of constructing

the temporary log cabins and clearing the forests in preparation
for plowing and planting of the land. The building of the cabins
required much teamwork as did the measuring of the various family farms, the clearing of the land and the building of fences. It was
decided by lot how the cabins were distributed among the families as they were completed and all families shared the cabins already constructed and the land that had been cleared until enough
cabins and land were available for all.

Within several weeks the men had constructed and covered
enough cabins for every family. The cabins were elementary in
construction, built with felled logs and though they were caulked
with mud containing straw to keep out the winds they still had
dirt floors. It was not necessary to arrange them in the form of forts
for the land had been purchased by its former owners from the
native Indians who were friendly and anxious for trade.

Though the Banta family had been on this continent ninety-
three years when Hendrick's family and his sister Wyntie's family
came to the new frontier in Bedminister in 1752, the family, except for Hendrick II, had never settled in one place since they had
arrived in the New World. Thus they could be called professional
frontiersmen. Hendrick and his brother, Albert, had helped their
uncles clear much forest land in Bergen County. The frontier was
in their blood and they instinctively knew the ways of the frontier.
Wyntie's husband, Samuel, likewise was at home in the wilderness.

Clearing land was a technique learned by frontiersmen just as
blacksmiths learn the tricks of their trade. The wild-woods are not
tamed into farmland in a day, week or month. It takes years to
turn virgin forests into plowed fields with growing crops. After the
first crop is planted, the yield will be disappointing because the
first year's wheat will grow to straw with little salvageable wheat.
This is because the eons of falling leaves have turned the soil into
mulch so full of nitrates that the heads never develop.

The pioneers first job was to remove all the small trees and
underbrush from the land they were preparing. They also cut off

the larger branches off the giants of the forest. Next they girdled the larger tree's bark a few feet above the ground depriving the tree above the girdle of life-giving nutrients. The tree would then die, and the next year the men would build a heap of dried brush around its trunk and set fire to it. The tree being dead would burn fiercely down to its stump. Many farmers left the stumps in the ground and plowed around them for several more years until the stumps decayed. Only then did they pound them to pieces with sledge hammers and remove them. Though this method left ugly fields until the stumps were removed, it saved the terrible effort that had to be expended by men and draft horses to remove the stumps immediately. This was the method of preparing the large tracts of land needed by the colony. That common land needed for the colonies present use was cleared immediately the hard way by removing the trees and trunks by the axe and a team of horses.

The men were pleased to find that a saw mill and a grist mill were already built on Peapack Creek the year before they arrived by a William Allen. Thus, they were able to start building their permanent homes with milled lumber. As the Spring turned into Summer, some fields were cleared and crops planted. One of the first crops planted was flax which the women needed to spin into thread to make linen or to mix with wool to spin into thread to make linsey-woolsey. Since the looms were too bulky to transport by wagon, each household needed a new loom in Bedminister. With the saw mill on Peapack Creek, the carpenters had lumber available to build the new looms so that cloth could again be woven.

As the colony built its permanent houses and barns, they took on the look of those they had left in Bergen County with the large kitchen which was also the great room. As before, one wall of the great room was taken by the enormous room-wide hearth. Built into the hearth was the great oven made of brick in which all the bread, pies and other bakery goods were baked. The metal cranes, hooks, pots, trammels and other necessities for a Dutch housewife were either taken with them from Bergen County or were made by Hendrick in his blacksmith shop. Next to the great room was the cellar on the same level with the living room but separated from it by a door. The big, clumsy loom was kept in this cellar along with apples, potatoes, and other stored fruits and vegetables.

The houses of those days had no closets. All clothes were hung on pegs arranged along the top of the walls just below the beams.

Hendrick built his permanent house in Bedminister as he did in Bergen county with his blacksmith shop attached to his house. The other craftsmen often did the same. With all the trades represented in the colony, within two to three years all items needed in a civilized village were readily available. By 1755, much of the land was cleared and under the plow. The first crop, which mainly turned to straw, was reaped and tied into small bundles to make the thatched roof for the houses and barns.

The farm animals increased and multiplied. Hogs were grown in the woods fattening on acorns and hazelnuts and all sorts of other herbs and roots. The second year the men gathered for a killing of the hogs at each others houses in the autumn and the women turned this into a party coming in the late afternoon with supper prepared. After eating at a well-laden table, the long clay pipes made their appearance as well as the musical instruments and the men and women danced till late into the night. On the frontier whenever the men or women gathered for a work party the event was turned into entertainment. For women, these work parties consisted of quilting bees, apple paring, spinning parties and corn husking. For the men they were held after hog killing, barn raising, and other events of the farm where the men gathered for community effort.

As permanent houses were completed and as trades were set up, the community took on the look of an established village. Family life was returning to its normal course. Each house had its smoke chamber where the family smoked fresh pork, bacon and other meats. The hams made from the young hogs who had been fattened on the fruits of the forests were especially tender and succulent. The women brought their two spinning wheels, the large one for wool and the small one for flax, into the living room. These they used for spinning the thread used in weaving cloth on their looms for use in making everything from clothes for the family to curtains for the windows.

The fields were producing excellent crops. With the great old Dutch hearth covering a full wall of the new living room and the housewives cooking, spinning, weaving and cleaning as they did in Bergen County, family life became less austere and more normal. The early years of the colony had been very rigorous and required maximum effort by every man woman and child. The worst was over and a bright future could be seen ahead.

Tanning vats were built close to the mouth of the Peapack Creek along with a mill to grind the black and red oak bark used in the tanning of the leather. As when Teaneck was carved out of the frontier forests, the Dutch way of dressing in New York, Bergen and New Hackensack, again gave way to dress that could better stand the strenuous tasks required on the edge of civilization. Here, traditional dress was saved for the Lord's day or for socials. At all other times the men again wore a great deal of buckskin and leather for it held up against the tears and snags of the wild woods and the work of clearing land that destroyed clothes made of cloth. They made their hats out of Beaver skins. Leather was also essential for shoes and most frontiersmen were able to cobble the shoes for their entire family. They also made and repaired their own bridles, saddles and other leather items needed on a farm.

As the frontier settlement grew into a thriving community, so also did the families grow year after year with a new crop of babies. Hendrick and Anna arrived at the frontier with six living children. Today that would be a large family but it was just the beginning of theirs. A year after their arrival at Bedminister, a son, Samuel, was born and Pieter joined the family in 1755 while they were still living in the log cabin. John was born in 1756 as they were moving into their permanent home.

The Dutch who had come over into New Amsterdam had split into two groups since the English takeover of the New Netherland colony: Those who willingly adopted the English culture and those who vehemently opposed being absorbed into it. To those who opposed absorption, such an idea became a crusade, something for which they were willing to undergo great hardships for themselves and their families. It was equal to the quest for the Holy Grail or to Moses leading the Israelites to the promised land. Father Hendrick solidly stood behind this group.

The Low Dutch Reformed Church had also split along the same lines. One branch of the church insisted that Dominie be ordained in Holland and the American church must remain dependent on this remote source for its ministers. This branch also did not oppose the absorption of the Dutch community into the English culture. This was the conservative branch and was called the "Conferentie." The other branch of the church desired autonomy and believed that arrangements had to be made to ordain Dominie on this continent or the Church would not be able to supply ministers in numbers required for the new churches being organized on the American continent. This branch believed that the Dutch culture on this continent must be preserved. They were called the "Coetus."

During this controversy that rocked the Dutch Reformed Church in America, a split in the Sommerset County church occurred in 1752, the same year the Dutch Bedminister immigrants had arrived. Father Hendrick was against the European powers and believed that those in America should not be dependant on them but should do things for themselves. Thus he split with the Conferentie side and joined the Coetus who had erected their own church building that year.

In 1759, seven years after the founding of the Dutch settlement at Bedminister, the village decided that it was time for them to build their own church which would follow the Coetus philosophy. Two sites were proposed, one at the Larger Cross Roads about a mile and a half west of Bedminister, the other at the Lesser Cross Roads which was Bedminister itself. Those seeking to build the church in Bedminister prevailed. In 1758, Jacobus Van der Veer and Hendrick Banta were appointed elders for the proposed new church and Rynier Van Neste and Cornelius Lane were appointed as overseers. This was accomplished at a meeting in the parsonage at Raritan attended by the consistories of North Branch, Neshanic, op de millstone, Raritan and Bedminister,

With teams of oxen and the talents of the many tradesmen in the village, assisted by the strong arms of the farmers of this religious community, its members built the new church the next year. Jacobus Van der Veer donated two acres of land, fifty pounds sterling and one third of all the lumber. Guisbert Sutphen donated the same amount of money and one-half of the lumber.

This Low Dutch Reformed Church completed the Dutch community. The church was austere in its structure and interior, unpainted and plain, but to the community it was beautiful. The Domine stood high on the plain pulpit while below him sat the presenter, or lining deacon, who passed notes to the Domine as necessary and lined out the words to the songs and psalm tunes which the members repeated after him. The Pulpit was in the center of the hall with the adult congregation facing the Domine while the children sat to his back and the young people sat to both his left and to his right.

Hendrick and Anna continued increasing the children in the family by one almost every year. Cornelius Banta arrived in 1762 and was baptized at the Bedminister church while the community celebrated the tenth anniversary of its coming to Bedminister. Then followed Daniel in 1765, Jacob in 1766 and Mary in 1767. Hendrick and Anna's family had grown to thirteen children. Their family, the village and the church were all well established and growing rapidly.

Hendrick Jr., Hendrick's oldest child, who was but twelve years old at the time of the immigration, married Maria Stryker in 1761 when he was twenty-one. They were married in the new Bedminister church which had been completed less than two years before their wedding. Hendrick and Maria's wedding was the social event of the year with the entire town entering into the celebration as was the custom in Dutch communities.

Although the price of land around the Dutch Bedminister

CONQUEST OF A CONTINENT

colony was escalating rapidly as the best land was already put under the plow, Hendrick Sr. had a thriving blacksmith business and
farm. He could well afford to, and did, purchase a farm for his
newly married son. With help from Hendrick's father, his brothers
and others in the village, a new house and barn were built for the
newly-weds. A year later, with the birth of their first son, a new
family and a new generation entered on the stage of this epic. His
son, Hendrick Jr., was the fifth generation of Bantas born on the
North American continent and the fifth in this line to bear the
name Hendrick. This can cause much confusion in our story so we
will call Hendrick who migrated with Anna and their six children
to Bedminister Township, Father Hendrick. We have just referred
to his son simply as Hendrick and to Hendrick's son as Hendrick
Jr. Hendrick Jr.'s birth in 1761 was followed by Peter in 1763,
Rachel in 1764, Abraham in 1766 and Anna in 1767. At this date
he had five children for, since their marriage, he and Maria had
been matching Father Hendrick and Anna, child for child.

In 1763, Father Hendrick's first daughter was married to Jacob
Montfort in the Bedminister church. Father Hendrick and Jacob's
father arranged to set the newly married couple up with a house
and farm. By 1767, they were blessed with two children. Prices
for land had climbed higher than at the time of Hendrick's wedding. Father Hendrick could see that with Abraham at 23 years of
age, Albert 21, and Geertruid 19, his money for land would run
out before five of his thirteen children would need land to start a
new family. Foremost in his mind in coming to Somerset County
was to find land sufficient to maintaining the family community
without his children being forced to split up in search of new
farms on the frontier.

New immigrants had come in such large numbers that in
eleven years all the good land was taken. Again the idea of moving
to the new frontier where a new Dutch settlement could be set up
entered his head for there would not be enough land for this next
generation and the one to follow. The men who gathered at his
blacksmith shop were discussing land in Pennsylvania where the

government was advertizing for new settlers. It would mean starting out all over again but it would also mean keeping the large
family together. Also, Bedminister, as had Teaneck, was becoming
Anglicized for Dutch families were selling their farms to those
outside the Dutch community. Old Dutch Road and Holland
Road, the roads along which the Dutch farms were located, were
divided now between Dutch and English farms.

Being of the Coetus philosophy, the Dutchmen of Bedminister
thought it was essential to preserve their Dutch culture. As the
plan developed, it was refined into a mission the goal of which was
to establish a socially independent Dutch colony somewhere on
the western frontier. This goal caught the rapt attention of Dutchmen of the Coetus viewpoint throughout the Raritin Valley and
spread to friends in New Jersey.

Father Hendrick, who so strongly opposed integration of the
two cultures, found himself questioning the wiseness of the course
on which he was leading his family. He decided to have a family
conference with Anna and his oldest son, Hendrick. He arranged
to have all three of them meet in his great room one day at two in
the afternoon so that they would be alone except for the youngest
children who were not in school.

As they sat around the table Father Hendrick began the discussion by saying, "I've told you many times how while sitting in
my father's and my grandfather's laps, they told me the story of
my great-grandmother's request on her death bed for my great
grandfather to raise her sons as good Dutchmen and to not let
them become little Englishmen. Perhaps this picture, implanted
in my mind as a child, has become an obsession with me. We have
watched those Dutchmen who have integrated with the English
become part of the establishment and become wealthy in New
York and New Jersey while we are still frontiersmen chasing a dream.
I want to bring this matter into the open and discuss it with you,
Anna, for you bear the hardships of raising a family on the frontier.
I also want to hear your view point, Hendrick, for you are the
oldest of my children and will speak on their behalf. The question

before us is as follows. Is it sensible for our family to pursue this dream of forming a Dutch nation on this continent? Other Dutch families who have accepted assimilation into the English culture and accept the rule of the English king have been blessed with many material things and have become wealthy. We, on the other hand, live on the edge of civilization and will be soon forced to emigrate again if we are to follow our dream."

"Hendrich," Anna replied, "You know that I wholeheartedly share this dream with you. Though my family is of French Huguenot origin, through inter-marriage I have as much Dutch blood in my veins as you have French Huguenot in yours. The Dutch culture must survive on this new continent. We must do everything we can to assure that it does. I believe you are following the right course and will support you wherever our goal takes us."

"I've been thinking," Father Hendrick went on, "about this problem of the survival of our culture and ask myself this question which I now put to you. With a whole continent of frontier land lying to the west, why could we not find enough land for a Dutch colony where we could live to ourselves in our own ways without constantly fleeing from being taken over by the English language and culture? Perhaps, Pennsylvania is the land where we could set up such a colony."

"Let me answer on behalf of my generation," Hendrick said entering the discussion. "The answer to that question is obvious. We should do just that. We can't have my brothers and sisters running off in all directions and losing their Dutch church and customs. We will find new fertile soil where land is cheap and abundant. We've already been through the trying times of establishing a new settlement and we have learned how to do it. This time, everything will not be new. The skills we have mastered will be put to good use."

The discussion continued with all agreeing on finding land for a new colony on the Pennsylvania frontier.

"Then it is agreed," Father Hendrick said in conclusion. "We will seek out the new land for our colony."

As this idea was turned into spoken words and spread among the New Jersey Dutch families who had joined with the Coetus, many Dutchmen from Bedminister, the Raritan Valley, Bound Brook and Millstone as well as those in east New Jersey who agreed with this line of reasoning began planning a new settlement in Pennsylvania where there would be ample land for their Dutch culture and growing families. It would be a sizable colony with all the trades represented. The Dutch families had made a substantial amount of money on the new continent and if their farms and businesses were sold there would be enough money available to reach the goal of rescuing their culture and keeping their families together. The women could see that it was not that their men had itchy feet but rather that their motive was to hold their families and the Dutch community together. Hendrick was a principal instigator of this plan to establish a new Dutch colony on the western frontier and he was very eloquent in his presentation. He persuaded many men to join his crusade to create a new Dutch nation on the frontiers of Pennsylvania.

Father Hendrick's brother-in-law, Samuel Durea, and his sister, Wyntie, were also enthusiastic about moving to Pennsylvania with the newly proposed colony. By 1765 their family had grown to nine living children. Their ages ranged between Geertje, who was twenty-one, to Annaetjen, who was newly born. With their oldest daughter of marriageable age and their next two boys, Peter and Abraham, seventeen and fourteen, they were facing the same problem of Bedminister losing its Dutchness and the price of land in east New Jersey scattering their children as they married.

Anna's mother and father, Samuel and Leah Demarest, decided that they would cast their lot with Hendrick and Anna in search of a Dutch nation on the Pennsylvania frontier. Samuel was sixty-one and Leah was fifty-five at the time of the migration to the Pennsylvania frontier.

Father Hendrick was also instrumental in encouraging three Westervelt, four Demarest and six Brinkerhoff families as well as many other families to enlist in this crusade to maintain a Dutch nation on the North American continent.

In 1765, scouts for this movement were sent ahead along the Old Dutch trail to locate land in Pennsylvania for the migration. Hendrick was one of the men chosen for this task. He was forty-seven years of age and one of the community's leaders. The other two men selected for the task were Cornelius Vanarsdale and Francis Cosart, both of whose families were close friends of the Bantas. They traveled along the Old Dutch Road to the Delaware River which they crossed at a point above Philadelphia. Here they left New Jersey and entered Pennsylvania and continued westward along the road to the vicinity of where York now lies and discovered that the Germans and Irish had established settlements a few miles west of York just south east of the hills named Conewago by the Indians. These were the farthest settlements along the Old Dutch Road. As they crossed south of the Conewago Mountains they found that the way ahead was blocked by the South Mountains which were rugged enough to be very difficult to cross with a wagon train. They were now over one hundred and fifty miles from Bedminester.

Beyond the Conawago mountains lay an area in-between and west of the Irish and German colonies. In this area, there were many streams flowing through an area of rolling hills. The main creek was also called Conewago by the Indians. Some of this land had been settled but for the most part it was available for original entry. The price of land was cheap on this new frontier if purchased from current owners or, if the new settlers preferred, they could purchase land not yet entered by seeking an original warrant from the Pennsylvania government.

This land was within four miles east of where Gettysburg is now located. They discovered that this area had soil they thought to be similar to that in Bergen County from its red color, consistency and feel. At this time in history there were no scientific means of testing soil for its fertility other than from its appearance and the growth of the wild-woods that covered it. From both these tests, the men who were mainly farmers felt they had found the ideal location for the new colony. Since a creek named the Conewago flowed through this area and mountains to the north-east bore the same name, they named the area with the melodic Indian name of Conewago.

Cornelius van Arsdale purchased from Robert Latimore, by deed of transfer, 200 acres of land for a consideration of three hundred and fifty-five pounds with Father Hendrick and Francis Cossart as joiners in the deed. This would be the first land in the Conewago area bought by the Dutch from Somerset county. This is the area where the colonists would first settle while they were surveying and entering land that was still un-entered. In looking for this two hundred acre plot of cleared land, they had visited other settlers and looked at various plots of land to find the best value available.

While looking over the land , Father Hendrick found a two-story log cabin already built alongside a pretty little brook named Swift Run Creek. He found that Sam Miller, the owner, was anxious to sell the cabin along with the three hundred and twenty acres of land surrounding it. The cabin had been built fourteen years earlier and many improvements made to it. The house had a great room which had been built in the English style with no great hearth across one wall, It also had a cellar on the first floor and a spiral staircase which led to three bed-rooms on the second floor. This would accommodate his fam-ily if all the boys were to sleep in one bedroom while all the girls slept in another leaving the third bedroom for him and Anna. There was ample land cleared next to it and a barn erected that would perfectly serve as his blacksmith shop. This he real-ized could save Anna and his eleven children still living at home the stress of starting a new house from scratch. He made a offer to Sam Miller for his rights to the land, offering to paying him a small amount at the time with the remainder due at the time he arrived with his family. The owner agreed to this arrange-ment.

The men had accomplished their task of finding land for the new colony and returned to Bedminisrer to relay to all the families along the Raritin Valley and in New Jersey who were ready to join in the migration the news of locating what they believed to be good farm land. With this news, old Jersey wagons that could be rebuilt or repaired were restored to a condition equal to that in which they were when they carried the immigrants to Somerset County. Other families constructed new wagons for the journey. All the same preparations that had been made thirteen years prior were again made for the new migration. The Dutch families from Bedminister were joined by other Dutch families from the other Dutch communities along the Raritan. Some had been in Somerset County longer than those in the Bedminister wagon train. Some came from as far away as Bergen County.

The total number of Dutch men women and children was over one thousand. Most were experienced frontiersmen. All were Dutch or Huguenot. All were searching for the same dream; a dream to save their culture and their ethnicity for their families on a continent which their ancestors had called home for over one hundred years. In late Spring of 1768, three years after the scouts had found the land for the new colony, the wagons followed by the families and their livestock again headed west along the Old Dutch Trail.

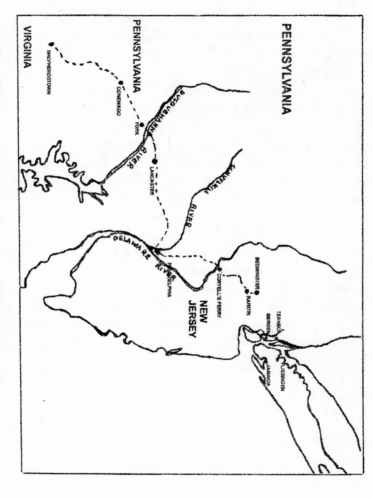

THE LOW DUTCH MIGRATION TO CONEWAGO, PENNSYLVANIA

CHAPTER 9

THE CONEWAGO COLONY

At sunrise, on a cold Spring morning in 1768, the wagon train was assembled at Raritan with families from Bedminister, the Raritan Valley and the Bergen and Hackensack areas of New Jersey. Over one-hundred families with their Jersey Wagons drawn by oxen and their livestock following each family were lined up on the trail. The number of emigrants was over one thousand. Every man, woman and child in the train recognized that three weeks of unknown hardships and total commitment lay ahead of them. .While traveling the Old Dutch Road, now known as the Old York Road, to the County of York and their final destination, Conewago, they would be traversing over one-hundred and fifty miles of frontier road that would become no more than a trail after they passed Philadelphia and ultimately an Indian trace as they approached their destination.

The trip would require crossing three major rivers, the Delaware, Schuylkill and Susquehanna, as well as myriads of lesser rivers and streams. Those who had made the arduous journey from Teaneck to Bedminester knew they had been through a warm up for this major emigration. The road was better kept to Philadelphia than the Old Dutch Road they had taken to Bedminister had been, but then it deteriorated to a condition as bad as the Old Dutch Road and the distance was three times as long.

Father Hendrick was a robust fifty years of age when he took his wife, Anna, and his thirteen children, three married with their own families, on this perilous journey. His sister Wyntie's husband,

Sam Duryea, was fifty-six with nine children as he entered on this mission. Anna's Parents, Samuel and Leah Demarest were sixty-one and fifty-five respectively at the time.

Because of the size of the emigration, there were many mishaps, such as lynch pins vibration out of their sockets allowing the wagon axles to crash to the ground or wagons getting stuck up to their beds in mud holes, causing the entire train behind the mishap to grind to a stop until repairs were made if the incident occurred in an area where the road was too narrow to allow the other wagons to pass around it. Because of this, the wagon train split into several groups often with miles between them. Men on horseback rode between the gaps in the train to hurry those falling behind and to warn of accidents ahead. They also rode ahead of an accident to slow the train in front of it. The train's length stretched several miles and it took hours to pass by a single point such as a village. Since Indians were not hostel along the Old York Road, keeping the wagons in close order was not required for defense.

Father Hendrick, Cornelius Van Arsdale and Francis Cozart alternated at the point of the wagon train as they had previously been over the route three years prior. The road was good as the train moved westward along the Old York Road. Many villages dotted the route in this well traveled area. Between the villages much of the virgin forest had been cleared and there were established farms. On their way to where they would cross the Delaware, they passed through the villages of Centerville, Three Bridges, Reaville, Larsons Corner, Ringoes, and Mount Aire. Finally the wagon train reached Lambertville on the banks of the Delaware just a few miles upriver from where George Washington crossed the same river on Christmas Eve only a few years later to accomplish his stunning defeat against the Hessians. At Lambertville lay the ferry they would use to cross the river.

The journey to the Delaware River was executed with no casualties and with few serious incidents. The three men who had been advance scouts three years before knew that the ferry had sufficient craft to make the crossing relatively easy though the size of the wagon train exceeded any the ferry owner had seen before. He was amazed to see a group of over one thousand Dutchmen heading for the farthest frontier.

It took two days to complete the crossing of the Delaware by the entire wagon train with its over one-hundred wagons, one thousand people and their livestock. There were no casualties to people, wagons or livestock though there were several hair raising moments.

After crossing the river, the road turned south towards Philadelphia. This section of the Old York Road was also in good condition and the train made good time. The Dutchmen, with their wagons and livestock, amazed villagers as the wagon train moved through their village. On its journey to Philadelphia it passed through the villages of Lahaska, Buckingham, Furlong, Bridge valley, Jamison, Hartsville, Warminister, Hatboro, Willow Grove, Abington, Jenkintown and Elkins' Point.

The train stopped at Philadelphia for a day to restock perishable supplies. How the emigrants relished this day's break from the rigors of their journey. The next day they were off again to the banks of the Schuykill River at its tidal basin only a mile or two from the river's mouth. Here, just south of Philadelphia, where the flow of the water was less rambunctious, lay another ferry to carry the Dutchmen, their wagon train and their animals across the river. Again the crossing went without serious incident.

The Old York Road on the west side of the Schuylkill deteriorated badly. The well-kept farms still stretched along the road on both sides and the wild woods had been tamed and removed but they could tell by the condition of the road that this section was far less traveled. As they moved farther from Philadelphia, they saw that the farms had been recently cleared from the forests with areas of virgin forests between the farms. The villages were farther apart and some still contained rough log cabins but some structures were built of finished lumber. They were only half way along their journey and yet they could see that they were on the frontier with miles of wild woods encroaching in on the road interspersed with farmers in the process of clearing their land. They knew that this land had been passed-by by the scouts as the colony needed thousands of acres for the building of the new Dutch nation.

As they moved westward, the road became unmaintained and miserable. The Old York Road closely paralleled the current Lincoln highway of today but at that time was barely wide enough for the axles of the wagons to pass between the trees of the forest that encroached on both sides of the trail. It had been raining on and off since the train had left Raratin but now the rain began to pour down making the journey almost impossible considering the condition of the road.

Puddles along the road came together forming lakes where the road went through low sections of the surrounding terrain. The streams rose to the point where it was impossible to ford them until the water receded. The train came to a complete stop. With everyone miserable and trying their best to keep as warm and dry as possible, a little Dutchman in the womb of his mother decided this was the time to enter this world. The women and men quickly set up a lean-to and made it as secure and dry from the storm outside as they possibly could.

It was a remarkable effort and soon the new mother was able to sleep in a warm dry place while regaining her strength. The baby boy was robust and healthy and greeted the world with lusty crying that showed all the emigrants that life was tough and could overcome all the problems they faced. The new arrival brought smiles and laughter to those who had almost given up hope just hours before.

"We've done a good job so far," Epke joked with his family. "We've had no casualties and with the new baby, we've got a larger population in our train than when we left Raritin."

It rained all the next day, but the following day the sun broke through and a glorious Spring day emerged. The streams were still too high to ford so the men and women went about repairing wagons, clothes and tending to people and animals that needed attention due to injuries that couldn't be attended to while the wagon train was moving. The next day the stream was forded and the wagon train proceeded along the Old York Road toward the city of Lancaster which lay approximately three days journey ahead of them, according to the three scouts that had traveled the road three years before.

The next three days remained sunny but cold. It was perfect weather for a wagon train on a trail that served as a road. The work was hard but the cool weather permitted the men to exert extra effort without becoming over-heated. The three trying days passed and the immigrants found themselves coming out of the road through the wild woods to beautifully kept farms with all the houses and barns white washed a brilliant white. It stunned them to see such a scene in the middle of nowhere on this edge of the frontier. They had reached the Mennonite colony of Lancaster.

Lancaster was one of the first inland cities on the continent. It had been settled by German Mennonites in 1709 and the borough of Lancaster was laid out in 1730. It was a clean and prosperous village and the Dutch immigrants in the wagon train took heart when they saw what had been accomplished so far west of what was at the time considered the frontier. They felt certain that within a few years they could duplicate this remarkable achievement.

The Lancaster villagers had witnessed the immigrations of the Germans, English and Irish who had settled east of where the Dutch were now going. They were clannish but not to the point where they didn't enjoy showing the passing wagon trains the wonders of what they had accomplished so far from civilization. The Dutchmen watched in rapt attention as they were escorted around the bountiful farms that surrounded the village.

Then the leaders of the train again assembled the wagons to begin the last portion of their journey to the land of the Conewago mountains and creeks. From Lancaster, the trail became even more difficult to travel for very little traffic moved between the next village of York and Lancaster. The name given the road, "the Old York Road" indicated that it ended at the next village of York in York County. Beyond that lay what? This was the question in the minds of the Dutchmen. Only Hendrick Banta, Cornelius van

Arsdale and Francis Cosart who had scouted the area before had seen the answer to that question.

The next physical barrier that lay before them was the Susquehana River which lay half way between Lancaster and York. The wagon train reached the river at a point where Columbia now lies. Since there was far less need to transport passengers and goods across that river on the edge of the frontier, the ferryman was ill prepared for the crossing of one-thousand Dutchmen with their wagons and livestock. He simply didn't have the equipment for the task. Therefore, the men in the train set to building rafts from timber cut in the forest. The men in the Wagon train came from all trades and professions. With their various skills, the rafts were constructed in a very expeditious manner. After crossing the river, the rafts were given to the ferryman for his assistance in directing the safe crossing of the Susquehana River.

On the west side of the Susquehana River, the Old York Road remained deplorable but passable. The terrible strain on the immigrants began to show in their physical conditions. A flu-like sickness swept the families which was very hard on those men who had to keep the wagon train moving by repairing the wagons and heaving them out of mud holes. The intermittent rain storms kept the trail soggy the entire route. Illness hit the elderly the hardest and two of those who were in their seventies succumbed and went to there reward just days before the immigrants would reach York where rest and shelter would be available. These two venerable old Dutchmen died among their own, but the normal Dutch burial customs had to be forgone for expedience sake. With Hendrick conducting the services, they were laid to rest in graves along side the Old York Road.

Two days later, the wagon train arrived in the farthest village on the western frontier, the village of York, in York county, Pennsylvania. York was situated alongside a beautiful creek, the Condorus creek. It had been surveyed and laid out as a village in 1740, twenty-eight years before the Dutch immigrants entered it on their way to the Conewago Creeks twenty miles to the west.

York would be the closest bit of civilization to the land that the three scouts had picked out for the Dutch settlement. The village had grown far beyond the felling of the giants of the forest and the clearing of land for farming. Permanent houses had been built over the last twenty years and the trades established. It would be the village where the new immigrants would get needed supplies for the next several years until their village was established. York was a town built by English pioneers.

After a days rest and recuperation just outside of York, The Dutch immigrants pushed on toward their final destination. Beyond York, the road, such as it was, became no more than an Indian trace, and the job of clearing the trees and underbrush wide enough for the wagons to pass through put the final test to the grit of the Dutchmen. The thought of being so close to where they would erect their new Dutch nation gave them renewed vigor as they hacked their way through those final miles. As they crossed through a pass between the Conewago Mountains and the Pigeon Hills, the trace split into a Y. On the scouting trip three years before, the three scouts had taken these two traces and found an Irish settlement to the north and a German settlement to the south. Directly ahead lay the land through which the Conewago Creek with many other smaller creeks flowed. This was the land the scouts had picked out for the Dutch nation. It had taken these brave Dutchmen over three weeks to make this epic journey. It had taken the lives of two ancient patriarchs and one of the newest generation had joined their number. They had arrived where they would establish their colony which they named Conewago.

The wagon train arrived in the land of the Conewago Creeks with every member of the new colony completely exhausted but in a state of euphoria. They had survived a long and difficult journey to form a new Dutch nation in a beautiful setting. The land was forested with large areas of meadows that would be relatively easy to put to the plough and much of which would be simple to turn into pasture land for their livestock. The land was gently rolling with many creeks in the crevasses between the rolling hills.

They arrived on a beautiful spring afternoon with the low sun giving all of the lovely surroundings a rose red glow. There was a feeling of unbridled optimism and certainty that they would accomplish their goal in this wonderful land of gently rolling hills.

Their first stop was at the two-hundred acres of land purchased by Cornelius van Arsdale. Here they set up their base camp and prepared to sow their first crop since it was now mid-spring and planting had to be done as soon as possible. Scouting parties were assembled by the various families to seek land for their own farm. Father Hendrick's farm was in the northern section of the land they planned to colonize and the plan was to arrange their farms in the five mile area stretching south of his property.

As families located their farms, a road they named the Low Dutch Road ran north to south through the middle of these farms. Along the road were located the various trades with Father Hendrick's blacksmith shop at the northernmost point in the colony. One of the first objectives of the Conewago colony was to construct a church. Father Hendrick donated land in the middle of his farm for that purpose while at the opposite end of the five mile long Low Dutch Road an inn and tavern were built.

Since the Indians in the area were not hostile, it was not necessary to concentrate the families in a fortified village. While the English did not follow the tradition of the Dutch of buying the land from the local Indian Chief, the Indians accepted the immigrants and desired to trade with them. They had no idea of the European concept of private property and this did cause difficulties between the two cultures. The lack of hostility did, however, permit the Dutch families to build their homes on their farms and thus no central village was necessary. Instead the shops were located along the five-mile road from the church to the tavern.

There were many streams in the area where the colony

settled such as Plum Run, Rock Creek, Beaver Dam, Brush Run and Swift run which supplied ample water for the colonist's use. Swift Run Creek ran alongside Father Hendrick's farm and supplied sufficient power for a grist mill as did several other of the creeks. All these streams flowed into Conewago creek, then into Big Conewago which emptied into the Susquehana River.

The new colony did find a vexing problem of finding a good mill site for its saw mill for rough cut lumber. None of the streams in the colony had a steep enough drop-off in the stream bed to power a first class saw mill. For this reason, the Dutch community was required to depend on the English, German and Irish settlements for much of their rough cut lumber. Many lived in well-constructed cabins of striped and smoothed logs that were well caulked and finished inside with plaster while using cut lumber only for floors and partitions.

Since there were meadows among the forests, the families found it easy to bring a good bit of acreage under the plow that first spring. In the past when new land was brought under cultivation, they had found the first crop of wheat grew to straw because of the fertility of the topsoil. Their first indication that their optimism for this new land might be overstated was the first year's crop of grain that grew on this new land. It did not grow to straw and the yield was less than normal, far less than could be expected from the land they left in New Jersey. The top soil, they found, could be measured in inches instead of feet as the land had not been repeatedly renewed by the alluvial soil deposited by the flooding of the land from rivers and streams.

Hendrick Banta's house in the Conewago settlement. Built
in 1743, he purchased it a few years later. He and his family
lived in it for thirteen years before going to Kentucky. The
one story room in the front had been the front porch until
recent remodeling.

With the reaping of that first crop in the fall of 1768, the
farmers recognized that the land they had chosen for their new
Dutch nation was not the fertile land they needed but instead
rather poor in quality. Thus, the warning flags went up even before many had purchased or claimed land or finished building
their temporary log cabins. The two warning flags were a lack of
good saw mill sites and the poor quality of the land. In spite of
this, the spirit of the new community remained high for everyone
thought they could overcome these deficiencies and that their
migration to the frontier of Pennsylvania would surely save for
posterity their Dutch culture and ethnicity on this continent. They
believed that with the strong Dutch work ethic and tenacity these
shortcomings could be overcome.

The central symbol around which this new Dutch nation was
organized was the DRC, Dutch Reformed Church. The church

was uppermost in the mind every member of the community. Thus, its construction came before other vital earthly projects. With the help of every able-bodied Dutchman in the colony, the church was completed the following year in January, 1769, out of rough lumber on the land donated by Father Hendrick.

Since everyone in the colony belonged to the DRC and there were over one-thousand in the community, The church building was a large structure for a frontier church. It was not fancy but well and efficiently constructed for its required heavenly function. At the opposite side from the entry door, stood a hour-glassed shaped pulpit that was very high. The space between the pulpit and the pews was of ample size to accommodate the communion service, marriages and baptisms that would take place within these solemn, holy walls. A broad middle isle ran down the center of the pews to within ten feet of the entrance. Two narrow isles also ran along the walls to the right and left of the pews. Extending around all four sides of the church, a bench was constructed for extra seating and the bench was always filled during services.

From the church, the Low Dutch Road ran south through the middle of the Dutch boweries (farms) for five miles to where the village inn and tavern was located. With this arrangement there was little temptation for Dutchmen to drop into the tavern to quench their thirst during the lunch recess of the Sunday service.

Following Lea's marriage to Jacobus Montfort, the Montfort family became very close friends of the Banta family. The children from both families fit in age and sex perfectly as potential romantic interests. Because of the uncertainty of the future, the migration was similar to a great war where things are put off until its conclusion. This was true of young couples who were in love and wanted to get married. Just following the formation of the new Conewago church on the new frontier, the presiding minister of the Classis of New Brunswick, Dominie John M. Harligen of Millstone, New Jersey, visited his new flock on the frontier. When he arrived, he found that all the young people who had fallen in love and wanted to get married were waiting for him to preform wedding ceremonies in the new church.

Abraham and Albert, Father Hendrick's next two oldest sons, asked Father Hendrick's permission to marry their sweethearts, two of the Monfort sisters. When Father Hendrick and the Montforts agreed to the marriage, the two couples decided to have a double ceremony. Geertruid Banta, the next youngest in Father Hendric's family had fallen in love with Francis Montfort and decided to make it a triple marriage. Abraham married Margrieta Montfort, Albert married Styntie Montfort and Gertruid married Francis. Marriage after marriage followed or preceded theirs because the young couples wanted to take this opportunity to have the nuptials preformed while the dominie was there so that they could be with their sweethearts during the building the new Dutch nation. It was the baby boom of the new colony after the rigors of the migration.

Following the organization of the new church, the Montfort and Banta families were joined by marriage between Father Hendrick's second, third, fourth and fifth oldest children and the Montfort children.

Through these newlyweds, many brand new families joined the well over one hundred families in the migration to the new settlement with the musical, lilting name of Conewago. What unique honeymoons were had by these couples on the edge of the Pennsylvania frontier. This rash of marriages took place upon completion of the church in January, 1769.

Father Hendrick with his oldest son and confidant, Hendrick, became the driving force of developing the three-hundred and seventeen acres Father Hendrick purchased on the scouting trip three years before the migration. Under their direction, these acres were developed into farms on which all the Bantas, married and single, with the exception of Abraham, Father Hendrick's second oldest son, resided. The work was backbreaking and unrewarding for the land simply wasn't fertile. Father Hendrick named his bowery, "Loss and Gain." The Loss stood for exchanging the fertile soil of

Somerset County for the poor quality of land in Conewago. The Gain stood for the development of a new Dutch nation on this new Pennsylvania frontier.

Nine months after the rash of marriages, a crop of Dutch babies inundated the new colony. Incredibly, Father Hendrick had three grandchildren born on the same day. One to each of the newly married couples. All three babies were born on October 23, 1769. He felt certain that his decision to move to this new frontier was justified by the formation of these three new families for here there was ample land to accommodate all of his children.

Within two years, Hendrick moved from his father's farm and became the owner of ninety-five acres of his own land. He moved his family onto it, prepared some land for planting, and constructed a new house. Upon planting his first crop he found the fertility of the soil to be less than acceptable. The condition of the soil on his farm are told by the name he gave it, "Mount Misery."

As the other families located their farms, each family told their hope or disappointment by what they named them. Francis Cozart named his "Cozart's Dream." David Cozart named his "Barren Hill." Francis Montfort's was named "Walnut Bottom." Peter Cozart's was named "Turkey Range." David van Dyne called his "Broken Land." David Hornet named his "Delight." It's easy to recognize the pleasure or displeasure of each farmer by the name he gave his farm. Though some were pleased, most recognized that the land didn't seem worth the great effort they were investing in it.

With the first crop being far from a success, questions arose among the Dutch families as to the advisability of continuing in Conewago. It was decided among the leaders, a group in which Father Hendrick was becoming predominant, that some families should continue the search for the land where the Dutch nation should be established. It was decided that Father Hendrick's brother in law, Sam Duryea and his, sister, Wyntie, would again form a wagon train with several other families to continue to search for better land.

Only a year after they had arrived from the long hard trip

from Bedminister. Samuel and Wyntie and the other Dutch families began anew the search for better land by wagon train Their search took them forty miles to the south into Berkley county, Virginia, to where Shepherdstown, West Virginia, now lies. Here they established farms to see if that land held more promise for the colony's future. These two communities kept in close contact with each other. Sam and Father Hendrick traveled regularly between these two colonies to visit each other's families and coordinate the business between these sister communities. Other families in the two new colonies also kept in touch with each other.

The seriousness of the conditions of the Conewago colony can be read between the lines of a letter written by Anna's mother, Lea Demerest, to her brother back in New Jersey. The entire letter follows as it poignantly describes the emotions and thoughts of those enduring the hardships of this sub-marginal land on the Pennsylvania frontier.

Connewagen, Aug.6.1772

Respected and much loved brother and sister,

I must not let this opportunity of writing you something slip by; and so I let you know that, by God's grace we are all reasonably well and hope that these lines may find you in health. I should rejoice to see you, but I do not ever again expect to do so, unless you happen to come here for our days are passing by. I do not think that I shall abide here much longer, my time is almost gone. I am here in a strange land, away from all my friends and acquaintances and I have never yet been in a place where it would have cost me less pain than to die here. I pray the Lord may prepare us both that we may see each other hereafter. My dear brother, my desire and wish from you is that you would forward me the money left me by my deceased father. I am in great need of it. Nothing further, except greeting from me and Samuel to you and your wife, and to Maria and Abraham and all my brothers and sisters. Greeting also from Trientie and Jacob.

Lea Demerest

This letter was written while Lea and Samuel were still in their fifties. Their despair in the frontier conditions they were enduring is clearly evident in Lea's sad words pleading for the money her parents left her. Unfortunately, she was not to receive the pittance she requested and joined Sam and Wyntie Duryea in Shepherdstown, Berkeley county, Virginia, shortly after this letter was written.

By 1774, the Conewago settlers had established their colony and church by their tenacity and stubbornness. While life was difficult they were committed to achieving their goal and to that end Father Hendrick was entering into the politics of York county. His primary objective was to raise support among the other settlements towards breaking off the area settled by the Dutch colony into a county of its own. He was elected a member of the York County Committee of Safety which was the committee made up of freeholders of York County, Its purpose was to establish laws governing the transaction of business. In this capacity, he worked for the support of a separate Dutch county. He was greatly disappointed to find no support for his dream among the other colonies.

At this time, 1774, the people of Boston were engaged in the preliminary struggles that led to the Revolution. This was the time when the Boston Tea Party took place in anger against the English taxes. While he and his second oldest son, Abram, were on the committee, it, under chairman, James Smith, sent a letter to the Committee at Boston siding with "the unfortunate people of Boston." The letter was accompanied by 246 pounds for "relief of the suffering people of the city." The Dutch colony of Conewago strongly supported the Continental Congress that met to resolve the matter.

To those in Conewago, these matters seemed far away and incidental to the daily problems of trying to keep their own heads above water on this inhospitable frontier. None the less, in 1775, when hostilities broke out between the American patriots and the British army and Loyalist Americans, many from Conewago, including Bantas, served in the Pennsylvania Militia and saw action on the Pennsylvania frontier. When the British occupied Philadelphia in the winter of 1777-78, the Continental Congress was forced to move to the City of York for protection. The American capitol was in Conewago's front yard. Meanwhile, the British and Revolutionary American soldiers marched back and forth across east New Jersey through Hackensack township as battles were won and lost by the two sides. The Dutch in Conewago learned of the scorched earth around Teaneck and how many of their relatives homes were burned by the British as the battlefield moved through their cities and towns.

Families back in New Jersey were split between the Tories and American patriots. There were Bantas on both sides of the conflict, some Tories, some patriots depending on the branch of the schism in the Dutch Reformed Church to which they belonged. Hendrick Banta and the Conewago colonists stood firmly behind the Continental Congress.

While the war raged, life on the frontier became even more difficult. The families back in New Jersey were fighting for their own lives and could offer little help financially. Supplies in the City of York dried up and the frontiersmen had to build their community with no outside help. Living on the frontier had always been dangerous and hard but with a Revolutionary War being fought, daily existence became even more difficult. With no outside help, the colonists had to look to themselves for every necessity of life. In spite of this, with Dutch determination, the farms and the community continued to improve in farm lands under cultivation and in better housing.

Father Hendrick's own family continued to expand at the rate of a new baby every eighteen months. In addition, his married children were producing offspring at the same pace. By 1776, he had added four more children to his ever growing family. These four children were; Antie, born in 1769. David, born in 1771. Isaac born in 1773 and Angentie born in 1775.

At the time of the beginning of the Revolutionary War, his family numbered twenty living children with all six children born of his first wife, Rachel Brower Banta, now married with families of their own. Hendrick was now 58 and the Banta family had been on the North American continent for one hundred and seventeen years. After all these years he and his family were still battling the rigors of frontier life. Many of the family who had stayed in Hackensack township were now wealthy but were undergoing the tragedy of watching their homes and precious possessions ravaged by the war that was sweeping back and forth across their land. It is difficult to determine which part of the family was undergoing the greatest trauma. These were "the times that tried men's souls."

His eldest son Hendrick's family now numbered nine children. They were in the process of clearing the last of their farm land from the primaeval forests. Their family home had been completed and "Mount Misery" was producing a crop that was not abundant or profitable from the viewpoint of energy expended but adequate to keep the family afloat.

Hendrick was Father Hendrick's closest son and confidant. He had come to rely on him as a sounding board for his hopes aspirations and goals. They had worked as a team in building the family's new life in Conewago. Suddenly, Hendrick was taken from his family by a Smallpox epidemic that swept through the colony. In frontier villages such epidemics struck every few years. This time it left Mary, his pregnant wife a widow, his nine children without a father, and Father Hendrick without his oldest son and closest companion.

There were several deaths in the Dutch community from the

disease and burials were not public because of the virulence of the epidemic. Hendrick was buried in the new cemetery near the Dutch Reformed Church. Dominie George Brinkerhof presided at the family graveside service. He had succeeded Dominie Cornelius Cosine who had been appointed the first resident minister by the New Brunswick classes.

Dominie Brinkerhoff was a descendant of the family that had purchased part of Epke's farm in Teaneck, becoming one of their first neighbors on that frontier. Two Bantas had inter-married with the Brinkerhoffs, one of which was Father Hendrick's great aunt Angenitie. Dominie Brinkerhoff was one of the first ministers of the Coetus fork in the schism of the DRC to be ordained in America rather than in Amsterdam. The congregation was pleased to have as its domine, one of the first ministers ordained on this continent. The Banta family found it very comforting to have as the dominie presiding at the grave site a relative who embodied the colonies Coetus beliefs.

The family rallied around Mary, Hendrick's widow, with her now fatherless family. Hendrick's brothers took turns at the tasks required to keep the farm operating so that Mary could tend her family and prepare for the delivery of her expected child. Her sisters and sisters in law tended her housekeeping chores as the loss of her husband during her pregnancy left her despondent and lethargic with little energy. The family pitched in to help her through these trying days. They became a support group that carried her through the valley of despair that follows such a tragedy.

Albert, Hendrick's second younger brother, had been especially close to Hendrick and stepped in to oversee the management of "Mount Misery." Hendrick Jr., Hendrick's oldest son, who was now sixteen and had been working with his father since finishing grammar school, had taken over as head of the family. His Uncle Albert, who was similar to

Father Hendrick in that he was very religious and liked to preach, laid out the work to be done during the following week.

The new baby, a boy, was born on September 3, 1777 about six months after Hendrick's death. He was named Albert after his uncle. This was Hendrick and Mary's tenth and last child. With the birth of her new baby, Mary's depression waned and in its place exhilaration filled her spirit. Her family and its well-being became the focus of her life. She was thankful for the Banta boys who, with her oldest son, Hendrick, were continuing the operation of her farm. She would often go out to where the boys were clearing the trees from the forest in order to create new farm land. She would fix them a basket lunch and share it with them when they took their lunch break from the exhausting work.

About six months after Hendrick's death, she left baby Albert with Uncle Albert's wife, Stynie, who would take care of Albert and her two other children who were too young for school. She went out to watch the men clear trees from the forest. The men consisted of her oldest son, Hendrick Jr., his Uncle Albert, Uncle Jake and Uncle Dan. She laid out a blanket on the meadow where they could share lunch at mid-day when they took a break from their work. The men were felling a giant of the forest and as they always did made their cuts so that it would fall in the area intended. All thought that where Mary was sitting was perfectly safe for they thought that she was far enough away so that the tree couldn't possibly strike her even if they miscalculated and the tree fell her way.

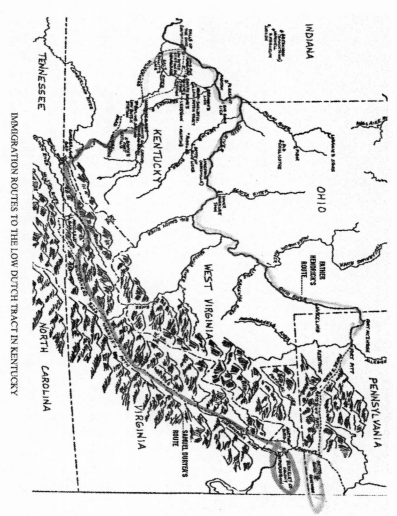

IMMIGRATION ROUTES TO THE LOW DUTCH TRACT IN KENTUCKY

This was in March 1778, and one of the first sunny Spring days. Mary, who was dressed warmly for the chill in the air, laid down beside the basket of food and, in the warmth of the Spring sun, fell fast asleep. The tree was cut and began to fall in the direction intended. Then, it inexplicitly twisted at the cut and began to fall towards where Mary slept. Too late, the men could see that the tree might fall on Mary and all screamed to Mary to get up and run. Mary heard the screams and sleepily opened her eyes and began to sit up as the tree smashed into her with a gigantic branch striking her shoulder and head.

Her son, Hendrick Jr., was over to her in an instant followed by Albert, Jake and Dan. Climbing through the branches they reached her side and could see she was unconscious from the blow to her head. They could also see she was still breathing. With all the combined strength of their muscles, hard as steel from the work they had been doing, they were unable to lift the branch to free Mary. They dared not use their axes to directly cut the branch to free her for the striking of the axe on the branch could crush her skull. They therefore had to remove all the side branches. Then through leverage of a long straight branch they lifted the limb off of Mary while Hendick Jr. pulled his mother out from under it. When they had completed the rescue, Mary was no longer breathing. They carried her lifeless body back to her house where her other children who were not in school were awaiting her return.

As they neared the house, Hendrick thinking of what he must tell his brothers and sisters broke into uncontrollable sobs while he kept repeating over and over, "Mount Misery, Mount Misery. Father surely chose the right name for our farm."

Uncle Albert carried the dead body of Mary into her cabin and laid her upon her bed. Albert's wife, Styntie, rushed to his side asking, "My God in heaven, What has happened to Mary?"

"She has been hit and killed by a falling tree," cried Hendrick Jr. who had entered the room with his two other uncles. "What is to become of my brothers and sisters. We are all orphaned. Father died only a year ago and now mother has been killed. Our lives have ended!"

Six of his brothers and sisters were at school. Of the three at home, only little Maria at age six could comprehend the tragedy that had happened for Leah was only three and Albert was an infant.

"Styntie, you must take care of matters here while I go and tell father what has happened." Albert said. "Then, I will go to the school and prepare Peter, Rachel, Abraham, Anna, Sarah and John for this terrible disaster."

With this, he quickly saddled and mounted his horse and galloped the mile to Father Hendrick's house. He found him in his blacksmith shop and told him of the awful event that had happened and that he must be off to prepare the children who were in school for the terrible shock. Father Hendrick stopped the work he was doing and ran to saddle his horse while calling over his shoulder, "Tell your mother to come quickly. We must ride over to be with the children as soon as possible."

Anna came running out of the cabin and Father Hendrick picked her up and placed her behind the saddle on the horse. He mounted the horse and the two rode off toward "Mount Misery" with Anna holding tight to his waist.

Albert reached the school as it was letting out for the day and climbing down from his horse called his nieces and nephews aside to tell them the sad news. There was no easy way to do it and the children were shattered when he told them what had happened as gently as he could. He picked up the two youngest children, John who was eight and Sarah who was nine, and put them up on his horse. He then climbed into the saddle with his niece and nephew in front of him. Together, Albert and the children headed to "Mount Misery" with the other four running along beside his horse weeping in stunned silence.

When they arrived home, grandfather and grandmother were waiting outside the front door for them. The six children ran to them and buried their faces in the familiar smell of their clothing as the grand-parents tried to hug all of them at once. Weeping they went inside where their four brothers and sisters along with their and aunt and uncles were talking quietly. When they went to their mother's bedside and saw her lifeless body the anguish in the room was unbearable.

Hendrick Jr., who had witnessed his mother's death, again voiced his innermost concern, speaking to everyone and to no one, "Mount Misery, how well father named this farm. We are all orphans. What will become of us on this inhospitable frontier?"

Without a moments hesitation, Anna firmly answered his question. "Hendrick, you and your brothers and sisters have nothing to fear of the future. Your grandfather and I have adopted you as our children from this very moment on."

Tears filled the eyes of her husband, the tough old frontiersman. "What a wife the good Lord has given me," he thought. "She raised her cousin's children as if they were her own and now she will raise these ten children of her sister's oldest boy. She is a woman like no other. She is a rock that has stood by me through two frontiers and has never complained. Now she welcomes this additional chore with all the love that is in her heart."

"Yes children," Father Hendrick continued, "You have nothing to fear. You are now a part of our many children. Our families have become one."

From that day forward, Father Hendrick never talked of his nineteen living children, nor did Anna or his children, for these ten children were no longer grandchildren but part of his immediate family of twenty-nine.

During the war years, news from relatives in east New Jersey was full of dreadful tails of destruction and battles. Homes of some relatives were burned to the ground. At one point, the Bantas were proud to write to the family in Conewago that General Washington had bivouaced his army on the Banta farm in Teaneck.

The English held the Northwest Territory which was not part of the land being fought over since it was not a colony. A rumor circulated in the colony that the English were seeking to take hold of the land to the south of the Ohio River in northern Virginia known as Kentucky. They were stirring up the Indians to the west in that area in order to lay claim to the land which Virginia claimed as part of its colony. The rumor had it that settlers could claim land there as a means of holding it from the British. The American patriots who were seeing action against the English in the Revolution felt a strong loyalty towards their new nation for which they fought so bravely. To many of them, settling the land south of the Ohio in Kentucky in order to hold it from the British was a noble cause.

Daniel Boone had made his way into Kentucky by way of an Indian trace which he called the Wilderness Trail, then through the Cumberland Gap. He then set up a fort in eastern Kentucky at a place he called Boonesborough. He was elected as a captain of the militia. During the Revolution, he and thirty of his men were captured by Shawnee Indians who took them to the British headquarters at Detroit. The Indians had great respect for him and he was elected as a member of their tribe. He then made them believe he was on their side and would prevail on American settlements to surrender to them but instead he escaped and hurried back to Boonesborough where he prepared the fort for the Indian attack. The Indians, of course, were repulsed and despised Boone for his deception. Thus the relations between the Indians and the white man couldn't have been worse. Daniel Boone's experiences were the talk of the newspapers throughout the colonies. His capture and escape happened in 1778.

When Sam Duryea read of Boone's exploits, he traveled to Conewago to confer with Father Hendrick. Both brothers-in-law sat at the table in Father Hendrick's great room in his old log cabin and entered into discussion about the their disappointment as to the Conewago area as the site for a Dutch nation. With their long Dutch clay pipes lit and smoke surrounding their heads, Sam brought Hendrick up to date on what he had read and heard about the Kentucky section of the Virginia colony.

"I believe," he said to Hendrick, "that we have found the right place to establish our Dutch nation and at the same time save the Kentucky country from the English. If that country is to be saved for the American cause, settlers must migrate there and establish colonies. I have been talking to several Americans of English decent who are planning to go there and claim land. I've told them that I will go with them. If I find fertile land, will you abandon Conewago and lead a colony of Dutchmen to settle it?"

Others were already abandoning Conewago for greener pastures. Its future looked bleak yet they had invested ten years in building their farms and it was not an easy decision to make. Father Hendrick set about to determine the attitude towards such a migration with Anna and his family. All agreed that Conewago had not lived up to its promise due to its poor soil. Anna was ready to move again for she saw no future in the section of York County where they had settled. Their non-Dutch neighbors were dead set against allowing the Dutch to break from York County to form a new county.

After these discussions with Anna and his family. He told Sam that if he could find good fertile land in Kentucky, he would lead an emigration from Conewago to the new land despite the distance and dangers involved.

"Good," Sam said. "Then I will go with the band of Englishmen to see what kind of land is available in the Kentucky country. I'll report back to you as soon as I return."

The word spread among the Conewago families that Father Hendrick was looking into moving a settlement to the Kentucky land. Many felt as he did and were ready to give up all they had built and move to better land. At the time of this discussion, Father Hendrick was sixty and Sam was sixty-five, a time when most men would be preparing for retirement.

CHAPTER 10

KENTUCKY

AND THE LOW DUTCH TRACT

Sam Duryea returned to Shepherdstown and informed the men who were going to scout the Kentucky country for land to settle or sell that he would join them. They expected to be able to acquire thousands of acres of fertile land there and claim it which by law meant they must build a cabin and clear a small area of land for each claim they would make. Sam was the only Low Dutchman in the group and at sixty-five the oldest. He made known to them that his mission was to acquire land for a Low Dutch colony.

The men that would travel with him on this dangerous adventure were Ralph and William Morgan, John Taylor, John Strode, George Bedinger, John Constant, Thomas and Benoni Swearingen, and two Africans belonging to the Swearingen brothers. All these men thought Sam, who appeared to them to be in his seventies, was eccentric. None the less, they admired his knowledge of the frontier and welcomed him warmly to accompany them into this unknown territory.

After careful preparations, they left Shepherdstown, Berkeley County, Virginia, on March 1,1779 for Boonesborough knowing that the Indians in the area were hostile. Their journey took them along the Wilderness Road which was still the Indian trace that Daniel Boone had followed just a few years earlier. This trace took them through Powell Valley, then through the Cumberland Gap and finally to Boones Trace that would lead them to Boonesborough.

Here miraculous good fortune turned what they thought at the time was bad fortune, into an event that probably saved their lives.

Unknown to Sam and the scouting party headed for Boonesborough, a Captain Starms, leading a group of ten to twelve men, left Boonesborough headed for Virginia. Boonesborough had been under siege from the Shawnee, under Chief Black Fish, for seven months and the fort was barely able to keep the enemy in check. This group of men had had enough and were ready to quit the Kentucky frontier. Their leaving the fort left it badly under-manned. When Captain Starm's group left for Virginia, the Indi-ans surrounding the fort split into two groups and some twenty five followed on the trail behind Starms and his group.

While Starms group was only a few miles from Boonesboro, Sam's scouting group lost the trail and wandered through the cane for about a mile. As they again neared the trail, their horses caught whiff of scent of the white men followed closely by the Indians and began snorting and rearing, warning the scouting party of danger. As they carefully entered the trail, they found signs of the Starms party having passed and of the Indians following it. Through providence they had just missed the passing of these two antagonists. This was on April 6th just before dark.

Though they were only a short distance from the fort, it was decided to stop and set up camp for the night leaving the comple-tion of their journey to the next morning. Sam informed his group that they should move off of the trace for perhaps a hundred yards to set up the camp and then they should sleep without fires due to the Indians in the area. Colonel William Morgan countered Sam's advice saying, "Let us not worry about this. If it is our time to die, we shall die. If not, our time has not yet come."

No one questioned the Colonel's strange logic and showing they were as brave as he was, lit a very large bonfire right in the middle of the trail. With it crackling cheerfully, they ate their suppers and went to sleep around its warmth. The next morning the men arose, loaded their packs, mounted their horses and set of on the final short trip to the fort. Within a few hundred yards of their camp, they found where Indians had been observing them the night before, but, thinking they had set up some sort of trap to ensnare them, they did not attack the foolhardy scouting party. Thus in twenty-four hours they had twice unconsciously avoided almost certain slaughter.

When they reached Boonesborough the following day, they were greeted with great jubilation for now the loss of Starms group was replaced. The entire fort was in the middle of this celebration when the sad news was delivered by Jacob Starms, son of the Captain, who arrived back at the fort terribly worn and exhausted, that his fathers group had been attacked and annihilated by Indians less than thirty miles from the fort. He was the lone survivor having saved himself by hiding in the cane and had cautiously hurried to the security of the fort. This was less than two hours after Sam and the scouting group had reached Boonesborough.

The men in the fort placed themselves on full alert and did not leave Boonesborough in groups of less than five. Even then they would hide during the day and hunt only at dusk and dawn. Though the woods were crawling with Indians, the scouting group still continued to cautiously go into the forest to find fertile land for their land claims. As improvements were made, the land was assigned among the men by ballot.

This company of land seekers that was headed by Swearigen traveled cautiously to an area a few miles northeast of Boonesborough. Here they found a very fertile area of rich top soil which surrounded a creek named Muddy Creek that was a tributary of the Kentucky River. They made three improvements along this creek for which the men balloted. On May 5th, an improvement was made on a part of upper Muddy that had a considerable fall. Due to the rapid fall in the creek no one but Sam was interested in it. Sam recalling the problem of setting up a good saw mill in Conewago, recognized that this fall in the creek would solve that problem if the Dutch moved here. Since the other men thought the site too poor, they let old Sam have it with no ballot. Sam told them this would be the site of the new Dutch nation that he would lead here. After this improvement the scouting party returned to Boonesborough following the east fork of Otter Creek.

Swearington joked to the other men at the fort that Duryea's choice of land was the least desirable of all they had improved. Sam, with his age, broken English and brusk Dutch manner, was called the "old man" by all his contemporaries, while he called them "the boys." Most continued to think of him as an eccentric. He, however, considered his choice a perfect one and would so report to Father Hendrick when he returned to Virginia.

The scouting party from Shepherdstown continued to live at Boonesboro through the summer raising corn near the fort and then returned to Virginia in the fall. Sam was favorably impressed by the land he had claimed and told his fellow Dutchmen he had found rich fertile land in Kentucky. A few days after his return to Shepherdstown, he and Wyntie went to visit his brother-in-law, Hendrick, at Conewago to tell him also about the rich, fertile land he had found in Kentucky ideal for the Dutch nation that they had so often talked about establishing on the western frontier.

Their dream was within reach, he told Hendrick. They then came up with a plan to settle this new Low Dutch community. The plan was to divide the migrating party into two sections. One party led by Duryea would migrate with the Dutch families from Shepherdstown, Berkeley County, Virginia, overland by means of the Wilderness Trail to White Oak Station. This station had been built by Nathaniel Hart about three-quarters of a mile north of Boonesborough the year before Sam's scouting party had traveled to Kentucky. Hendrick would, at the same point in time, lead a second party from Conewago across Pennsylvania to the head of the Ohio River where Pittsburgh now stands. From there, his colony would take flat boats down the Ohio to the Falls of the Ohio where Louisville is now located. Hendrick would establish a Dutch station near the Falls. Here his contingent of colonists would build cabins and plant, grow and reap a crop to provide food for both parties. Then Hendrick would lead his group in the Fall of 1780 ninety miles east to Boonesborough and White Oak Springs Station.

When both groups were together they would then make preparations to build the Dutch tract on the land Samuel had picked out on Muddy Creek.

Here they would fulfill their goal to build a Dutch nation where the Dutch families could raise their children and their children's children with Dutch customs, language and, most important, where they could praise God through the Low Dutch Reformed Church. This was their motivation for this dangerous step in the lives of the Dutch families that would join them. They would find and settle enough good fertile land to make it possible for their sons and daughters to raise their families without being forced to leave the community to look for land on a new frontier. Both men agreed immediately to start preparations for a migration of Dutch families to Kentucky.

Sam recruited his group from Berkeley County, Virginia. These Dutch families included over thirty-five individuals and included the families of Sam, Peter and Henry Duryea, Peter Cosart, Frederick Ripperdan, John Bullock and Cornelius Borgart, plus the following single men, Daniel and Albert Duryea, Albert and John Vorhees and Dan and Peter Banta. In the Spring of 1780 these pioneer families traveled down the valleys of the Alleghenies, then through the Cumberland Gap and then followed the Wilderness Road, which Daniel Boone had just hacked out of the primeval forests following an ancient Indian war path. At that time, it was not a road but simply an Indian trace through the virgin forests where Indians ferociously defended their land, and wild beasts were threats to life and limb.

His party set off for Kentucky in the spring of 1780. On this migration, this small band of Dutchmen tested their skills and bravery as true men and women of the frontier. They passed through the Shenandoah Valley of Virginia, between the Blue Ridge and Alleghenies, and across the mountains through the Cumberland Gap and then into Kentucky. As they were passing through Powell Valley, they were ambushed by hostile Indians and Peter Banta, a son of Father Hendrick, was murdered.

They were compelled to travel on foot with pack horses. The "pack-saddle" was the forked branch of a tree fastened to the horse upon which were hung all their household goods and provisions. One historian pictures the journey thus:

> Men (were) on foot with their trusty rifles on their shoulders, driving stock and leading pack-horses. The women, some walking with pails on their heads, others with children in their laps, and other children swung in baskets on horses, shouldered equal, if different, responsibilities with their men. Encamping at night, expecting to be massacred by Indians, subsisting on stinted allowances of stale bread and meat, encountering bears, wolves and wild cats in the narrow bridle-path overgrown with brush and underwood, they continued their perilous journey with no thought of abandoning it.
>
> An account tells a story of when the colony reached within a half dozen miles of the first settlement in the territory. Several families stopped and made camp for the night while the rest of the train moved on. The Indians that night attacked the families and slaughtered all but one man who escaped into the underbrush.
>
> After enduring three weeks on the trail suffering many other hardships and terrifying incidents, the party arrived in White Oak Springs in March of 1780, three weeks after leaving their homes in Berkeley County

CHAPTER 11

THE FALLS OF THE OHIO AND THE

BEARCREEK LOW DUTCH SETTLEMENT

In the winter of 1780, Father Hendrick organized his party or emigrants who were leaving from Conewago, York County Pennsylvania. His own family of Banta children, the families of his married daughters plus his sons' wives and children would have, by themselves, made up a party of 38. Of these, sixteen children were twelve or under. In addition, The party included the families of Samuel, Peter and John Demaret, John and Christopher Westerfirld, Simon VanArsdale, Sophia Voris and Catherine Dorland. In all, the emigrants totaled over 100 of which half were twelve or under. Though other parties of Dutch would follow in the next few years, this first group was the largest Dutch group to ever migrate to Kentucky by way of the Ohio River.

Once again the Jersey wagons were taken out of retirement or new wagons were built to accommodate the families on their arduous journey across the Appalachian Mountains to Fort Pitt. Fort Pitt was located where the Allegheny and Monongahela Rivers merged to form the headwaters of the Ohio River. Other Dutch families had already emigrated from the beautiful but unfertile land of the Conawegos to greener pastures but this emigration was the death knell of the Conawego colony. Over the next few decades it simply faded away. Today all that remains is the church graveyard, Father Hendrick's log cabin and a five mile long road named the Low Dutch Road. The tavern outlasted the church and its owner bought the church property. The proceeds were used to construct a stone wall around the graveyard.

This Low Dutch cemetery is all that remains of the
Conewago Colony.

The distance they would cover in going to Fort Pitt was just under 200 miles. There was an unkept road that they followed which closely paralleled the route that U. S. Highway 30 and

parts of the Pennsylvania Turnpike now follow. The journey over
the mountains was difficult and with all the hardships they had
endured on previous migrations they covered it in two weeks.

Upon reaching the fort, the families set about constructing
flat boats for the trip down the Ohio River. These were built from
rough cut logs which they bought from a local saw mill and caulked
with pitch. Each flat boat was rectangular in shape, with a two
and one-half foot wall around all four sides. A gate was provided so
as to permit their livestock and possessions to be loaded and
unloaded. A shelter was built in the center and the craft had a long
sweep pole at the stern to act as a crude rudder which was used to
steer the craft. Each craft differed per the desires of its builders but
averaged about thirty feet in length with a sixteen foot beam. Since
the floor of the craft was built out of heavy timber they had almost
no draft and traveled easily over shallow water. Row boats were
constructed and tied alongside each flat boat to take the occupants
to the shore, to scout ahead for shoals or rapids and to use as a
lifeboat in emergencies. The building of these flat boats consumed
about three weeks. It took fourteen craft to accommodate the entire
party.

In mid-February, Father Hendrick and his party of Dutch immigrants, started the navigation of the craft over the seven hundred miles of the twisting and turning Ohio River lying between
Fort Pitt and The Falls of the Ohio. The trip was extremely perilous due to the hostile Indians who roamed the wilderness at that
time. In addition, there was the hazard of shoals where the river
widened and on which the craft often got stuck plus the areas
where the river narrowed and the water became rapid.

The Indians were a constant menace, causing the Dutchmen
to be cautious as to where they beached their boats so that the
livestock could graze. All other times they kept the flat boats as
close as possible to the middle of the river. At one time Indians
traveled beside the flat boats in birch canoes creating a terrible
noise with their war cries. They made no attempt to attack when
they saw that every man aboard carried a long rifle and that the

pioneers could take refuse in the center cabin. Fortunately, the trees and bushes had shed their summer leaves permitting the frontiersmen to see into the forests that lined the banks. Nonetheless, the crafty red man set traps to lure them to shore where they could be ambushed. The shrewd Dutchmen fell for none of their tricks.

After two weeks on the river, Father Hendrick and the Dutch families found themselves at the end of their journey, The Falls of the Ohio. The Northwest Territory lay to the north, and Kentucky lay to the south of the river. They made the final beaching of their flat boats on the Kentucky side of the river just above the falls. At that time there was nothing where Louisville now stands except a few log cabins. After disembarking and forming a prayer group, all bowed their heads while Father Hendrick offered thanks to the Lord. Only one life had been lost on this incredible journey which was miraculous considering the distance they had covered and the dangers they had endured. The colony of Dutchmen arrived in Kentucky in mid-April of 1780.

As per their plan, Father Hendrick's section of the two pronged immigration was to find land to grow a crop along the banks of the Ohio for the colony's sustenance before setting out to meet Sam's contingent at White Oak Station in the Fall.

The colony's first priority was to find a location to build log cabins and clear fields for planting a crop. Hendrick found that a man named Colonel John Floyd owned several thousand acres of fertile land and had built a fortified station along a creek named Beargrass Creek. This creek flowed into the Ohio River near the falls. Floyd had built this station about six and one-half miles north of the falls in 1779. Hendrick had his colony build their Low Dutch Station half a mile below Floyd's Station for safety from the hostel Indians. They called their station the New Holland Beargrass Station. The Revolutionary War was still in full progress and being ardently fought by the Americans and the English. The English enemy had stirred up the Indians in the area and were using them as a military weapon against the Kentucky settlements in the War of Independence.

Flat boats similar to those used by the Low Dutch
migration down the Ohio. Courtesy of Elsa M. Banta

There were other settlements along Beargrass Creek which had been built in the year since Floyd had established his station. Land along the creek could be rented from Colonel John Floyd very inexpensively if settlers were willing to clear the land. Floyd had a two-thousand acre grant which he had no way of clearing except through the labors of those coming down the Ohio River to locate in Kentucky. Hendrick negotiated for sufficient land to build the colonies' homes and to grow their crops.

Hoagland had built a station about half a mile farther down stream at the site of present day Big Springs Country Club in Louisville. Spring Station, Sturgis Station, Sullivans Station and Linns Station were also built during late 1779 and early 1780 prior to the Dutch arrival. Linns Station was the station farthest east of the Beargrass group of stations This Beargrass group of settlements was relatively safe from the Indian menace as the settlers in the area were in such numbers that they posed a formidable foe when marauding Indians threatened.

However, traveling the ninety miles between Beargrass and White Oak Springs was very dangerous and usually done with an escort of militiamen if families were involved. Experienced frontiersmen could cover the distance in safety by knowing all the signs and techniques of the red man. Therefore, contact was made by cautious frontiersmen between the two Dutch stations during the time between the planting and the harvest of the crops at the New Holland Beargrass station. News was relayed between the two stations by means of these frontiersmen. One bit of news relayed to the Beargrass Dutch station heavily impacted the Banta families. They learned that the first Banta to be lost to Indians on this new migration had been killed during the Duryea migration when Hendrick's son, David Banta, was killed in an ambush as the group moved through Powell Valley on their way to Kentucky.

CHAPTER 12

WHITE OAK SPRINGS STATION AND

BANTAS FORT ON MUDDY CREEK

In the Fall after the crops at the New Holland Station on Beargrass Creek were harvested, Hendrick, with his sons Abraham, Albert, Dan, Henry, Jacob and John along with Simon VanArsdale, traveled to White Oak Spring Station and met with the Sam Duryea and his contingency that was settled there. It was time for both groups to join together to begin to build their dream; a Dutch Colony on the thousands of acres of rich Kentucky soil that had been found by Sam Duryea on his journey in 1779. During the fall and early winter, they made plans for building the Dutch Colony on Muddy Creek, sixteen miles from Boonesboro.

Sam and Hendrick again sat at the table in Sam's great room as they had thirty-six years earlier in Teaneck to plan the building of a Dutch nation. They had been in their early thirties then. Now the two Dutchmen were in their sixties and had been through two trials and errors in searching for this goal. Along with the other Dutchmen at White oak Springs Station, they laid plans for the building their final dream; a nation with enough fertile land to accommodate its future for many generations to come.

In February of 1781, their plans were set and the call went out for twenty volunteers to set out for Muddy Creek and establish a station there. More than enough volunteers came forward so Father Hendrick picked the twenty he felt were most qualified for the task. The men included six Bantas: Father Hendrick and his sons Abraham, Albert, Daniel, Jacob, John and his adopted son Henry,

Jr. (He was the same Henry that had witnessed his mother's death in Conewago,) four Duryeas: Samuel and his sons Albert, Daniel, Henry, and Peter; three Voris: John, Sr., John, Jr. and Albert; Peter Cosart, Frederick Ripperdan, Corneliou Bogard, Simon Vanosdale and John Bullock. These twenty men set out with Sam Duryea leading them to where he had improved the land and established his claim on Muddy Creek. They traveled about sixteen miles into the wilderness to Muddy Creek and the land chosen by Samuel Duryea in 1779. Little did these twenty men realize that six of them would fall victim to the vengeance of the Indians in the next few years.

The Kentucky settlements. Courtesy of Vincent Akers

The men set to work improving this land by building a station on Muddy Creek, a tributary of the Kentucky River, and called this station Bantas Fort. They spent five weeks in the area starting fourteen cabins. Seven cabins were placed in the form of a fort, three of which were completed to the extent of being covered. During the time the men were building these cabins, Abraham Banta, Father Hendricks oldest living son, went to Estelles Station, which was about five miles west of Bantas Fort. This fort could be reached from Bantas Fort by following Muddy Creek and a trace called the Mulberry Lick Trace. He negotiated with Captain Estelle to rent fifty acres of cleared land for Spring planting since the land around the Banta cabins could not be cleared in time for the 1781 planting.

While the other men were working on Bantas Fort, Sam Duryea and his sons decided to also build a cabin about four miles from Banta's Fort as a start for his family' station. At the end of three days they had a cabin up and covered that was to serve as the Duryea home and fort. Since their cabin was completed, Sam decided to leave two men and their families to complete work on clearing land around the cabin. They had brought their wives and children with him to set up housekeeping. Hendrick felt it was dangerous to leave families alone among the hostile Indians for even a short period of time. Sam disagreed, saying that they would be alone only a short time as he would have other Duryea families with them in a few days. Then the rest of the men returned to White Oak Springs Station in late March, leaving Peter Duryea, John Bullock and their families at the Duryea cabin. With it completed, these two men moved their families into the cabin. The others returned to White Oaks Spring station to bring out the other Duryea families that intended to also stay in the cabin while they built other cabins at this station.

The families settled-in on a Friday and the Indians attacked them on Monday. Inside the cabin, they were safe from the Indian attack. In due course their corn meal was used up and since they had no mortar on which to grind corn into meal, the two men left the safety of the cabin to cut a block to make a new mortar on which to bruise their corn. While cutting the block, they were attacked by the Indians.

Bullock ran towards the cabin but fell and was caught by a quick young brave who cleaved his skull with the tomahawk. He died instantly and lay in a pool of his own blood. Duryea was mortally wounded with a ball through his chest but made it back to the safety of the cabin. Bullock's wife looked out the door at her fallen husband questioning whether he was still alive. While she was looking out the doorway, she was shot through the breast by the Indians and fell dead across the doorsill. Anna Duryea, the only adult left unhurt, caught Mrs. Bullock by the feet and pulled her into the cabin barring the door. She then in rapid succession stuck her rifle through several of the cabins rifle ports. This caused the savages to believe there were several other adults in the cabin with her and they did not attack.

Anna Duryea used every means she knew to stop the bleeding from her husband's chest. Finally in desperation she pushed her handkerchief into the wound. This stopped the flow of blood and her husband recovered to the point where he regained consciousness. Recognizing the hopelessness of the situation, Duryea pointed to the door and said in a soft voice with devotion and sincerity, "Save yourself and the children. Go, go, while the Indians have retreated."

Anna Duryea stood with her sister-in-law dead at her feet and her husband barely alive trying to decide what to do. The three children clung to her skirt and as she looked at them she knew she must save them. Carrying her three year old child and with the two other children following, she made a dash for the woods since she dare not take the trace for fear of the Indians. Then she ran through the woods for almost a full day completely losing her direction. Exhausted, she located a familiar landmark and found herself only a mile from the bloody cabin she was trying to escape.

Near the point of complete discouragement, Anna decided to

follow the trail at any expense. Almost immediately she met the other Duryea families who were coming out with a small guard to join the two families who were already at the Duryea cabin. She told them of the terrors she had been through and as they were discussing how best to resolve the situation, the Indians let out a war whoop in the distance. The men realized they could not make a stand in the wilderness with the women and children present. They, therefore, drove the horses into a canebrake where they cut their packs loose and mounted the women and children on the horses. They returned to White Oak Springs as quickly as they could. The next morning seventeen men returned from White Oak Springs to the scene of the battle to retrieve their packs and bury the dead.

The following is quoted from a newspaper article describing the incident:

> A few years afterwards, the brave and somewhat reck-
> less Captain Dan Banta met the widow, Anna Duryea. Hav-
> ing heard of her remarkable adventure, she exactly suited
> him. He courted and married her and she bravely stood at
> his side while he played a conspicuous part in reclaiming
> Shelby county from the wildness of nature.

That same spring, old Samuel Duryea and his son Henry were killed by Indians at the White Oak Springs Station. Thus ended the charmed life of Hendrick's beloved brother-in-law. Four of the twenty men, all from the Duryea family, who had gone to Muddy Creek to build the new colony, had already been slaughtered by the Indians. The building of cabins on Muddy Creek had become an impossible nightmare. In May, the Bantas, discouraged and defeated, gave up the plan to organize the Low Dutch Colony on Muddy Creek and returned to the Low Dutch Station on Beargrass Creek ninety miles to the northwest.

The idea of settling on Muddy Creek was not completely abandoned. The Dutch families who had come to Kentucky over the Wilderness Trail continued to stay at White Oak Springs. In the Summer of 1781 nine of them rode out to Estelles Station to see the land Abraham Banta had negotiated to rent from Captain Estelle. They also intended to rescue tools that had been left at the half-built cabins the year before. Captain Estelle was leading this group which included his brother Sam Estelle, along the Mulberry Lick Trace through the cane with Sam Estelle in the rear.

After they had covered about one-half mile from Estelles Station, they came upon a large red oak tree that had fallen close to the trace. This oak had been felled by the Indians as cover for an ambush of the pioneer party. Indians lay in wait behind the camouflage of the trees leaves. Sam Estelle noticed a moccasin beneath the oak tree leaves. He instantly fired his rifle and shouted "Indians!" as he threw himself off the opposite side of his horse from where the tree lay. The Indians fired at the same moment with one shot hitting Captain Estelle in the right arm, badly breaking it. His horse, becoming frightened, turned and bolted for the Estelle Station with Captain Estelle holding the reins in his teeth unable to control the animal.

Meanwhile, a large fierce-looking Indian, painted black and holding a tomahawk over his head, leaped from the oak tree toward Frederick Ripperdan, another of the ten men who had been building the cabins.

"Shoot the son-of-a-bitch," Frederick shouted to Sam Estelle.

"Why don't you shoot him yourself, damn you?" Sam shouted back "Your gun is loaded while mine is empty."

Ripperdan quickly brought his rifle to his shoulder and fired at the Indian at point blank range. The muzzle almost touched the red skin's chest as the gun fired. Mortally wounded, the Indian let his tomahawk fall to the ground, clutched a sapling for support and a loud noise like a bear's roar came from his throat. He fell to the ground dead at the hooves of Sam's horse. The other Indians who were part of the ambush hurriedly retreated from the scene.

This skirmish was referred to by the local people as the "Dutch Defeat" for it convinced the Dutchmen that they could not settle the land on Muddy Creek because of the hostile Indians. Later

Captain Estelle's arm, which had been badly broken by the Indian rifle ball but had healed itself, gave way in a fight with Indians and it cost him his life. When his arm gave way, the Indian buried his tomahawk in the captain's skull. This incident happened March 2, 1782, and was known as "Estelle's Defeat."

The "Dutch Defeat" ended all thought of settling on Muddy Creek. A new source of land for their community had to be found though some of the Dutch families continued to live at White Oak Springs Station until after the Fall harvest. The Banta men, discouraged by the slaughter at the Duryea cabin plus the Dutch Defeat episode, left the area and retraced their steps to the safety of the New Holland Beargrass Station.

One more of the party of twenty men who were building the cabins on Muddy Creek was to fall victim to the Indians before all the Dutch vacated White Oak Springs Station. In July 1781, when most of the colony had vacated the station, some of the Dutch stayed on to harvest the crops they had planted. Peter Cosart, the fifth man from that band of cabin builders was killed by Indians as he was gathering blackberries for his family.

Later in the year, Father Hendrick took many of the Dutchmen from the Dutch Station at Beargrass Creek and set up a second Low Dutch Station a few miles south of Harrods Station at Boiling Spring. This station lay between the Salt River and the Kentucky River, about two thirds of the distance from Beargrass Station to Boonesboro. It was located near Cove Springs about ten miles south of Harrods Fort. Harrods Station was a well established station and this second Low Dutch Station had rented land from Colonel James Harrod. The Dutch colony intended to remain at this second Dutch Station for only a short time until the problem with the Indians settled down.

Sam Duryea's contingent of the Dutch colony decided to completely abandon their settlement at White Oak Springs Station and joined the many families who had come to the new Low Dutch station near Harrods Fort from the New Holland Station at Beargrass Creek. With their arrival, all thought of establishing their colony on Muddy Creek was abandoned. With both Dutch parties here, the conditions at the Dutch station below Harrod's Fort became extremely crowded. They were renting land from James Harrod, but he was unable to fulfill the needs of the growing community with his limited land. With Kentucky land tied up by speculators, the situation was becoming desperate.

The American Revolution had concluded for all intent and purposes in October of 1781 with the surrender of the English General Cornwallis, but the Indian menace did not subside in the least. The white man and the red man continued to be mortal enemies around the settlements in Kentucky. The Dutch families had been forced by the Indian menace into crowded stations, "Where the air seems to have lost all its purity and sweetness . . . and a kind of flux is common of which numbers die . . . living in dirt and filth." This period at the Dutch station below Harrods Fort was the most distressful that the Dutch families had endured in their long history on this continent. Many died from contagious diseases during this trying period. This was a devastating time for the Low Dutch pioneers who in the past were used to cleanliness and spotless housekeeping.

CHAPTER 13

SQUIRE BOONE AND THE PROMISED

LAND "THE LOW DUTCH TRACT"

Upon their arrival in 1780, the Dutch immigrants discovered that the stories of the available, rich farm land in Kentucky they had heard about in Pennsylvania was a myth. The Virginia legislature had handed out most of the tillable land to speculators making it almost impossible to buy large parcels of land at a reasonable price. Back in 1780, a petition to the Continental Congress began circulating among the Kentucky settlements which sought their approval to open settlements across the Ohio River in the territory held by the English enemy during the War of Independence. Among the 400 signers were the names of Abraham, Albert, Cornelius, Jacob and John Banta.

This course of action was quickly eliminated by an English military man named Colonel Byrd who incited his Indians on the north side of the Ohio River to attack and capture Ruddle's and Martin's forts in Kentucky in June of 1780. This panicked the Kentucky settlers and any thought of settling on the north side of the Ohio was out of the question. This added to the normal irritation between the Indians and the settlers who were invading the Indians' hunting grounds. With the English inciting the red man to attack the Americans and the Americans establishing settlements in their hunting grounds, the Indians were extremely hostile towards all settlers including the Low Dutch colony.

In 1783, The group of Dutchmen under Father Hendrick Banta decided again to petition the Continental Congress to redress the problem of expensive land. The following petition was drafted and forwarded to the Congress signed by 46 "Inhabitens" and 105 "Inten Frinds." The "Inhabitens" were Dutch families who were already in Kentucky while the "Intend Frinds" were those families planning to come to Kentucky. Eleven of the "Inhabitens" signing the petition were Bantas which constituted 24% of the "Inhabitens" who signed it. The following is the entire wording of the petition as it clearly explains the ethnic motivation of the colony and the plight in which they found themselves.

To the Honourablee President and Deligates of the Free United States of America in Congress Assembled.

Gentlemen. A Memorial and Petition of a number of Inhabitants of Kentucky Settlement of the Low Dutch reformed Church Persuasion in behalf of themselves and other intended Settlers was brought to me by one of those Petitioners desireing me in the name of the rest to give a Testimonial of their Character to the Honorable Congress because I was Personally acquainted with them. Some have lived amongst us and belonged to my Congregations. They were a Plain honest peaceable Sober and Industrious People remarkable for Agriculture and by Current reports we have of them they are all hearty friends to our Glorious Revelution and the Honorable Congress

Gentlemen, I Remain with due Respect your Most Humble Servt.
J. M. Van Harlingen,
Minister of the Gospel at
Sourland and New Shennick.

To the Honorable President and Delagates of the Free United States of America in Congress Assembled:

The Memorial and Petition of a number of Inhabitants of Kentucky Settlement of the Low Dutch Reformed Church

persuasion, in behalf of themselves and other intended settlers.
Humbly Sheweth.

That in the Spring of the Year 1780 they moved to Kentucky with their families and effects with a view and expectation to procure a Tract of Land to enable them to settle together in a body for the conveniency of civil society and propagating the Gospel in their own known language; when they arrived there to their sorrow and disappointment they were thro' the dangerousness of the times by a cruel savage Enemy obliged to settle in Stations or Forts in such places where there was the most appearance of safety, not withstanding all their precution numbers of them suffered greatly in their property, several killed and others captivated by the Enemy, living in such distressed confined way always in danger, frequently on Military duty, it was impossible for them to do more than barely support their families with the necessaries of life, by which means they are much reduced, and what adds more to their disappointment and affliction is, that contrary to their expectations before their arrival and since, the most of the Tillable Land has been Located and monopolised by persons that had the advantage of your Memorialists by being acquainted with the country, and your Memorialists being strangers and confined as aforesaid, and being so reduced are unable to purchase Land at the advanced price, and especially in a body conveniently together agreeable to their wishes. Whereas Providence has been pleased to prosper and support the virtuous resistance of the United States in the glorious cause of Liberty, which has enabled them to obtain an Honorable Peace whereby they have obtained a large extent of unappropriated Territory. And whereas it is currently and repeatedly reported amongst us that the Congress has broke or made void Virginia's right to claim Land in Kentucky Settlement.

Your Petitioners therefore humbly pray, (in behalf of themselves and other intended settlers of the same persuasion,) the Honorable Congress would indulge them with a grant of a Tract or Territory of Land in Kentucky Settlement. If the Virginia claim thereto should be made void, or otherwise in the late ceeded land on the northwest side of the Ohio river, whereto there is not any prior claim, to enable them to settle in a body together, on such reasonable terms as Congress in their wisdom and prudence shall see just and reasonable, they complying with, and performing all reasonable conditions required, to enable them to put their intended plan and purpose in execution, they having principally in view the Glory of God, the promotion of civil and religious society, educating and instructing their raising generation in the principals of religion and moriality: hoping the Honorable Congress will give all due encouragement to such a laudable undertaking. The premises Duly considered, your Petitioners as in duty bound shall ever pray, &c.

Inhabitens

Hendrick Banta, David Allen, Peter Demaree, Benedick Yury, Cornelius Bogart, Henry Yury, John Demaree, John Voreis, **Cornelius Banta**, Simon Vanosdol, Samuel Durie, Sophia Vories widow, Albert Dueie, Francis Voreis, Marga Cozart widow, Aaron Mon Four, Antje Durie widow, John Ryker, **Daniel Banta**, Cornelius Vories, Albert Vorhis, **Henry Banta**, John vorhis jr., **Abraham Banta Jr.**, Luke Vorhes, **Peter Banta**, Samuel Demaree jr., **John Banta**, Peter Demaree jr., William Vancleave, Henry Shively, Catherine Darling widow, Saml. Demaree jr., Lambert Darling, John Vancleave, John Darling, John Harris, James Voreis, **Peter Banta**, Johanna Seburn widow, Samuel Westervelt, **Albert Banta**, Mary Westervelt widow, **Jacob Banta**, Samuel Lock, **Abraham Banta**.

Intend Frinds
[There were 105 signatures of intend frinds]"
[Banta names highlighted for emphasis]

The hopes of acquiring land for the Low Dutch colony through action of the Continental Congress were dashed when the committee to which it was sent reported on September 27, 1783, "That it would be improper for Congress to take any grants of land in the Western Country, til they compleat their general arrangements as to the ceded territory."

The new search for land at an affordable price for the colony's settlement started again in earnest. In their search for the thousands of acres of fertile land on which to establish their colony, the members of the Low Dutch colony at Beargrass Creek came in touch with Squire Boone who had been awarded a Virginia Treasury Warrant, which authorized him to survey 12,335 acres of unclaimed land. Squire Boone was the brother of the legendary Daniel Boone. In search of the land he would survey for his land warrant, Squire Boone had established a station at Painted Stone in 1780 as the base of his operation. The Painted Stone Station was the closest station east of the Beargrass stations. It was in Shelby County about twenty-five miles east of the Beargrass Creek settlements and was the eastern-most station in the area.

In 1781, the Indians in the area of Painted Stone became hostile and he had maintained the station with great difficulty. A few of the families from the Beargrass Creek stations, including the Demarests, had joined Squire Boone at his Painted Stone Station. The Indians attacked in the Spring of 1781 and badly wounded Squire Boone. His wounds were so severe that he did not recover until the Fall. Several of the Beargrass creek families decided to leave Painted Stone and go back to the safer Beargrass Creek stations. This loss of manpower caused Squire to abandon Painted Stone temporarily. He called on the Jefferson Militia to accompany the families through the dangerous twenty one miles they had to travel to the nearest Beargrass station. Since there were not enough horses, Squire Boone's and widow Hinton's families stayed at Painted Stone until the militia could return for them.

The group of families who were being escorted by the militia became badly scattered along the very difficult trail. One of the men became ill and ten of the militia fell behind to protect him.

With the company in a weakened and disorderly state, the Indians attacked from ambush. Contrary to an earlier agreement by those families going back to the Beargrass stations that they would stay together if attacked, the leading families cut the packs from their horses, mounted them and took off for Linns station, the closest of the Beargrass Creek stations. This seriously reduced the number of men available for fighting the enemy. With the ten militia men protecting the ill frontiersman and the leading families running for Linns station, the remaining families and militia were left in an under-manned position and were unable to protect themselves adequately. They fought off the red-skins long enough to cut the packs off the horses and mount the women and children for a race to Linns station eight miles away. The Indians continued the attack and packs were strewn for more than a mile along the trail.

When the families reached Long Run Creek, they had to cross its swollen waters while trying to control a savage enemy. As night fell, the remaining members of the party straggled into Linns station. This battle became known as the Long Run Massacre. Many members of the families involved were slaughtered by the Red skins.

The Indians were not the only threat to life for the frontier families. Meat for the Dutch stations was mainly provided by men finding game in the uncharted forests that made up the Indian hunting grounds. It was on these hunting trips that the Dutch colonists became acquainted with the quality of land in the large areas they covered on such trips. They were ever on the lookout for fertile land that might be acquired as the large tract of land they needed for a site for the Dutch Colony. Such trips were dangerous not only from the point of ambushes from Indians but also from the wild animals they encountered on such hunting trips. Following is a verbatim account of one such encounter as contained in an article from the Shelby Courant, Shelbyville, Ky, May 15, 1873.

A hunter, named William Gordon, married a sister of
Daniel Banta and became a member of the Dutch community
about the year 1800. [This is the same Dan Banta who courted

and won the widow heroine of the Duryea cabin massacre. Ed] Among the many adventures with wild beasts, I give the following, which are in every way reliable: Gordon and his brother-in-law, Dan Banta, were out hunting and had separated temporarily, when Banta heard the crack of Gordon's rifle, and knowing that the latter never wasted his powder and lead for nothing, hastened to the spot from whence the sound came. When he arrived, he found Gordon lying on the ground terribly mangled and nearly lifeless. A few feet from him a large bear wallowing in its own blood was already stretched in death; and a short distance from the two, Gordon's faithful dog was whining and tumbling about, badly used up. Gordon was carried home on a liter and so dangerous were his wounds thought to be that his friends sent to Shelbyville for Dr. Morse— if I am not wrongly informed, the first physician located in that place—who dressed his wounds, and gave encouragement of his recovery.

As soon as Gordon was able to converse, he gave the following version of his adventures: He had left Banta but a little while when he met the bear and shot him, but the ball failing to do its work completely, he was attacked furiously by the bear before he could reload his gun. He drew his hunting knife, and the fight commenced in good earnest. When the bear would close on Gordon, the dog would assault him in the rear with desperate courage and force him to divide his attention between him and his master. After several rounds in this way, Gordon, cutting and hacking all the while, got in a deadly thrust with his knife and ended the conflict—but not till after himself and dog were terribly used up, as above described. He always gave his faithful dog the credit of saving his life.

Some time after the above occurrence Gordon was a few steps in advance of his wife, when he heard a scream behind him. On turning around he saw a panther crouched on a limb of a tree in the act of springing on his wife. He commanded her to stand still, knowing that his wife's life

depended on his skill as a marksman. Gordon was equal to
the emergency; raising his gun, with quick eye unerring
touch, a sharp report, and the once dangerous animal
tumbled to the ground harmless at his wife's feet.

In 1782, Father Hendrick and the colonists at the Dutch Station ten miles below Harrods Fort as well as those at the New
Holland Beargrass Creek Station became acquainted with the land
Squire Boone planned to survey for his land grant. Daniel Banta
and two others from the Dutch settlement traveled through the
land Boone was surveying when they joined him on a hunting trip
that took them to the upper branches of Clear Creek. Other Dutchmen about the same time had explored Six Mile Creek and what
later became Bantas Fork. All who had seen this country agreed
that it was desirable, fertile land that would be an ideal location
for their Low Dutch colony. If they could buy Squire Boone's entire land grant at a reasonable price, their search for the thousands
of acres of fertile land necessary for their colony would be over.

The Dutch colonists unanimously appointed Abraham Banta,
the oldest living son of Father Hendrick, to open negotiations with
Squire Boone. Boone was delighted to find one purchaser who
wanted to buy the entire tract. A purchase contract for all of Squire's
land was negotiated in 1783 by Abraham but immediately rescinded when it was discovered there were conflicting claims to
the land he had surveyed.

In 1784, Abraham Banta agreed to a new contract for all of
Boone's land not contested by other claims. He also began negotiations for 3,000 acres of land adjoining Boone's tract. This nego-
tiation resulted in a purchase contract for all 3,000 acres from
Richard Bird in 1785. The total number of acres covered by these
two contracts totaled 7,610. The master plan of Father Hendrick
Banta and Sam Duryea had become a reality. After traveling many
hundreds of miles across unbroken wilderness and seven hundred
miles down the Ohio River the Dutch colonists had found the
land for their dearest dream, a Low Dutch Colony of their own.

After over twenty years of wandering, Father Hendrick Banta, and his son Abraham, had brought them to the promised land.

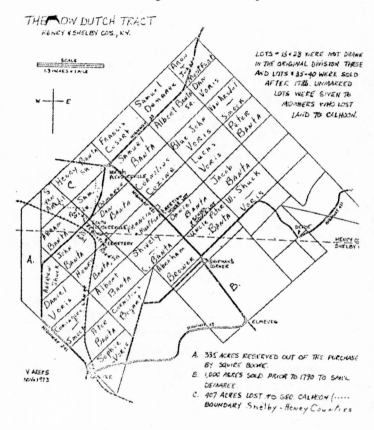

Map of the Low Dutch track in Kentucky. Courtesy of
Vincent Akers

Squire Boone signed the contract assigning his tract to Abraham Banta, who was now sharing leadership with Father Hendrick, on March 13, 1786 and the contract with Richard Bird was also concluded. There was great rejoicing in the two Low Dutch settlements upon the signing of the two contracts. This was undoubtedly the most joyous occasion this group was to know.

They had accomplished their objective. Their expectations had become a reality. In this case, as is so often true, their anticipation was greater than realization. Father Hendrick was sick at heart that old Sam Duryea had not lived long enough to rejoice with him on this day.

Two stations had been recently built abutting the Low Dutch tract: Hoagland's second station just west of the southwest corner of the tract and Ketcham's station, a few miles further south. Both of these stations were unfortified cabins. The closest fortified station was Painted Stone six miles to the south.

In 1786, after Abraham had signed the contract but prior to the company's Articles of Agreement being drawn up and signed by members of the company, Daniel, Cornelius, John Sr. and Jacob Banta wanted to have a closer look at the tract Abraham had purchased for the colony. About six miles northeast of the Pained Stone station, they entered the wilderness forest. Here they decided to build a log cabin which they constructed out of blue ash logs. They had become experts at building such lodgings and it was built so sturdy that it stood the rigors of the harsh Kentucky winters for eighty years before it was torn down. At the cabin, they cleared land and planted crops, the first in the Low Dutch Tract. Daniel and Jacob Banta traveled the buffalo trail that bisected the tract exploring the quality of the land.

The following account of what happened is taken verbatim from the Shelby Courant, Shelbyville, Kentucky, May 15, 1873:

> The colonists were eager to explore their new land and therefore Captain Daniel Banta, Cornelius Banta and John Banta, Sr., [All sons of Father Hendrick] followed the "trace" leading from Harrods Station in Mercer County to Hoaglands Station in what was afterwards Shelby County to within a few miles of the latter place where they boldly plunged into the wilderness, and built a cabin two miles northeast of Hoagland's station . . . This was the first cabin built in the limits of the Dutch tract. It was built of blue ash logs and was torn down after braving storms for eighty

winters. The Bantas on their hunting expeditions, doubt-less saw a considerable part of the tract of land though hardly all of it, as it was no child's play to explore such a vast wilderness.

. . . The Bantas had enjoyed their novel position but a short time when one of those periodical storms of wrath burst in upon the frontier settlements, and they wisely re-tired to Hoagland's station. This station was poorly manned and provisioned at the time and was threatened daily by the red-skins. So squally did the times become that the little garrison determined to send to Harrod's station for rein-forcements. Jake Banta, an officer of the fort (Brother of the other Bantas) volunteered to perform the dangerous mis-sion. [Harrod's station was forty miles to the south. Ed.] The wilderness being full of prowling savages, he chose the dark-ness of the night to pass through the "narrows" on the wa-ters of Benson Creek, near where Hardinsville now is. But poor Jake never reached Harrod's station. As he crept all alone in the darkness of the night through the dreaded "narrows", the red-skins pounced upon him from ambush and cleaved his skull with the tomahawk. They left Captain Banta on the tragic spot with his own tomahawk buried in his skull as a token of their fierce vengeance. The loss of this brave man was deeply felt by the frontier settlement. As soon as the storm had subsided our three heros, who had taken an active part in the exciting scenes with which they were surrounded, went back to Harrods Station fully satis-fied that their attempt to take possession of an isolated wil-derness at that time was immature . . .

The Banta family was both dreaded and hated by the Indians. Being men of wonderful strength and constitu-tion, and brave to a fault, they had taught the savages many lessons in their own mode of warfare. If all their conflicts with the Indians, the heroism of their women, etc., were traced by the pen of an able writer, a book of truly thrilling adventures would be the result.

Jake was the sixth of the twenty men who started the Banta Fort on Muddy Creek to be killed by the Indians. He had just married Catherine Voorhies prior to going on this journey with his brothers and volunteered for the dangerous mission partly to be with his new wife. This left the Dutch colony with yet another widow.

Because of the long delay in acquiring the tract, some families had lost faith and had purchased small plots of land for their farms on their own. Thirty four families signed the Article of Agreement at the Low Dutch station below Harrod's Fort, on March 13,1786. Fourteen of these families were Bantas. This agreement served as the constitution and by-laws for the new Low Dutch Colony company.

Out of the eighty-five Low Dutch families that had come to Kentucky, forty percent joined the company. Over the years, the number of families in the company grew until in 1840 there were fifty-six families in the Low Dutch colony. Though it was signed by but forty per cent of the Dutch families in Kentucky at that time, all Dutch families were in favor of the project and backed it fully. A portion of the tract was cut into thirty-four parcels and these parcels were allotted to the different families who had signed the Articles of Agreement by drawing lots.

The principal commitments to which the signers of the Article of Agreement pledged themselves are summarized as follow:

1. That each signers would pay his proportionate share of yearly payments to Abraham Banta until all payments to the grantors of the land were completed. Proportionate share would be based on "The quantity and quality of land each of us shall hold to the whole quantity of land . . ."

2. "That we will subscribe to and support the Low Dutch Reformed Society . . ." by giving a call to a Low Dutch minister and endeavoring to have their children taught and instructed in the Low Dutch language so that they would understand the Gospel when read or preached to them in Dutch.

3. That each would accept their proportionate share of the cost of land and building for a parsonage for the minister.

4. That neither Abraham Banta, in whose name the property was recorded, or any of the signers would sell or dispose of any of the land to any other person unless that person agreed to comply with the above article.

5. That each signer would accept his proportionate share of defending the title of the tract. If title to any portion of the tract would become void all signers would bear their proportionate share of the lost land.

These articles defined the purpose of the colony which was to maintain the ethnicity and religious heritage of these Low Dutch families.

The tract they had bought from Squire Boone straddled the Henry and Shelby county line with the northern half in Henry County and the southern half in Shelby County. On today's map it covered the area from half a mile above State Highway 22 on the north, to State Highway 43 on the south. U. S. Highway 421 would have run down the center of it and U. S. Highway 241 would have been its western boundary. The tract ran just as far east of Highway 421 as Highway 241 was to the west of it. This land lay about forty-two miles north of Harrods Fort and twenty-five miles east of Linns Station which was the closest Beargrass settlement.

Each of the families who had signed the pact sent contingent parties ahead to prepare for settlement of the portion of the tract they had chosen by lot. For safety, many of the families moved as a group. The first part of the journey from Harrods Fort north to Shelby County was along Harrods Trace. In Shelby County they had to leave the trace and hack their way north through virgin forest to the Dutch tract. The Banta brothers had been to the tract the year before when Jake had been killed by the Indians and were acquainted with the area and terrain. They suggested Daniel Ketchums Station and Hoaglands Station as the headquarters for the Dutch settlement until land could be cleared and cabins built.

When they were located at these two stations as their headquarters, the families began the cooperative clearing of the land and building of cabins.

The tools used were owned in common by the community. The tract was pristine virgin forest where no white man had tread before, and the clearing of it had to be a community effort where all families could share cleared land of others until it became their turn to have their land cleared. When they first arrived, the entire tract was forested with the exception of a plot of about one hundred acres which was as clear as a prairie without so much as a single tree trunk. Everyone thought that this land must be no good due to minerals in the soil. To the surprise of all, it proved to be excellent fertile soil and provided cleared land for early planting.

While the colony was still using Ketchams Station as their headquarters because of marauding Indians, Rachel Van Arsdale gave birth to a baby girl, Eleanore, on May 4, 1786. Eleanore Van Arsdale married Rev. Henry D. Banta, who was the son of Daniel Banta (Daniel had married the widow Duryea after the massacre at the Duryea cabin.) Her version of the Duryea cabin massacre varies from the accepted historical version previously related in this story. The following are portions of a sketch of Eleanor's life written for her son and presented by him to the editor of a newspaper.

AN OLD PIONEER

Having some time since promised you that I would give you a short history of the life of one of the oldest settlers of this county, viz., that of my mother, Eleanor Banta, I therefore proceed to redeem that promise, and as much as possible will give it in her own language.

She was born in Ketcham Station, or Fort, in Shelby Co., Ky., May 4, 1786, and of course is 92 years old today, this being her birthday, and therefore as suitable a time as any for such history. When she was nine days old the Indians drove her mother, with the other women in the fort, six miles back to the nearest settlement at that time, and they had to retreat in the night for fear of being shot or tomahawked and scalped by the Indians, as she was afterwards informed by her parents. . . . [Partial quotation of her words. Ed.]

My parents told me that the morning I was born one of my uncles was shot near the Fort, and the woods around the fort were full of Indians. They were driven off, however, and we had peace for a spell again. We remained in that section of the country until the year 1817 . . . .

Before we built the horse mill we had to grind all of our corn on hand mills. They were a very simply constructed affair. The hopper, as it was called, would be a portion of a trunk of a large tree, two or three feet in diameter and three or four feet high; one end of this block would be securely fastened in the hopper, and a small hole cut in the side of the hopper, just at the top of the bed stone, and a small spout attached to carry off the meal; the top stone, or runner as you would call it now, had two holes in it, one in the center to receive the grain to be ground, the other near one side, in which was placed an upright pole, two or two and a half inches thick; the top end of the pole was placed into a timber or beam overhead for that purpose, and the operator would take hold of this pole and turn it round, much the same as the apothecary would his pestle in a medicine mortar, turning with one hand and feeding the mill with the other at the same time. Many and many times I have ground my meal on the hand mill, and that was the way we got all our corn in those days, for we had no wheat then. . . .

I recollect of hearing my parents tell that my uncle Samuel Duryea and his brother's wife were out some little distance from the house, and two uncles were cutting a tree for the purpose of building a hand mill, when they were surprised by the Indians and fired upon, and all three fell mortally wounded and died in a few minutes. Dear me, folks now-days know nothing about trouble and hard times, for the Indians would frequently come into the settlements of nights and kill the milch cows and cut out a slice or chunk for their hams, and leave the balance for an aggravation to the owners. Talk about hard times, you know nothing about it.

After the Indians were driven from the country, so there was not so much danger, I used to take my little spinning-wheel and go many times of nights and spin flax by the light of the brush heap fires that my husband was burning in the clearing. . . .

Eleanor was born at Ketcham's station. The Indians were prowling the woods around Ketcham's at that time and her uncle had been killed by them. At the age of nine days, she, her mother and all the other women and children at Ketcham's station were evacuated under the cover of night to Squire Boone's Painted Stone station as it was much better fortified. Such were the conditions at the Low Dutch Company tract in May of 1786. These marauding Indians were not peculiar only to the area where the tract was located. The situation was pervasive throughout this entire area of Kentucky. Abraham Lincoln's grandfather was killed by Indians at this same moment in history only twenty miles to the west.

In spite of the hazards of Indians and wild beasts, land was cleared through the colony's common efforts and cabins were built. As the work was completed, families moved on to their allotted farms and the community began to take shape. They established their permanent headquarters in a village they called Bantatown, now renamed Pleasureville, Henry County. Their taking possession of this tract was somewhat premature as the Indians still contested the frontiersmen in their communal hunting ground. The various tribes just as vigorously contested other Indian tribes use of this communal hunting ground and wars between tribes were just as ferocious as were skirmishes between the Indians and the frontiersmen. The major difference was that the frontiersmen believed in private ownership and turned the hunting grounds into privately owned villages and farms which upset the communal use of the hunting grounds by the various tribes.

As the Indian squalls would occur, it was retreat, await the settling of hostilities and then reclaim their farms. In 1788, during one such squall Indians attacked Tyler's station on Tick Creek and slaughtered most of the Bland Ballard family. This drove most of the other families to the better fortified stations but as soon as hostilities died down spirits of the families would rise and they would return to their farms. These trying times destroyed the confidence of many of the families and due to the periodic scattering of the company by the Indians, the community lost much of its cohesiveness and suffered greatly. In spite of this, it continued as a Dutch ethnic and religious community, sharing together in the Company's rewards and defeats.

It was not until the late seventeen-nineties that the community was free from the Indian menace. While Father Hendrick tried to hold together the religious context of the community under the Low Dutch Reformed Church and maintain the Dutch customs and traditions, problems in having an ordained minister sent to them by the Synod and the periodic scattering of the colony by the Indians made this a difficult goal to achieve.

As we have seen, the Low Dutch Reformed Church was beset by the schism which had occurred in its membership brought about by one group insisting that ministers be ordained in Holland while another faction insisted that they could be trained and ordained on this continent. This schism was further exacerbated when one faction of the church backed the Tories in the War of Independence while the other was firmly behind the revolution. Thus, members of the Dutch community and members of Dutch families found themselves fighting on different sides of the war.

With these problems tormenting the church, with a shortage of ordained ministers and little desire of the ordained ministers to go to such a primitive, hostile environment, the colony elders wrote letter after letter asking that they be sent an ordained minister to care for their urgent religious needs such as baptisms and marriages.

The following extract from a letter sent to the Reformed Church at New Brunswick, New Jersey, by a seventy-six-year old Elder, January 20, 1794, explains the problems faced by its members in Kentucky.

> As I viewed almost every settlement in the Kentucky country, and tarried some time at different places, I had a very good opportunity to learn the state of religion and what progress the Gospel had made there, an account of which I doubt not but will be acceptable to you.
>
> The concern and work of ministers of various denominations which I saw there, to form congregations, was such that I was astonished. The people in general seem to be more concerned about their eternal welfare than any place I have been in. I have seen much devotion among them and heard many of their preachers, some whom made use of expressions that would by no means be acceptable to our congregations. I have never seen more preachers and traveling preachers in my life than I did there for the term of time— Consisting of Presbyterians, Regular Baptists, Separate Baptists, Methodists and two Universalists, with several of whom I had the pleasure of conversing and thus got much intelligence, the particulars of which would be too much for a letter. I shall therefore be particular only in regard to our Low Dutch in that country, with the most of whom I am acquainted and with whom I principally resided while there. They were very numerous, scarcely credible considering the time the country has been settled. There are nearly 500 families, the major part live well, and no wonder they consider themselves as a people forsaken by the church to which they formerly belonged and from which they have long waited for help. They would have before now fallen in with other denominations, but many of them are firm friends to our church constitution and very loth

to part with our church forms, besides still entertaining some
hope our Synod will yet provide for them.

They have at present no public worship of their own
excepting the lecturing of old **Henry Banta,** and praying
societies, which is not attended to by many, especially when
within reach of praying of any kind whatever. They are
much exposed to be led astray by hetrodox preachers, viz:
Separate Baptists and Methodists who are doing all in their
power to gain them over to their churches, but have not as
yet been able to effect it. They gained one person, viz: **Mr.
Albert Banta,** [We will follow him in the next generation of
our story. Ed.] **who joined the Separate Baptists, and without
license commenced preaching, and for some time made
much disturbance among them, some favoring but the
greater part opposed him, and by what I could learn he
would no more be permitted to officiate for them. The
opposition he met with made him move to a considerable
distance from the Dutch settlement. But notwithstanding
this, some of their leading men entertained sentiments
which, to me, were altogether new and strange, and which
I firmly believe the presence of an orthodox minister would
easily remove.** A particular affair to which I was an eye-
witness I cannot help mentioning:

A number of them had children to baptize; They
procured a minister of their own choosing on condition he
should use our Form of Baptism, though only as far as he
should think proper. He only read the explanatory part and
then, without answer or promise of any kind, baptized
seventeen children.

Some of the people who were present expressed their
dissatisfaction at this; but one of their leading men, and the
principal one among them, stepped up and said that the
minister had done right, and that it was wrong to cause an
unconverted person to make an answer of that nature. After
hearing and seeing what I have mentioned, and especially

the trouble and cost of other denominations to extend their churches, I was astonished and much dissatisfied at the conduct of our Synod—that they have never sent one missionary into that country. This led me to question myself in the following manner: Whether other denominations had not more concern for their churches than we have for ours? Whether our young ministers; have not the same courage and resolution, and zeal for the cause of Christ that others have? Whether our Synod could not do a part of the same trouble and cost that others do? And whether that rising generation in the Kentucky country, originally of our church, were to be a forsaken people.

I heard several ministers of different denominations, who were acquainted with the situation of these people, express their surprise at the conduct of our Synod—saying "Their people are in general very moral, they are strict in their observances, they have their church forms of which they are very tenacious, and yet we see no provision made for them." Other preachers there, especially Separate Baptists and Methodists, often endeavor to break their attachment to our church by saying that our Synod have sufficiently shown by their conduct that they pay no attention to them, and that waiting longer will only be in vain—and in reality they are almost out of patience. However, they have now sent a call to the Classis of New Brunswick for any minister of our church they can get, but in my opinion one is required who is very well qualified for the business. Many of these people have not subscribed for this call, giving the reason they might hear him first. I sincerely pray they may be successful, for if they do not get one soon, or if nothing else is done for them, they are without doubt lost to our church; but I am persuaded that if our Synod were acquainted with their real situation they would do more for them than they hitherto done."

[Bold print was used by editor for emphasis.]

This seventy-four-year old Elder of the Synod eloquently expressed the plight of the Low Dutch Reformed Church members. What he did not know or perhaps did not express in his letter was that these families had braved the dangers of a hostile frontier to form a colony of believers for their church. They had brought the church to the Kentucky frontier at great cost of life and property and the church could not or would not complete their mission by sending them a minister. Without a shepherd they were a lost flock. Without a shepherd, many other Christian societies sought them as members.

Albert Banta was the second oldest living son of Father Hendrick and was the most religious of his children. In this respect, he closely resembled his father. Due to the lack of an ordained Domine, the Dutch Reformed Church was required to hold prayer services conducted by laymen. Father Hendrick usually conducted these meetings but others filled in when he was unable to do so. Albert felt that he had a calling and preached often. He reasoned that just as Abraham had taken over the secular duties of his father, he was entitled to take over the religious duties his father fulfilled. However his Theology leaned towards the Baptists while the Dutch congregation was made up of ardent Calvinists. Albert tried to sway the congregation towards the Baptist form of preaching, causing strife in the Kentucky colony. The following letter explains what can occur when preaching is left to lay ministers and a son assumes he is entitled to take over duties that the group had assigned to his father.

From a letter John Cozine wrote to Rev. G. G. Brinkerhoff
August 30,1805, Mercer County, Kentucky

Mr. Demeree goes on to tell his friends what happened here twenty years ago. At that time a Mr. Banta [Father Hendrick. Ed.] was predominant ruler here . . . And after that, if I am rightly informed as to time, Mr. Swope came among them. . . . At that time Mr. Albert Banta rose, and did much as you have been informed; but please to understand that when Mr. Banta came forward with his heavenly call, Mr. Demeree said he also had a call. It was agreed on by the society that they both might exhort, and go on as probationers and improve their talents, and he who was the most approved of by the Society should go on to the Synod for approbation and license. Nevertheless, although Mr. Banta was most approved of, our Society still thought it would not do, and expresses themselves to that import. Thus said, Mr. B left them and joined the Baptists.

Albert was not understanding as to his rejection by the church that held his father in such high esteem. In fact, he was downright angry and expressed his anger to the congregation. Then he and his family moved out of the Dutch nation his father was building, which led to bitter feelings between Father Hendrick and his son. This was the first break in the solidarity of the Bantas who until this point in time had been united in seeking the same goal as Father Hendrick. Both were hard-headed Dutchmen and there would be no compromise on either's part.

Albert, his wife Styntie and his nine children became Baptists and joined the growing Baptist Church. They took up residence in the Baptist community and severed all relations with the Dutch Reformed Church. He did however keep in contact with his father and brothers and those few in the congregation who felt he would have made the better lay minister.

Father Hendrick's dream of a Dutch nation and Church was disintegrating before his eyes. His second eldest son was adding to the confusion by becoming so disturbed from the communities rejection that he had removed his family from the Dutch Colony and deserted his father's life long goal. His goal of thousands of acres of land for a Dutch colony had been achieved but the wrath of the Indians and the lack of an ordained minister from the Synod were causing his dream to become a nightmare. The Indians were a known enemy but the apathy of his church was a tragedy he had not anticipated. He felt that this desertion by Albert would have been avoided if the church had an ordained minister rather than relying on lay ministers. Again he turned to the petition but this time not to the congress, but to his own church. The entire petition is now quoted:

> **To Rev. Jno. H. livingston, D. D.**
> Reverend Sir: On request of a certain minister of our Reformed Dutch Church, together with our lamented circumstances in the cause why we, your humble petitioners, take the freedom to acquaint you with our present calamities, which we hope, kind sir, you will pardon when you have examined your suppliant's petition.
>
> We are, reverend sir, at present in a precarious situation in regard to church affairs, and have been so for a number of years past. We are surrounded by a number of societies who are of different confessions. We are a numerous people who are destitute of Devine service. We are a people who scarcely know the difference between our and other church constitutions, which makes it difficult to keep them united. We are so situated that we can have supply at almost any time on making application, which we allow is dangerous, as we shall mention hereafter. We are a people who have the same feelings and possess the same degree of ambition as these, our neighbors. We are hurt that there is no more done for us; we suspect that it is caused among ourselves by men who formerly have intimated that we were not like to become a church or nation; we are satisfied and must reasonably suppose that all future efforts will be of no effect unless a speedy remedy takes place.
>
> Therefore we pray you, in the name of Him who has all power to will and do, that you will assist us if in your power. With submission we crave your aid and assistance with all possible speed. We have sent a call to the Rev. Classis, of New Brunswick, likewise a letter of expostulation, and wrote to some others of the clergy, which we hope may have the desired effect. If not, we are a scattered people, as there are numbers among us at present that say we can wait no

longer—our children should and must be baptized, besides, great numbers that have been baptized by parents to whom it is a matter of indifference by whom it was done. Others have the boldness to say that, when there is no regard or attention paid to us, why should we wait longer? Others say: our neighbors societies, and some who are much inferior to us, are great care taken of, such as missionaries sent and churches established, etc.,—and we, who are superior, there is nothing done for us. Our neighboring clergy have made several offers, and have sometimes preached, which only serves to weaken us and break the bond of unity; but we wonder how we have united as long as we have—we may view it as something almost supernatural.

Therefore, Rev. Sir we have thought it a duty incumbent on us to inform you with our present circumstances, to enable you to form a just idea about us; and further, we are almost become a reproach by other nations on account of persevering and adhering to our church forms, constitution, etc., and not as much as a supply.

It is needless to tell you the reflections we endure; but our nation here in general are liberal and generous, and look upon themselves to be superior to a number of others. They are daily increasing; we expect soon to be able to make up 500 dollars yearly as a salary.

We have now made up 300 dollars and if well united might do more, but we hope that God shall forbid that we should be any longer without a minister. This much for your consideration, praying that if you have it in your power to help us, to let no means pass by, so that we might once more become a church and nation. On expectation of your aid and assistance, your petitioners shall pray.

Signed: **Hendrick Banta**, Garret Dorland, **Albert Banta**, [Hendrick's brother. Ed]. Lucas Van Arsdalen, John Smock, Simon Van Arsdale, Isaac Van Nuys, Isaac Van

Arsdalen, Abraham Brewer, Laurence De Mott, Cornelius
A. Van Arsdalen,.

The flock was being scattered. Living and doing business with the English without any assistance from the Synod to hold the Dutch community together was combining to stir the great melting pot. Not only was the rising generation accepting other persuasions, but even Father Hendrick's own children were joining other flocks, many of them leaving for other frontiers that were opening up in the Northwest Territory.

In addition to Albert's abdication, several of his other children and their complete family left the Dutch colony and joined a new sect called the Shakers. John Banta was one of the first to accept their beliefs. He held meetings in his house which induced other members of the Dutch community and sometimes entire families, to join their colony. A brief quoted statement of the origin of Shakerism in Kentucky follows:

In the year 1800 began that extraordinary movement known as the "Kentucky Revival," during the progress of which religious meetings were held attended by as many as twenty thousand persons at one time, the meetings were being continued day and night for several days. The most singular manifestations characterized at these meeting. Boys and girls of twelve years of age exhorted with wonderful eloquence and power, and many of the worshipers were so affected that they shouted and leaped for joy, while others fell upon the ground "like those who are shot in battle," and lay for hours as in a trance.

A history of the time (The Kentucky Revival, by Richard McNemar, p.24,) says of one of the meetings: "On this occasion, no sex nor color, class nor description, were exempted from the pervading influence of the Spirit; even from the age of six months (!) To sixty years, there were evident subjects of this marvelous operation." As an outgrowth of this awakening, Shakerism had its rise in Kentucky. A delegation from the Community at New Lebanon, N. Y., visited the State and found a hospitable reception at the house of John Banta, who was one of the first to embrace their teachings.

The work just quoted says (p. 85), 'The same faith produced by the preparatory work of God, began to also break out at Eagle Creek, sometime in the six month; which gave occasion to the testimony being opened there. A few at first embraced it with full purpose of soul, as the only way to God. Through the faith and special light of Matthew Houston, Samuel, Henry, John Bonta, Elishia Thomas, etc. The testimony entered and was received on the south side of Kentucky (river), about the middle of the eighth month, and continued to spread until it embraced as many as were willing to embrace it in Mercer, Shelby, Paint-lick and Long-lick. In each of which places there are a number of families who have denied ungodliness and worldly lusts, taken up their cross, lived together in the unity of the spirit and bond of peace, and while with open eyes they are traveling from death into life, they shine as lights in the world.

Father Hendrick's and Sam Duryea's dream of a Dutch nation with Dutch customs, language and religion had come within a hair's breadth of achieving its goal. It vanished and become lost in the smoke and confusion of Indian massacres and an unresponsive church. The flock was scattered. Now that dream could be seen only in old Father Hendrick's failing eyes. This old pioneer had fought for a goal that he believed in with every fiber in his great body. He was certain his plan for a Dutch nation would succeed but even with the heart of a lion and his awesome spirit, he could not control the destiny of his people because of a savage enemy and a lethargic or overtaxed church. Father Hendrick passed from this earth in 1805, aged 87 years. He had fought the good fight for his dream from the day he left for Somerset County in 1752 to his death, a span of fifty-three years on the American frontier. He was buried on George Bergen's farm and was the first burial in that graveyard.

CHAPTER 14

OHIO IN THE NORTHWEST TERRITORY

Albert Banta was the fifth of Father Hendrick's twenty-one children and his oldest living son. His second eldest brother had died in infancy in Teaneck. He was two when his mother, Rachel Brower Banta, died in childbirth giving birth to his next youngest sibling, Gertrude; three, when his father remarried Anna Demarest Banta; and four, when Father Hendrick moved his family to Somerset County. He had no memory of any mother other than Anna and barely remembered the wagon train trip to Bedminister. He was twenty-two when Father Hendrick and the one-thousand other Dutchmen started the Conewago Colony and had been there when his oldest brother, Hendrick, died of smallpox in Conewago. A year later, he had witnessed the death of Hendrick's wife, Mary, by the falling tree. He was thirty-four, married to Styntie Montfort and the father of five children at the time of his father's migration from Conewago by way of Fort Pitt and the Ohio River to Kentucky. He had spent his entire life, except for his first three years, growing up and raising his family on the edge of the frontier in a colony of Dutchmen. After his family's having lived five generations and one-hundred and thirty-nine years on this continent, his primary language was Low Dutch, and he spoke English in a broken manner with a strong accent.

Albert had been a child of the frontier and was a professional frontiersman from the age of three. It was the only life he could recall. No one knew the ways of the frontier better than he did and its dangers had been an intimate part of his life. As one of the twenty men who had helped construct Bantas Fort on Muddy Creek, he had seen the treachery of the Kentucky Indians and was a skilled Indian fighter. He was at home matching his fighting skills and wits against his arch enemies, the red-man and the large cats, bears and wolves in the forest.

At the same time, he was a good husband and father, and believed from the depths of his soul that he had a calling from God to preach the Gospel. As a farmer, he was familiar with all the ways of the land, the plow, the sowing and reaping of crops. The rejection by the congregation of his former church, the DRC, had stung him badly. Leaving it meant turning his back on all his friends, his ethnicity, which he prized highly, and his farm. It had caused friction between his father and himself. He paid a great price for what he believed to be necessary in order to maintain his self-esteem.

He was the first to break from the Dutch ethnicity and traditions of this line of the family. His rejection as lay minister by the community of the Low Dutch Reformed Church explains why this line of the family left the Church. After five generations and one-hundred and thirty-nine years of his ancestors maintaining their Dutch ethnicity in America, he was leaving his Dutchness behind and emphasizing the fact that his family was American. The melting pot was working and all thought of a Dutch nation was dead. It was amazing that the Dutch dream lasted as long as it did and that its zeal had carried his family this far away from civilization into a dangerous and inhospitable frontier in Kentucky.

As a result of the Revolutionary War, The United States had acquired the Northwest Territory from the British through the Treaty of Paris in 1783. The Indian tribes in the territory, spurred on by the English during the Revolutionary War, were hostile to the United States. General Arthur St. Clair was appointed the territory's first Governor. He established his capitol at Cincinnati and was appointed by President Washington to be the Commander In Chief of the army forces in the Territory. The United States

Government wanted peace with the Indians so that the territory could be safely opened to settlement. His attempt to negotiate a treaty with the hostile Indians was to no avail and therefore he attempted to defeat them with his troops. In the battle that ensued, his troops were badly defeated by the Miami tribe under their chief, Little Turtle. This defeat caused him to resign his commission as Commander in Chief of the troops in the territory.

President Washington replaced St. Clair with General Anthony Wayne, known as Mad Anthony Wayne during the Revolutionary War. General Wayne, with a force of about three thousand men consisting of equal numbers of mounted riflemen, Kentucky volunteers and troops brought together from around Pittsburgh, began a march into the Indian country in October of 1793. On August 20, 1795, he and his troops decisively defeated the Indian forces at the Battle of Fallen Timbers. Indian hostilities were at an end and a treaty was perfected at Fort Greenville, General Wayne's headquarters. With peace with the Indians, the Northwest Territory was ready for settlement.

During General Wayne's campaign against the Indians, the men who composed the Kentucky contingent of his forces saw much of the area along the northwest side of Ohio. General Wayne's march took him through impenetrable undergrowth as his army hacked-out its trails wide enough for army wagons northward from Cincinnati. From Fort Hamilton, his road passed through what is now Preble County, Ohio, just east of Eaton and after crossing Banta's Fork near the forty foot pitch followed the route of Ohio State Highway 503 to Fort Greenville. Along his way, the General named the creeks as Three Mile Creek and Seven Mile Creek according to their distance from Fort Hamilton. This became an easy road for settlers to follow through the dense undergrowth and was known as Wayne's Trace.

The Kentuckians who were part of his army saw that this country was composed of rich soil with ample water from the streams. When they returned to Kentucky, the word quickly spread that marvelous land was now available free of the Indian menace in

CONQUEST OF A CONTINENT   229

the Northwest Territory. Now that Albert had left the Dutch nation and church, there was nothing to hold him to this land of disappointments and tragedies.

The Land Ordinance of 1785 established a new system of distributing Government land. Virginia's system of distributing land had led to nothing but contested land claims. The Virginia method was to issue a Land Warrant in advance and then let the party with the Land Warrant stake out his claim not knowing whether someone else had already done so. In Washington, our new nation's leaders came up with a much better idea. Under this plan, at a point where the Ohio River crosses the Pennsylvania border, a north-south line was to be run as the principal meridian. At the same time a base line known as the geographer's line was to be surveyed. From these two lines, Parallel lines were to be surveyed at six mile intervals. The north-south lines were to be called "Range" while the east-west lines were called "Township." This formed a system of squares, six miles by six miles. Each Township was divided into thirty-six sections each of one mile square.

Judge John Cleves Symmes, a land speculator from New Jersey, purchased a total land area of 311,682 acres from the Federal Government. This land was known as the Symmes (or the Miami) Purchase and ran approximately twenty-four miles north of the Ohio River and lay between the Great Miami and Little Miami Rivers. Excluding land reserved for Fort Washington, schools, religion and Congress' future use, the amount of land actually patented (deeded) to Symmes on September 30, 1792 by President George Washington was 248,250 acres. This purchase initiated much of southwest Ohio's settlement.

Symmes had this land surveyed according to the Federal Rectangular Survey System which divided the land into six mile square townships as established by the Federal Government. He, however, had his Ranges running east and west while his Townships ran north and south contrary to the government plan. His section numbers also were numbered north to south contrary to government practice. Symmes numbering system for Range, Township and Section still carry his survey practice making the land between the Miamis different from all other original surveys.

In late 1795, Symmes sold ranges 7 and 8 of his land to four men including Jonathan Dayton who had been his agent in dealing with Congress and these ranges east of the Great Miami and north of the Mud Rivers became known as the "Dayton Purchase." This tract included what is now eastern Montgomery County including what is now the city of Dayton. On April 1, 1796, settlers arrived at the Dayton town site and began setting up a town. Dayton was located on the Great Miami River where the Mud River flows into it. The land between the Miamis south of this junction of rivers was being sold by Symmes.

Surveyors had been sent out by Symmes to lay out the Range, Township and Section lines and post markers at their corners in 1787. His maps showed natural phenomenon such as rivers and streams in relation to these markers. This survey was made prior to General Wayne's victory over the Indians at Fallen Timbers. Thus, the surveyors had to be excellent frontiersmen as well as good in their relations with the Indians for the hazards they faced were formidable. Symmes, himself, had courted the good will of the Indians and forbade his surveyors to stir up trouble or fight with them. He recruited some of the surveyors from the hardened pioneers in the Low Dutch colony. Symmes had purchased this land from the Government for sixty-six cents per acre and he and Dayton were selling it at a cost settlers could afford.

Albert knew one of the surveyors and had asked him to be on the lookout for good bottom land along the Great Miami River while he was conducting the survey around 1789. He had surveyed a broken section along the Miami which contained only two hundred acres of Great Miami River bottom land, an amount Albert could afford. He marked them with clearly visible corner markers and located their position on a surveyor's map which he gave to Albert.

In 1796, Albert heard that Symmes had started selling land in his patent north of the Ohio River and between the two Miami rivers in the Northwest Territory. He and his brother Dan were among the first to purchase land from Symmes and he knew the land they purchased would be fertile because his surveyor friend had picked it out for them. He no longer had any reason to stay in Kentucky where land was now costly and titles to land questionable. He had sold his land in the Dutch Tract at a handsome profit now that it was a productive farm land with clear title and the Indian menace had been eliminated. He knew that if he moved quickly he would have the "pick of the litter" on the land just newly acquired and opened for settlement by Symmes and Dayton.

Albert talked to his wife, Styntie, and his children about the wonderful opportunities that had just become available in the Northwest Territory. Styntie, who endured the Dutch community's rebuke of her husband with great empathy, felt ostracized from her old friends and saw this as a means of finding a new community and life.

"Why should we remain in Kentucky with all the litigation concerning land? Albert asked Styntie. " The Loose laws of Virginia have permitted almost every piece of land to be contested by several parties claiming to have good title. The land in the Symmes Purchase was sold to Symmes by a patent signed by President Washington. What better proof of ownership could there be than this land delivered to Symmes under our President's signature?"

Hendrick, their oldest son, was twenty-nine and was mentally handicapped. He was not capable of supporting a family life of his own though he was capable of doing a good day's work under supervision. Peter was twenty-seven, and was seeing Effie Hole with the intentions of marriage as soon as the problems between his father and the Dutch community settled down and their future was more assured. Albert Jr. was twenty-six and courting Mary Ackerman, while Abraham was twenty and courting Catherine Nutts. Both intended to get married when their futures had become settled. Both had talked with their fiances about their intentions of moving to the Northwest frontier with their family. The girls had spoken to their fathers, and all thought the move to be a great investment in the future.

All four boys were very excited about pioneering the newly opened territory. They saw it as the chance of a lifetime and an opportunity to escape the hostile atmosphere. Albert's four youngest children, Rachel, eighteen, Hanna, sixteen, Isaac, fifteen, and Christina, thirteen, were also very excited about the prospects of a new adventure.

In spite of his falling out with the Dutch community, Albert had stayed close to his brother Dan, who remained the consummate frontiersman and could also see the benefits of buying the rich, fertile land in the Northwest Territory. The land Albert's surveyor friend picked out for Dan was bottom land along the Little Miami River twelve miles northeast of the bottom land Albert had chosen along the Great Miami River. Dan bought what he thought were two partial sections. One was Range 4, Township 3, Section 19 while the other was Range 4, Township 4, Section 19. He was told by Symmes that these were in the same Range and adjoining Townships, within a few miles of each other. Symmes had made a mistake and the land in Township 4 was not between the Miamis but instead in the Congress lands east of the Great Miami River. Symmes had run the Ranges in his survey east to west while all other surveys ran Ranges north to south. Because of this discrepancy, he had sold Dan a section that was not in the Miami Purchase. Actually, the second listed section Dan had bought was out of Symmes purchase in the Congress land west of the Great Miami. Symmes had accidentally sold him a section he had no right to sell. It had been an honest error on the part of Dan. He didn't discover this error until he later visited his section along the Little Miami.

Both he and Albert and his boys planned to travel together north up the Kentucky River to the Ohio River and then they would follow the Ohio east to where the Great Miami became a tributary to the Ohio. Here, Albert and his boys would travel north up the Great Miami to the section he had purchased from

Symmes, while Dan would follow the Ohio River past Cincinnati for another twenty miles to where the Little Miami River joined it. Then he would follow the Little Miami north to where his property was located. The land between the two Miamis was covered by impenetrable forest undergrowth. Thus, each party had to take separate routes in search of the land they had purchased.

In late Spring of 1796, Dan and Albert set out on their scouting trip. Albert was accompanied by his four oldest sons, Hendrick, Peter, Albert and Abraham. Dan traveled by himself. As planned, they both followed the road along the Kentucky River north to the Ohio River and then followed the Ohio River to the Great Miami. Here the two parties split with Albert following the Great Miami north and Dan continuing along the Ohio to the Little Miami and then following it north.

Alongside the Great Miami River, except for Indian traces and animal paths created by the larger animals of the forest, a thick layer of brush was woven together beneath the trees. Albert and his four sons had to hack their way through areas when natural forest byways could not be found. The forest and its undergrowth was heavier than any they had ever encountered in Kentucky.

The Indian menace had dissipated after General Anthony Wayne's overwhelming victory at the battle of Fallen Timbers and the Indians reluctantly accepted their lot. Immigrants now entered land with lessened fear of skirmishes with, and ambushes by, the Indians. Frontiersmen and their families built their cabins and plowed their fields with less fear though they were still very cautious of the Indians. The larger cats, wolves and bears were still formidable foes but to well-trained frontiersmen like Albert and his sons, they were unlikely to surprise them and do them bodily harm.

The terrain was not spectacular in a majestic way but the river was attractive and its surroundings were absolutely beautiful when Albert and his sons stood in meadows where they could see more than the immediate trees and underbrush that made up the great forests. The land was undulating with the Great Miami River flowing through its channel and providing water to almost any spot where a farm might be laid out. The forests were full of game and the river and its tributary streams full of fish. As farmers, they could see that the loam on which they walked alongside the river was waiting for the plow of a settler to produce bountiful crops.

They followed the river northeast all the way to Dayton, a distance of about forty-five miles as the crow flies but over seventy miles with the river's twists and turns. On their trip up the river they found the markers left by surveyors and discovered it was the very best bottom land they had seen. It was the ideal place for their new farm. They found that on their surveyor's map it was located about midway between Hamilton and Dayton. They erected a lean-to for shelter and explored the surrounding land.

Consulting their map, they determined that this partial section, outlined by surveyors markers, was the one for which they had been searching, Section 36, Township 2, Range 5. Since this section lay along the edge of Symmes Purchase, it was an odd sized section rather than a complete section and contained only two hundred acres along the east side of the Big Miami River in what is now Montgomery County, Ohio.

This was the land they had bought, so they built quarters for better living while they explored the section to their best ability. They constructed as their home a pole shed, open on one side, so that they had some shelter from the elements as they went about their business of surveying. They then cleared about six acres of land around what they had picked as their cabin site. This provided a rifle-shot sized ring around the proposed cabin for safety from marauding Indians and the larger dangerous wild animals. It also provided land for sowing next spring when the whole family would be coming here as their new home. They remained here until the fall. Their last act before returning to Kentucky was to build a large, substantial double log cabin with space available for a loft for the family's comfort upon their arrival in the Spring.

Upon his return to Kentucky at the beginning of Winter, 1796, Albert, met with Dan to compare notes on what each had observed.

It was apparent from their discussions that both men were enthused about the possibilities of the land they had purchased. Dan had also found one section of his land alongside the Little Miami River. Its legal description was Section 19,Township 3, and Range 4 in the land between the Miamis that Symmes had purchased and he had glowing reports on the land in this vicinity. Since the other section for which he had paid was in the Congress lands on the west side of the Great Miami, he had been unable to locate it.

Now that two-hundred acres alongside the Great Miami River belonged to Albert, he hastened to prepare his family for their move to their new farm on the very edge of the new frontier. In the Spring of 1797, Albert, his wife, Stintie, and their nine children hitched the oxen to four wagons filled with their belongings and accompanied by the livestock they were taking with them set off on their immigration to their new land alongside the Great Miami River. They followed the road along side the Kentucky River to the Ohio River and then followed the Ohio to the Great Miami. Here they turned north and followed the Great Miami to their land. This was a distance of about forty miles through the most difficult underbrush they had ever encountered. His family was moving up this river by themselves through the wild untamed forest and they had only the narrow trail Albert and his sons had hacked out of its entangled underbrush to follow. The boys had to widen this trace so that it was wide enough for the oxen and the axles of the wagons to pass. Each mile was torturous. Muscles throbbed from swinging the axe and cutting with the knife to widen the path from that where a single person could pass to one that would accommodate a team of oxen and a wagon.

While the men struggled with the clearing of the underbrush so the wagon train could proceed, the women cleaned, dressed and then cooked the game that the men brought them from the streams that were teeming with fish and the forests that were teeming with animals. With the men doing such strenuous work they had ravenous appetites and Styntie was cooking a good portion of her day. In addition, the women had to keep the men's clothes washed and repaired for the work the men were doing was terribly hard on clothes. They also tended the livestock and a myriad of other frontier-women's tasks.

While the Indians were not unfriendly, bears and wildcats posed a formidable foe. At night these animals came close to the wagon train and a guard had to be posted all night to keep them at bay. The long rifle had to be used on occasions, sometimes hitting the encroaching animal sometimes missing it but always scaring the bear or cat away.

After ten strenuous days on the trail the little wagon train reached the cabin that had been built by Albert and his four sons in anticipation of the families arriving in spring. Albert had been on seven migrations but this was far different from any he had been on before. On all previous migrations he had been with a wagon train with many other families. Among the families there were men of different professions. Each new colony had all the various trades represented. This time, all support available was from the eleven Bantas. However, like all frontiersman he and his sons were jacks of all trades. In addition to Hendrick being a farmer, the three other oldest boys had apprenticed out to various trades. Peter knew black-smithing, Albert knew carpentry and Abraham was a tinsmith. They were capable of living comfortably using their own knowledge of how to exist all alone on the frontier. It was a daunting task, however, to start from nothing and as a family create a home with no white men or stores within many miles.

With the tools they brought with them in the wagons, they improved the cabin by putting in a rough-hewn floor. Logs had been laid lengthwise across the room so as to create beams to lay a ceiling for the great room. Clapboard of about six inches by four inches was split from oak limbs and laid across and fastened to the beams so as to create a ceiling for the cabin big room and a floor for the loft which lay between the ceiling and the gabled roof. A ladder was built to permit climbing into the loft. Albert, Styntie and the girls would sleep in the great room while the men would sleep in the loft.

The logs that formed the cabin sides were thoroughly caulked with clay mixed with straw until it was completely sealed from what would be the freezing temperatures of winter. The door was heavy clapboard held together with wooden pins. A wooden latch beam was raised and lowered from the outside by a strong latch string which traveled from the inside of the door to its outside by means of a hole. The latch string was only taken in when danger lurked from unknown strangers in the area be they Indian or white intruders. From this latch string used by the pioneer frontiersmen comes the saying, "The latch string is out," meaning "You are welcome in our house."

They also created a substitute for window glass by covering paper with bear grease till it was opaque and let light into the room while keeping out the cold and the insects. Styntie and the girls took the furniture and personal belongings they had brought in the wagons and began to turn the cabin into a home. The large and small spinning wheels were placed in front of the fire ready for the first crop of flax from the fields and the first coat of wool from the sheep.

The family had lost the technique of constructing the great hearth and brick oven the Dutch families had known prior to the migration to Kentucky. Instead they built the fireplace outside the wall as did the English. This was built of small logs similar to the way the cabin was constructed and then plastered on the inside with clay mixed with straw to make the chimney fireproof. Styntie had learned the English way to cook from the years the Dutch tribe was lost in the wilderness of Kentucky, being shuttled from place to place as conditions required.

The eleven members of the family were very crowded in the double cabin. However, they felt far better off than when they were living under the intolerable conditions of the Dutch Station above Harrods Fort. Those were terrible, tragic and terrifying years with the Indian menace and the rampant epidemics that swept that overcrowded station.

The men immediately planted the six acres that they had

cleared the year before and along with the crops of corn and vegetables, they planted a patch of flax so that the women could spin
it into linen for cloth to make clothes for the family of eleven.

Splitting rails for fences to keep the livestock contained took a
good part of their time. The pigs were allowed to roam the woods
and grew fat on the fruits of the forest. The milk cow produced
ample milk for the family and the sheep had abundant grass to
grow and increase in numbers. The game of the forest and the fish
in the river supplied more than enough meat and fish without the
men going but a few hundred yards from the farm.

After the crops had been planted, the men removed the brush
from about a hundred acres of land and girdled the giant trees so
they would die above the girdle and could be burned to the stump
the following year. In addition, they cleared ten more acres the
hard way so that they would have sixteen acres ready for planting
next Spring.

Fall came and the crops were ready for harvest. They now saw
what fine land they had chosen. The corn was gathered and husked
creating a supply of it for the winter. The wheat had grown to
straw because of the land's fertility and was harvested and tied into
bundles for use as thatch for the cabin roof. Even with a closely
thatched roof, rain would seep through to the attic and that made
it an uncomfortable place to sleep. The flax was ample for the
ladies to begin spinning it into linen. Wool from the sheep would
be available for shearing in the spring. The family was ready for
the Winter.

They now needed a loom to weave the linen thread into cloth.
Looms were far too cumbersome to carry with them in the wagons. There was not enough room in the small cabin for a large
loom so a lean-to enclosed shed was attached to the cabin as a
cellar to hold the loom and their produce and meats. After the flax
crop was harvested, the men went to work under Albert Jr.'s guidance, hewing rough lumber from timber so that he, as a carpenter,
could build a loom. The women spent their days and evenings
spinning flax into thread on the small spinning wheel and in due

time they had enough linen thread to start weaving it into cloth on the loom.

They had accomplished an amazing amount of necessary work during the spring, summer and fall and were prepared for the severe Northwest Territory winter which was now upon them. The Winter was harsh and lonely beyond the edge of civilization. No family could be more capable and prepared for survival under this bitter Northwestern Winter than were the eleven Bantas. The cabin was too small for simple comfort but its smallness made it easier for the ever-blazing fireplace to raise the freezing temperatures outside to a chilly but tolerable temperature inside.

The men had made sure that the cellar was full to brimming with corn, vegetables, sun dried fruits of the forest, gathered nuts, and meat and fish. The temperature in the lean-to was freezing which kept the meat and fish fresh. Albert had cut a block to grind the corn into meal. This block was also placed in the cellar room. There was a salt lick within a few miles of the cabin from which they had stored enough salt for the winter. Syrup boiled from the sap of the maple trees served as their sugar.

To pass the time during the Winter months, members of the family played frontier parlor games in the cabin. The spinning wheel was kept constantly busy. With eleven people occupying the cabin there was always something going on. Even so, cabin fever soon began to take over when the weather kept them inside for days on end. Hunting was a favorite sport for the men when the weather permitted. Also splitting wood gave a body a chance to exercise muscles.

Two Dutch cultural items had been passed down through one hundred and twenty six years on this continent to Albert of the fifth generation. This is because this line of the Banta family maintained their Dutchness through all this time. As part of their ethnicity, the art of making and using klompen (wooden shoes) and ice skates had passed generation to generation. This was the last generation of which this would be true.

Concerning klompen, they proved to be much better adapted

to the wet fields than Indian moccasins which quickly became sodden and were of little protection from the wet earth or snow. The English made foot coverings for the wet weather and snow from birch bark with hickory bark soles strapped over heavy home made woolen socks. These contraptions worked far better than moccasins in the snow. The old Dutch klompen were far better than birch and hickory bark shoes.

The pleasure and exercise of ice skating was just as enjoyable on the frozen ponds alongside the Miami as it had been for the Banta's forefathers on the canals in Holland. What a delightful way that was to spend freezing winter days on this godforsaken frontier. The sight of these white men and women gliding effort-lessly on the frozen stream was a spectacle of great interest to the Indians who gathered along the banks to witness a sight they had never seen before. With these diversions the winter was not easy for the Bantas but it was tolerable. Time did not pass quickly that first winter of 1798, but it did pass and for its harshness, spring was all the more joyous.

As spring came and winter left, the family looked forward to their new life. They knew they were poised for a beautiful future in a new country and a new culture. They had the best land on this new frontier. Here their applied grit and tenacity would have no bounds. There would be no fight for ethnicity or with Indians. This was the land of the free and the home of the brave and on this frontier and in this family there was no lack of either.

As soon as the earth thawed and the days warmed beyond the days of frost, Albert and the boys were planting the sixteen acres ready for the plough. In addition to farming, they had many vital things to get done in order to live comfortably on the far frontier. Tanning vats were constructed so that the animal skins could be tanned into leather for shoes, pants and coats as well as saddles, harnesses, bridles and the dozens of other places where leather was used on a frontier farm.

When spring came in 1798, they found that the path they had created to their farm from Fort Hamilton was now used by a

string of immigrants to this new land. There was a constant stream
of settlers passing by their farm on their way to land they hoped to
settle. Most were squatters but some had purchased land from
Symmes. Throughout the year, the family continued to improve
the farm and increase the tillable acreage. By winter the farm was
well established and the stream of new settlers looked on it with
awe.

In early 1799, Albert was suddenly faced with a terrible dilemma. An U. S. marshal for the Federal Government came to
their farm and told them that the land along the Great Miami
River which they had bought from Symmes had been returned to
the government as Symmes had not lived up to his agreement in
paying for it. Symmes had not paid the Federal Government per
his agreement nor met other obligations under which he had obtained the patent and therefore all land he had sold was being
illegally held by those who had bought it from him. For this reason, he told Albert, he was a squatter on government land. All the
other settlers who had bought land were in the same position.

"What is this you tell me," Albert said to the agent. "We come
here and sweat blood to build this farm from the dangerous frontier, and we don't own it. How can that be when George Washington signed the paper saying Symmes could sell it. I been swindled
and President George Washington was a party to the swindle."

"Don't yell at me," the marshal said to Albert, "I'm just the
messenger bringing the bad news. I don't make the laws or the
policy. You can't blame President Washington. Symmes reneged
on his deal and never paid the Federal Government for the land."

"Who else I got to yell at," Peter responded. "You be the only
one here. Why do you take such a terrible job where you got to tell
honest farmers that what they bought is not theirs. I bet you catch
hell from all the farmers. You could get shot and I wouldn't blame
who did it."

"I've been shot at," said the marshal. "If they meant to kill
me I'd be dead but being honest, God fearing men, they just
meant to scare me. Why don't you join them in what they are

doing. They are going to Cincinnati to meet with their congressmen and senator."

Albert decided to join the other farmers who were now squatters and go to Cincinnati to argue his point with his elected officials. All the other settlers throughout the Symmes purchase found themselves in the same position. Some had bought land that Symmes had no right to sell. Others had bought land in the Symmes Purchase but he hadn't paid the Government and the patent had been rescinded.

Albert and Dan had blazed a trail between their two farms on the Great Miami and Little Miami Rivers, a distance of about twelve miles, so that they could visit each other. Dan came to Albert's farm and they decided to go together to Cincinnati. Dan, was also caught up in this disaster and in an even worse dilemma since one section he had bought from Symmes wasn't even in the Symmes purchase. The two brothers were leaders in the fight to hold their land against the Federal Government.

Washington was flooded with complaints by irrate settlers who had poured their body and souls into the land they thought they owned. Congress was quick to note it would be unjust to take the settlers improvements and move them off the land. Therefore they passed Relief Acts on March 2, 1799 and March 3, 1801, which gave these settlers who had purchased land from Symmes in good faith the first right to buy the land from the Federal Government if the purchaser had made improvements on it. The congress even included in this preemption land mistakenly sold by Symmes outside the land between the Miamis if the purchaser had improved it. This was the first time the right of preemption was granted by Congress. The government also pointed out to the swindled farmers that they still had rights in a court of law to recover from Symmes what they had paid him.

Dan found that the second section he had purchased from Symmes was not located along the Little Miami River. He had discovered Symmes mistake when he found his land along the Little Miami and learned that there was no Range 4, Township 4 anywhere nearby. In talking to surveyors of the Congress Lands west of the Great Miami, he learned that such section was located in the Congress Lands west of the Great Miami about two miles east of Twin Creek. Dan was anxious to retain his title to that section but had no time to go and improve that section himself. He, Therefore asked Albert to send one of his sons to improve it so that he would have preemptive rights to purchase that section from the Federal Government when it was opened for sale. Albert told him he would see that it was improved as soon as he possibly could.

"What a crazy thing," Albert said to Dan. "Symmes got nothing and we're supposed to sue him for something. That don't make sense." Albert was right. No farmer ever received a dime from Symmes who ended up completely broke from his land purchase. Albert was furious that he had relied upon the Federal Government in purchasing the land from Symmes but delighted that no speculator could buy from under him the land he and his boys had improved.

"We took this challenge of tearing these beautiful farms from the edge of the frontier to avoid the land problems in Kentucky and then we walk right into the middle of one here in the Northwest Territory," he said to Dan, "but by buying the land again from the government we know for sure we have good title."

He and Dan had to lose the money they had paid under the Symmes Purchase and, in addition, they had to pay the Federal Government two dollars an acre for the land they already thought they owned. Albert purchased for the second time his two hundred acre farm in Section 36, Township 2, Range 4. When the Land Office opened in Cincinnati in 1801, he not only paid the government for the land he had purchased from Symmes, he purchased Section 35, which was also an irregular small section alongside the Miami. This increased his land holdings to six hundred and forty acres of the very best bottom land along the Great Miami River. He thought this would be ample to take care of all his children when they got married.

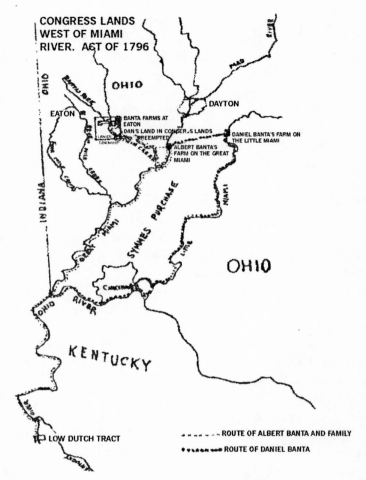

MAP OF ALBERT AND DAN BANTA'S EXPLORATION OF AND LAND PURCHASES IN THE NORTHWEST TERRITORY, 1798

While this upsetting problem was being resolved, 1799 passed with much improvement to their farm. Dayton had become a village and a few of the rough edges were worn off the new frontier. The year 1800 saw the farm really come into its own, producing bumper crops.

In the spring of 1800, Albert Sr. and Peter set out to improve

Dan's land by Twin Creek in the land the Government had just opened west of the Great Miami River. They had heard from veterans of the battle of Fallen Timbers of excellent land along the road General Wayne had cut from the undergrowth for his war wagons. This land was along side Twin Creeks about sixteen miles northwest of their farm. They left the farm on the Miami in charge of Albert and set out to travel to this new fertile land of which they had heard such glowing reports. They followed the Great Miami southward for several miles to where Twin Creek became its tributary. Here they traveled northwest about eighteen miles up Twin Creek to where Dan's land lay about two miles to the east. Here they left the river and found Dan's section. Although not bottom land the soil was excellent and they set about building a cabin and clearing the forest around it so as to establish preemptive rights for Dan.

After completing the task, they returned to Twin Creek to follow it back to the Great Miami. At the creek they met some friendly Indians who stopped to visit with them. Through sign language, the Indians told them they had just come from a creek that flowed through rich forests and land about two mile farther up Twin Creek. They decided to follow the trace that had been used by the Indians to check out the land the Indians had described for from what they had understood this land and creek sounded very interesting.

They followed Twin Creek north and after an additional two miles, they discovered a tributary that exactly fit the image of what they imagined in their mind's eye. Both men knew at first sight that this creek and its surrounding land was bottom land and had great promise. They set up camp where this new creek entered Twin Creek and began exploring the surrounding area. After two days of tracking through the area, both agreed that this land was too good to let pass by. On their survey map they determined that its legal description was Section 10, Range 3, Township 5. The land was well drained yet had forest mulch for as deep as they could drive a stake into it. The stream was full of trout and the forest teamed with game. The beautiful creek that ran through it emptied into Twin Creek and the eons of flooding by these two creeks had turned the soil into rich loam.

They had seen no other white men in the area but on the third day they met a frontiersman who had been told of their coming by Indians. The word had spread among the natives that a group of white men were heading up Twin Creek. The frontiersman told them his name was Jacob Parker and asked them their names. Then he told them that he had arrived in the area prior to 1800. He said he was the only white man within many miles according to the Indians and spoke of the fertility of the land in glowing terms.

"You've come to the right place," he said. "I been lots of places but this is the best land I ever saw. I found it when I was in the army under General Anthony Wayne heading for the battle of Fallen Timbers and swore I would return and make my farm here."

"You been in the army with General Wayne?" Albert asked Jacob. "You've been some sort of real man. I admire you."

Jacob had been intrigued by Albert's broken English and Dutch accent so he continued by asking, "You must be new here from Germany. How'd you get a-way out here? This is no place for a greenhorn."

"Take good look at us," Albert replied. "Do we look like green foots? I been a frontiersman all my life. I been born on a frontier as was my father and his father."

"Don't let his accent fool you," said Peter. "Our family came to this country when the Dutch owned New York and I don't recollect when that was. Guess we was here near as long as the Indians." By now, except in a general way, family history had been lost to this sixth generation.

Albert told Jacob that they had decided to purchase this land where the smaller creek entered Twin Creek and the land to the north up the smaller creek.

"Then I guess we should call this smaller creek Banta's Fork since you are gonna own it," Jacob said and that has been its name since his official sanction.

The author stands on a bridge over Banta's Fork, Lanier Township, Preble County, Ohio

Since they had decided that this was the land they planned to buy, they built better quarters for better living while they surveyed the land to their best ability. They constructed another pole shed, open on one side, so that they had some shelter from the elements as they went about their business of surveying. Albert thought so much of this land that he decided that Peter should buy this location and that Peter, Albert Jr. and Abraham would move to it and improve it as soon as the family could spare them from the farm on the Great Miami. Its official description was Section 10, Range 3, Township 5. This section included the portion of land where Banta's Creek becomes a tributary of Twin Creek and was only five miles from where the City of Eaton now stands.

They followed Twin Creek down to a point opposite their farm on the Great Miami. Then, in order to avoid a longer triangular trip down Twin Creek and up the Great Miami, they blazed a direct trail between Twin Creek and their farm on the Great Miami River, a distance of about four miles. They returned to their farm alongside the Great Miami and continued to improve the farm until the boys could be spared to migrate to the land on Bantas Fork near Eaton.

By 1801, it was time for Albert Jr. and Abraham to go back to Kentucky and warm up their romances with the ladies they loved. Because the cabin in which they had been living was small even for Albert's family, two additional cabins were built for the prospective new families. Since they had already talked to their sweethearts and their sweethearts fathers about settling the Northwest Territory, they were sure enough of themselves that they took two wagons and two sets of oxen to carry their brides' goods on the return trip.

As soon as young Albert and Abraham arrived back in Kentucky, they both undertook a whirlwind romance with the two ladies they had chosen for their intended brides. They first, of course, told their sweethearts how they had been so very lonely for their company while they had been gone and that the pain was almost unbearable. Then they told their intendeds of the unbelievable opportunities on the new frontier and how they had the first pick of the best land. Both young ladies and their parents again said, "yes." The girls' families hastened to prepare for the wedding ceremonies. Albert and Mary and Abraham and Catherine were married in a double ceremony in the Baptist church in early spring.

When the two boys returned with their two brides and their trousseaus, spinning wheels and other personal items, everyone helped in setting up the two newly married couples' cabins so that they could live in a comfortable fashion. The Banta settlement now was composed of three cabins and three families.

Several other personal things happened to the Bantas on their farm alongside the Miami River in 1801. The cabins of Abraham and Albert Jr. were both blessed with the beginnings of the seventh generation of the family on the North American continent in

December. Albert and Mary had the baby girl of the seventh generation whom they named Elisabeth. Abraham and Catherine had the first baby boy of the generation and they named him Solomon. No one could foresee as this baby boy entered the family epic that he would become the model for this line of the family to follow, leaving their world of uneducated frontiersmen behind and becoming a well educated man.

1801 also was the year that Peter, Albert's second oldest son, left bachelorhood behind at age thirty, and married Effie Hole. He had met her at the Baptist church in Kentucky. At his wedding in Kentucky, everyone wanted to know about the farm on the bottomland alongside the Great Miami. It was a major point of interest to everyone at the wedding but especially to Peter van Ausdel who had been one of Peter's best friends when the family lived in the Low Dutch colony. Peter van Ausdel said he was very interested in buying land in the Northwest Territory and asked Peter to divide Section 10 at Bantas Fork with him when he purchased it from the Federal Government. The truth was that Peter van Ausdall was smitten by Peter's sister Rachel and felt if he could be near her he could woo her and win her. Peter told him he would love to have him as a neighbor and would divide section 10 equally with him, each taking two quarter sections.

When the newlyweds returned to the farm on the Great Miami, a new cabin was raised for them and the Banta settlement on the Great Miami River now consisted of four cabins. Now, only Albert Sr.'s oldest son, Hendrick, age 31 and his youngest son, Isaac, age seventeen, remained unmarried while all five of his daughters still were single. Since Hendrick was mentally handicapped, he preferred to stay at the Great Miami farm and Peter became Albert's business partner. As Albert Sr. grew older, he put Peter in charge of the family's fortune and the two became the financial heads of the family.

Hendrick loved farming and was very content to stay with his parents and do the farm chores. He remained a bachelor until 1833 when his mother, who was then widowed, died at the age of eighty-three. The following year, though he was sixty-five years of age, he married the Widow Piatt and they had two children, a son, Henry, who died at age fourteen and a daughter, Belle, who became a teacher in Cincinnati.

There were many settlers who could not afford to buy an entire quarter section from the Government Land office. These immigrants were willing to pay much more for a smaller number of acres than the two dollars per acre charged by the land office for those who were wealthy enough to buy a quarter section or more. The land the Bantas had bought and cleared along side the Great Miami River was especially attractive.

With the influx of settlers rising each year, they had newcomers bidding for that bottom land. They sold a portion of the three hundred and sixty acres alongside the Great Miami in small parcels at good prices. This put them in a cash rich position and allowed the family to enter into the buying of the land at Bantas Creek in Township 5, Range 3 which later was named Lanier Township in Preble County. They were now in the business of land development. It was a foolproof way to make money as few of the pioneers had enough money to buy more than one-hundred acres.

In 1803, Peter bought Section 9 and one-half of Section 10 on and near Bantas Creek. He split section 10 with his best friend, Peter van Ausdel. With the purchase complete, the familiar story of this line of the Banta family once again repeated itself. Peter, Albert Jr. and Abraham set out to improve the blazed trail to Bantas Fork to accommodate the wagons in the wagon train. Albert would supervise the migration but he, Styntie, Hendrick, Isaac and the girls would continue to operate the farm on the Great Miami while the other three boys would move to and make improvements to the land on Bantas Fork. This was the eighth migration in which Albert Sr. participated during his fifty-six years of life and he had become as familiar with the procedures of migration as he was in the profession of farming. The wagons were packed with the three families' farm and personal goods and the oxen attached to the yokes. The farm animals were herded behind the wagons and with the Bantas walking behind, the wagon train they were on the move to Bantas Fork in Lanier township.

With the men hacking and cutting the blazed trail into one that could carry wagons, the wagon train followed the tracks that Albert Sr. and Peter had blazed a couple of years earlier to their new purchases. Here, the three Banta families planned to make their permanent home. They arrived in late summer of 1803 and began to build their cabins and clear the forests to start their new farm alongside Banta's Fork. They had the cabins built and a few acres cleared for planting the next Spring before the first winter snows fell. The next year was spent in repeating all the things they had to done to make life comfortable on their land on the Great Miami River.

While they were doing this, Peter van Ausdel, who had brought his father and family with him, was conducting the same efforts in building his farm. It was comforting to have as neighbors a family that had been close friends of the Bantas for generations.

With the essentials accomplished, they saw the economic possibilities of building a saw mill. Albert Sr. learned the value of a good sawmill from the sad lesson the Dutch colony had suffered in Conewago. He had located a site on Bantas Creek where there was a forty foot pitch and purchased that section from the government. Albert Sr. sent Abraham, Albert and Issac with three wagons to go back to Kentucky for equipment for the mill. When they returned, Albert Sr. set out to build a saw mill at the pitch in order to be ready to produce the rough cut lumber the new families would sorely need. Other new pioneer families were asking about lumber as the area grew steadily in numbers of new settlers.

It was soon apparent that the sawmill would be economically very profitable with new families arriving weekly in the area. By 1805, the people in the county increased to the point where all the trades were represented in the small village of Eaton. With the numbers now in the area, it was time to begin the organization of a church. The Bantas were active in organizing a Baptist church

and were among its first members. Abraham was not much interested in farming. Like his father he felt he had a calling from God
and preached in the Baptist church while practicing his trade as
tinsmith.

With fertile land so inexpensive in the Northwest Territory
and the sawmill and the land sales increasing their wealth, Peter,
Albert Jr., Abraham and Isaac purchased other sections in Lanier
Township in their own names. In addition to his purchases of
Section 9 and half of Section ten, in 1803 Peter bought Section 19
and Section 14 in 1804. Isaac bought Section 12 and Albert bought
one half of Sections 1 and Section 4 the same year. In 1805, All
four boys bought additional land, Peter buying the other half of
Section 1, while Abraham bought Section 8, Isaac bought Section
12 and Albert bought Section 30. In 1815, Abraham purchased
Section 13 and in 1816 he purchased the land set aside as school
land which was Section 11. Each of the boys now had his own
land except Hendrick, who lived with his parents, and each built a
cabin and established their family farm on their section. Much of
this land was sold at a profit to new settlers. Isaac was twenty-one
in 1804 when he purchased his section and married the girl next
door, Peter's sister, Mary van Ausdel. All five farms were contiguous to each other and were laid out like a string of pearls. Albert
and his five sons now owned eight square miles of Lanier Township
with their farms located a few miles from Eaton.

The land in Ohio was so attractive that while it had been
inhabited only by Indians with a very few white settlers in 1801,
by 1803 the population had grown to such an extent that it was
admitted as the seventeenth state in the Union. With its admis-
sion, the population grew even faster. Immigrants were flowing in
from all over the world. Log cabins were being built everywhere
while the dense forests were being cleared and brought under the
plow. Cincinnati was becoming a large city. Dayton, twelve miles
to the east of their farms, had also become a medium-sized city. In
1806, Eaton was incorporated as a city. Eaton had become a respectable town with all the trades established. In 1808, the first

school was opened and paid for by the School Land Section set aside in each Township. Church services had been held in local cabins from the outset but a formal church was constructed in Eaton in 1806.

In 1808, Rachel, Albert Sr.'s oldest daughter, married Peter van Ausdel. Peter's plan had worked. Now two of Albert Sr.'s children had married two of their neighbors, the van Ausdels. On the frontier, where families were so large and the population so limited, when unmarried men and women of the opposite sex and of the same age lived as neighbors, romances often occurred resulting in marriages. We've seen this several times at intervals of this epic story.

By 1809, the boys had purchased eight additional square miles in Montgomery county between the Miami River and the Ohio-Indiana border but outside Preble County and Lanier Township. They were now heavily into land development as well as milling and farming.

A large number of Bantas who now live in Ohio and Indiana have descended from Albert Sr., who like Epke, spread the family name by five sons. Hendrick only produced a daughter but the other four were as prolific as Epke's boys were. Peter had eleven children of which five were boys. Albert Jr. had nine children of whom five were boys. Abraham had thirteen children of whom five were boys. The record is not clear as to how many children or boys Isaac and Mary had but the number was likely similar to his brothers. If it was, then the generation of five boys that came to Ohio quadrupled in the next generation to twenty young men who were to pass on the Banta name. Is it any wonder then that Ohio is a leading state in the number of Bantas that reside there?

Abraham Banta of the sixth generation and whose line we follow in this story, was the fifth of Albert and Styntie's nine children. He was born on June 27, 1778 in Conewego, Pennsylvania. In 1780, as a two-year-old, he was one of the thirty-one children and grandchildren of his grandfather, Hendrick, to take the hazardous journey across Pennsylvania to Fort Pitt and then down the

Ohio River to Kentucky. Abraham Banta then lived with his family on the Kentucky frontier until the fallout between his father, Albert, and the Low Dutch Reformed Church at the Low Dutch tract at Bantatown.

Abraham had spent all his early years moving from place to place following his father and his family across the wild frontier. Here on the Great Miami, his father finally settled down with his wife, Stintie, and his nine children. With hard work the family had created a successful home and farm. Abraham had had enough of migrating. All he wanted in life was to settle in one place, develop both the section he purchased from the government along side his brothers and pursue his trade as a tinsmith. In addition he wanted to preach at the Baptist church for like his father he felt he had a calling from God.

He and Catharine raised thirteen children in the log cabin on his farm, five boys and eight girls. All of Abraham's children were impressed by his oldest son, Solomon, who was the first in seven generations of this line of the Banta family to move from being a frontiersman and an Indian fighter to being an educated man with a profession.

Here on the northwest frontier, the Bantas were not shackled by ethnic ties. The family had found their "promised land" but it was not a Dutch nation. The four boys raised their families in log cabins for much of their children's lives. The children, like their parents were professional frontier's men and women. They were as much at home in the forests of Ohio as were those who had been raised all their lives in New York at home in the big city. They could make soap from lard and lye taken from ashes, tan their own leather, make their own shoes, saddles, halters and leather and home spun cloth frontiersmen clothing, make candles, spin linen and lindsey woolsey thread which they could weave into cloth for every conceivable use and a myriad of other things that made them self sufficient on the edge of civilization. But unlike their city cousins they had no education beyond simple ciphering, reading and writing. They were educated to live on the frontier not to make a living in the city.

It had been this way for six generations before their generation came into being and no one saw any need for further "edication." None, that is, until Abraham's first son, Solomon, entered the family. He had been named after a man of great intellect in the Bible: the great Judge Solomon. He was raised as a contemporary of another great intellect whom had lived in Kentucky until his father moved his family to Indiana in the Northwest Territory, Abraham Lincoln. Abe pulled himself up from splitting rails to the President of the United States by his own bootstraps.

Solomon was from the same mold. He studied by the light of the cabin's fireplace. He did his ciphering with charcoal on the back of a shovel. He loved learning. He never became president but he did raise himself to be a lawyer and the mayor of Eaton. He was accepted in the finest society as a leader in his community. He lived with his brothers and sisters on his parent's farm and received as did they a limited education in a log schoolhouse. When he was about twenty years of age, a teacher from the east came to the area and taught the classics. Solomon's mind caught fire with the information this teacher made available to him. Under his direction, he studied Greek and Latin and the Arts. After working all day on his father's farm, he would pursue his studies at night by the light of the wood fire on the old-fashioned hearth.

Upon completion of these studies, he studied law in the office of Thomas Corwin, Governor of Ohio, at Franklin, and was admitted to the bar. With his formal education completed and his profession established, he married Malinda Small on Christmas day of 1828. They moved to Danville, Illinois, where they resided for three years. Able-bodied men between eighteen and forty-five were required by law to join the militia reserves and practice drilling two times a year. The penalty for not doing so was one dollar. Solomon did his duty and showed up for drilling as required.

Trouble had been brewing with Black Hawk, chief of the Sac Indians, who had sold their domain to the white man after General Wayne defeated the Indian forces at the Battle of Fallen Timbers. This was the land in Illinois that was now being settled. When the Sac moved west across the Mississippi they infringed on the territory of the Sioux and skirmishes ensued between the two tribes. Black Hawk believed his tribe had been tricked out of their land in Illinois. He said the white man had brought whiskey to the negotiations and got the chiefs drunk then took advantage of them. He crossed the Mississippi with five hundred braves. A large contingency of U. S. troops under General Atkinson convinced Black Hawk to return across the river. For this he was given sixty thousand bushels of corn. With this payment Black Hawk promised he would never again threaten the families establishing their farms in the Northwest Territory.

Black Hawk's brother, "The Prophet," predicted that the Ottawas, Chippewas, Winnebagos, Pollowattomys and Fox tribes would join him in a final battle against the United States and he would be provided with guns and ammunition by the English if he would initiate a war. The Prophet convinced him he would win, for the Great Spirit would be with him, so in spite of his promise to General Atkinson, he again crossed the Mississippi with five hundred braves.

Dressed in his battle arraignment with painted face and a cap of eagle feathers, he and his braves traveled about forty miles into Illinois burning settler's crops and homes while killing whole families and taking scalps. General Henry Atkinson advised all families to take shelter in the forts and then sent a letter to the governor asking for volunteer reinforcements. Men rode through the towns asking for volunteers. Solomon volunteered to serve in the militia and set out in April, 1832, with a group of militia men to find Black Hawk and his army.

After a difficult march through swamps and streams, they set up camp at the edge of the Mississippi River. Black Hawk realized by this time that the other tribes were not going to join him nor were the English going to provide him with rifles and ammunition, therefore he sent a party of three braves under a white flag to negotiate with the enemy. The Illinois militiamen who were undisciplined frontiersmen had gotten drunk on the Company' stock of whiskey and set upon the peace party of braves and beat them senseless, leaving them for dead.

Five braves were on a high spot observing the peace party and upon seeing what happened reported to Black Hawk. Black Hawk upon hearing the report became so angry that he attacked the Militia of twelve hundred men with less than five hundred. In spite of having superior numbers, the Illinois militia troops put up no fight but took off as quickly as they could run into the woods. They ran back across the swamps and rivers, hills and valleys to from where they had started their march in search of Black Hawk.

The first men back to the base reported that the militia had been overrun by hordes of crazed Indians and that most of the militiamen had been killed. However, by midnight, all but eleven men had been accounted for. Because of this instance and other similar ones, the United States Army under General Atkinson became disgusted with the volunteers and took a vote as to whether they should be sent home. After the vote, which turned out to be a tie, they discharged the entire company.

U. S. troops under General Atkinson caught Black Hawk and his warriors at Bad Axe on August first and slaughtered most of his forces. Black Hawk slipped away during the battle but was followed and captured by Sioux Indians friendly to the government. He was taken to Washington where he met with Andrew Jackson for a meeting between these two old warriors. Black Hawk told President Jackson that there would be no more wars between the Indians and the white man. The battle of Bad Axe was the last of the Indian wars.

The war was won by the U. S. Army and most volunteers never saw an Indian though they suffered hardships at the hands of the elements, hunger and frustration. Solomon was glad to have this battle behind him and pleased that this saw the end to the Indian menace. He returned with Malinda to Eaton, Ohio, in 1837 and practiced law. Here, he served two terms as Prosecuting Attorney of Preble County, was elected several times as Mayor of the City of Eaton, and was for years, Justice of the Peace.

Solomon was the first in seven generations of this line of the Banta family to move from being a frontiersman and an Indian fighter to being an educated man with a profession. Is it any wonder that his younger brother, Frederick, who we will follow in the seventh generation of our story, was inspired and influenced by his education, profession and acceptance in the society of Eaton. While Frederick was unable to obtain an education for himself, he promised himself, as we have noted earlier, that one would be provided to his children of the eighth generation.

We spent a good deal of time following the career path of Solomon though Frederick, his younger brother, is the one who will be followed in this epic story. Frederick was born in house Abraham had built to replace his original log cabin near Banta's Fork, Preble County, Ohio, October 17, 1815. He was the eighth of his father's thirteen children. Frederick was fourteen years younger than his oldest brother, Solomon. He grew up watching Solomon grow in intellect. Solomon was an idol to this rough farm boy. As he grew older, he watched in awe as each step in Solomon's life seemed to move him, as if by magic, away from his father's frontier farm into a social life wholly strange and glamorous to this frontier boy. Solomon's and Frederick's father, Abraham, died December 4, 1864, on Banta Fork, Preble County, Ohio, at the age of eighty-six.

While Frederick was unable to acquire a higher education for himself, he was convinced that education was the route from the frontier farm to the good life. He determined that he would, by the sweat of his brow, provide a college education for all his children. The life of a college educated man could not be his for what he knew how to do was to be a farmer. This he had learned on the frontier at his father's side. At this profession, he knew he was the best.

CHAPTER 15

INDIANA

Frederick, born in 1815, entered the family fifteen years after they had moved to the new frontier in Lanier township and settled their farm along Banta's Fork. Ohio had become a state in 1803, while Eaton had become a a city in 1808. Abraham and his family lived on their farm when Frederic was born, but the log cabin had been torn down and in its place Abraham had built a substantial home. By the time of his birth, settlers had purchased almost all of the land in Lanier township and had turned it into farm land. His earliest memories were of an established farm and of his father's practicing his trade as a tinsmith. He also remembered his father's preaching at the meetings of the newly organized Baptist church which he was trying to estab-lished in Lanier township. He had never been in a wagon train or opened a new frontier, but he had heard his father's stories around the fireside at night so many times that he longed to move to a new frontier as his forefathers had done.

As a young adult, he realized, that if he was to continue as a farmer, and farming was the only occupation he knew, he would have to do just that. With Abraham's large family of twelve living children, even the square mile section he had bought from the government was not large enough to support his children's twelve families. Since the abandonment of the idea of a Dutch nation, the Dutch no longer migrated as a unit. With the country's growing up and the dangers from Indians and wild beasts a thing of the past, an entire family was not needed for safety in moving to a new frontier. No longer was it necessary for the community or family to migrate as a unit.

For the first time in the history of this line of the family, an individual, Frederick, set out alone to locate land to purchase from the government. He intended to carve a farm of his own from frontier land where he could raise a family. In 1836, at the age of twenty-one, Frederick headed for the new frontier in northwest Indiana. At this time, the government, under President Jackson, was opening land for settlement at auction at the minimum price of one dollar and twenty-five cents per acre on a cash or land script basis. If land was not sold after it had been offered at auction, it was open to entry in any amount of acres at the minimum price.

Prior to 1836, President Jackson had proclaimed a large potion of land opened for auction, and in 1836, sales reached a figure never to be exceeded. Land was opened in northwest Indiana and Frederick traveled across Indiana in search of land for his prospective farm. He kept his ears open for leads to good land. In his travels, he had talked to some men who told him there was land close to the western Indiana border that was swampy but contained hillocks of excellent land. These hillocks were often many acres in area which would make them suitable for farming. They told him to keep traveling until he reached an area which had a certain species of oak trees whose branches hung down to the ground. They said the trees would look like a hanging grove. He followed their directions and found the grove just as they had described it. There was only one family in the area, the McCoy's, when he arrived and they agreed to name the township in which the grove was located Hanging Grove Township.

In 1836, Frederick purchased at auction about one hundred and eighty acres of land on several of the hillocks that rose above the swampy land. The land he purchased from the government was about fifteen miles east of Manon, Indiana and about forty miles south of Valpariso. On one hillock, he built a home and improved the land. The land proved to be of excellent quality. Because the land was swampy, with tillable hillocks arising from the swamps, his acreage was not contiguous, but his hillocks were as close together as topography would allow.

As his father and grandfather had been before him, he was very religious; and as new settlers came to Hanging Grove Township, he became involved in establishing the Christian Church of Hanging Grove. During its organization he met a young lady who sparked his

romantic interest. Her name was Sarah Gray whose family had come
from Pittsburgh. On March 1, 1843, at the age of twenty-eight, he
married Sarah Gray, age nineteen. They had a typical large family of ten
Banta children, seven girls and three boys. Katherine was their first child
and was born December 12, 1843. Little Clarissa, their third child, died
when she was two years old, while their other nine children lived full
lives. Frederick and Sarah were also aunt and uncle to fifty-three nieces
and nephews by Frederick's twelve brothers and sisters.

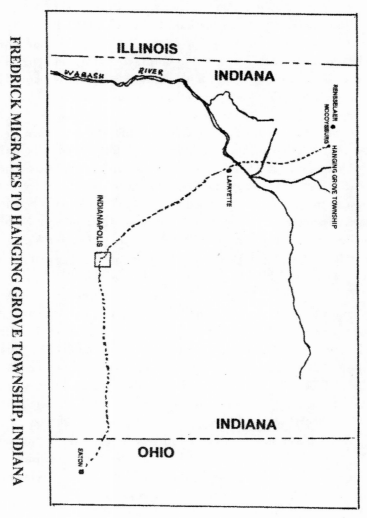

Old Banta homestead
1836

T. P. Banta's mother, Sarah Banta, in front of their sod house
in Hanging Grove Township, Indiana, in or about 1860

Frederick and Sarah raised this large family on the farm near
Monon in a frontier sod house similar to many other frontier homes
in the area. These houses were typical log cabins with sod roofs.
Frederick's family's life was similar to the lives of the seven generations on this continent that preceded his. Certainly life was very

hard, working a frontier farm where luxuries were nonexistent and most necessities of life were home-made. All items, homemade or store bought, had to be carefully conserved. After almost two hundred years as a frontier family, this new shoot of the Banta family continued as all seven generations had before it by building a farm from the wildwoods on the North American Continent's frontier.

By 1862, eight of Frederick's and Sarah's children had been born. This year their ninth child, Robert, was born, and their oldest daughter, Katherine, married Charles Orcutt in Rensselaer, Indiana. This was near the beginning of the great Civil War. When war was declared, Charles, among many of Indiana's young men, volunteered to form the 87th Indiana Regiment. He was in Company A. Katherine became pregnant in the first two months of their marriage, just prior to Charles' leaving Indiana with his regiment. December 20, 1862, she gave birth to a daughter whom she named Emily. Just one month later, Katherine was notified by the War department that Charles had died in combat November 21.

Theodore P., known all his life as T. P.—Frederick's sixth child, second son and the family member we will follow as the next generation in this story—was only nine years old at the time and was deeply moved by the loss of his brother-in-law. The whole family was in mourning over this tragic loss and the widowing of their oldest sister.

This war brought the specter of death to most families in the young nation. It was a very emotional and stressful time for all of the nation's families, but especially for a young impressionable eight year old like T. P. In addition to losing his brother-in-law to the war, he also lost two cousins: James, Aunt Louisa's oldest son, and Warren, Uncle John's oldest son, who lost their lives in the service of their country. Warren was killed at the battle of Shiloh, April 6, 1862.

April 9, 1865, General Lee surrendered to General Grant, and that terrible conflict concluded with a glorious victory for the Union. With the end of the war, the nation's families resumed everyday life.

In 1865, Frederick and Sarah, through frugal savings, became successful enough to be able to purchase a home in Rensselaer, the largest city near their farm. Frederick and Sarah had already started providing for their children's college education, as Frederick had promised himself he would do prior to his marriage to Sarah. They would send all nine children who reached adulthood to college. Frederick wasn't to see his children graduate; three years after moving to Rensseler, Frederick met an untimely death at age fifty-three. Sarah continued the process of college education for six of their children after his death.

Both Frederick and Sarah were advocates of good grammar schools. When the local school district needed land to construct a one room school house in 1875, widow Sarah Banta donated five acres from their farm land to the school district for its site. The school was named the Banta school and was in active operation from 1875 to after the Spring term in1921. The one room school's first two teachers were daughters of Sarah and Frederick who had graduated as teachers.

In Hanging Grove Township by Nancy Meyer, Blanche Cook McDonald wrote an article with the title of "Memories of the Banta School." She told what it was like to be a child in a one room school house in 1896:

> I attended the Banta School in Hanging Grove Township for eight years, starting in 1896. Ola Dodd, driving her horse and buggy from Lee, Indiana, was my teacher for the first three years . . .
>
> We lived one-half mile west down the road from the school and walked every day unless the weather was bad and then Dad took us with the bobsled. Our fathers enjoyed visiting while waiting for the school to be let out.
>
> The schools at that time consisted of only one room with a coal and wood burning stove in the center. School patrons cut, sawed and piled wood in neat cords outside. The bigger boys would carry it in for the teacher. The teacher usually tied her horse behind the wood pile. The stove was surrounded by

double seats and desks—usually one pupil was a good house-keeper and the other wasn't. The pupils who sat closest to the stove sometimes had blistered faces and the ones sitting on the outside were cold. In the back of the room were two nice shelves where we put our lunch pails. There was also a row of hooks to hang our wraps on. A water pail and dipper which was purchased new in the fall sat on a bench. It's a wonder we didn't get sick drinking after one another, but we didn't.

We had a library shelf put in our room and held box socials to pay for the books. We had a talent show to pay for an organ. These were the social events of the year. All the parents came and brought the little ones in the family.

We too enjoyed our fifteen minute recesses, one in the midmorning and one in the afternoon. We had our hour of play at noon. In the winter, we enjoyed skating on the ice and the younger students would just slide. "Fox and Geese" was the popular game just after a fresh snow. During the stormy weather, we played inside and a game I won't forget was "Fruit Basket." Many times the ink bottles were spilled as the game got rather rough when the basket was upset. We played blackboard games too.

Some of the pupils attending Banta during these years were . . .

The Parker School was closed in 1909—1910 and five pupils were hauled over to the Banta School.

I remember one family who came to our school for a short time. The father hunted skunks for a living and in the evening his children would help him skin them. They came to school the next day and the teacher took one big whiff and home they went.

After college, I taught school at Banta for one term; I received less than three dollars a day.

We could read, write and spell when we finished with school. I look back on my school days and teaching as very educational with many good times.

Ruins of the one room Banta School, Hanging Grove
Township, Jasper County, May 1988

Many of Frederick and Sarah's children attended Valpariso
University. This university was established in 1874 and was known
as the poor man's Yale. At the time it had a very large student body
averaging several thousand students. Nearly all of their children
graduated as teachers, while two became medical doctors. Their
daughter, Margaret, was one of the first women in America to
graduate from medical school. She was fond of telling stories of the
pranks the other medical students played on her as the only female
student in the medical school.

In 1875, young widow Katherine, again fell in love and married
Daniel Jenkins. She and Daniel were the first of Frederick's and
Sarah's family to try their luck homesteading property as her
forefathers had done for the last seven generations. Their problem
was that the earlier pioneers had filed on all of the best lands in the
new country. She, Daniel, and little thirteen-year-old Emily became
the new generation's first pioneers by searching among the remnants
of the last marginal land available on the eastern high plains of
Colorado just west of the Kansas border. Their searching took them
to Chivington, Colorado where Daniel homesteaded one hundred

and sixty acres, built a house and barn and through hard work turned the land into a productive farm.

Only Barbara, their second child who lived to be only thirty-three years of age, and Mary, their eighth child, continued to live in the Midwest. Six of their children moved west to the eastern side of the arid Great Basin which was the closest thing to a frontier left by 1890. Even here all the good land had been filed upon. There were vast stretches of desert but without water the land was useless. Five of their offsprings moved to the Arizona Territory while one moved to New Mexico. Sarah sold the farm and house in Indiana and joined her children in Arizona, living with her daughter, Miranda, who had married Job Moore whom we will learn more about in the next paragraph. These six children and Sarah went to the eastern edge of the Great Basin where rivers and streams from the mountains to the east flowed into its arid deserts. Here they hoped to find land of their own suitable for farming.

The first member of the family to try her luck out west in the Arizona Territory was T. P.'s next older sibling, Miranda. She was the fifth child and fourth girl in this family of ten. Miranda married her cousin, Job who was Aunt Julia's second oldest child. T. P. was especially close to Miranda, for in a large family such as his where ages spanned more than twenty-three years, a sister within two years of his own age had much in common with him during childhood.

His oldest sister, Katherine, who was the first to leave home and who homesteaded the land in Colorado, was nine years older than he; and, because she had the responsibility of raising the younger children, was considered more as a second mother than a close friend. His youngest sister was fifteen years his junior and here again they had little in common. Miranda, two years his senior, and Margaret, two years his junior, were especially close to him during his childhood. T. P. was also very close to his younger brother, Robert who was born in 1862, the same year his oldest sister, Katherine, married. With the birth of her new baby girl, Emily, she had little time to spend as second mother for her baby brothers and sisters. Thus, much of the bringing up of little Robert was left to his older brother T. P.

Miranda's husband, Job, had graduated from Knox College in the class of 1872. Shortly after their marriage in 1877, they set out for the Arizona Territory where they made their home in Prescott, Arizona. There, Job became President and General Manager of the Arizona Ore Company. He was a member of the Arizona Legislature and became acquainted with the important political figures in what was then the Territorial capitol of Arizona. She and Job were instrumental in bringing two of her brothers and two of her sisters to the Arizona Territory. With Job's success in the Territory, other members of the family wanted to try their hand way out west.

Sarah died December 17, 1889, at the age of sixty-five in Phoenix, Arizona Territory, nine years after she had moved to the Territory to live with her daughter and son in law, Miranda and Job. Thus T. P., whom we follow in the next chapter, the eighth generation, lost his father when he was fifteen years old, while his mother lived until he was thirty-three.

PART II
THE STORY OF
THE LAST FRONTIER

CHAPTER 16

T. P. BANTA OF THE EIGHTH GENERATION

From the progenitor of the Banta family name, Epke Jacobs, who arrived in Vlissingen, New Amsterdam, New Netherland, in 1659, through Theodore Parker Banta (T. P.) of the eighth generation on this continent, there was a constant movement by each following generation to the frontier's edge. For eight generations, this line of the Banta family was a frontier family. It was always pushing the edge of the envelope in its odyssey of two-hundred and forty-one years across a new continent from Flushing on the Atlantic coast to the Imperial Valley fifty miles from the Pacific Ocean.

T. P. and his wife and sons were the last of these generations of frontiersmen. His story is the story of the conquering of the last frontier in the contiguous United States of America. His frontier was the Colorado Desert, the most God-forsaken and dead world imaginable. Who, in their wildest dreams, could foresee that this desolation could be made to bloom in an abundance of luxurious green and become the vegetable garden of the nation.

T. P. was born in Hanging Grove, Indiana, Northwest Territory, as the sixth of Frederick and Sarah's ten children. He was born on his father's farm, and as a child lived in a sod house similar to the sod house shown in the television series "Little House on the Prairie." When T. P. was thirteen, Frederick and Sarah bought a house in the City of Rensselaer, Indiana, forty miles to the east. He and Sarah had made enough money so that the family could live very comfortably. Two years later, Frederick passed away.

When the new world was brand new, and even up to Albert's

generation, The Banta family was a Dutch family living in America. The Dutch way of settling a new frontier was to form a colony of Dutchmen who would purchase a tract of land from whoever was in charge of it, whether an Indian tribe, a local jurisdiction or, after it had become the sovereign entity controlling the undeveloped frontier, the United States Government. The first thing the colonist did in their new community was to build a church of the Low Dutch Reformed denomination and then a grammar school. All children were taught their three R's but beyond this, education was unavailable on the frontiers where Frederick's forefathers had always gone in search of their fortunes.

Solomon had been the first in seven generations to receive a higher education in the Arts. It is not surprising that T. P.'s father, Frederick, was inspired and influenced by Solomon's education and profession as a member of the bar. It seemed to Frederick that education was the way to escape the long, hard days of farming on the frontier. He envied Solomon's gracious life and his ability to socialize with the most important men in his community.

Frederick died when T. P. was fifteen and while four of his other children were younger than that. His youngest daughter, Sallie, was only two at the time of Frederick's death. Even after Frederick's death, Sarah kept Uncle Solomon as the family's role model for success. Sarah continued to expect all her children to acquire a higher education and a profession.

In 1876, when T. P was twenty-three, he enrolled at Valpariso University. The university in northwest Indiana, had been established in 1874, just two years earlier. He entered the College of Education and planned to be a high school teacher after graduation. While attending Valparaiso University he met a beautiful young co-ed from Lansing, Michigan, named Carrie Lott. Carrie was not only beautiful but one of the most intelligent persons he had ever met. She was not only intelligent but also practical and yet she was unassuming and approachable. T. P. was right off the farm and had no social graces, while Carrie had completed finishing school and knew all the proper things to do and say. She possessed all the skills that T. P. longed to acquire. He realized she would make the perfect life partner. Best of all, she was interested in him though he couldn't understand why, so he asked her to social affairs at the university.

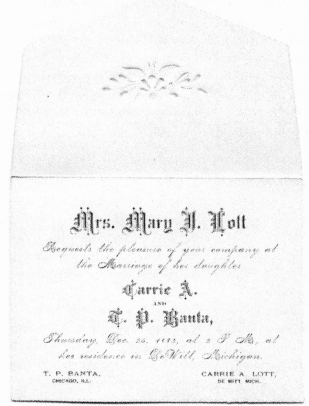

Wedding invitation to the marriage of Carrie A. Lott to T. P. Banta

There couldn't have been a more disparate couple than they were when they first met; he the farmer, she the socialite. But T. P. was a fast learner. He felt like an idiot at the first dean's tea, but he watched Carrie and imitated her every nuance. Soon he was socializing with the best of them. He had a keen wit and a charisma that made him popular. Carrie found herself smitten with this farm boy turned socialite.

They fell in love and were married shortly after graduation. Their wedding was held at the residence of her mother, Mary Lott, in De Witt, Michigan in 1884. T. P. was residing in a bachelor apartment in Chicago, Illinois, where he had accepted a position as a teacher at a local high school. The newly married couple found a larger apartment near the high school and set up housekeeping. Their life seemed to be settled with a fine apartment and a job he thoroughly enjoyed. Within the next four years they were no longer a couple but instead a family of four when two little boys, Earl and Al, were born a year and a half apart.

As a teacher, T. P. was a self assured, strong-willed disciplinarian. He was an excellent teacher but this was to be a short-lived profession. In his fifth year of teaching, he was discharged for knocking-out cold, in a fist fight, a senior who was a star athlete and the high school bully. When he saw the bully attacking a smaller boy, he grabbed the bully by the shirt collar. When the bully turned and swung at him, he knocked him out with a single blow. T. P. was six feet tall and very muscularly built from his many years of working on his father's farm.

Unfortunately for T. P., the bully's father was a very rich and politically powerful man. After this incident, T. P. decided, he was not cut out to be a teacher. He decided it would be far better to achieve the position of a very rich and powerful man like his Uncle Solomon. He realized that the school officials considered him to be of less importance than the bully's father because he didn't have money or political power and that bothered T. P. What a difficult moment it was for him for he had to come home and tell Mama, which was what he now called Carrie because of their two sons, that he had lost his job. Carrie was terrified by the news, for with raising a young family, they had saved nothing and had many bills to pay.

With no job, T. P. and Carrie were considering various alternatives. His brother-in-law, Job, who had married his sister, Miranda, his next youngest sibling, had great success in Prescott which at that time was the capitol of the Arizona Territory. Job was in the Arizona legislature and had become acquainted with many prominent men. T. P. learned through his sister Miranda and her husband Job that a Mr. Myron McCord, who owned a large ranch in Mesa, Arizona Territory, was looking for a foreman. Mr. McCord was later to be appointed governor of the Arizona Territory by President William McKinley. T. P. approached Carrie and told her that he felt that he could put his education to benefit as a farmer as he would have an edge on other farmers who almost never had more than a high school education.

"Mama," he said, "I know there's a lot of money to be made out on the last frontiers of our country by a man with a good college education and a lifetime of knowledge learned by hard work on a farm. I shouldn't run from my upbringing on the farm. I should harness it to my college education and use both to make our fortune."

Carrie still thought of Arizona as a lawless territory with gun fights going on daily. The newspapers had been filled just a few years before with accounts of the gun fight at the O. K. Corral in Tombstone, between Wyatt Earp and a band of thieves and murderers. "Papa," she said, "The Arizona Territory doesn't sound like a good place to raise two young boys."

"Carrie," T. P. answered, " you know that I wouldn't expose you or the boys to any danger. Mesa is a Mormon settlement and you know that they are God-fearing people who wouldn't put up with any nonsense. I expect they will have far stricter rules there than we have here in Chicago. My family has always been on the frontier and I know that with my experience on the frontier and any luck we can homestead some land and end up handsomely wealthy."

T. P. convinced her that a move to Mesa, Arizona Territory, offered the best opportunity for the family's future. Secretly, down deep inside, though she had been raised in the city, she had the heart of a pioneer and welcomed the chance to live the life on the frontier. In 1890, T. P. applied for the position and Mr. McCord hired him. Thus, he and Carrie packed up the family belongings and headed for the City of Mesa in the Arizona Territory. He hoped that he might, as his forefathers had done, be able to file on land of his own when he became familiar with the new territory.

Carrie Allen Lot, age 21

T. P.'s mother, Sarah, who had moved to the Arizona territory in1880, passed away in 1889, just a year before T. P. Carrie and their family came to the Arizona Territory. She had lived in the territory long enough to realize that there were wonderful opportunities in this Territory and she would have been pleased that T. P. and his family had chosen to make their home there. T. P., as related earlier, recognized that an educated farmer had many advantages over an uneducated farmer. His education served him well throughout the rest of his life. He had another advantage in life; for, in addition to his education, he had an educated, practical wife in Carrie. They made a good team and, from the very first, he always made decisions after seeking her council.

CHAPTER 17

ARIZONA

Mesa, in the Arizona Territory, had been reclaimed by the Mormons from the Arizona desert by diverting irrigation water from the Salt River flowing down from the mountains east of Mesa on the edge of the Great Basin. The Mormons used many traces of irrigation canals constructed in ancient times by a long extinct Indian tribe. Mesa is a suburb of Phoenix and the entire area around Phoenix had been reclaimed from the desert by irrigation water from this same source.

What a vast difference was this irrigated land scratched from the desolate and hostile desert as compared to the Indiana and Michigan farm lands that T. P. and Carrie had left behind. There, the rain caused crops to grow. Here, on the edge of the Great Basin, it almost never rained and the crops grew because the canals brought the water to them. The Arizona weather was both a blessing and a curse. Here, the winters were delightful, while in Indiana, Michigan and Illinois, winters were cold and filled with snow storms. But the summers in Mesa were almost unbearable with the temperatures well over one-hundred degrees each day during the summer months. A compensating feature was that during the summer months the humidity was very low making the heat more bearable.

As foreman of a large ranch, T. P. needed an assistant he could count on. He wrote to his younger brother, Robert, whom he had helped raise and asked him to join him in Mesa. Robert, at the time, was a teacher in Indiana. He had married Mary Anderson,

004204204204204204204204204ী4204204204204204204204204204204204204204204

and they had three small children, Grace, Myra, and Pearl. Robert was also struck with the desire to have his own land and accepted his older brother's offer as a means to that end. Thus the two brothers ran the McCord ranch while looking for an opportunity to homestead their own land.

Margaret, T. P.'s younger sister who was a medical doctor, and Sallie, his youngest sister, had already joined Miranda and Job, who had found jobs for them in Prescott. As we have related, their mother, Sarah, had also moved her home from Rensselaer to the Arizona Territory to live with Job and Miranda in Phoenix and be near her other two daughters. Thus, Miranda and Job were instrumental in bringing four of Miranda's siblings and their mother, Sarah, to the Arizona Territory.

T. P. learned a great deal about irrigation farming in his service as the foreman of Myron McCord's large ranch. The job permitted him to keep his wife and family properly, but T. P. longed to have his own land as did his father before him. The premium land around Phoenix available for irrigation was already filed upon and therefore had to be bought on the open market. Good land was too expensive for a young foreman of a ranch. He saved what he could from his wages but homesteading government land as his forefathers had done no longer seemed possible. The country had grown up. Year after year he continued in his job as foreman making the best of the life he had.

Carrie was also ambitious and longed for a farm of their own. She had a real pioneer's heart and knew she could be a helpmate to T. P. if he could acquire land for a farm. He had learned the skills of irrigation farming during his seven years as foreman and his oldest son, Earl, would be a tremendous help to his father in such an adventure.

Robert was also getting itchy feet. They both looked at land around the Mesa—Prescott area. After working for several years with T. P., he decided to file under the Desert Land Act on a half section of marginal land on the Aqua Fria Creek near the small village of Stoddard. This he did using up his rights under the

Desert Land Act which permitted any U. S. citizen to file on a half section (three hundred and twenty acres) of Government land and upon meeting certain criteria to own that land. Since the land was marginal, Robert worked the land while T. P. continued as foreman of the McCord ranch.

In 1896, T. P. decided that he would also file for a half section of marginal land where the city of Gilbert, Arizona, now stands. He quit his job as the foreman of the McCord ranch; and, after building a cabin on the land, moved his family there. He started irrigation farming almost immediately since the land had been barren due to lack of water. The soil was somewhat alkaline and he knew it would take several years of irrigation before the alkalinity would be leached out and it would produced good crops; but he felt, with patience, it would produce amply. Being vitally interested in his boys education, he, as his mother had done, donated a portion of his land so that a school could be erected.

Carrie had decided that she was not going to continue the proliferation of the Banta family at the exhausting pace of the earlier generations. T. P.'s father had ten children, while his grandfather had twelve children, his great-grandfather had nine children and his great-great-grand father had twenty-one children. With the birth of Al in Chicago, Carrie decided that two children were sufficient for a proper family and thereupon terminated T. P.'s conjugal rights. We must remember that in the eighteen-nineties there was no effective method of birth control. Cut off from sexual satisfaction, T. P. was hopping around from one foot to the other and was very anxious to have his rights restored but, plead as he might, it was to no avail.

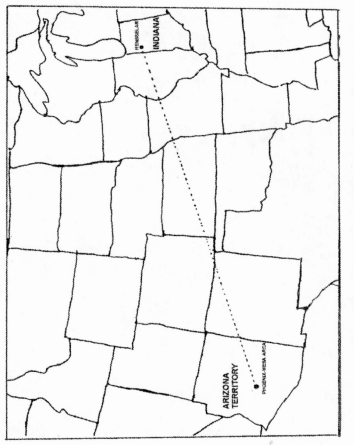

T. P. AND FAMILY MIGRATE TO THE ARIZONA TERRITORY
BY RAILWAY

Baby George, bought for a trip to Michigan

Earl and Al Banta in Mesa, Arizona Territory

Carrie grew homesick way out west in Gilbert, Arizona Territory, and longed to go back to visit her mother in Michigan. T. P., being a good horse trader, saw the opportunity for a swap beneficial to both parties. "Mama," he said, "I've got an offer I think you will find interesting. If you'll restore my conjugal privileges until one more child is born, I'll dig up the money for your trip home to see your family in Chicago. It won't be easy but I'll get it come hell or high water."

T. P. was right. It was an offer Carrie couldn't refuse. Carrie went home to see her family, and little George was born six years after Al. Though she was bribed into having George, little George was the apple of his mother's eye which obviously irritated his two older brothers. The Banta family now had three boys.

While waiting for his land to reduce its alkalinity, T. P. entered into local politics and became the populist nominee for probate judge but was defeated. Thereupon, he went back to his old profession as a teacher at the one room Lehi school. One of his political enemies was a school board trustee and worked public sentiment against him charging incompetency. The matter was brought to a head by the holding of an indignation meeting. There, a vote was taken and the matter of discharge was settled in his favor. T. P. knew that his political enemies would make it uncomfortable for him in the hopes they might make him resign.

About this same time, June 1900, the Phoenix newspaper, the Phoenix Republican, started carrying articles about a proposed project of gigantic proportions. The California Development Company was about to commence building the largest irrigation system the world had ever seen and would be hiring many workers to build the canals and gates. The articles told how hundreds of square miles would have the water from the Colorado River brought to them. Thus, settlers who acquired land from the Federal Government under the Desert Land Act in the area to be irrigated would be able to purchase water rights from the California Development company. The company would then be required to bring irrigation water in the company's canals right to the settler's claim. This would make it easy for settlers to satisfy the Act's requirement of bringing water to the land within three years of settlement.

The articles went on to explain that the area where this was to take place was the foreboding Colorado Desert. This desert was actually the delta of the great Colorado River. The river had been depositing its silt into the Gulf of California for untold millennia until it eventually had cut the Gulf in half by forming a dam of silt across its width. Prior to this cutoff by alluvial fill, forming a dam across its width, the Gulf of California extended all the way to Indio, 160 miles north of its current northern shore. The river, then for more millennia, poured its silty but fresh water into the cut off portion of the Gulf north of the silt dam. This continued for thousands of years until the lake, formed north of the silt dam, became a fresh water lake. The silt dam grew higher and higher until it stood forty feet above sea level.

The river then changed its ambivalent mind and once again flowed into the Gulf of California, leaving the fresh water lake to the north to slowly dry up over the centuries. The great Colorado River continued flowing in its self-made levies along the top of this silt dam and pouring its fresh water into the salt water of the Gulf of California.

The engineers of the California Development Company had completed surveys that conclusively showed that irrigation water could be taken from the river and caused to flow by gravity to the Salton Sink in the Colorado Desert. This was the lowest portion of the old fresh water lake, forty miles north of where the Colorado flowed along the top of its self-made dam. All of this land subject to irrigation was alluvial silt many meters deep. All that was needed to make this sandy loam, which currently was the dead Colorado Desert, bloom was water. This water could be inexpensively diverted from the Colorado river.

CHAPTER 18

THE IMPERIAL VALLEY,

CALIFORNIA THE LAST FRONTIER

THE CALIFORNIA DEVELOPMENT COMPANY

Mr.Charles R Rockwood was one of the first to recognize the potential for irrigating the Colorado desert with water from the Colorado river by gravity flow. He observed from a personal survey of the area that the cost would be very reasonable. Flood channels had been created from water overflowing the Colorado river's self-made levies on the north side during flood stages. These channels ran all the way from the Colorado river down the slope of the dry freshwater lake bed to the Salton Sink, two hundred and thirty-two feet below sea level and forty miles to the north. They could be improved and used as canals for an irrigation system saving the major cost of a project capable of irrigating hundreds of square miles.

The Southern Pacific Railroad skirted the east side of the desert. This would provide a transportation system to carry produce grown in the desert to anywhere in the United States. It could easily supply the growing Los Angeles area with fresh produce.

Rockwood approached Mr. Anthony H. Heber, a well known and well thought of promoter in Chicago, to raise the capital needed to finance the venture. He convinced Heber to associate with him. Heber and Rockwood made an excellent team; Rockwood on technical matters and tenacity, Heber with enthusiasm, ambition, confidence and business ability. They organized a capital stock corporation under the laws of the state of New Jersey named the California Development Company. It was chartered on April 26, 1896. They were permitted under its charter to sell $1,250,000 of stock for financing the project.

In order to proceed with the project, they needed an option to purchase land in Mexico on which to build an international canal. Unpassable sand hills ran the full length of the valley on the east side all the way to the Mexican border. For this reason, it was necessary to carry the water by canal through Mexico to the United States border near where Mexicali now stands. This Mexican land was owned by General Andrade. Rockwood purchased a limited time option for buying the land from the general. He also made arrangements with the government of Mexico for permission to build the canal. There was only one feasible site for the heading gate on the Colorado river. This site was owned by a Mr. Hanlon. He also purchased a limited time option from Mr. Hanlon for the heading gate site.

The two promoters had many disappointments. Each time, just as it appeared the capital needed was at hand, the deal fell through. With practically no assets and liabilities of $1,365,000, it appeared the project would be abandoned. The two options were ready to expire. They had not paid the state of New Jersey their corporate tax and application for an injunction by the state was set for March 20, 1900.

The months of September, October and November 1899, were full of despair. At the last moment, in December, Mr. Rockwood received word that their capitalist had been found. This was Mr. George Chaffey of Los Angeles. Mr. Chaffey was a skilled and experienced irrigation engineer. In 1881, Mr. Chaffey founded the colony of Etiwanda, developing his first irrigation system. He also devised the first Mutual Water Company which became the model for all future Southern California water companies. In the same year, he founded the colony of Ontario, organizing and endowing Chaffey College. The Australian government was so impressed with his irrigation projects that they commissioned him to construct reclamation projects in Australia's great deserts. As a result of his work he was elected a member of the Institute of Mechanical Engineers in London.

Upon his return from Australia, Rockwood and Heber induced him to look at the Colorado Desert Project. From Mr. Chaffey's past work, he was charmed, rather than repelled, by the Colorado River and the Colorado Desert, newly renamed the Imperial Valley by the California Development Company.

Mr. Chaffey was fully familiar with the engineering problems of the project but failed to examine the company's books or make himself familiar with its financial condition. He did not know how close it was to closing down. He did not know that the state of New Jersey was prepared to withdraw its corporate charter in a matter of days. Purely on his survey of the river and the engineering feasibility of the gigantic proposed irrigation project, he entered into an agreement with Mr. Rockwood and Mr. Heber to perform the actual construction of the gates and canals.

The contract with Mr. Chaffey was signed in March 1900. Although the contract called for the sale of water stock on fifty-thousand acres before he should be required to begin construction, Mr. Chaffey plunged at once into the building of the gates and canals. By the fall of 1900, he had expanded the company's survey camp at Cameron Lake in the Imperial Valley into a work camp for building the irrigation project.

The California Development Company had renamed the Colorado Desert the Imperial Valley for esthetic reasons. They reasoned that it would be much easier to induce settlers to come to a place called the Imperial Valley than to a place called the Colorado Desert.

Cameron Lake had been chosen as the headquarters for the California Development Company camp because of the fresh water available from the lake. The lake was a beautiful blue oasis in an unbelievably desolate land. The lake was one of several that had been formed by the Colorado River during each year's flood stage. At flood stage, the river would overflow its self-made levies on their northern side. That is the side toward the dry lake bed. The water from this overflow would flow down the easy northward grade of the Valley to the Salton Sink, two hundred and thirty-two feet below sea level and the lowest point in the old dry lake bed. The channels formed by these flood waters had been worn by countless floods over the centuries. Cameron lake was one of two lakes that consistently maintained their water between flood seasons.

CHAPTER 19

T. P. AND THE IMPERIAL VALLEY

In the fall of 1900, the California Development Company's recruiter's of experienced irrigation project workers for the proposed Imperial Valley system found a bonanza of trained men in the Mesa-Phoenix area. They prepared a wagon train to transport men, animals and equipment to the work camp at Cameron Lake in the Imperial Valley just north of the Mexican border.

The route the wagon train would take would follow the Gila River banks to the Colorado River of which it was a tributary. Then they would traverse the few miles along the Colorado until it flowed through Yuma. From there, they would cross the Colorado and travel the few miles through Mexico in order to skirt the impenetrable sand dunes on the east side of the valley. Finally, from Mexico, they would cross the United States border into the Imperial Valley. This was the only route by wagon train from Mesa to the Imperial Valley.

Ultimately the recruiters for the Imperial Land Company, the sister sales company of the California Development Company, approached T. P since he had acquire years of experience in irrigation farming as foreman of the McCord ranch. They told him of their need for someone experienced in irrigation farming. They flattered him by telling him that none was more highly thought of by his fellow farmers than he was.

T. P. explained to them that he had exhausted his rights under the Desert Land Act. If he had not, he said he would have gone with them and would have developed his land in their irrigation project as a model farm. He told them that he did not want to develop the land for someone else for he was better off developing his land in Gilbert than taking the risk of working as a employee of theirs with the prospect of making others rich by his experience.

The Imperial Land Company men said they would have to check with their principals as to whether anything could be worked out under the circumstances. In a matter of days they were back with the solution to T. P.'s problem. In June of 1900, 320 acres had been selected by Mr. Rockwood and Mr. L. M. Holt This property lay alongside where they intended the main canal of their irrigation project to run shortly after the canal would leave Mexico and enter the United States. They had checked the soil and it was excellent for raising crops.

This 320 acres had been filed upon by a Mr. John F. Leighton as applicant and L. M. Holt and C. R. Rockwood as witnesses under the Desert Land Act of March 3, 1877 as amended and was intended to be the model farm. Mr. Leighton was not interested in developing the model farm and if T. P. would develop it for the company, the company would sell the farm to T. P. for the amount the company had put into its development. This way T. P. didn't need to be entryman on his own land and the fact that he had already used his entry rights would be of no consequence.

T. P. talked to Carrie about the potential of this new venture. "Mama," he said, "I'm discouraged by this political mess in which I find myself. I've examined this new irrigation project as carefully as I possibly can and it looks good to me. I don't want to downplay the rigors of what will lie before our family if we migrate to the Imperial valley. It's as desolate a piece of the United States as exists anywhere on the continent. It will be one hundred and twenty in the shade a third of the year and there will be no shade till the water comes in and we plant the trees. But the upside is that it's going to succeed. I know this from what I've learned these last ten years in Mesa with its irrigation system. This might be our last chance to have really good land of our own. This will be prime acreage on the irrigation canal just after it comes into the United States. The Land Company is behind me. It can't fail."

"Pa," Carrie answered, "I believe in you and if you think this is the thing for us to do, I'll back you all the way."

Neither of them had any idea of the unbelievable hardships the family would face in the next three years. They would leave an area where they had many friends and with their three boys take the gamble on this last frontier in the contiguous United States. The two older boys, Earl and Al, were delighted as they saw this as a way out of the schoolroom. In this, they were dead wrong. T. P. had earned his degree as a teacher and had no thought of letting their schoolwork slide. He made special trips to meet with their teachers and arranged to copy their lesson plans for the remainder of the year. Throughout the remainder of the 1900-01 school year, Carrie and he taught the boys both on the trail and while the family called a tent their home. He made a special effort to obtain the school books for the following year just in case no school was available in their new surroundings. No matter how tired the boys, Carrie or he was during the next two trying years, learning was not neglected.

As pioneer settlers, they would not be an official part of the wagon train of recruited construction men and would have to provide their own transportation. The men from the Imperial Land Company, however, assured T. P. that they would assist him in developing a model farm along the main canal where water would first be brought into the Valley. He, therefore, would be the first, or one of the first, to bring in a crop from the new irrigation project.

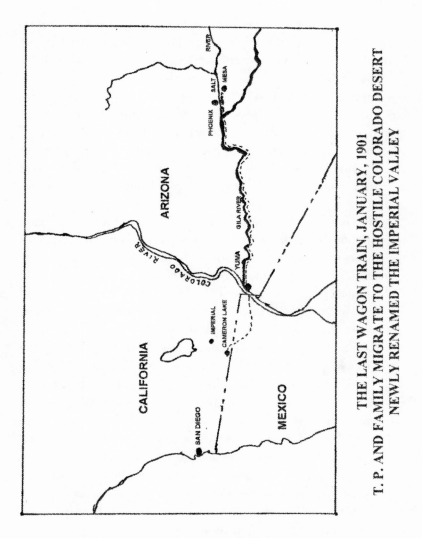

THE LAST WAGON TRAIN, JANUARY, 1901
T. P. AND FAMILY MIGRATE TO THE HOSTILE COLORADO DESERT
NEWLY RENAMED THE IMPERIAL VALLEY

T. P. assembled two wagons for the trip. He would drive the team of mules pulling the first wagon with Carrie and little George as passengers. Earl, now fourteen, would drive the team of mules pulling the second wagon. Earl had experience driving mule teams on the Governor's ranch. Al would be his partner. Al was twelve. The two wagons were packed full of the necessities of life as there would be no means of obtaining supplies until they reached Yuma. Tied to the back of the first wagon were two horses. Tied to the back of the second wagon were two Keg Tail ponies and a cow.

Space and weight were so precious that Carrie tore the genealogy pages out of her family Bibles and was forced by weight restrictions to leave the Bibles, themselves, behind. Carrie's great-grandfather on her mother's side was the son of Ethan Allen, of Revolutionary War fame. The first page of the family's history in the Allen Bible was written in Ethan Allen's son's hand. Carrie was rightfully proud of this heritage and could not leave these pages behind.

The morning for departure arrived. To the sound of mule and horse hoofs, the rattle and squeaking of the wagons and shouts of the drivers to their teams, the last of the thousands of wagon trains in American history lurched forward on its journey toward the Colorado Desert, now renamed the Imperial Valley.

This was in early January of 1901. The wagon train containing the workers, animals and implements, with our little family of five tagging along, moved its tedious way down the banks of the Gila river, thence, a short distance along the Colorado River, finally arriving in Yuma. They drove to the banks of the muddy Colorado where workmen constructed rafts to ferry men, animals and equipment, and the Banta family across the river into Mexico.

It was late afternoon of the fifteenth day of their journey that the dusty and tired pioneers pulled their wagon train to a halt at Cameron lake, the headquarters camp for the California Development Company in Imperial Valley. The camp was already abuzz with activity from company people who were already working on construction of the irrigation project.

Other than for the lake, the green growth along the flood channel in which the lake lay, and the company camp, T. P., Carrie and the boys saw that they had arrived at the quintessence of desolation. They had driven into a dead world of sand with not so much as a green leaf for as far as the eye could see. It was so desolate it was fascinating. The shock would have been unbearable to those not aware of what irrigation water could do when brought to sandy loam like that on which they were standing. As a man experienced in irrigation farming, T. P. recognized the richness of the soil.

That night, T. P. and his family slept in the open between their wagons as they had done since the wagon train left the Mesa area. Early next morning, T. P., Earl and Al started building, with material supplied by the California Development Company, their temporary living quarters which consisted of a ramada shed constructed a couple of feet over a canvas and wood tent. The purpose of the ramada shed was to keep the direct ray's of the sun from striking the tent. The floor and a wainscoting of the tent were of wood as well as was the frame of the screen door. A wood frame held up the canvas of the tent which had a pitched roof.

The frame of the ramada shed was constructed of what lumber could be found, a limb of a mesquite tree, cast off construction lumber, whatever. Arrowweed, which grew in abundance around the flood lakes and in the flood channels, was used to make the roof of the shed. These were tied together and closely bound so that they not only acted as a sun screen but also shed the rain water that fell during the infrequent rain storms. Without the ramada shed, the sun shining directly on the tent could raise the temperature inside the tent during the hot months of the year to over one-hundred and eighty degrees. With the ramada shed over the tent, the temperature in the tent remained about what it would be in the open shade. That seldom exceeded one-hundred and fifteen to twenty degrees. The Imperial Valley was obviously no place for powder puffs of either gender.

In addition to the cooling of the tent by the ramada shed, the sides of the tent could be raised to permit whatever breezes that might exist to flow through the tent. This method of keeping the rough living quarters of the early settlers and workmen marginally livable was used throughout the valley. Preparing these living quarters for the family took only a few weeks. It felt wonderful to have a roof over the family's heads, no matter how crude, after spending weeks in the wagon train sleeping under the stars.

Word of T. P.'s arrival soon reached Samuel Ferguson, President of the Imperial Land Company, in the newly created "City" of Imperial. Sam drove a spring wagon down to Cameron lake to meet T. P. and have a talk with him. Sam pledged to support T. P. in every way in establishing his farm so that the Imperial Land Company would have, at the earliest possible time, a working farm to show prospective new settlers the produce that could be grown in the valley.

Charles R. Rockwood, founder of the California Development Company, had just arrived at the Cameron Lake construction camp in November to begin engineering surveys for the water distribution system within the Imperial Valley. He chose Thomas Beach as his superintendent for the great work of constructing of the Imperial Valley canal system. Tom Beach had arrived at Cameron Lake just a few months prior to T. P.'s arrival. T. P. had known Tom in Phoenix for he had also come to the valley from the area around Phoenix by wagon train, using the same route down the Gila River bed to Yuma, across the Colorado River, then up through Mexico and entering the valley near Cameron Lake. Accompanying him was Mobley Meadows, who joined his company in Yuma. Tom was Mobley's brother-in-law having married Mobley's sister.

Mobley had been a close friend of Yuma's famous sherifff, Wyatt Earp. who was best known by Carrie for his gun fight at the O. K. corral in Tombstone. In Yuma, Mobley had been known as Kid Meadows. He was a crack shot and had entertained audiences in Yuma with a marksmanship show in which he preformed marvelous trick shots with his revolver and rifle. One of his famous tricks was to squarely hit a silver dollar thrown into the air by an assistant with a rifle bullet.

Also, in the same wagon train with Tom and Mobley were the Gillette family and the families of the Van Horn brothers. Accompanying the Gilettes and Van Horns were their seventeen children. These were the first three families in the Imperial Valley. Everyone in that wagon train went to work for the California Development Company. T. P., Carrie and the boys were the fourth family to immigrate to the Imperial valley.

Sam Ferguson arranged a meeting in which he, Rockwood, Tom Beach and T. P. could discuss preparation of a model farm on which T. P. could commence farming as soon as water became available in the valley. He, Charles Rockwood and Thomas Beach met with T. P. in Mr. Chaffey's office quarters. The three of them met for several hours. As the main source of income for the development of the irrigation system would come from the sale of water stock, Charles Rockwood saw the necessity of having an operating farm to show prospective settlers. Prospective settlers would want to see crops being grown in the Valley before they would be willing to buy the stock.

He told Sam and T. P. that he would supply them with guidance as to where the 320 acres lay along the main canal where it would cross into the United States from Mexico. He would also supply the labor at cost to level the soil and make whatever improvements would be necessary to establish T. P.'s farm. Tom Beach agreed to accompany T. P. to where John Leighton had applied for his tract of desert land just northeast of where the canal was to enter the United States T. P. knew the soil and Tom knew the layout of the proposed distribution system for the irrigation water and the location of Leighton's tract. Between them, they could decide whether this was the ideal location for the farm. Tom said he would like to have Mobley Meadows accompany them as he and Mobley wanted to file on Government land also. Since T. P. had experience in what constituted good soil, he could give them advice as to where to file their patents. T. P. told Tom that he was available to commence the search for the location of his farm at any time. Tom agreed they would start the search the second following day. He said he and Mobley would meet T. P. at his tent at sun up.

T. P. was delighted with the arrangement between the con-struction company, the sales company and himself. T. P. assured Rockwood and Furguson that he would proceed with the inspection of the land and commence its preparation as soon as possible. He assured Ferguson that he would be able to sow a crop as soon as water was brought into the valley. T. P. now knew that he would be one of the first to grow irrigated crops on the banks of the proposed canal immediately on this side of the border. With Tom Beach's assistance in determining where the main canal would be located and his own knowledge of soil, he knew that he could supply the Imperial Land Company the productive farm they wanted and needed.

Workers were direly needed by the California Development Company as the project was moving ahead at full steam. T. P. was unavailable due to the work necessary to prepare the model farm. T. P.'s boys, however, did take advantage of the critical need for workers. Because he had experience driving teams of mules, Earl was hired as a handler of a Fresno scrapper, which was the bulldozer of its day. Al also went to work constructing the gates and canals. Even little George was put to work though only five years old. His job was as a water boy. He carried water on horseback to the workers. This was a critically important task. The safety of the workmen building the irrigation system in the scorching desert heat depended on his reliability. Being so small, Carrie insisted that he be tied to the saddle so that he would not accidentally fall off the horse and be injured.

Little George saw nothing unusual in his having a job just as his older brothers did. This job left him with a feeling of responsibility that he never outgrew. Ever after, he could always be counted upon to arise to any responsibility entrusted to him. If your life depended on one man, this is the man you would choose. Working in the desert heat, water was an absolute necessity, and five year old George was always there when a workman needed water. Their lives depended on a five-year-old boy, and he never let them down.

CHAPTER 20

IN THE IMPERIAL VALLEY

It took T. P. about two months to complete the tent house and ramada shed, get acquainted with the men in the camp, familiarize himself with the layout of the valley and then have his meeting with Sam Ferguson, Charles Rockwood and Thomas Beach. Now he was ready to determine where Leighton's filing on desert land was located. The next day passed quickly and in the evening he met with Tom Beach to prepare for the next day's journey. Tom had surveyor's maps of the valley on which were drawn the proposed main canal where it entered the United States, first flowing north west for about three miles and then flowing directly west for about four miles before heading north again. The canal took its western path about three miles north of Cameron Lake where they were located.

"I suggest we travel north to where the canal passes closest to the work camp in an east-west direction," Tom said to T. P. "I can then locate the stakes I've laid out for the canal and you can locate Leighton's filing and examine the soil and determine if the soil is good for farming."

After his meeting with Tom, T. P. went back to his tent house and prepared his saddle pack for the next day's journey. He prepared for three days out on the desert to allow plenty of time to lay out the stakes indicating the location of the land he was to develop. Carrie and the boys helped him get his pack together and were very excited at the thought of having land of their own. Everything was working out even better than their fondest dreams. Creating his farm from the raw desert where he knew the main canal would first flow just a few miles after crossing into the United States would assure his family of having their farm where the company would first make water available for farming. Thus he would be one of the first farms to have water available from the new irrigation system.

T. P. arose before dawn the next morning and went out to feed the cow, mules, horses and ponies. In the light just before dawn, he could see that it was a perfectly calm and beautiful morning. As T. P. went about his tasks, he looked out to the north east and noticed that he could not see the horizon. Instead he saw way off in the distance a giant brown cloud stretching from north to south as far as his eyes could see. He had been told by the men who had been in the Valley longer than he about the great sand storms that arrive unannounced and cause havoc, sometimes lasting several days.

Others in the camp had also noticed the menacing cloud. All about the camp, men were scurrying about tightening and securing every thing in the camp as best they could. T. P. called Carrie and the boys to come see the sand storm approaching. Carrie rushed inside to cover or put away all the things that would be ruined or damaged by the sand. T. P. and the boys took the cow, mules, horses and ponies around behind the more substantial company tents on the side away from the direction the wind would be blowing as quickly as they could. They covered the hay and feed for the animals so that it would not be adulterated by the sand. Then they set to bracing up the ramada shed and finally making the tent as sand resistant as possible.

Tom arrived at this time and they both agreed that they would have to postpone their journey because of the approaching sand storm. T. P., though disappointed, realized that was the only possible course of action. There was little time to think of anything other than preserving what could be saved from the storm.

The cloud got bigger and bigger as it came closer and closer to the camp. Finally, with a noise like a giant threshing machine, the storm was upon them. The entire family sat inside the tent house. This was the month of March and with no sun, due to the dust storm, they grew quite cold to the point that they bundled up in their coats. There they sat all day afraid to light the stove for fear the embers would escape and start a fire in the tent or in the Company structures. The stove pipe even blew away once and T. P. tied a handkerchief around his nose and mouth, jumped on a horse and chased it down across the entire camp and out into the desert before he caught up with it.

There was no lunch or dinner that day as the dust made it impossible to eat. The dust was an inch thick on every thing in the tent house. When darkness came, everyone slept in their clothes so that if the tent house blew down they would be properly dressed. All the next day the wind howled and they sat bundled up in the tent. Finally, they got so hungry that Carrie opened tins of canned vegetables and all five of them ate as quickly as possible to avoid pollution by the sand.

At six the following morning the wind ceased its fury. The dust died down as quickly as it had come up but the sand was in drifts around the walls and in the corners. It was two inches thick on the blankets on the beds, on the table, on the floor, everywhere. Outside, the sand had drifted two feet deep against the windward side of all the Company tent buildings and all the tent houses. Sheltered by the tent buildings, all the animals had survived the dust storm with no difficulties.

First on everyone's agenda was to eat a hearty breakfast to make up for the lunch and dinner that had been missed. While T. P. fed the cow, mules, horses and ponies and assessed the damage to the ramara shed, Carrie and the boys cleaned the table and chairs, washed the pots and dishes, started a fire in the stove after reattaching the chimney and opened and heated canned foods. A banquet at the finest hotel never tasted as good as that hot canned food to these survivors of the storm.

The day turned so beautiful that it made up for the horror of the dust storm. In short order the storm damage was cleaned up and repaired as if it had never happened. T. P. found his friend, Tom, the surveyor, and asked if he could reschedule their trip for the next day. Tom agreed and they agreed to meet at sun rise for their journey out into the desert. T. P. wanted to see the soil at the location that had been chosen. From his years as ranch foreman he knew soil. He wanted to be sure they had not picked a plot that had large alkaline patches or contained too much clay.

He arose the next morning to put things in order for the trip. Earl helped him get ready. Carrie prepared them a good breakfast of eggs bought from the Gillette's and Van Horn brothers. These were the three families that had come into the valley from the Salt river just south of Mesa by the same route used by T.P.'s wagon train just weeks prior to T. P.'s arrival. They had encountered trouble from the very officious Mexican officials because they had not entered their chickens on their written manifest prior to entering Mexico. They had to send their chickens back to Yuma and then have them sent by train to Flowing Well, which was the Imperial Valley junction on the Southern Pacific rail line. Since then, they had retrieved their chickens from Flowing Well and had the only eggs for sale at Cameron Lake. She also cooked some bacon from McPherrin's general store, and made some homemade biscuits.

Just before sun up, T. P. and Earl saddled his horse, and attached his pack to the back of the saddle. At sun up Tom and Mobley arrived prepared for the pending journey. Carrie kissed T. P. goodby and the boys excitedly hugged their father knowing that when he returned the land for their farm would have been analyzed by T. P.'s expert eyes.

There were no roads across the desert other than the ruts left by the wagons as they moved between the construction camp at Cameron Lake to where the canal was being built from the Colorado River heading at Hanlon's Landing across Mexico to where it would cross into the United States. To the north, where they were heading not even tracks existed as they were going the opposite way from where the canal was being built.

As the three men rode their horses away from the Cameron

Lake construction camp, endless nothing stretched before them. Nothing, absolutely nothing, except the desert sand and an azure-blue sky. Behind their horses arose a cloud of dust that stretched back to the camp as they rode further into the desert. There was not so much as a green twig to be seen as they moved out of sight of the construction camp and Cameron Lake.

In about an hour they arrived at the area Tom said was the site where Leighton had applied for his patent. It was also the point where the main canal would pass closest to Cameron Lake. T. P. examined the soil. It was a fine sandy loam perfect for farming when water was brought to it. They also examined adjoining sections for application by Tom and Mobley. It took them three days to establish the corners of their new claims. Then they retraced their tracks back to the construction camp at Cameron Lake.

He told Carrie and the boys of his impending trip to the "city" of Imperial to visit Sam Ferguson to make final arrangements concerning the establishment of the model farm. The news was greeted with much exuberance by his family. Only a family such as his that had lived on the irrigated desert at Mesa could have felt happiness at hearing his news of settling and turning into an irrigated farm three hundred and sixty acres in this land of stark desolation and ugly dust storms.

That night, T. P. worked on the paper work containing the information that he wanted to give to Sam and the commitments he wanted from the land company. He decided to waste no time and prepared to take the trip the next day. Tom and Mobley, who planned to farm their entries as soon as water was available, agreed to accompany him to Imperial. With the excitement, T. P. got little sleep that night.

He arose early the next morning and, again, Earl and he saddled his horse and attached his saddle pack. In his saddle pack he had his paper work and a jug of water. He and his friends set out on their journey to the only town in the valley, Imperial. Imperial was about eleven miles north of Cameron Lake and was in the center of the area the California Development Company planned to irrigate. Again there were no roads but there was ample traffic from mule teams hauling heavy wagons full of construction materials for the canal and construction camp. They followed the wagon tracks across the desert sands in the direction of Imperial eleven miles to the north of Cameron Lake. It was March and the weather was wonderfully invigorating. The air was so clear that the coastal mountains to the west and the sand dunes and Chocolate Mountains to the east looked like you could throw a rock and hit them. Only the dust from the mule teams and heavy wagons marred a perfectly clear morning.

T. P. was pleased that every thing was going as he had planned and he thought pleasant thoughts they moved briskly across flat desert sand. Before he knew it, through the crystal clear morning air, he could see a large canvas structure with two gabled wooden roofs, some smaller similar canvas structures and two frame buildings far off on the horizon. Imperial was in sight but the clear desert air made it appear closer than it really was. The men slapped their horse's flanks to quicken their pace. Soon they arrived at their destination.

Imperial was awash with activity though the city was in its earliest stages of development. Men in overalls and western garb were everywhere. They were building structures and fences, loading wagons, digging trenches and doing a multitude of other things including just watching and kibitzing. The cool time of the year was when most work could be done and everyone was making the most of it.

The California Land Company intended Imperial to be the center of activity for the valley and had big things planned for it. However at this time these were future plans and T. P. saw that Imperial was still mainly just plans. The entire city, at that time, was composed of a large frame building with canvas walls with two gabled wooden roofs called the hotel, two smaller but sizable rooms also of frame construction with canvas walls and wooden roofs which served as a kitchen and dinning room for the hotel, a small frame structure serving as a real estate office for the California

Development Company, a larger frame structure which was a general merchandise store, and a corral and feed yard constructed of rough posts and covered with arrow weed. Between these structures ran a well rutted and dusty dirt road.

Material was on the ground for the erection of what he later was told would be the home of the future Valley newspaper to be called the Imperial Press, together with building material for living quarters for the editor and his family. Also on the ground were the presses which would publish the newspaper. That was it. That was downtown Imperial. Around the edge of the town were tent houses which were the homes of the town's residents. Even so, it looked beautiful to T. P. for it broke up the endless sands of the desert. It told him that there was a company with the where-with-all to change these surroundings from desolation to a land of plenty.

T. P., Tom and Mobley rode their horses to the corral and feed yard. They climbed down from their horses and tied the reins to the hitching post. A tall, well tanned, lanky cowhand came over to them and asked if he could be of help. T. P. introduced himself and then told him that he was from the Cameron Lake Construction Camp down south and was going to Sam Ferguson about creating a model farm down by the border where water would first enter the valley. He asked the cowhand if this was the livery stable and told him that, if it was, they wanted to leave their horses with him. His new acquaintance said that the corral was the town's livery stable and for the use of the McCaulley Stage Line. He told them that they could board their horses with him until they completed their business.

The three men walked over to the shack that was serving as the office for the Imperial Land Company and entered it. Once inside they saw that the shack was sparsely furnished with a couple of desks, some chairs and filing cabinets. On the wall was a drawing of a map of the valley and the proposed canal system. In the land office were two men, one seated at a desk and one standing talking to him. T. P. immediately recognized the man seated at the desk was Sam Ferguson. Sam greeted the three men with a friendly smile and introduced them to the other man, Lawrence Swayne, who was the company's notary public. Sam knew Tom and Mobley.

The paper work was completed about lunch time and Sam Ferguson suggested that they have lunch at the tent hotel. He said he would introduce them to the local business men. The three men thought this would be a good idea and accompanied him out onto the dusty dirt street heading for the tent that served as the hotel dinning room. T. P. stopped and watched as a long string-team of mules hauled a freighter wagon in front of the small group of men. While waiting for the picturesque driver and wagon to pass, Sam caught sight of Leroy Holt, A. W. Patton, W. F. Holt and H. C. Reed, all standing near where the material which would become the Imperial Press building lay on the ground. Sam invited them to accompany T. P., Tom, Mobley and himself to the hotel dining room. He wanted to introduce the three men to the business men of Imperial. The men accepted Sam's invitation and joined them in their very short walk to the hotel tent dining room.

On the way, T.P. asked Leroy and W.F. Holt if they were related to Luther Holt with the Imperial Land Company who had talked him into coming to the valley. They said they knew Luther but they were not related. They further explained that the two of them were brothers.

Upon entering the dinning room, Sam spotted Dr. Hefferman already at a table and the seven men pulled tables together so they could join him. Sam introduced the three men from the south to the men from Imperial.

Leroy Holt had arrived in Imperial in November 1900. He had come to the desert for his health. He had been a banker by trade and had become so enthused by what he saw in the valley that he decided to enter business and stay here. W. F. Holt had been persuaded by his brother, Leroy, to come see what was occurring in the Colorado Desert. W. F. was so taken with the California Development company's project that he decided to stay in Imperial and put his considerable business acumen to work as an entrepreneur. T. P. noticed from the conversation that he was an excellent businessman and was into everything that was going on in Imperial.

A PICTURE OF THE IMPERIAL HOTEL
IMPERIAL PRESS, MAY 3, 1902

Dr. Hefferman owned the general store they had passed on their way to the hotel dining room. Mr. H. C. Reed was to be the editor of the Imperial Press as soon as the Press building was erected and the press machinery was installed. He had brought Mrs. Reed with him to the valley. Mr. A. A. Patton worked for the California Development Company.

During their lunch the men talked about the great future of the valley and how fortunate they were to be in on its beginning. Little did they know the difficulties the immigrants to the valley faced during the next seven years. The Imperial business men told

how they intended to start immediately on building the Press
building, and, then their next project was to build a house of
worship, painted white with a tall spire, which would be the first
thing new visitors would see.

The Imperial businessmen were thrilled to hear about the proposed farms the three men from down south were preparing to
level and plant as soon as water was brought into the valley. Mr.
Reed waxed poetic about how pleasing to the eye the green fields
would be, surrounded by barren waste. He said that this subject
would be one of his early headline stories. T. P. offered that he was
thinking of putting in a couple of wells in the hope that the water
might be good enough to give him a head start on his planting.
Everyone wished him well on this new endeavor.

As they ate, "Chinese Charley" Nunn, the hotel proprietor
came by the table. Sam introduced him, to T. P., Tom and Mobley.
They all complemented him on the fine lunch his dining room
had served in the middle of the Colorado Desert.

"We do best we can with what we got," Chinese Charley said.

T. P., Tom and Mobley, after finishing their lunch, said goodby
to their new friends and walked over to the livery stable and retrieved their horses from the lanky cowhand. They paid him for
keeping the horses, rubbing them down and feeding them while
they were about their business in Imperial.

They started back toward Cameron Lake about two in the
afternoon. All three were in top spirits as they headed south into
the desert following the wagon wheel ruts of the freight wagons
carrying their heavy loads to the construction camp. They struck
up a wager as to which one would bring the first crop to harvest
and sale. They were almost giddy with excitement at the prospects
of the ranches they would have as soon as water was brought into
the valley by the Development Company. T. P. again thought of
his idea of drilling wells and silently thought that, if the water was
good, it might help him win the bet as to who would bring in the
first crop.

Around four thirty in the afternoon, they arrived at the

Cameron Lake construction camp, each heading for his own tent home. Carrie was anxiously waiting for T. P.'s return. The boys were still on their various jobs for the company. T. P. grabbed Carrie around the waist and joyfully swung her around and around. "We will own three hundred and twenty acres of the best farm land in the country," T. P. proudly proclaimed. "All we need do is to bring water to it, and that's a sure thing with George Chaffey building the canal."

Around five thirty the boys returned from their chores and as each returned T. P. told him of his exciting trip to Imperial and of the company agreeing with his every request. Carrie had prepared an especially nice dinner that evening and the Banta family celebrated the prospect of farming their new land with much excitement and levity, for from this night on there would be a great deal of hard work before the land could be called a farm.

CHAPTER 21

THE BANTA RANCH

Only true pioneers could be excited about the prospect of turning a square mile of desert in the middle of the worst desert in the United states into a desert oasis. The Banta family was a true pioneer family and they were delighted at the opportunity to do so.

T. P. purchased two well-used Fresno scrapers. He and Earl loaded them onto their two wagons and their mules pulled them out to their ranch. They proceeded to build a ramada shed and corral for the mules with used lumber and arrow weed they had found around Cameron Lake and the construction camp. With the corral, they could leave the mules at the ranch and ride their horses daily from the construction camp. Day after day they rode the horses out to the ranch and spent the day from morning to dusk leveling the soil in preparation for planting seed as soon as the canal brought water to the land.

T. P. also hired Cocupa Indians, indigenous to the area, to sink three wells. They struck water at a depth of forty feet, but the water was not much good. It did provide water for washing them selves and for non-drinking or non-irrigation purposes. Towels wet with water from the wells and placed around their fresh water jugs also helped keep the water cool enough to drink. T. P. was disappointed that the well water was not good enough for growing crops. If it had been, he could have won his bet with Tom and Mobley by growing a saleable crop before canal water entered the valley. He would have to wait for the canal water just as they would.

On two of the wells, T. P. installed the typical hand pump.

The third, he lined with adobe brick and installed a wench and rope typical of the wishing well. To this he attached a cage covered with wire mesh and fitted with several shelves. This he used as a cooler for he had found from living in Mesa during the heat of the summer, that such a devise made a marvelous cooler to keep perishable foods cool during the dog days of June through September. They would keep the cooler just above the water line and would raise or lower the cage to put in or take out perishable food. This kept the produce cooled to about seventy degrees, Fahrenheit;

The Imperial Land Company was seeking to set up a site for a border city that could be used as a new work camp in place of the work camp at Cameron Lake. They knew that the elevation of the land around Cameron Lake was to low and subject to flooding during the overflow of the Colorado River during flood stage. This was a wise decision for in the floods which would take place following 1905 the lake bed and the camp site were completely engulfed by the flood water.

George Chaffey donated one hundred and sixty acres of land he had filed upon for the new camp. It was on high ground just east of the New river channel in which the camp lay. The donated land lay just north of the Mexican border. The camp was moved at his orders in March of 1901. Mr. Chaffey ordered a town site platted on the donated land. The platting was done by Fred Hall, Pete Gaines and Paul McPherrin. T. P.'s friend, Luther Holt, publicity director for the Imperial Land Company, named the town Calexico and named the town's counterpart in Mexico, Mexicali. These names, found no where else in the world, are unique combinations of the words California and Mexico.

The work tents of the surveying party were the first buildings assembled in the new city. The tent of the chief clerk and store keeper, J. D. Hoffman, was the very first tent erected. Soon this was followed by tent houses for chief engineer Perry and his family and Tom Beach and his family. Tom, as we related earlier in this story, was the superintendent of surveying. Permanent commercial buildings in the new townsite followed. Dr. Hefferman opened a

second store for hay feed and general merchandise. The C. D.
Company built a large adobe building for their headquarters. An
adobe building was erected by Ed Aiken as a bank. The business
section of the city was taking shape.

T. P. moved his tent house from Cameron Lake to his ranch,
which was only a couple of miles north the new town. T. P. could
see, however, that the newly platted town could not help but grow,
and he therefore invested in several lots which he purchased from
the Imperial Land Company. This was T. P.'s first involvement
with real estate, a profession he would fully enter shortly thereafter.

With the family tent house now on the ranch, T. P. and Earl
could work on leveling the land from sunup to sundown with no
time wasted in travel.

Time moved quickly and the word around Calexico was that
water would be turned into the main canal some time in June. A
small ditch had already been brought into Calexico. What a relief
that was, as prior to this water's arrival, water had to be hauled
four miles for all purposes including the making of the adobe bricks.

Al and George quit their jobs at the California development
Company so as to have their full time available for getting the land
ready for planting as soon as the water came into the main canal.

T. P. had brought the agricultural planting equipment and
seed with him in the wagon train from Mesa. When water was
turned into the main canal in early June, he immediately started
seeding the leveled fields with milo maze. Using a weir to raise the
water level in the main canal, he turned the water through pipes
in the canal banks onto his land and flooded the land to water the
seed.

His boys, as did all the other workers, received half of their
wages in water script and the other half in cash. The Imperial
Land Company had borrowed money using water stock as collateral.
In addition to the rights his boys had earned as salary, T. P. purchased
some of these rights for fifty cents on the dollar. So many water
rights had been issued to finance the California Development
Company during its time of distress that water rights on the open

market were selling well below the price being charged by the Imperial Land Company.

George Chaffey had to finance much of the International Canal construction himself in spite of the fact that his contract stated he was not required to start construction till fifty thousand dollars of script had been sold. When Chaffey discovered the terrible financial shape of the California Development Company, he decided that he would start building the canals immediately with his own money. He was not required to build any canals in the Imperial Valley as his contract called only for bringing the water to the United States boundary line. However, with the terrible financial condition of the Company and their complete lack of credit due to their financial condition, George Chaffey had to use his own credit, which was excellent, to continue the construction work. It is doubtful that the California Development Company could have continued in business without George Chaffey's credit.

Within days of planting the milo maze seeds on the Banta ranch, they had sprouted. T. P. also experimented with cantaloupes with wonderful results. Many, from the construction camp at Calexico and from the city of Imperial, came to see with their own eyes what T. P. had accomplished on his ranch. This prompted H. C. Reed, editor to the new Imperial Press newspaper, to write an article waxing eloquent where under a scare headline, he painted a word picture of the valley's near future concluding with these lines, "Imagine how pleasing the green fields surrounded by a barren waste will be to the eye."

Tom and Mobley also sowed their fields with sorghum and Barley and the California Development Company planted rows of Egyptian cotton on T. P.'s model ranch at the request of the Federal Government. With the weather, the water, and the fertile soil, the crops planted along the main canal grew rapidly showing that the confidence of the early pioneers was amply justified. A Bermuda lawn was also sown and trees were planted around the California Development Company headquarters building in Calexico.

In August, T. P. and Carrie were in Imperial shopping and met editor Reed on the street. They told him that the corn they had planted in June was now higher than his head and that T. P. had a wonderful cantaloupe and melon patch. Mr. Reed wrote an article carrying this information in the next week's newspaper. Certainly, this was a very fertile land once water was brought to it. Tom Beach and Mobley Meadows had also planted the leveled portions of their farms and their crops were developing beautifully. The race was on as to which one would win the bet as to who would be the first to bring his crop to sale.

The Imperial Land Company ran regular tours from Imperial to these three farms located seven miles to the south. Prospective immigrants were amazed at what they observed. The greenery on the farms acted as editor Reed had predicted. The lush green against the dead desert background was awe inspiring. It caused many settlers to file on Government desert land and purchase water rights on land that would soon be supplied with water from the Colorado River. The Imperial Land Company was well repaid for helping T. P. develop his farm along the main canal for it caused many shares of water stock to be sold.

Unfortunately, much of this stock was offered at a discount by Rockwood while he was trying to get the project off the ground or was used as partial payment to the workers on the gates and canals in Mexico. As mentioned before, the workmen were paid half in cash and half in water stock. Those workmen not wishing to locate a farm in the Valley sold their stock on the open market for what they could get.

Even when stock was sold by the Imperial Land Company, it was sold for eight dollars and seventy-five cents a share, one dollar down and one dollar a year. The Imperial Land Company received the one dollar that was paid in cash to pay for actual advertising expenses, the cost of salesmen showing the prospective immigrants the land and helping them to file on it, and to sell them water stock. This left only the discounted contracts on the promise to pay the remainder for George Chaffey to use in payment for construction.

These contracts were sold to investors in order to get immediate cash for construction for fifty cents or less on the dollar. The contracts also offered the buyers a five percent interest rate on the unpaid balance. Clearly, this was not a lucrative investment on the part of the stockholders of the California Development Company. At this time of development, there was barely enough cash available to continue construction. This is why Mr. Chaffey had to use his own name to get credit to keep cash coming in to cover disbursements.

T. P. was blissfully unaware of the C. D. Company's financial woes and that George Chaffey's name and credit were keeping it afloat. The sweat and labor of the boys, Carrie and himself involved his entire days and nights. Similarly, all the men working for the Company or trying to get their land ready for planting were equally ignorant of the fact the Company was actually insolvent and was being subsidized by George Chaffey. The glorious side of the equation was that the land was all that the promoters had promised and where water was brought to the desert, the desert bloomed in excess of all expectations.

As July moved into its second half, the weather topped one hundred and fifteen degrees daily with some days well into the one hundred twenties. There were days when the body seemed to have taken all it could take and was ready to quit. As obnoxious as that word "quit" was to T. P., it often seemed the better part of valor. But, though the family's body was weak, its sprit was indomitable. The spirit being willing the body was forced to follow. In these early days it must be remembered that there were no trees or bushes. The only shade was the Ramada shed. Yet work had to go on. T. P. had planted sixty acres of kaffir corn which had to be tended despite the heat. He also had fields of Barley and his melon patch. He planted 140 acres in crops that first year.

There was not an ounce of ice to be had in the entire south end of the valley. There was no electricity, only oil lamps. All drinking water was canal water which either had to be filtered or allowed to stand in barrels or tubs till the silt settled to the bottom. The only wood to be found for the cooking stove was bits of cast off construction lumber, a small amount of brush from along the New river channel in which Cameron Lake lay and Mesquit wood from the Mesquit forests by the Salton in Mexico. It was costly but simpler to use an oil stove.

Simply doing the washing, ironing or cooking meals were tasks that took Carrie all day from morning to night. All this, during temperatures exceeding one hundred and fifteen degrees for four months of the year, had to be done in order to support a family of five in this Colorado desert. As we recall, the Banta family's home was a tent stretched over a wooden frame under a ramada shed. Every time the wind blew, with no wind breaks and the new land being broken for farming, it was like a hurricane filled with dust. Keeping a tent home clean was a never-ending job. There were no bridges across the canal. One simply drove the wagon up on one bank, took a dive and if you were lucky, up the other bank. There was no farm machinery except the mule, plow and hoe.

In spite of the heat the crops did not wither. With the abundance of water, the crops grew in such a lush manner that it was awesome. Since no weeds had grown there before, weeding was easy as there were no weed seeds to sprout for the first two or three years.

All farming is like a game of chance where the farmer can make a killing, break even, or lose his entire expenditure of money, time, sweat and tears. Thankfully, as the weeks passed by, the crops of T. P., Tom and Mobley grew ever more luxurious.

In late spring politics in the California Development Company caused T. P.'s friend, Sam Ferguson, to be replaced by Anthony Heber as the president of the Imperial Land Company. Anthony realized the vital part the active ranch of T. P. was playing in sales of water stock in the valley. He made several trips to the Banta farm and became well acquainted with T. P. Anthony Heber as president of the Imperial Land Company arranged to have T. P. photographed in his fields standing among the corn, holding a sugar beet, standing in a field of barley, so as to have visual proof to send to papers all across the nation. A picture is worth a thousand words and most people have very little ability for imagining lush green fields when looking at one of the world's most desolate deserts. These pictures were also printed in the local Imperial Press which was given to all prospective immigrants who visited the valley. At this point, with so few residents in the valley, the newspaper's primary purpose was as a propaganda devise to help the company take some of the bleakness out of the desert confronting the prospective settlers arriving in Imperial.

The tour to T. P.'s model farm and Tom's and Mobley's farms along the main canal, conducted by the Imperial Land Company, was the best possible method of promoting visitors to settle in the valley. Sam Ferguson's faith in T. P.'s abilities was repaid in full measure, pressed down and flowing over.

Finally, it was fall and the crops were ready for harvest. Since there was no harvesting equipment. T. P., the boys and hired hands harvested the crop. T. P. already had a buyer and sold the crop of Kafir corn for fifteen hundred dollars which tripled his investment in land, water rights and other costs. Best of all, he won the bet of ten dollars each from Tom and Mobley.

In October, the heat was dying down and, in the exuberance of the moment, the rigors of the summer seemed not to have been so great. Such is the human spirit that difficulties and agony are quickly forgotten and only the good memories remain. T. P. looked over his farm after all the produce had reached maturity and had been harvested. The stubble, he thought, would be excellent fodder for livestock. He visited the Van Horn brothers and the Gillettes to see if they might pay a small fee for grazing their cattle on his harvested land. They agreed to a price and brought their animals over to his fields. T. P.'s mind raced to the conclusion that he could make much more fattening his own cattle than he could by leasing the land to others. He, thereupon decided to take a trip to Mesa and see if he could purchase some cattle and chickens of his own.

He and Carrie discussed the idea that night and decided he would do just that. Plans were laid out for Earl and Al to ride their horses to Flowing Well while he accompanied them in the wagon.

There they would board the Southern Pacific train, and travel to the Southern Pacific whistlestop for Phoenix. Then they would rent horses and a wagon to ride to Mesa, purchase the cattle and chickens and return home with them. The date for the trip was set two weeks hence.

The boys were delighted that they were included. The trip would be fun. They would get to see their old friends again, and they would get to drive the cattle from Mesa to the Southern Pacific Phoenix whistlestop and from Flowing Well to the ranch. Earl had been on a cattle drive on the McCord ranch in Mesa but Al had never been on a cattle drive before.

There was much to do in very little time. T. P. wanted to telephone his friends in Mesa, telling them of his plans and asking them to check out livestock available for his purchase as well as a couple of crates of chickens. He also wanted to check with the Southern Pacific to have cattle cars ready for the return. Since there were no telephones in Imperial, he would have to take a trip to Flowing Well, the Southern Pacific junction for the Imperial Valley, to make the telephone call on their line. He could also make arrangements at their station for the cattle cars he would need to transport the cattle and chickens from Phoenix to Flowing Well. Flowing Well was about thirty miles north of Imperial. He found out from Tom Beach that the stage from Imperial to Flowing Well would leave at seven thirty A.M. the next morning. Rather than riding his horse from Imperial to Flowing Well, he planned to take the McCauley stage.

T. P. was up before dawn the next morning and ready for his ride to Imperial, about eight miles north of the Banta Ranch. He arrived at Imperial about seven in the morning and boarded his horse with the lanky cowhand who ran the livery stable. The cowhand also sold him his ticket for the McCauley stage coach. He was told that four other passengers would be riding in the coach with him.

"If I were you," the cowhand said, "I'd be first to board the coach and get the seat next to the driver. There's a lot less dust up there than in the coach."

T. P. noticed the driver and two other men had almost completed hitching the horses to the stage. With no further delay, T. P. climbed up into the seat alongside where the driver would sit. T. P. figured he would get a better view in addition to the fact that it would be less dusty than inside the coach. One by one, the other four passengers arrived. The cowhand assisted each in putting their baggage in the rack on top of the stage coach. Then each entered the passenger compartment. The passenger compartment was arranged with two upholstered bench seats, one in front and one in the rear facing each other. The cowboy collected the fare from each of the four passengers and handed the money to the driver. When the horses were properly hitched, the driver climbed up into his seat. T. P. introduced himself. In turn, the driver introduced himself to T. P. and with a call to the horses and a crack of the whip the stage moved forward out of Imperial and into the desert.

The driver followed the wagon tracks of previous freight wagons and stage coaches going to and from Flowing Well. The morning was brisk and absolutely beautiful. The air was so clear that visibility was unlimited. T. P. was delighted he had taken the seat next to the driver. It gave him a three hundred and sixty-degree view of the valley. The flat lifeless desert sand stretched to the horizon both front and back and mile after mile to each side until it reached the dry mountains on the east and west sides of the Valley.

"Guess the trip gets tedious after repeating it day after day." T. P. said to the driver.

"Well, there are times we get more excitement than anyone would want," the driver shouted back.

"What excitement could happen out here with nothing around? It's so barren and dry that even the jack rabbits have to wear canteens," hollered T. P.

"For starters, let me tell you what happened to my boss, George McCauley during that sand storm last February or March.

McCauley has several teams at Flowing Well that he hires out, with drivers, for those who don't want to go by stage. A couple of very religious and elderly people came down from L. A. and hired a wagon to take them to Cameron Lake. McCauley didn't have no drivers available, so's he decided to take 'em his self. On the way back, that terrible dust storm that hit in the early spring caught them. Well, you know how with nothing' out here but sand those dust clouds make it impossible to see anything. McCauley, as well as he knows this desert, completely lost his way. He wandered around the sand dunes till the horses were near used up. He and his passengers were choking on the sand. It was in their eyes, their noses, their ears and they were thirsty as all get out."

"The elderly lady says to Mr. McCauley, 'Driver, please stop and I'll pray for deliverance.'"

"McCauley didn't know much about praying' but he thought it was worth a try, so he pulled the buggy into the lee of a sand dune and reined the horses to a stop. The elderly lady climbed down from the carriage, dropped to her knees and offered one of the longest and sincerest prayers you ever heard for deliverance from the terrible dust storm. Then she got up and climbed back into the wagon. Then, by golly, as McCauley sat there, all of a sudden the wind slowed to a breeze and the dust blew away from them. McCauley was astonished."

"As he started the wagon the elderly lady leaned over and said to him, 'Sir, What do YOU think of THAT?'"

"McCauley was at a loss for words, so he just sat there driven' the team . As he rounded the sand dune and headed in the direction he thought was Flowing Well, for the wagon tracks were obliterated with drifting sand, the wind renewed at ten times its original force. It almost upset the buggy. The elderly lady's bonnet was blown away. McCauley's mouth was filled with sand before he could retie his handkerchief around his face."

"He turned to the elderly religious lady and shouted to her over the roar of the wind, 'Pardon me ma'am, but WHAT THE HELL DO YOU THINK OF THAT!'"

T. P. laughed heartily at the story. He recalled the dust storm at Cameron Lake and thought how puny man is when compared to nature. He hoped that the California Development Company could subdue the violent forces of nature in this hostel domain which mere man hoped to dominate.

As they traveled toward Flowing Well, they passed several freighters fully loaded and heading for Imperial or Cameron Lake. Everything used in the Valley had to be brought in by mule team from the Southern Pacific Flowing Well depot. Up ahead a lone mesquite tree came into sight.

"That's what we call the Fifteen Mile Tree. We call it that because it stands about fifteen miles from Flowing well," the driver told T. P. "It may not look like it, but that's the US Post office."

T. P. nodded assent but didn't follow the drift of the post office remark. As they drew closer, he saw what the driver meant for hanging on the tree was a typical U. S. mail sack.

The driver said, "They leave sacks of mail on that tree for Boswell camp on the Eastside."

"Isn't that dangerous?" said T. P. "Couldn't it be stolen."

"We been doin' it nigh on nine months and ain't nothing happened yet. If something does happen, I pity the poor feeler who does it. He'll get strung up sure as shootin'.'"

As time passed, they arrived at the Alamo River crossing which was a dry river channel traversing the Valley from south to north on its east side. It was dry as a bone almost all of the time except occasionally at flood stage on the Colorado River. During heavy floods the river would overflow on its north side sending water all the way to the Salton Sink. Over the years this occasional flood runoff created the Alamo channel. As they drew nearer, T. P. noticed barrels lined up three deep, side by side, by the channel. The driver told him that this was the only water between Imperial and Flowing Well. He stopped, filled some buckets and gave the horses a drink. It was a four-hour trip and the poor horses seemed exhausted.

Of course there were no bridges in the valley at this early time in its history. Wear by wagon wheels had worn down the natural, steep channel banks to a more gentle incline so the wagons could cross with less effort by the horses. In spite of this, the tired horses trembled as they went down one bank, holding the stage back, and strained to their utmost pulling the stage up the other bank. After crossing the Alamo channel, the driver told T. P. the journey was almost over and that they should be in Flowing Well within an hour.

"That's great," said T. P., "I'm going to drink a bucket of water out of that flowing well. Hope it's nice and cold,"

The driver laughed uproariously. "That there well ain't flowin'. Matter of fact there ain't no well at all."

T. P. felt embarrassed. He felt like a greenhorn that had been taken in. He wanted to ask, why, then, did they call the whistlestop Flowing Well, but he just let the subject pass.

As they approached Flowing Well, T. P. saw that the whistle stop along the Southern Pacific Railroad line from Yuma to Los Angeles was nothing but a smaller edition of the canvas-covered frame hotel in Imperial. Besides the hotel there was nothing but the livery stable which accommodated the freight wagons and McCauley's horses and wagons. There was nothing else but the desolate train tracks across a barren waste.

The driver pulled the horses to a halt in the shade of the livery shed for they appeared completely exhausted. The cow hands quickly unbridled them and immediately set to rubbing them down. A worker came to the coach with a hand cart and helped the passengers unload their belongings from the rack on top of the coach. T. P. followed the worker as he pulled the cart over to the front porch of the hotel which was covered with a wooden roof and ran the full length of the canvas building. The building, as well as being a hotel, also served as the train station. T. P. entered the canvas walled building and went over to the telegrapher and gave him the wording for the telegram requesting four cattle cars to be available at the whistlestop that served the Phoenix area on the day he intended to load the cattle he would purchase in Mesa. He also made his telephone calls to his old friends in Phoenix, telling them when he would arrive and his proposed purchase of cattle and chickens for his ranch. He asked them to be on the lookout for a good buy on cattle and chickens.

The telegrapher, who also served as ticket agent and station master, telegraphed Southern Pacific Railroad headquarters and made arrangements for the four cattle cars. He guaranteed the cars would be there the day T. P. needed them.

It was now a quarter to one and T. P. suddenly realized how hungry he was, for he had eaten nothing since four A. M. He found the dining room and ate a hearty lunch. Then he went to the livery stable to find when the next stagecoach would be leaving for Imperial. The news was not good for he was told that there would be none until seven thirty the next morning. T. P. had to get back to the ranch as he had told Carrie that he would be gone only that day and she would worry to the point she might start a search party looking for him. Since Carrie knew he would be all alone on the desert with no one around for miles for a good part of the journey, not being back by the appointed time could mean serious trouble.

He went over to where a freight wagon was being loaded and asked the freight driver if he might ride with him to Imperial. The freighter was a large muscular man that looked like he would fear no man but he answered, "Can't do that! McCauley would skin me alive for taking a fare away from him."

"Well, tell him you hired me on as your assistant," T. P. said.

"Naw, that wouldn't work. You don't look like no mule skinner," replied the freight driver.

The team of eight mules was already hitched to the wagon and the wagon was packed, ready to roll out.

"Give me a pair of gloves and I'll show you how to drive a team of eight mules! Hell, I've driven fourteen mule teams," T. P. countered.

The driver pulled his gloves off and gave them to T. P. T. P. put the gloves on and then put the left reins for two mules between each pair of fingers on his left hand and did the same with the right reins in his right hand. The driver knew from just watching him that he knew what he was doing.

"Let's get going!" he said. With that, T. P. slapped the reins against the mule's flanks, shouted, "Haw! Git up," and the team headed out of the freight yard.

The two men traded-off driving the mules all the way back to Imperial. T. P. found the freighter's stories to be most entertaining and the freighter found T. P.'s story of his new life in Imperial Valley equally interesting. The four hours and fifty minutes the trip took passed very quickly.

"Thanks for the ride." T. P. said as he left to get his horse at the livery stable.

"Thank you, for your help and conversation," the freight driver responded.

The livery hand put the saddle on T. P's horse and brought him to the hitching post in front of the livery stable. T. P. mounted him and headed back to his ranch just as it was getting dusk. In about an hour and a half he reined his horse to a stop by the ranch corral gate. Earl was by the corral waiting for his father. T. P. dismounted and Earl unsaddled the horse, rubbed him down and fed him while his father went inside to tell the family the story of the trip. After eating a hearty meal, T. P. slipped into his night shirt. He was so tired from the exhausting day that he was asleep as soon as his head hit the pillow.

CHAPTER 22

CATTLE FOR THE RANCH

T. P., Earl and Al prepared for a two-week trip to Mesa, Arizona. It was the fall of the year and they had completed the winter planting so that Carrie, George and the hired hands could take care of the chores of the ranch. Al and Earl would ride the horses to Flowing Well while T. P. would drive the wagon. The wagon would be needed for the crates of chickens they would be bringing back with them and to carry feed. The horses would be needed for the two cattle drives that would be required on the trip: one, twenty-five miles from Mesa to the Phoenix railway station on the Southern Pacific Line; the other, forty plus miles from Flowing Well through Imperial to the ranch.

By early October 1901, the family had prepared everything for the trip. From Flowing Well to the Phoenix station, they would take the train. The Phoenix station on the Southern Pacific line was about twenty-five miles from Mesa. They would rent horses and a wagon to take them those last miles.

The trip to Phoenix went just as planned. The boys enjoyed seeing Imperial and the ride from Imperial to Flowing well was a long ride but better than doing farm chores. At the Phoenix station, they rented the horses and wagon as planned. They drove out to Mesa where T. P.'s friends had lined up cattle for them to inspect. T. P. and the boys visited several ranches in the area and decided on the eighty head of cattle they would buy. They also purchased thirty chickens and two crates in which to carry them.

All of T. P.'s old friends wanted to know about the Imperial

Valley and how he was faring there. T. P. boasted about the water coming into the Valley during May, about the fine crop he had brought in and about the fine price for which he had sold it. Everyone he talked to was extremely interested and wanted more information about this wonderful new irrigation project that was now a reality. Several of his friends invited him to a meeting of cattlemen to tell of the wonders of the Imperial Valley.

So much interest was shown that the entrepreneur in T. P. saw the possibility of money in what he knew about the Valley and the many acquaintances he had in the Phoenix area. He was in a position to benefit both the Imperial Land Company and his friends around Phoenix in a win-win situation. He would talk to Heber as soon as he returned to the Valley about an agency with the Imperial Land Company so he could receive a commission for bringing new settlers to Imperial. T. P. had a quick eye for all possibilities of making money. The Phoenix Stockman newspaper ran an article on T. P. and his success in the Imperial Valley.

The week in the Phoenix area passed very quickly for T. P. and the boys and now it was time to return to the ranch with the cattle and chickens. His friends from whom he had purchased the cattle had them cut out from the herd and ready for the trip. They had branded the cattle with a bar B brand and knowing that these were T. P.'s first cattle for his herd on the Banta ranch, made a present of the branding iron to T. P. for branding the descendants of the eighty head. T. P. and the boys loaded the rented wagon with the chickens and feed for the eighty head of cattle and chickens and started the twenty-five-mile cattle drive from Mesa to the Phoenix station on the Southern pacific line. Both T. P. and Earl were old hands at driving cattle for they had been on many cattle drives on the McCord ranch in Mesa. They both were well-seasoned cowboys.

Upon their arrival at the Phoenix train station they returned the rented horses and wagon to the coral that served as a livery stable. They found the cattle cars awaiting them as had been promised. They watered and fed the cattle and chickens and awaited

the next freight train going west. The station master said it would
be by in a few hours.

The freight train arrived within an hour of the time expected.
T. P. and the boys had loaded the cattle and chickens into the
cattle cars. In no time the railroad had the cattle cars off the siding
and attached to the freight train. T. P. and the boys rode in the
caboose with the railroad men to the Imperial Valley station at
Flowing Well. Here they unloaded the cattle and put the chickens
and feed onto their own wagon. Now all that remained was the
forty plus mile cattle drive back to the ranch. Driving the cattle
down to the Banta ranch was exciting for the boys and they loved
every minute of it. How proud they were as they drove the cattle
through Imperial on their way back to the ranch.

While in Imperial, T. P. showed his cattle to Anthony Heber,
and discussed the matter of his setting up an office in Phoenix for
recruiting settlers to the Valley. Anthony agreed that this was a
good idea and he appointed T. P. as an agent for the Imperial Land
Company. T. P. would receive a commission on all water stock sold
to settlers he would bring to the Imperial valley.

Then T. P. and the boys were off on the last leg of their journey. They arrived back at the ranch at about four P. M. on the
twelfth day of the long and arduous trip. Carrie and George were
about their chores and dropped what they were doing to run to
greet T. P. and the boys, and to inspect the eighty head of cattle
and the chickens. T. P., Earl and Al with Carrie and George's help
drove the cattle into the coral and the chickens were placed in the
coop that had been built for them in anticipation of their arrival.
The chickens could not be left to run wild because the coyotes
would soon finish them off.

Afterwards, they sat down to the grand dinner that had been
prepared for the weary travelers by Carrie. T. P. gave thanks for the
fine ranch they had acquired through hard work and providence,
and especially for the new addition of the cattle and the chickens.

"Now," T. P. said, "This is a real ranch and every bit of it will
be ours."

T. P. had every right to be proud of himself and his family for bringing cattle and chickens to the ranch. But little did he know that the most important thing he had done on his trip to Phoenix was his decision to go into the real estate business as an agent for the Imperial Land Company. His decision to be an agent for them in Phoenix changed him from being strictly a farmer to being the first real estate man in the Valley, which business was to take over the majority of his future life.

1901 quickly moved through November and into December. The entire Banta family was pleased with all they had accomplished in the year since they had first arrived in the valley. They had created a lush farm from the deadly Colorado desert now replete with chickens and cattle and had grown, or had growing, crops of sorghum, melons, corn, barley, wheat, alfalfa and many vegetables.

They greeted the new year 1902 with exuberance and enthusiasm. With new settlers filing on land wherever new canals were built and purchasing water stock from the Imperial Land Company, the California Development Company was getting healthy. Everything was going their way and beyond the horizon of the New Year there appeared to be nothing in the future for them but a beautiful life on their new ranch.

CHAPTER 23

THE DUAL CRISES OF 1902

The New Year was greeted in the valley with much shouting, dancing, singing and a few pistol and rifle shots. No one in the valley could imagine anything other than a bright future for valley settlers and the California Development Company. Crops had been harvested and winter crops were in the fields. No farmer had anything but success with the land when water was brought to it. All Imperialists were waiting for a report to be published by the United States Department of Agriculture which they were sure would bring a flood of new settlers to the valley.

In February, the Department of Agriculture released its report, prepared by two young "experts," J. Gannett Holmes and Thomas H. Means, known as "Circular No. 9." To the shock and chagrin of Valley residents and the California Development Company, the Circular, in brief, said that most of the soil in the valley was impregnated with alkali to the point where agriculture was very improbable. One paragraph stated, "One hundred and twenty-five thousand acres of this land have already been taken up by prospective settlers, many of whom talk of planting crops, which it will be absolutely impossible to grow. They must early find that it is useless to attempt their growth."

These young "experts" had completed their research with only forty days spent in the field to cover one-hundred and sixty-nine square miles. They had made only four borings of any depth. This report, known as Circular No. 9, was published as a pamphlet and broadcast across the nation. Its purpose was to warn people not to immigrate to the Imperial Valley. Not only did the government mass-distribute the pamphlet, but it also conducted interviews across the continent using every means to persuade prospective settlers not to go to the Imperial Valley. Newspapers devoted much space to the report and it's recommendation due to these interviews. This action by the Federal Government caused an immediate stop in the settlement of the valley, to the great distress of the early settlers. In addition, the report destroyed the credit of both the California Development Company and the settlers.

At almost the same time, Rockwood and Chaffey got into a battle for the control of the California Development Company, with Rockwood, Heber and their group buying out George Chaffey. George Chaffey had been the savior of the company and had done all the work in building the tremendous amount of construction work that had been completed during late 1900 and all through 1901. In twenty-two months, George Chaffey had built more than four hundred miles of canals and laterals, more than one hundred thousand acres of land was made ready for water, two thousand settlers had been attracted to the valley, the town of Imperial and Calexico started and the debt ridden and bankrupt California Development Company turned into a concern worth millions. He had also been instrumental in keeping the company solvent by using his own credit to keep the construction work going.

It is doubtful that Rockwood, et al, would have bought out Chaffey had they known that Circular No. 9 would have been as derogatory to valley land as it turned out to be. At the time it appeared to Rockwood that the Company had come through its financial struggle. He and his friends moved George Chaffey out at the exact moment the crisis of Circular No. 9 reared its ugly head. Charles Rockwood had looked for eight solid years for George Chaffey. He had found him in the nick of time when the California Development Company was bankrupt and he was ready to terminate the venture. Yet, at the first moment it looked as if the Company would be profitable, he bought Chaffey out.

These two incidents caused great worry to the settlers in the

Valley. Although they knew that Circular No. 9 was in error and that they were having great success in raising crops in the Valley, they were up against the might of the United States Government with its unlimited financial resources to distribute the findings of Circular No. 9. This government action resulted in the immediate shut-off of new settlers. This occurred when the California Development Company was most dependent on the new settlers' purchases of water stock to keep money coming in to continue building canals under previous obligations to earlier settlers. At the same time, without George Chaffey's personal credit, Los Angeles banks had discontinued purchasing California Development Company commercial paper.

T. P. respected the knowledge and abilities of George Chaffey but it meant little to him who was chief engineer of the irrigation project as long as it moved ahead in it's building of the canal system in an efficient manner. T. P. had become aware through his company connections of the financial weakness of Charles Rockwood and his group. This became of great concern to him.

T. P. and his family did all they could to reverse the bad effects from Circular No. 9. He wrote to his friends in Phoenix and sent them samples of crops he had grown. The Imperial Land Company released pictures they had taken of T. P. standing among his lush crops and the pictures made editors across the nation sit up and take notice of these emphatic contradictions of the message contained in Circular No. 9.

A picture is worth a thousand words. This picture of T. P.
in his fields was taken by the Imperial Land Company to
debunk the false information in Circular #9

Empirical evidence by the Imperial Valley's earliest farmers overcame the ridiculous pseudo-science of the Department of Agriculture's youthful experts. How and why did the Federal Government make such a terrible and avoidable mistake? As we note, the circular was distributed after the first cash crops had been grown and sold by T. P. and Tom Beach. Was it possible that the Department of Agriculture was in league with the Federal Reclamation Service in attempting to dispose of this, the largest of all reclamation projects being built by private enterprise? In the eyes of the government, wasn't this their job? Shouldn't private enterprise keep its hands off of projects that could be better accomplished by an agency of the Federal Government?

Certainly, if this report of the Department of Agriculture had been published before lush crops were being grown in the valley, it is likely that Imperial Valley would not exist. But the growing crops put Circular No. 9 on the scrap heap and informed the nation that the conclusions of the Circular were another case of government misinformation. However, the damage to the California Development Company had been done. Money, needed to construct canals under obligations to settlers who had already purchased water stock, was delayed in coming into the books of the Imperial Land Company. Thus, construction and maintenance money for the canals was in short supply. The scene was set for the terrible tragedies that befell the Imperial valley starting in the winter months of 1905.

At this time, though money was in short supply, the building of canals by the California Development Company continued and settlers saw little difference between the Company under Rockwood as compared to Chaffey as chief engineer. The specter of Circular No. 9 was eliminated by exposing the American public to the truth about the productivity of the Valley land. But the financial scars remained even after new settlers were flocking to the new land opened by the waters of the Colorado river flowing through the irrigation canals. The future of the company gave T. P. concern since his agreement with the company, regarding his purchase of the John Leighton filing on which his farm lay, was verbal with the present management. If the management changed, the new principals might not keep the agreement to sell him the tract after the entry was perfected. Then all his work would go to the benefit of the company.

CHAPTER 24

T. P., THE REAL ESTATE AGENT

As T. P. worked to erase the scar of Circular No. 9, he induced friends from the Salt River Valley to come to the Imperial Valley. Through his foresight of becoming an agent for the Imperial Land Company, this resulted in commissions being paid to him by the Imperial Land Company. As water stock was sold by the company to those T. P. induced into coming to the Valley, T. P. received his commission on the sale. This became so profitable that he started to leave the management of the ranch to Carrie and Earl while he pursued the profits from the real estate business.

Earl had turned sixteen in April of 1902. On this wild frontier, that made him a man. Earl was very bright and well capable of accepting responsibility. Still it was tough on a lad of sixteen to be saddled with the work of handling all the problems and hard physical labor required to manage a large working frontier farm. Also, Earl had missed almost two school years. T. P. knew he was being unfair to his oldest son and vowed to make it up to Earl in the future. For now though, the family needed him to manage and work on the farm and that's what T. P. insisted he do.

Earl resented working so hard and later when the U. S. Government started to hire men to build the Panama Canal, he often thought of going to Panama. He was well trained in canal construction due to his experience in working on the International Canal bringing water to the Imperial Valley. The government was paying big salaries to the Panama Canal workers. He heard of others leaving the Valley for the big money in Panama and lay awake nights planning on leaving, too. T. P. read Earl's mind and one day talked to him about what Earl was thinking.

"Earl," he said, "I know that if I was a young man like you are, I'd be thinking of going to Panama for that big money. I won't blame you if you go though the family greatly needs your help at this critical time. Promise me one thing." he continued, "If you plan to leave don't run away on your own. Let me know and I'll stake you to the trip and give you enough money for the first few months till your pay checks start coming in." This took all the fun out of running away to Panama and made Earl realize his duty to his family. Suddenly there was no romance to the thought; and T. P., by being alert to his son's needs, forestalled Earl's taking early leave of his family. T. P. thus saved his son's valuable services for their present and future benefit.

In March of 1902, T. P. returned to Phoenix with a friend from the Salt River Valley, C. C. Long, who was also an agent for the Imperial Land Company. He had a duel purpose for the visit. First, as agent for the Imperial land company, he wanted to look at the possibility of purchasing an ice plant in Phoenix which could be moved to the Imperial Valley. With the large crops now being grown in the valley and not a piece of ice to be had, there would be a great demand for such a product. He recommended the purchase of the plant and arranged to have it shipped to Imperial where it was installed in the summer of 1902. Second, he and C. C. opened an office in Phoenix at 218 Washington Street where they displayed samples of grain and alfalfa grown in the Imperial Valley. By their confidence in Imperial land and the company reclaiming it, they were successful in inducing many farmers from the Salt River Valley to settle in the Imperial Valley.

T. P. also noticed that some of the first settlers in the valley simply could not make the adjustment to the harshness of valley life and, after filing for land and purchasing water stock, wanted to get out. Again, seeing an opportunity to make his knowledge pay off, T. P. became the first real estate man in the Imperial Valley, opening a full time office in Imperial in a frame building. Thus he was one of the first businessmen to establish an office in the City of Imperial. He worked in conjunction with the Imperial Land Company as they wanted an orderly disposal of such land and water stock. To have no market for such land and stock would not be in the best interest of the Company as it would be a detriment to selling new stock.

As the real estate agent in Imperial, T. P. had first notice of snap bargains coming on to the market by quitters who were leaving the Valley. Where the property was next to his farm, or where no buyer was readily available, T. P. would purchase the property in his own name. The property adjoining his farm he would purchase and add to his farm. The other property he would purchase and hold for a buyer. So strong was his faith in the land and the Company that he would bet his family's entire fortune on their future. With such confidence, it was easy to sell new prospects on settling in his Valley. T. P. found himself putting more and more of his time into his real estate business and leaving more and more of the management of the ranch to Earl who in essence acted as foreman carrying out T. P.'s, general plans. Earl had, of course, hired hands, both Cocopah Indians and men who had come to the valley wanting a salary rather than the potential future profit from the work of starting a new farm from scratch.

To establish his real estate business, T. P. started running real estate adds in the local paper listing properties of pioneers who had given up and were selling their property. He spent much of his time taking newly arrived prospect to show them property for he knew the Valley like the palm of his hand. T. P. also worked under his arrangement as company agent for the Imperial Land Company taking new arrivals who wanted to file on land under the Desert Land Act to property that had not been filed upon but had water available, or where water soon would be available, from the California Development Company canals. Following is a verbatim account told by a new arrival describing just such a transaction and the results it had on the new pioneer's life. The account is from the book "The First Thirty Years in Imperial Valley, California", by Otis B. Tout.

Pg. 63. September, 1902. T. D. McCall. Imperial:

Was a traveler in Mexico when I read a spread in a Los Angeles Sunday paper. Wired Mrs. McCall from Guaymas, Mexico, to sell furniture in her San Diego home and meet me at the Flowing Well junction. Mrs. got the wire after dark but sold out and caught the midnight train and made connections per schedule.

Drove down into a dead world, not a green leaf anywhere, so deadly it was fascinating. Imperial was the big town, there being no other. A tent hotel, a few campers and a church, a little box with a spire. The best piece of advertising I ever saw. Took some desert out of the picture. Bought a bottle from Bob Davis and went with T. P. (Texas Pacific) Banta in a rattle trap rig and a pair of kegtail ponies. Located our farms, and when we filed on them, we had $14 left and owed $5000 for water stock. Made a house of adobe, our only building material. Graded every inch of our land. Fought contesters that sent us into the red some $20,000. Planted trees and converted a square mile of desert into a grapefruit grove and don't owe a thin dime. Thirty years of unfaltering, laborious grind, but we did it. How I don't know. Quitters helped a lot. They sell cheap and on credit—About ninety-nine percent of mankind are quitters.

CHAPTER 25

THE BANTA'S PLAN THEIR DREAM HOUSE

THE FIRST FRAME HOUSE IN THE VALLEY

In June of 1902, the Banta's had been in the Imperial Valley a year and six months. All this time they had lived in a tent house with a ramada shed over it. It had been hard on all five of them to live in one room and Carrie had to do all her chores in keeping the family fed and clothed in clean clothes under the most difficult of conditions. All water for domestic needs came from the canal and had to be settled before being used as the canal water carried much silt. Hot water for washing clothes or bathing had to be heated over a wood fire. Preparing dinners for the family was very tedious involving picking the vegetables from the vegetable garden, washing and preparing them under very primitive conditions.

A chicken dinner meant catching and killing the chicken, plucking the feathers from the bird after dipping it in a large pot of scalding water, drawn from the settling tank, that had been brought to a boil over a wood fire, cleaning it and finally cooking it in a primitive outdoor kitchen. Washing, ironing, housekeeping and every other chore a mother had to do were equally as difficult in a tent house on a frontier farm.

In the same time period, T. P. had leveled and sown their land. He had reaped and sold crops. He had become an agent for the Imperial Land Company with a frame office building in the city of Imperial. The family had become prosperous in their new home, and the Imperial Valley was their new home now. Carrie finally announced to T. P. that it was time to think of the family and build their permanent home in the Valley. They had become well-to-do in the valley and she saw no reason for not building a home representative of their new wealth. No one had yet built a frame house anywhere in the valley.

"By God, Carrie," T. P. said, "you're absolutely right. It's just the thing to do to show the new settlers how convinced we are in the future of the Valley."

Being in real estate, T. P. also saw a chance to make some money. He would open a subdivision just outside the city of Imperial. He had purchased some land from a quitter just to the east of the Imperial city limits extending north and south of eighth street. He filed with the county to subdivide this property and called it the Banta subdivision. With this done, he set out to find a con-tractor he could trust to build their dream home. His friend, Irwin, had built his real estate office in Imperial so he talked to him about building his house.

"Sure," Irwin said. "I can build a frame house as easy as a frame office building. All I need are the plans. The Imperial Land Company can get the plans for us if you tell them what you want."

T. P. talked to Carrie about what she wanted in a house. Carrie had been thinking about a house for a long while and had pretty well decided what she wanted for the family. She wanted a house just like all the city houses that were now being built in the new twentieth century. Except that to accommodate the hot desert climate, she wanted large screened areas covered by the roof for the six hot months of the year. Of course the house must have indoor plumbing, plumbed both for water and sewage, in the kitchen and bathroom. Three bedrooms would be adequate: Earl and Al in one bedroom, George in another and the master bedroom for T. P. and herself. There would be a front room, with a fireplace for the cold winter months, and a dining room right off the kitchen

On the long summer evenings, T. P., Carrie and the boys sat, outside their tent house talking and writing out what the new family home would be like. T. P. made several sketches, finally settling on a rectangular one story bungalow, with large screened rooms at each end for the hot summer months. It would have a brick foundation to raise the floor off of the ground. The roof would be gabled in the center but it would slope down at each end. On each of the four sloping sides of the roof there was to be gabled attic vents. In all, it would cover fourteen hundred square feet. Though it would be a small house, it would be a house that would fit into any neighborhood in any modern city. And of course it would have the modern plumbing as Carrie had requested. To have this, the house would have to be built on the banks of a canal. T. P. would have a settling tank constructed on its banks. A farm windmill would pump the water from the canal into the settling tank. Then the clear settled water would be pumped up into a raised water tank next to the windmill. The water would be brought into the house by gravity flow. A cesspool would be dug and connected to the house by sewer pipes so that the house would have all the plumbing amenities of a city home. Lighting, cooking and heating would be accomplished by fuel oil. The house would also have a brick fireplace in the front room to make it cozy on the cold winter nights.

T. P. took his writing and sketches to Irwin, the contractor, and Irwin had plans drawn which T. P. approved. T. P. had decided where the house would be built. He would build it on a dirt road extension of eighth street just outside the city limits of Imperial right next to the Dalia canal which was a feeder canal off of the main canal. This position would put him close to the ranch and almost next door to his real estate office in Imperial.

His next project was to purchase the materials necessary to build the house and then have them delivered by train and freight wagon to his chosen location beside the Dahlia canal. This would require a trip to the big city of Los Angeles where he could get the best prices on building supplies. He would take Carrie and Irwin with him. Irwin could help him pick out the building materials while Carrie could look for furniture in the large furniture stores.

The three planned their trip with great care, talking with the purchasers for the California Development Company and Imperial Land Company to determine where they might get the best prices. The Company gave them letters of introduction to suppliers in L. A. and wrote ahead so that they would be welcomed when they arrived. They also recommended a hotel where they could stay in Los Angeles. T. P. picked up schedules for the Southern Pacific trains from Flowing Well to Los Angeles. T. P., Carrie and Irwin prepared a detailed list with great care so that they would remember everything needed for constructing and furnishing the first frame dwelling in the Valley.

On the day before the great adventure to Los Angeles, they loaded the wagon with their suitcases for the week's trip. T. P. told Earl that he would be in charge of the farm and his two younger brothers till they returned. Carrie cooked a fine diner for the family in anticipation of the wonderful adventure that lay before her.

T. P. and Carrie arose well before sunup the morning of the trip. The boys got up at the same time for they had their chores to do. Carrie prepared an ample breakfast as she did every morning, for life on a frontier farm was hard labor and required lots of vittles. No one ever got fat on a frontier farm for no matter how many calories or fat one ate, they worked them off.

Irwin arrived Just before sunup. He had been raised in Los Angeles but the trip to L. A. was a first for Carrie and T. P. T. P. of course had been to Flowing Well while Carrie had been no further than Imperial. She enjoyed the trip from Imperial to Flowing Well in their buggy rig pulled by the two keg tail ponies. As they drove through the desert, T. P. pointed out the fifteen mile mesquite tree that still served as the U. S. Post Office. He commented on the rows of drums of water along side the dry Alamo channel, the sand hills along the east side of the valley and all the other points of interest along the flat desert plain to Flowing Well.

As they approached Flowing Well, Carrie saw that the station along the Southern Pacific railroad line from Yuma to Los Angeles was nothing but a smaller edition of the canvas-covered frame hotel in Imperial. Besides the hotel there was nothing but the livery stable which accommodated the freight wagons and McCaulley's horses and wagons. There was nothing else but the desolate train tracks across a barren waste.

T. P. pulled the ponies and buggy rig to a halt in the shade of the livery shed for the ponies appeared completely exhausted. The livery stable cow hands quickly unbridled them and immediately set to rubbing them down. A worker came to the coach with a hand cart and helped them unload their belongings from the buggy rig. All three followed the worker as he pulled the cart over to the front porch of the hotel which was covered with a wooden roof which ran the full length of the canvas building. It was about four in the afternoon when they entered the hotel to register for their rooms. T. P. knew that the next passenger train wouldn't arrive till five-forty the next morning. "That's if it's on time," he told Carrie. T. P. asked the room clerk how he could make arrangements for boarding the train due by the next morning. The clerk told him to buy the tickets now and that several other guests were boarding that train and the flag would be up for it to stop. All he had to do was be beside the track by the flag. T. P. purchased the tickets for Carrie, Irwin and himself from the railroad agent.

They all went up to their rooms to clean up before dinner. Their rooms were similar to the rooms at the Imperial Hotel. There was the dresser with a porcelain bowl and pitcher. The pitcher was filled with water. There was a drinking glass beside it. T. P. and Carrie filled their glasses with water, drank them in one gulp, then filled and drank two more glasses before their thirsts were quenched. Then they washed the grime from their hands and faces and sponged off as best they could in the porcelain bowl. As in Imperial, every drop of water had to be hauled in to Flowing Well from the overflow lakes miles south on the Alamo gulch which were filled yearly by the overflow of the Colorado River.

T. P. and Carrie went down to the dining room for dinner and on the way asked the room clerk to refill their water pitcher. They met Irwin in the dining room and dined with him. After dinner they told him that they would meet him at four thirty the next morning to catch the train to L. A. All three of them were exhausted from the day's trip and immediately after dinner, Carrie and T. P. went to their room and fell asleep almost immediately.

It seemed like seconds and their alarm clock awoke them. While T. P. shaved, Carrie dressed and packed their bags. Then they went to the dining room for breakfast. Irwin was already in the dining room when they arrived.

T. P. had been told that the train was never early but often late. Nevertheless, they were out at the track at half past four. By four-forty, the other passengers going to L.A. had also congregated by the track. At five-forty everyone anxiously looked up the track for the train's head light. Dawn came at six thirty and they still stood anxiously waiting. By seven they had all moved to the shade of the hotel porch.

At seven forty five someone shouted, "I see smoke from the engine on the horizon!" A while longer, the chugging of the steam engine could be heard, then the clickety-clack of the wheels on the rails. The screeching of the brakes followed as the train pulled to a stop along side the raised flag. With a deafening roar the engine released the steam from the steam brakes. The porter climbed down the vestibule steps of the day coach that the passengers were to use and carefully placed the platform used for mounting the steps to the vestibule. One by one, the passengers, including T. P., Carrie, and Irwin climbed up to the vestibule and entered the day coach passenger car. The coach was almost new. The bench seats were most comfortable. The rich mahogany wood used throughout would have just as well adorned a capitalist's mansion. The electric lights used to light the car after dark were of brightly polished brass with Victorian stained-glass lamp shades. The massive steam locomotive lurched forward. As the engineer slowly opened the throttle, the couplings between the passenger cars creaked in sequence as each after the other felt the pull of the engine.

Some of the windows in the passenger cars had been opened to ventilate the car in which they were riding as the summer sun warmed the valley. With the windows open, the sounds of the steam pistons applying power to the drive wheels filled the car. At first it was a slow chug . . . chug . . . chug as the passenger train slowly picked up speed. This was replaced by a rapid choo, choo, choo, as the train arrived at it's cruising speed. T. P. could hear the clickety-clack of the steel wheels passing over the rail couplings.

He had traveled by train only twice before from Chicago to Phoenix when the family moved to Mesa, and from Flowing Well to Phoenix to pick up the cattle and chickens with the boys. He again experienced the comfort of the sounds of a train. It was amazing, he thought, that these noises should be comforting rather than irritating, but their rhythm made them seem cozy and reassuring. He knew the train was traveling at a speed of over fifty miles an hour. An unbelievable speed! He was amazed to see the desert floor next to the train fly by the window while the Chocolate mountains in the distance stood almost motionless.

He moved to the left side of the car as the train passed the almost dry Salton sea where he noticed men working at a salt mine. The vastness of this dry lake bed, the remnants of the fresh water lake that had filled this valley in past ages, filled him with awe. He had seen nothing like it before. Soon the dry lake was out of sight behind him and again endless desert stretched to the distant mountains. The speed of the train slowed slightly as it passed the lowest part of the valley and started it's gradual climb towards the mountains in front of it to the west. As time passed he heard the engine straining as the grade steepened.

It was now noon time and the three passengers were beginning to feel hungry. The conductor who had collected their tickets when they boarded the coach had told them that there was a dining car three cars forward. They found their way to the dining car and sat in a table toward the center of the car. The dining car was well occupied with other passengers. Unoccupied tables were already set with a white tablecloth and fine china and silver. A colored waiter in a gleaming white uniform with a tall chef's hat greeted them, filled the crystal glass in front of them with water and gave them large menus from which to select their lunches. The three of them all agreed that nothing was as elegant or as luxurious as dining on a moving passenger train.

The waiter took their selections from the menu and shortly returned with their orders under beautiful silver covers to keep the food warm. T. P. ate leisurely so as to prolong the pleasure he was experiencing in such luxurious surroundings. He looked out the dining car windows and he noticed the mountains on both sides of the valley were getting closer and closer.

The engine was straining much harder as the grade ahead steepened. Looking ahead, he saw that the train was approaching a narrow pass between two towering snow covered mountains. He arose from his dining table and hurried to the dining car's vestibule the better to see this awe inspiring spectacle. Carrie and Irwin accompanied him to the vestibule to enjoy the view.

"What is this we are seeing" he asked Irwin.

"We are passing between two mountains that are over ten thousand feet high." Irwin replied. "Mount Gorgonio is the mountain on our right. Mount San Jacinto is the mountain on our left. This pass is known as the San Gorgonio Pass and the portion we are now passing through is known as White Water because of the way the white sand flows between the mountains. This is the high desert country and is thirty-five hundred feet above sea level. I've taken this trip a dozen times but never tire of the grandeur of this view. We're passing out of the desert and we'll descend down into the Los Angeles basin on the other side of the pass. The pass widens and continues for about thirty or forty miles at this elevation," he continued.

T. P. was delighted to have someone with him who knew the surrounding country so that he could understand what he was seeing. They returned to their dining table and ordered coffee. As the train continued its journey to Los Angeles, they visited and Irwin commented on the passing landscape, pointing out the small railroad junction of Colton at the foot of the San Bernardino Mountains, Etiwanda, which was George Chaffey's first irrigation project along the base of the San Gabriel Mountains and many other items of interest.

"In Spring," he told T. P. and Carrie "the base of the San Gabriel Mountains are covered with a mantel of the California Golden Poppies. The sight is so beautiful that Cabrillo, the first white man to see it, called it the Lord's altar cloth"

It was early July and the winter rye grass between the mountains was turning brown. During spring the grass was a beautiful green and it looked like a lawn covering all of the flat lands south of the mountains.

On such an interesting trip with such a knowledgeable friend time flew by and soon Irwin was telling him they would be in Los Angeles in less than an hour. T. P. was glad that he had taken Irwin with him as he didn't look forward to finding his way around a large city. Los Angeles had just passed the hundred thousand population mark.

T. P. had decided that they would stay at the Neadeau Hotel at First and Hill Streets. They had reduced their prices since the new elegant Van Nuys Hotel had just opened in the city.

"We'll arrive at the Southern Pacific Arcade Depot at Fifth Street and Central Avenue," Irwin told T. P., "where we'll hire a Handsome Cab since no streetcars run from the depot to downtown L. A. It's not too far from the depot to the Neadeau Hotel. Tomorrow morning it will be only a few blocks to the lumber yards and the hardware stores. The big Barker Brothers furniture store is also only a few blocks away."

T. P. thanked Irwin for removing that queasy feeling of arriving in a strange big city and for all the information about the country side through which the train had passed.

All three arose and left the dining car to return to the passenger car where they had left their suitcases. Presently, the train was slowing to a stop at the Arcade Depot. T. P. was pleasantly surprised at what a large and fine depot it was.

CHAPTER 26

THE CITY OF LOS ANGELES

The weather was perfect. The temperature was in the mid-seventies as compared to temperatures exceeding one hundred and fifteen degrees in the Valley. The air was crystal clear and the mountains to the north formed a crescent in which the city sat. To the south lay a broad flat plane as far as the eye could see.

After the train had stopped and the porter had placed the step stool on the platform beneath the bottom stair of the vestibule steps, the three travelers departed from the train and headed for the main entrance of the depot. When they left the depot, they found themselves on Central Avenue where Fifth Street dead ended into it. There, along Central, was a line of handsome cabs awaiting the arriving passengers. T. P. walked to the first in line and asked the fare to the Nadeau Hotel, which he found reasonable. The driver took their three bags and loaded them into the back of the carriage. With a slap of the reins against the horses flanks by the driver, the carriage started the short drive to the hotel. Upon arrival, T. P. paid the cab driver and their suitcases were unloaded and placed on the Spring Street sidewalk in front of the hotel.

It was now two-thirty. T. P. was amazed by the electric street light fixtures and the hustle and bustle of the intersection. People crowded the sidewalks. Electric streetcars were running on Spring Street. Scores of horses pulling carriages plied the streets between the electric streetcars. Above the streets, electric and telephone wires were strung by the hundreds between telephone poles with five and six crossbars.

The largest building on the block was the hotel which was four stories high. The doorman came and picked up their suitcases and carried them in to the registration desk. They registered and were assigned rooms on the fourth floor.

"Look," T. P. said to the clerk, "I don't want to climb all those stairs each time I go to my room. Give me a room on no higher than the second floor."

"Oh," the room clerk replied, "you won't have to climb any stairs. We have an electric elevator that will take you directly to your floor. The fourth floor is our best location as it is above the dust and noise of this busy intersection if you open your window for ventilation."

T. P. had never seen an "elevator" and wasn't sure he wanted to ride in one. The clerk assured him that it was perfectly safe. The elevator was the first in L. A. and had been operating for fourteen years without any injuries. T. P. thought for a while and decided that he would like to try one of these new fangled gadgets. The bell boy took their suitcases into the elevator and they followed him.

Inside the elevator, when the bellboy closed the safety gate, he was not so sure he had made the right decision. The elevator operator moved his lever to "up" and the car slowly rose passing two floors before arriving at the fourth floor. Why, it wasn't frightening at all. He could hardly wait to tell the boys about this amazing contraption. The safety gate was opened and T. P., Carrie and Irwin followed the bell boy to their rooms. The bellboy unlocked the door, entered, and placed T. P. and Carrie's suitcases on the dresser. After the bellboy had left, T. P. examined the room. He went over to the window and from the forth floor could see the electric street light fixtures and shop signs up and down Spring Street. He then examined the large walk in-closet, and wonder of modern miracles, the private bath room.

After two days of dusty travel and just sponge baths, he needed a good scrubbing in the tub. He drew a hot bath, removed his clothes and hung his one and only suit in the closet. Then, he entered the tub and laid back in the hot water. He didn't realize how tired he was, and as he closed his eyes for what he meant to be but a second, fell sound asleep.

Carrie knew how tired T. P. was and let him sleep. She would wait for her bath till later. She looked longingly at T. P. lying nude in the tub and thought what a fine hard body he had. He didn't have an ounce of fat on his lean and beautifully muscled figure from the many years of hard work he had put in at the hard life of a farmer. His stomach was as hard and flat as a young man of twenty though he was now forty eight years old. Being away from home in a beautiful hotel was a very romantic experience. She knew that T. P. would plead with her to once again have his conjugal rights restored for a night of passionate romance. But she also knew that she could not bear the thought of raising another child, especially on the bleak Imperial Valley frontier.

It was relatively easy to refrain from sex while living in the tent house on the farm with three young boys sleeping on bunks within a few feet of their bed. But what a temptation for a passionate night of romance was this beautiful hotel room in this big city. She knew if he asked she wouldn't have the willpower to say no. Well, so be it. She was forty-four and she knew that the chances of her getting pregnant would be slight. None the less she knew she would be in for several weeks of constant worry.

She also realized that this was going to be a constant problem when the new house was finished and they had their own private bedroom for her desire for T. P. had only increased over the years. Living as brother and sister rather than lovers only increased her passion for him. "Well," she thought, "we will have to face that temptation a day at a time when the time comes."

After an hour and a half she awoke T. P. and told him they had better get ready to go down to the hotel dinning room with Irwin for dinner. T. P. got out of the tub and commented to Carrie what a wonderful thing a bath tub was. It was one thing he definitely planned to have in their new house. Carrie then took a leisurely bath while T. P. put on his only suit and tie. After they both dressed in their best clothes they went to Irwin's room and the three of them went to the hotel dining room together. What a wonderful change this was from the Imperial tent hotel which was the only good dining room in the valley and one they seldom frequented. They spent almost two hours leisurely dining in the elegant hotel dining room.

When they had again returned to their room, it was dark outside. They went to the window to look at the big city at night and were amazed at the lights up and down Spring Street. The people were still moving in droves along the side walk. Horses and carriages filled the street between streetcars moving quickly up and down the street. What a magnificent place was this western metropolis of Los Angeles. They could hardly wait to explore it in the morning.

They hurried to bed so that they could get an early start to the busy day they had ahead of them. As Carrie expected T. P. pleaded for romance in such an exotic atmosphere.

Living the life of farmers, Carrie and T. P. were up with the sun. They hurriedly dressed and went to Irwin's room to have him join them for breakfast. At breakfast, they talked of the order in which they would accomplish their days work. Irwin and T. P. had to go to the lumber yard, the plumbing supply and the hardware store to make arraignments for the various materials necessary for building the new house in the Valley. Carrie would go to the big Barker Brothers furniture store to pick out the furniture for the house.

The city was well served by the electric street cars that crisscrossed it on several north-south and east-west streets. They could get within a few blocks of all their destinations on the street cars.

The California Development Company had arranged with their various suppliers to be prepared to help T. P. and Irwin in their quest for supplies. Surely enough, they were greeted at each place of business by friendly owners as the California Development Company was a large customer of each concern.

At the lumber yard, T. P. and Irwin spent hours choosing the most perfect of lumber and arranging to have it sent by the Southern Pacific Railroad to Flowing Well and then by freight wagon to the site T. P. had chosen for the new house. He was assured by the owner that the lumber would be delivered to the lot within a week. T. P. had the same good fortune at the plumbers supply and at the hardware store. Again, each owner assured them that the building supplies would be promptly delivered to the building site.

Irwin and T. P. had done such a good job writing out specification for each item needed that what could have been a difficult or even a disastrous task went off with marvelous ease. Building a house so far from civilization left no room for forgetting needed items. They felt sure that there would be some things forgotten no matter how hard they tried, but they hoped to keep such problems to a minimum.

They returned to the hotel as the sun was setting in the west. When they went up to T. P.'s room, they found Carrie waiting for them. T. P. was bursting to tell Carrie all that they had accomplished. He found Carrie was just as anxious to tell T. P. about her day shopping for furniture. The excited talk went back and forth between the two with Irwin kibitzing in the conversation in the room, continuing at diner, then again in the room till it was time to go to sleep.

What a wonderful time T. P. and Carrie had anticipating the wonderful new home they would have in Imperial. They say anticipation is as great as realization——and surely it was this night between these two who had been through so much together. They both thought how happy the boys would be after the terrible two years they had spent in the tent house under the ramada shed. The two years had been almost impossible but it had forged this family into a unit that could never be broken.

Before Irwin left for his room, T. P. decided that they would stay another day in Los Angeles to just see the sights. Irwin knew his way around the city and where the different streetcar lines went. He suggested they get up early in the morning and take the streetcar to Santa Monica, a beach city about fifteen miles west of Los Angeles. There had been a Southern Pacific Railroad line that went there that was so popular they changed it into an electric streetcar line just a year or two ago. The streetcars left every thirty minutes from six in the morning till seven in the evening.

"That will be great." T. P. said. "Carrie and I have never seen the Pacific ocean and we've been dying to see it."

"Going to Santa Monica, looking at the ocean, and returning won't take more than four hours." said Irwin. "It'll take an hour each way for the trolley ride and two hours of looking at the ocean will be enough. That will leave the rest of the day to take streetcar rides to some other the new suburbs."

T. P. and Carrie thought that was a marvelous plan for an excursion of the Los Angeles area. Tomorrow they would ride the street cars all around the city so that they could say that they saw more of the city than just the lumber yard and furniture store. The next day they did just that. They awoke early in the morning to get an early start. They hurriedly ate breakfast and then the three of them walked to Temple street where they would catch the Santa Monica streetcar. They were just in time to catch the seven o'clock trolley. The streetcars that ran on the Santa Monica line were magnificent cars, much larger than the trolleys that served the city streets. They ran on the full sized railroad tracks rather than the narrow gage tracks of the inner city lines.

The streetcar soon left the houses and buildings of the city behind. In no time they were traveling through orchards of orange trees and farm land. Just to the north was the Santa Monica mountain range that ended on its east side right at the edge of Los Angeles City. To the south, the land sloped away as a large coastal plain reaching as far as the eye could see.

As they traveled along the streetcar line, they passed dirt roads crisscrossing the ranches and orchards. Interspersed between the orange groves and farms were well kept, attractive, frame farm homes and large red barns. It was easy to see that these were prosperous farms and farmers. After about fifteen minutes of traveling through orchards and farm land, they came to a small town which Irwin told them was Hollywood.

"This is the town," Irwin told them, "where they are making those moving pictures that everyone's been talking about lately."

T. P. and Carrie commented on the beautiful area in which this little town of Hollywood was located, high on the Santa Monica mountain's foothills overlooking the coastal plain below. Next they passed the Sawtelle old soldiers home and cemetery which was nestled among the orchards of orange trees. Then, in just about one hour from leaving the Los Angeles terminal, they came to the terminal of the streetcar line in Santa Monica, high on a palisade overlooking the Pacific ocean. How excited they were as they got their first glance of the blue Pacific. As T. P. and Carrie gazed on the magnificent sight of the waves rolling in from the mighty blue Pacific, they could see a panorama reaching from the Santa Monica mountains to the north, across the broad coastal plain to the Palos Verdes hills far to the south. All this was in pristine condition without man made structures except for the small village of Santa Monica behind them.

As T. P. gazed at this awe inspiring sight, He had no knowledge of his family history reaching back to Epke Jacobse. He did not know that his reaching the blue Pacific ocean completed an odyssey of his line of the Banta family from their arrival in New Amsterdam in 1659 to his arrival at the Pacific Ocean in 1902. This was a journey consuming eight generations and two-hundred and forty three years always on the frontier. What Carrie and he knew was that they had had a long and trying journey from Chicago, Illinois, through Mesa, Arizona Territory, and the Imperial Valley, to reach the beautiful shores of California along side the great Pacific Ocean.

Steps had been built into the side of the two-hundred foot palisade so that people could descend the side of the cliff to the broad white sand beach below. Our three sightseers descended this long stairway to walk on the beach and approach the waters edge. They took off their shoes and stockings and allowed the waves to wash against their feet. After playing along the oceans edge for a half hour, they put their shoes and stockings on again and ascended the steps to the top of the cliff. They spent another thirty minutes looking around the small town of Santa Monica before boarding the streetcar for their return to Los Angeles. In an hour they were back in the big city. It was only eleven A. M. and they still had most of the day to see the other suburbs of the city.

When they arrived back at the Temple street terminal of the Santa Monica streetcar line, Irwin pointed out the majestic Los Angeles high school building which sat high on a hill overlooking the terminal just across the street from the Temple block. It was known as "the big red schoolhouse on the hill," being an architectural wonder of the city. The building was of gothic style, built of red brick set off with attractive white trim over many of its windows. Circular towers protruded from the corners of its roof and on the right front corner was a massive clock tower, which sounded the hours of the day. It was the pride of the city. On their way to catch the next streetcar which would take them to Boyle Heights, a new suburb two miles east of the city, Irwin took them by the new city hall which was built in 1888 in a similar style to the high school. T. P. and Carrie marveled at the beauty of the buildings in this west coast city. Boyle Heights was a new subdivision which was a small city in itself. Large signs were everywhere advertising lots for sale in the various subdivisions. T. P. commented to Carrie that Los Angeles was growing like corn on his ranch and was surely destined to be the metropolis of Southern California.

Returning from their trip to Boyle Heights, the three tourists stopped for lunch at the new Van Nuys hotel. It was the newest and finest hotel in Los Angeles having been built just that year. After an elegant lunch, Irwin told them that he would like to take them out to see the new University of Southern California which opened just sixteen years ago and had a lovely campus three miles south of downtown L. A. A street car would deliver them within two or three blocks of the campus. They decided they would spend the afternoon looking around that section of the city. They took the street car three miles to the point closest to the campus then walked the last three blocks. The main building was of red brick similar to the two previous public buildings they had admired. The front of the main university building had a bell tower to the right of center with gabled windows on either side of the tower. The building, itself, was very large and four stories high. Eucalyptus trees were growing around it, rising from a lovely green lawn. It was summer time and school was not in session though a few students were entering and leaving the building.

After looking around the campus, the three followed signs promoting subdivisions to the north in a neighborhood called the West Adams district. Here they noticed that, contrary to the earlier subdivisions they had seen, the lots were being subdivided into estate sized lots, and the homes being built were very large with some of them being mansions.

"Papa," Carrie said, "there will be a time when we will want, and will be able to afford, a house in Los Angeles so that we can get away from the terrible Valley summer heat. This is the area in which I want us to build that home. It's far enough out of the city and the climate is perfect."

"By God, Carrie," T. P. replied, "once again your absolutely right. When we get the money, we'll plan on building a house right in this area. Then you can get out of the valley during the terrible summer heat."

They had found the part of L. A. they loved and had a goal to work toward. Some day they would build a home in Los Angeles right in this neighborhood. The fertility of the Imperial Valley land would surely fill their pockets with gold if they were willing to put in the sweat to make their efforts pay off. T. P. and Carrie never doubted for an instant that they and the boys had the resolve to reach whatever goal they set for themselves.

It was getting late in the afternoon and all three were weary from the long day of sightseeing so they took the trolley car back to the hotel. The trolley stopped right in front of the hotel and they merely had to cross the street to get to the lobby.

The following morning, they were up bright and early to catch the train back to Flowing Well. The trip back to the ranch was uneventful but they had their wonderful thoughts about the delightful trip to the big city and passed the time recounting to each other the wonders they had seen and the fantastic things they had done. Though they were anxious to get home to the boys, The glamor of the big city made their desert, if possible, even more bleak.

Even so, they were happy to get back to the boys and their tent house, for this working ranch with it's growing crops, cattle, chickens and farm implements was home and home is where the heart is. They also knew that a lovely new modern home in the middle of this inhospitable desert lay just beyond the horizon.

CHAPTER 27

THE VALLEY GETS ITS FIRST

FRAME HOUSE AND ITS FIRST SCHOOL

Within a week and a half, all the supplies needed to build the family's house had been delivered by McCaulley's freighters to the lot T. P. had chosen on Eighth Street next to the Dahlia canal. The building of the house became the talk of the Valley. Irwin proudly began laying out the foundation of red brick and mortar. Many in the valley came out to see what was going on, to kibitz and to look at the plans. This didn't help the building process along but Irwin was so proud of what he was doing that he couldn't resist the temptation of going over every detail with the visitors.

As the work progressed, T. P. and his old friend Tom Beach talked about how nice it would be for them to be neighbors. While at Cameron Lake, Tom Beach and his wife had a baby girl, the first baby born in the Valley. They named the baby girl Cameron after Cameron lake. This was their third girl and increased their family to five. T. P. sold him the lot next to his on Eighth Street just west of the city limits of Imperial in the Banta tract

"By God," Tom Beach said, "I'm going to do it, T. P. We're going to be neighbors. Not only that, but I'll get my house ready before yours and I'll bet you ten dollars on it."

Even though Tom planned a clapboard cottage with no plumbing rather than the city style home T. P. was building, T. P. thought with his head start he had a cinch bet. It was August 30, 1902, and his house was all enclosed. "You're on," he said to Tom. Tom

took the bet seriously and had his building material on his lot in a
very short time. He was building his cottage himself just west of T.
P.'s place on Eighth Street.

Then bad luck fell upon T. P. Irwin broke his hand and there
was no skilled help to be had. Tom moved his family into his new
cottage on the twenty fifth of September while T. P. moved his
family into their new home on the twenty seventh. So the ten-
dollars T. P. had won from Tom by bringing in the first crop for
sale returned to its former owner. T. P. hated to lose the bet but
was partially compensated for the loss by the Imperial Press when
an article in the August 30, 1902, edition commented that his
house was "the most pretentious house in the valley and would be
an ornament in any city." Though the house contained only
fourteen hundred square feet, it brought a touch of civilization to
the valley. It was as unique to the valley pioneers as a house on the
moon would have been to moon beings. In the austere setting of
the Colorado Desert, it almost seemed out of place yet it was warmly
welcomed by those who saw the future in this God-forsaken valley.

Carrie, Papa, and the boys moved into the luxury of the brand-
new house with its running water and sewage disposal through
terra cotta pipes leading to a cesspool but with only the furniture
from the tent house. Carrie didn't want the new furniture from L.
A. delivered until the house was completed and ready for it. What
a delight it was for the Banta family to move from the tiny, dingy
tent to this fine house with its broad screened verandas. This was
truly pioneering in luxury. The icing was put on the cake for the
family when the freighter wagon delivered all the new furniture
Carrie had picked out on her trip to the big city. It was the dream
of their lifetime to have a real city house just a few miles from their
own farm.

Papa decided he would landscape his house with greenery similar to that surrounding any city house. From his former life as a
farmer, he loved growing-things and he loved to putter around his
garden. He not only had horticultural knowledge, he had a green
thumb. Every thing he planted turned a lush green and grew in

abundance. In the yard around the house, he planted a Bermuda grass lawn, shade trees close to the house and citrus trees surrounding the shade trees. All of a sudden, on the edge of this dusty, insufferably hot, dry desert town, a green oasis had sprung up and promised a beautiful future to those who would persevere the dreadful days the pioneers were presently enduring. This little plot of lush greenery was the talk of the city of Imperial and was shown to all prospective settlers.

Al and George Banta stand with the Dahlia Canal in front of them and the first frame house in the valley on Eighth Street, Imperial, behind them

IMPERIAL

"Water is King   Here is its Kingdom."

IMPERIAL, CAL., SATURDAY, JULY 16, 1904

AN IMPERIAL HOME

RESIDENCE OF JUDGE AND MRS. T. P. BANTA.

Above is a picture of what is some-times called the first "house" in the Imperial Valley, the habitations that had preceded it being little more than tents, or shacks. The people who had the good taste to build this are Judge their home. It is 28x40 feet in size, containing five principal rooms be-sides porches, baths, etc., and is hand-somely surrounded by lawns, flowers, and ornamental trees. The picture shows Mrs. Banta and some of the ...

FRONT PAGE OF THE IMPERIAL PRESS
JULY 16, 1904
Recovered from microfiche

T. P.'s great grandchildren, Ted and Michelle, stand in front
of the first house in the Imperial Valley in October, 1996

The new frame house was something new and interesting to
the Cocopah Indians who worked on the canals and as farm labor
on the valley farms. Prior to the canal's bringing water to the Imperial Valley, no indigenous people lived in the valley as it was so
barren and inhospitable. The Cocopah Indians were from Mexico
south of where the Colorado river flowed in it's self made levies.
There, the river formed its current delta flowing into the Gulf of
California. Thus, there was ample water and luxurious greenery to
support their existence. The Company hired the Cocopah Indians
to work on the canals and it is doubtful that enough labor could
have been recruited to build the irrigation project without their
help. The pioneers also used the Indians as farm labor. Relations
between the races were excellent since the company and the pioneers were reclaiming land useless to the Cocopahs and providing
salaries for their labor.

The Indians working on the canals and farms around the new
frame Banta house were intrigued by this new hogan made out of
bricks and lumber in a fashion no Indian had seen before. They

marveled at the greenery surrounding it that was so carefully tended. They were used to the ramadas, tents and clapboard cottages of the settlers but what was this imposing structure in which this family was living? They meant no harm but their curiosity got the better of them and occasionally an Indian would walk up to a window, cup his hands, and look inside to see how the white man lived in such a dwelling surrounded by greenery. This always made Mama nervous when she was alone in the house during the day so she would take the shotgun down from over the stove and hold it in her hands. Eventually, the Indian would have satisfied his curiosity and would leave. After the Indian had left, Carrie would then replace the shotgun over the stove and would feel foolish for her moment of fear, but then she would assure herself that prudence had been the better part of valor.

The Banta ranch grew bigger as T. P. purchased land from neighbors who had had enough of desert living especially in light of Circular #9; and therefore they sold their adjoining property to T. P. at an advantageous price. With the crisis brought about by the Department of Agriculture's Circular No. 9, frightened farmers were selling out cheap, and T. P. was one of the few buyers. The Imperial Land Company was playing up each evidence of the remaining farmers' faith in the future of the valley. The newspaper, which was actually a sales promotion vehicle of the company, was delighted to write articles about T. P.'s building a permanent frame dwelling, as it showed the family's dedication to the future of the valley.

Tom Beach, Mobley Meadows and T. P. continued their close friendship. The first weekend in September, while the homes of T. P. and Tom were nearing completion, the three men decided to take their families for a short vacation on the banks of the Salton in old Mexico. Tom, his wife and family including his baby daughter, Cameron, the first baby girl born in the valley, Mobley, his wife and family and T. P., Carrie, and their three boys went by wagon across the scorching desert til they reached a reasonably sandy beach on the edge of the Salton. Mesquit forests covered the landscape leading up to the Salton in Mexico and offered shade as well as cooking wood for the campers. Camping out was no new adventure to these frontier families, but the breeze off the water and the green growth on the banks of the Salton made the surroundings most hospitable and comfortable.

Al Banta had always been blessed with a keen eye when sighting across the sight of a rifle or pistol. His friends considered him to be a crack shot. Al had heard the many tales of the heroic acts of Mr. Meadows when he had been a side kick of Wyatt Earp in Yuma. He had seen Mobley Meadows shoot a silver dollar out of the air with his rifle at valley picnics. No question, Mobley Meadows was his hero and superstar. Now, here he was, spending a weekend in his company. Mobley took to Al as he recognized Al's talent with a rifle or pistol. He spent hours with Al giving him pointers which improved his skill as a marksman. Al almost jumped out of his skin with joy when he finely squarely hit a silver dollar in mid air with his rifle shortly before the families headed the wagons for home Sunday afternoon. The word that he hit a silver dollar in mid air made him a celebrity with his pals in the Valley.

The families brought back a sack full of quail; flocks of them were so numerous down at the Salton that you could almost get them with a club. Quail was the cuisine on the dinner tables of their many friends in the valley for the next few days.

THE FIRST GRAMMAR SCHOOL

With September arriving, school was foremost on the minds of the families with children of school age. For the Banta, Gillette and Van Horn families, who had arrived in the fall of 1900, and early January, 1901, their children had no formal schooling for a full school year. T. P. rallied the early valley settlers at a meeting at the Cameron Lake construction camp. At this meeting he told these pioneers that they had to make arrangements to have schooling available for the children by the 1901-02 school year starting in September. He told them that he had been trained as a teacher at Valipariso University in Indiana, and, as a past teacher, he recognized the great disadvantage at which their children would be placed if the matter was not resolved immediately

"We're here on the frontier," T. P. said, "to make a better life for our families, but how can our children have a better life without an education. Folks, our first duty is to our children. We have to start now to arrange to have a grammar school ready by September if they're not to miss another year of school. We must make arrangements to hire a very good teacher who has the potential of becoming a Superintendent of Schools in the valley when the valley grows as we know it must."

Everyone agreed. The Gillette and Van Horn families were large with many children of grammar school age. Tom Beach and Mobley Meadows also had children of school age as did other settlers from up north around and in the City of Imperial. The meeting had brought up an urgent matter whose time had come. Right there at the meeting they established the first committee to assure a teacher would be hired in time for the Fall school term. After examining the qualifications of those interested in the position, it was decided to hire Professor J. E. Carr, who later did become the first county Superintendent of Schools in the Imperial Valley. They also hired a young lady assistant teacher to help teach the school.

September came and the teachers were ready, but as yet, no school room had been constructed. T. P. rounded up the menfolk in the south end of the valley and some from up north in Imperial. He convinced them that since the largest number of school children lived in the south, which was the demographic center of children of school age, the school should be in the south of the valley. The families decided that the school should be built where the Dahlia Canal met the Main Canal. This was but a short distance from where the Banta Ranch was located.

In early September the men met early one morning to construct the structure that would serve as the first school in the valley. They proceeded to collect arrowweed from around Cameron Lake as well as cast off lumber and Mesquite limbs. They delivered this building material with their wagons to the banks of the main canal about five miles northwest of Calexico and five miles south of Imperial where they planned to construct the school.

It took the men about eight hours to erect a ramada shed (a roof with no walls) with a tent next to it. The ramada shed was about thirty feet long and about fifteen feet wide and was supported by six poles. The two center poles were slightly higher than the poles at each end causing each side to slope down from the center. Under this shed they placed hand-made benches and tables at which the children would sit. Next to the ramada shed they raised a moderate sized tent. Because of the weather, school would be conducted in the open shed most of the school year. During the incredible sand storms that often lasted several days, the school was closed. When it was too cold or during the very occasional rain storms the classes would move inside the tent. This was the valley's first grammar school! Fifty pupils enrolled for the first year though only about twenty-five attended regularly. Many of the pupils had to walk five miles or more to the school. Frontier living required work and chores by every member of the family simply to survive. Thus when work on the various farms required it, children would have to miss one or more class sessions.

The families had only provided for a grammar school. A high school at this point in the valley's history was out of the question. Earl had graduated from eighth grade in Mesa and since there was no high school, much to T. P. and Carries dismay, he had to miss school and continue working with Papa. He spent much of his time working on the family farm and acting as foreman since Papa was now in the real estate business.

Professor Carr, or his alternate teacher, Miss Glaskill, taught all eight grades. In the first school picture, in which Professor Carr did not appear, Miss Glaskill and her aid were the only ones wearing shoes. All twenty-three students in the picture were barefooted.

This schoolhouse was used until the 1904-1905 school year when a frame school building was constructed. Miss Mame McWilliams And Miss Lotteridge became the teachers. In the 1905 school year, the student body had grown to 113 students.

When the first school house opened September 8, 1901, George Banta was the youngest child in the school being six years old. Many mornings, as George and his brother, Al, walked to school alongside the Dahlia canal, they had contests to see which one could kill the most rattlesnakes. Usually, Al, who was six years older than George, won the contest, but one day George flung the door to the house open to shout to Mama that he had won the snake contest that day, killing five rattlers. Carrie squealed with delight then reached down and gave him a big hug, telling him what a wonderful snake killer he was.

The teacher was a strict but good teacher and every pioneer parent of each pioneer child backed the teacher one hundred percent. Woe to the child who had to take a note home reporting laziness, or worse yet, unacceptable deportment. If a pupil reported that Professor Carr had whipped him with a hickory stick he would get a second whipping at home for exasperating the good professor to the point where he lost his temper. Mr. Carr lost his temper at least a dozen times a day. Lessons were to be learned and were learned despite the primitive teaching facilities.

The teacher taught all eight grades and had a unique method of teaching arithmetic. When a problem was put on the slate at the front of the ramada shed, every child from the oldest to the youngest tried to work the problem out. Of course the oldest ones were asked to answer the question first and then explain how they arrived at the answer. If the oldest couldn't give the answer the next youngest was asked for the answer and if he or she couldn't solve the problem, the next youngest was asked and so on down the line of children by age until one could give the answer and show how to solve the problem. If no one could answer, the teacher would once again go over how the problem was solved. Thus, each younger student saw over and over how computations were done.

One day the teacher put a problem on the slate that none of the older children could solve. Eventually the teacher arrived at little George and asked him for the answer. He, of course, didn't have the slightest notion of how to arrive at the answer, so he just guessed. And, wonder of wonder, out of the millions of possible answers he guessed right! "Right," said the teacher. Then, knowing he had just guessed, the teacher did not ask him to explain how he arrived at the answer. But, instead, shamed the rest of the class by telling them that only the smallest in the class could answer a question that all of them should have been able to answer. Little George beamed to get such recognition and could hardly wait to get home to tell his mother that he was smarter than his older brother. Carrie once again squealed with delight, and, telling little George how smart he was, gave him a big hug.

Earl and Al chaffed at this attention George was getting, and, to their minds, unjustly so. The older boys called George "mother's pet" and other unprintable names, at which, little George would run to Carrie and tell her that the older boys were picking on him. Carrie, of course, would chastise Earl and Al telling them they must not bully their baby brother. This did not go down well with the two older brothers. At first, they argued with their mother that she was showing favoritism to George since he was the baby of the family. Carrie refused to listen for she felt certain she was treating all of her boys in a fair manner.

Since they got nowhere pleading with Mama, they decided they would have to take matters into their own hands. They lured George into the barn behind the house. Here they had set a rickety box on a table. From the rafter they had hung a rope with a hangman's noose just high enough above the rickety box for George to stand with the noose around his neck. They would show Mama's darling not to tell stories on his older brothers. They tied a gag across his mouth and strung him up. Then they ran out of the barn as fast as their legs could carry them.

Inside the house, Carrie heard muffled squeals and thought one of the horses had fallen and hurt itself. She dropped what she was doing and ran to the barn to see little George doing a balancing act on the rickety box and squealing like a pig in spite of the gag. Carrie ran back to the house and got a butcher knife, then, standing on a bale of hay, cut the rope and grabbed George as he collapsed into her arms. This time the older boys' chastisement was beyond her abilities and so papa delivered the lecture and punishment.

The first school in the Imperial Valley, 1901.
George and Al indicated by "X"

Earl and Al decided that if they were to give George his just deserts, they would have to punish him in a different fashion. George was leery of going into the barn with his brothers but they were so nice to him the next couple of weeks that he let his guard down and when they told him they had found a nest of baby mice in the barn, he wanted to see them so badly that he again went into the barn with them. The temperature was at least one hundred and fifteen degrees in the barn. This time they grabbed George and wrapped him inside a large old wool rug for which T. P. had traded something or other. Again, as soon as Earl and Al had left, George started screaming and once again Mama came to the rescue. This time T. P. really laid the law down to Earl and Al. He told them that if George had died of these foolish pranks, their lives would be ruined and, worse, they would never forgive themselves. This time he got through to them, and both boys promised each other to never do anything so thoughtless again. As a matter of fact the boys became good friends and enjoyed doing their chores together.

About two months after the rug incident, Earl and George had been watering the fields from the canal. They had driven the horses and wagon about a mile up the canal from the barn when the sun got low in the west and it was quitting time.

"George," Earl said, "I'd sure like to take a ride spread eagle on the back wheel, but I'm not sure you've forgiven me for those bad things that Al and I did to you and you'll whup the horses up till they're going so fast I'll be thrown off."

Spread, eagle was a ride they loved to do. It was like a ride at a carnival. The spread eagle rider would spread his legs and put one foot between two spokes of the wagon wheel and the other foot between two spokes about three spokes apart. He, then, would grab two spokes on the opposite side of the wheel with his two hands about three feet apart. This made him spread eagle on the wheel. As the wheel turned slowly around, it provided a wonderful spinning ride for the spread eagle rider.

"Heck, Earl," George said, "we're the best of friends now and I wouldn't do anything to spoil things so's they went back to the way they were before."

"Promise?" Earl said.

"Promise!" said George.

With this, Earl firmly fixed himself to the rear wheel of the wagon. George started the horses slowly till Earl was getting a good ride. Then, HE WHUPPED THE HORSES UP AS FAST AS THEY COULD GO! Earl was spinning on the wheel till he was just a blur. He hung on as long as he could, and then, like a boy doing the fastest cartwheels you've ever seen, flew off the wheel and cartwheeled across the desert at a remarkable speed till he collapsed in a heap. George drove the team and wagon over to where Earl lay. Earl was in a complete daze with blood coming from his ears, nose, eyes and mouth from the centrifugal force driving the blood into his head. George got down from the wagon and helped Earl to his feet.

"Let's call it even," George said.

CHAPTER 28

FRONTIER JUSTICE AND GRANDMA
ALLEN ENTER THE BANTA FAMILY'S LIFE

By the third quarter of 1902 the world was the Banta family's oyster. They had one of the largest and most successful active ranches in the Valley. T. P. was THE real estate man in Imperial and the only one running regular weekly ads in the Imperial Press. When it came to buying or selling farmland, his was the name that came to everyone's mind. He had also opened two tracts of land for subdivisions: one in Calexico and the other just west of the city of Imperial's west city limits at Eighth Street. The family was growing wealthy from his real estate business. The first grammar school had been opened and two of his three boys were back in school. They had completed and moved into one of the two first frame dwellings in the Valley. The Imperial Press had called their new home the most impressive home in the Valley and in the December 20, 1902 edition devoted the entire last page of the paper to a picture of their new house over the caption, "T. P. BANTA'S COTTAGE AT IMPERIAL."

In the fall of 1902, unnoticeable, like the tiniest speck on the horizon, the very first precursor of a terrible tragedy that would almost destroy the Imperial Valley was taking place along the banks of the Colorado River. Rockwood and his crew had won in the fight with George Chaffey for control of the California Development Company in the board room and on paper. But they had lost something far more important, his knowledge of the headgates

and canal system he had created. Rockwood's men thought that
the headgate installed at Hanlon's Landing by George Chaffey was
not low enough to admit sufficient water for the new farms during
the low cycle of the river. They, therefore, dredged an opening
around the gate known as a "by-pass." Through this narrow by-
pass they were able to get sufficient water to satisfy their contracts
with the valley farmers with crops in the field.

They would close this by-pass in spring, well before the floods
that arrived in the warm months caused by the melting of the
snows in Idaho, Wyoming and Montana, thus no harm would be
caused. It was obvious that this was a dangerous and expensive
procedure and that a deeper gate should be constructed as priority
number one. The California Development Company had no money
available for this imperative construction. They had to sell new
water stock to stay afloat financially. As new settlers purchased
water stock, they demanded new ditches to bring the river water
to their farms. The cutting of the by-pass was repeated in 1903
and 1904.

The irony of the situation was that years later it was discovered that the Chaffey gate was two feet lower than it appeared to
be to the Rockwood gang. Sand boards two feet wide had been left
in the gate according to Chaffey's plans which could be removed
at low water. Silt settling against these boards had given a false
bottom to the gate. Had these boards been known about and removed there would have been ample water and the future tragedy
awaiting the valley might have been avoided. Because T. P. new
nothing about the by-pass or its potential danger, this ominous
storm arising far to the south east along the banks of the Colorado
River could not cause him alarm. To his knowledge things couldn't
have been going any better.

As the year 1902 ended and the year 1903 began, two new
developments would impact on the Banta family's life. One would
make a substantial difference on their social stature in the Valley.
The other would change their mode of living. The first factor that
would influence the family's stature in the valley was the fact of

life that as an area becomes populated, the political arena must emerge. Each citizen in a frontier colony had to examine his talents to see where he might fit into an office where he could help govern the community. The second factor that would impact the day to day living of the family resulted from letters that Mama received from her family back in Lansing, Michigan, in September of 1902. The letters informed her that her mother was terminally sick and that if she wished to see her before she died she must plan to visit her within the next few weeks.

The death of her mother would evoke another unique problem, for her mother was caring for her own mother, Grandma Allen, who was Carrie's grandmother. Grandma Allen was ninety three years old and in good health. The problem was that when Carrie's mother died, Grandma Allen would have no place to go. T. P. insisted that, when the time came Grandma Allen should come to live with them now that they had their lovely new comfortable home. There was no big government to take over the responsibility of old folks. In those days families took care of their own and would have it no other way.

As to politics, T. P. considered where he might best serve the community. Although the county seat, San Diego, was only a little more than seventy miles away from Imperial Valley as the crow flies, with the rugged coastal mountains as a barrier, it might as well have been three hundred miles away. As far as law and order were concerned, the county court system was of no value to the valley. The valley relied on the police court, the Justice of the Peace, to meet out frontier justice to transgressors of the law, as had frontiersmen in previous frontier lands.

T. P. was one of the few college educated men in the valley. As such, his many friends encouraged him to run for the office of Justice of the Peace in 1902. Uncle Solomon, the first Banta with a higher education, was his guiding star. Uncle Solomon's being Mayor of Eaton, Illinois, did not impress T. P. nearly as much as his having been the Justice of the Peace. Forever after he had that elected position and title, everyone had referred to Uncle Solomon as Judge Banta. In politics, T. P. decided that the position of Justice of the Peace was the place where he would be most effective. Up until the elections in November 1902, the position of Justice of the Peace was an appointed position. The incumbent no longer wanted to serve; and therefore, the office would be open and would not be opposed by an incumbent. At the Republican convention, his friends put his name up for nomination and he was nominated for that office.

Because the Imperial Valley was then a part of San Diego County, the ballots had to be printed by the County, in the City of San Diego. Hence, the names of those nominated by the Republican convention were transmitted to the county officials in San Diego. Through some error, T. P.'s name was not listed under the office of Justice of the Peace, but, instead was listed under the office of Constable. T. P soon discovered that a transpositional error had been made. T. P.'s friend, F. G. Havens, who had been nominated for the position of Constable, discovered his name had been printed under the office of Justice of the Peace as a candidate for that office. This error caused great consternation in the minds of T. P. and H. G. Havens as each neither felt qualified nor wanted to serve in the office under which his name appeared. To say they were both distraught would be an understatement. They were furious! But the die had been cast and there was no way new ballots could be printed by the County and brought to Imperial in time for the election. The two men decided that their only hope was to take out an ad in the Imperial Press in an effort to start a write-in campaign to correct the typographical error. Thus, the following advertisement appeared in the November 1, 1902, issue.

IMPERIAL PRESS. November 1, 1902.

(Advertisement.)

For Justice of the Peace

T. P. BANTA

For Constable

F. G. HAVENS

When you vote on Tuesday be sure and write these
names in the 'Blank Column' exactly as they appear above.

The above is the way the nominations for those offices were made at the convention and there are excellent reasons why you should vote that way. Through some mistake in the County Clerk's office or else through ignorance on the part of the parties who certified the nominations to him, the Clerk has had the names printed just the reverse on the ballot and each one claims he will not qualify for the office for which their names appear on the ballot.

As is usually the case, the write-in campaign didn't work. Since the election was held November 7, voters became confused or didn't read the write-in advertisement, resulting in the following outcome of the election carried in the November 8 edition of the Imperial Press.

"Election in the Valley. A Republican Victory, No License, Win in all Districts."

"For Justice of the Peace of Imperial township the two precincts, Imperial and Silsbee, gave T. P. Banta 14, I. W. Van Dorn 15 and F. G. Havens 24, giving F. G. Havens a plurality of 9.

For Constable, A. W. Patton, the present incumbent, received 35 votes in the two precincts and F. G. Havens and T. P. Banta 6 each, giving Patton a clear majority of 13."

Thus, because of an error in printing the ballots, T. P. lost the election and H. G. Havens was elected to an office he neither desired nor felt qualified to serve. None the less, H. G. Havens agreed to serve as Justice of the Peace for the following year and next November T. P. could run for the office of Justice of the Peace with his name properly listed as a candidate for that office. Both men were, of course, disappointed but the injustice caused by the error in the County Clerk's office, or by those who certified the nominations to him, would be rectified in a year.

T. P. returned to spending his full time on his many other

activities, but especially his real estate business. The January 24, 1903 issue of the Imperial Press under "The Valley News," contained the following comment, "T. P. Banta, the real estate man, treated his office building to a new coat of paint."

In early October 1902, Carrie received an urgent call to come home to her mother's bedside. She stayed with her for some four months during her mother's lingering death. After the funeral, It became Carrie's task to bring her aged Grandmother Allen, to her home in the Imperial Valley. The following article appeared in the Imperial Press, January 24th, 1903.

> Mrs. T. P. Banta has returned home from an extended
> visit to her old home in Lansing, Michigan, where she was
> called some four months ago by the illness of her mother,
> who passed this world while she was at home. Mrs. Banta
> was accompanied on her way back by her aged grandmother,
> who is now nearly 93 years old. Mrs. Allen stood the trip
> remarkably well for one of her age, and is enjoying this
> beautiful climate immensely. It is needless to say that Mr.
> Banta is wearing the pleasantest of smiles.

The train ride from Lansing to Flowing Well was no strain on the old lady, but there was no way to get grandma from Flowing Well to the Banta home in Imperial other than by wagon across the thirty some miles of desert where no roads existed other than well rutted wagon tracks. Thank providence that the journey occurred in January as the trip might have proven lethal during the scorching hot months of the year. The old lady was as tough as a buzzard and enjoyed the trip immensely.

Papa brought his spring buggy to provide her and Mama the most comfortable trip possible. He tried to make the trip interesting for grandma by describing the points of interest as they passed them by but found there was little reason to carry on a conversation. Grandma Allen was as deaf as a doorknob. Another point he found most interesting was that the old lady smoked a corn cob pipe incessantly, tapping out the ashes and refilling with new tobacco as soon as one cob-full was used up. She should, he thought, do very well here on the frontier. Though none of the women in the valley smoked a pipe, none of them claimed to be high society either.

When they arrived at the Banta home, the boys greeted grandma Allen warmly, all three trying to hug and kiss her at the same time. Perhaps they would not have been so exuberant had they known of Papa's plans for putting up grandma. He and Mama had decided that George would give up his room for grandma's use. All three boys would share the same bedroom while grandma would have a room to herself. Earl and Al already felt crowded. Now they would have to share their bedroom with little George.

This was the least of the changes that were brought about by grandma's joining the family. Grandma claimed that she was unable to walk by herself and required someone from the family to help her up and escort her to where-ever she needed to go. This usually was to the toilet, the dinner table or to bed. The rest of the time she sat in her rocker in the front room and stitched on the crosspatch quilt she currently had in construction. If she needed anything from a glass of water to another pouch of tobacco for her pipe or more thread and material for her quilt, she would call on a member of the family to get it for her. This would usually be one of the boys if they were present or Mama if they were not.

The biggest change was to Carrie's life during the next five years til grandma departed this world. Prior to grandma's joining the family, Carrie had been a very social person, entering into the various ladies groups in the Valley. Since grandma needed constant attention, Carrie found herself house bound until the boys came in from their chores or from school. Being normal boys, they were none too enchanted at the prospect of sitting with grandma.

One day when necessity required grandma's being left alone because of other pressing duties by each other member of the family, George was the first to return, hurrying to make sure grandma was not left alone any longer than necessary. For some reason George decided to look in the window to see how grandma was getting along before going inside. To his utter amazement, he saw grandma walking to the cooler, opening it and removing a bottle of milk, and then going to the cupboard and retrieving a glass and then pouring herself a glass of milk. While he watched, she drank the glass of milk, then washed the glass and put it away. Then she put the milk back in the cooler leaving no sign that she had ever been out of her chair.

When Carrie returned, George called Mama aside and related how grandma had been pulling their legs, acting so enfeebled. Carrie told George that he must keep this to himself and not confront his aged grandmother with what he had seen. Mama said that it would not do to embarrass the old lady. So the charade continued but George couldn't keep this juicy secret from his brothers. When they were acting as grandma's sitters, they would pretend some urgent task so that they could go outside and peer in the window to see grandma get out of her chair to get something she wanted. This walking by their pseudo-crippled grandma caused them uncontrolled mirth with big belly laughs and much rolling on the ground. Grandma never heard any of this raucous laughter since, as we have informed you, she was deaf as a doorknob.

Grandma Allen was delighted with the wonderful winter weather that greeted her entrance to valley living. The cold, snowy, icy winter weather she had left in Lansing was hard on her rheumatism and other aches and pains acquired over ninety-three years of living. The chilly mornings and warm days that greeted her in Imperial reminded her of the wonderful spring days back home. She had lived much of her life on the frontier. Living in the big city had come about later in her life and, she was not quite comfortable with it.

She had never seen or imagined a place as stark and as desolate as the Imperial Valley, but being a pioneer most of her life, she welcomed change. She just wished she could go out and roam about the great wide-open spaces, but she was just too old and confined mainly to sitting in her rocking chair sewing on her quilts, smoking her pipe and looking at the four walls of the front room.

She worried about how she pampered herself at the expense of her grand-daughter's family, but she felt she deserved the pampering after the hard life she had lived and then being passed back and forth between her children and grandchildren in the last few years of her life. At the same time she was thankful for the loving care she was given by T.P., Carrie and the boys. Papa was always sure that she had the little things that made her life worthwhile. He always made sure she had thread and material for her sewing; and, though, she knew her pipe smoking embarrassed the family, he always made sure she had plenty of tobacco for her pipe. Back East, on the frontier, many pioneer women smoked pipes, but she noticed that these Western pioneer women had never taken up the vice.

One day when T. P. brought her a new pouch of tobacco, she said to him, "Son, though I've smoked for neigh on seventy-five years, don't buy me any more tobacco. I'm giving up the pipe."

"Why in the world would you want to do that," T. P. asked. "It's one of the few pleasures you have left."

"Because," said Grandma Allen, "it isn't ladylike." With that, grandma threw away her pipe and never smoked again, giving up a habit of a lifetime because she thought it embarrassed the family.

With sacrifices on both sides, grandma Allen became a part of the Banta family. T. P., Carrie and the boys no longer thought of the five of them. When they thought of the family, they thought of the six of them. Having grandma join the family was like when a new baby enters the family. Life changes as does the entire personality of the family. Contrary to society today, on the frontier family was everything. That feeling of family was the security net, not big government. People's lives were inconvenienced but there was a compensation for the inconveniences. Family really meant family, and welfare consisted of family love.

At the same time, one hand washes the other. While the Banta Family was good for Grandma Allen, Grandma Allen turned out to be a real asset to the Banta family. T. P. continued to worry about all the time he had put into the tract that John Leighton had entered under the Desert Land Act. He wanted to be sure it was his, yet he could not have the entry assigned to him while the patent was still being perfected, as he had used his entry privilege under the act. He had to wait until after the patent was finalized and then acquire title to the deed issued to John Leighton.

Grandma Allen had never used her entry right so there was no reason why the entry by John Leighton couldn't be assigned to her. Carrie was her sole heir so even if she were to pass away prior to perfecting the title, the land would be left to the family. T. P. decided to press the issue and succeeded in having the entry assigned to her on August 25, 1902. On that date John Leighton signed a contract stating,

> I, John F. Leighton, of Los Angeles county, State of California, for value received, hereby assign, transfer and set over to Margaret Allen of Imperial County, State of California, all interest acquired by me by virtue of that certain Desert Land Entry made by me on the 17th day of May, 1900 . . .

There was no question after that date that the land the family had worked so hard to develop would be theirs no matter what the composition of the management of the California Development Company. Ownership of the tract was safely in the family. All that was needed now was to for her to file final proof with the United States Land Office which she did on October 28, 1903. T. P. and Tom Beach acted as her witnesses "that said land has been properly irrigated and reclaimed in the manner required by law . . ."

Notice of intention to make proof was published in the Imperial Press once a week for the following six weeks as required by law. The paper carried a news article which said that at 93 years of age, she was the oldest person to file final proof to that date. She probably still owns the record.

For the next five years, until grandma passed on, there was a family of six. During those five years, grandma required the family focus just as much as if a new baby had been born. Grandma was not only a common object of annoyance and inconvenience but more importantly a common object of love.

In politics, the year sped by and soon the election of November 1903, was upon the people of the Valley. Once again The Republican convention nominated T. P. for Justice of the Peace. This time the ballots were printed correctly and T. P. easily won the election. He was delighted with his new office, and though the mix up eliminated historians from referring to him as the first elected Justice of the Peace in the Valley, that was the only disadvantage the lost year had cost him.

T. P. was correct in his assumption that he would assume the nick name of Judge by those in the Valley. From the day he was elected til the time of his death, all his friends called him Judge Banta. And he was a very good judge, fair in his decisions but firm in his sentencing. Everyone admired his dedication to this office. He was justice on this the last frontier in the contiguous United states. The Imperial Press devoted many articles to his decisions and actions in the Valley. Below are several articles chosen at random indicating how a frontier court met out frontier justice and the respect with which a police judge was held when preforming his various duties in the early days of the Imperial Valley.

THE IMPERIAL PRESS

April 1904

Justice Court Matters

The Tribunal of His Honor Justice Banta was the center of excitement, Friday and Saturday in disposing of the cases of six male defendants charged with various offenses in connection with whiskey selling and disorderly houses.

Two of the six pleaded guilty and were let off with $20 and $25 fines. The others fought stubbornly and "got it in the neck." They all had jury trials but no attorneys.

All were found guilty and punished as follows: Webb $250 fine and 6 months imprisonment: Frank Goar $100 fine; Antonio Abril $100 fine: Aat Reeder (recommended for mercy by jury) $25 fine. All four were taken Sunday (their Sabbath day's journey) by Constable Taggart to San Diego and there safely deposited in the county bastile until again called for.

A funny incident happened in the aftermath. Unwise friends of defendant Webb announced an intention of rescuing him from the local jail. To guard against this Justice Banta sent down Mr. Charlebois armed with a Winchester. Afterwards Constable Taggart, not knowing of this, took the same precaution and went down with another man to guard. The two found the first man there, and each supposed the other a rescuing party. Charlebois was the best armed, however, and the others retired in good order for reinforcements. When they got up town they met the Judge who hearing of the difficulty explained matters and the war ended.

April 1904

Priest—Clark Nuptials"

Imperial was pleasantly surprised Wednesday by the marriage of two of its most popular young people, Mr. Archie Priest and Miss Margaret S. Clark. Mr. Priest is a partner in the firm of Hawes & Co. Miss Clark, is the sister of our popular businessman. Wilber Clark. She is also prominent in business circles, having been our first postmistress, and school trustee.

The ceremony was performed by Justice T. P. Banta at the home of the bride's brother, in the presence only of Mr. Havens and Mr. Clark. Judge Banta performed the ceremony in his usual felicitous manner, Not forgetting the perquisite of his office. After the ceremony refreshments were served, and the happy couple departed by the 1:20 train for Coronado, whence after a fortnight's stay they will return to make their home in Imperial. The best wishes of a host of friends go with them.

July 2, 1904

Judge Banta has brought back from Calexico, where he has been pasturing his favorite 4-year-old sorrel runner, "Clip Springer," who can do time in a way to make a long road look like thirty cents. He weighs about 1,050, is a kindly dispositioned animal, and is from the celebrated Marcus Daly stock, the sire being imported by Mr. Banta.

July, 1904

Robbery Charged

John Doe Falkenburg was arrested Sunday by Deputy Constable Jacob Meadows, charged by George Miller with robbery. Miller slept Saturday night outside a tent near the big corral down Eighth street, and when he awoke found that $28.50 was gone from his pockets. He claimed that after awakening, defendant came and went through his pockets again but failed of results, as the original sum was the "demnition total" of his assets. Judge Banta heard the charge Monday morning on preliminary examination, and dismissed the prisoner for lack of evidence. Miller was in too hilarious a condition to know what was happening to him, and it was just as likely to be a blind pig as anything else that got the money.

IMPERIAL VALLEY NEWS. December 1, 1904.

(A New Newspaper Published in Brawley.)

Brawley.

Judge Banta from Imperial was the auctioneer Tuesday and sold everything in sight.

IMPERIAL VALLEY NEWS. December 8,1904

Imperial.

Justice Banta sent six men over the road yesterday. One got 60 days for stealing, one 60 days for carrying concealed weapons; Four, 25 days each for stealing railroad ties and burning them.

With the matter of Justice of the Peace rectified, T. P. joined the other men in the Valley in solving other pressing political problems, first most of which was the incorporation of Imperial as a city of the sixth class. This, the men of Imperial decided would be their next major political goal of 1904.

CHAPTER 29

1903—1904, THE END OF THE

BEGINNING AND ALMOST

THE BEGINNING OF THE END

1903 was the Year that marked the end of the beginning of making The Imperial Valley an inhabitable farming community. Much of the ground work had been done and much completed during the year. It could no longer be said that the valley was a desert. Canals crisscrossed much of it. In April 1903, the total acreage in crop was about 25,000 acres. Much more acreage was ready for crop, but the 700 miles of canals built at that time was incapable of satisfying the demand and the Development Company was unable to raise the money for the building of the necessary new canals.

Through every means possible, such as selling water stock in batches to investors at vastly reduced prices and borrowing by pledging company property, the company had increased the number of ditches opened to water. By the winter of 1903, more than 100,000 acres were put into crops and the population of the valley had grown from 4,000 at the beginning of the year to 7,000 that winter.

The company, being in disastrous financial condition, had no money to improve the Imperial townsite. Townspeople were becoming impatient with the townsite company for not providing means to irrigate lawns, grow trees and gardens. Except for the buildings, the town of Imperial was exactly the same as it was in 1900. The townspeople were becoming aware of the terrible financial condition of both the California Development Company and it's subsidiary, the Imperial Land Company. They were discovering that if they wanted things to be done they must wean themselves away from the company and find other means of accomplishing them.

Road dust was becoming such a problem, that the Imperial Land Company was induced in August by the town folk to make arrangements for irrigating the streets, half at a time, in order to allay the dust. By December, the Company was conducting its first experiments in road flooding to settle the dust on Eighth street, the street on which the Banta house stood.

T. P. had been greatly inconvenienced in his arrangements to get cattle for his ranch, due to the fact that there was no telephone line from Imperial. This caused him to take that trip all the way to Flowing Well to use a telephone in September of 1901. This was a common problem in Imperial. The problem could not be solved by the Imperial Land Company, who was responsible for the township, as there simply was no money available. Instead, it was solved by a very able businessman of early Imperial, W. F. Holt. Holt was the brother of the first banker in the Imperial Valley, Leroy Holt. Imperial was in dire need of a direct line with the outside world.

W. F. had sold a bank for twenty thousand dollars which he had started in Safford, Arizona, prior to coming to the Imperial Valley. That, by Imperial Valley standards, made him a capitalist. In 1901, Holt made the Imperial Land Company a proposition that they were in no position to refuse. He told them that if they would give him an exclusive franchise for telephone service in the valley and a bonus of water stock he would connect the Valley to the outside world in sixty days. For a minimum amount of money, he did just that and received his bonus and exclusive franchise. He organized and was manager of the Imperial Telephone Company. The company had four telephones: Imperial, Cameron, Calexico and Iris. He completed the line in October of 1901, just a month after T. P. had made his long stage coach ride to make his telephone call in Flowing Well. By the end of 1903 Holt had added ninety miles of telephone lines to his company.

T. P. had met W. F. on his first trip from Cameron Lake to Imperial when Sam Ferguson had introduced him to the men of Imperial in early 1901. On his second trip to Imperial two weeks later he had found him, along with his brother Leroy, constructing the frame building around the presses that would become the Imperial Press. At that time the presses had been delivered and left in the open desert and W. F. and Leroy were building with their own hands and with the help of fellow early Imperialites, a frame structure around the press machinery. W. F. was the owner of the Press and had hired an editor, H. C. Reed, who had not as yet arrived in the valley. W. F. was also postmaster, the only resident school trustee, and the appointed Justice of the Peace. T. P. immediately tagged him as an industrious and intelligent businessman who would be a boon to the development of the valley.

Next, Holt proposed building a church for the town if the Imperial Land Company would reimburse him with an additional bonus of water stock. The Company men agreed with W. F. that the addition of a church to the deadly atmosphere of the desert would take some of the starkness out of Imperial. They therefore traded a bonus of water stock for the building of a frame church.

In 1903 W. F. Holt again came to the forefront in solving a major Imperial Valley problem. The farmers were demanding a railroad line into the valley. Having the closest railway line in Flowing Well was just not acceptable. The Imperial Land Company had pleaded with the Southern Pacific to run a line down from Flowing Well through Imperial to Calexico, but to no avail. The Imperial Land Company did not have the resources to build the railroad line and they knew there was no hope of getting it financed by the troubled California Development Company.

Everyone in the Imperial Land Company felt certain that if private enterprise would form a company and start to build the line, the Southern Pacific would jump in to protect their interest and buy out the upstart company. The problem was that the credit of the California Development Company and all potential capitalists in the valley was completely worthless because of the difficulties resulting from the Department of Agriculture's Circular #9. Moreover, now, the Federal Government was foisting a new problem on the valley's credit. The government was claiming that the valley's rights to the water in the Colorado River was invalid since they preposterously claimed the river to be navigable. The Federal government seemed dead set on killing off this private enterprise irrigation development.

W. F. felt he could put together financing for the railroad, through a loan from his brother's bank, wealthy friends in Redlands and his own capital, in exchange for a bonus of water stock from the Imperial Land Company. In March 1902, he filed incorporation papers for the Imperial and Gulf Railroad in company with J. H. Braly, A. H. Heber, F. C. Paulin and E. A. Meserve. Note his close companionship with officers of the California Development Company and the Imperial Land Company. Mr. Holt immediately set to surveying and grading for the new railroad line.

It took but a short while for the officers of the Southern Pacific to come to their senses, realizing that an upstart corporation would own the rights to an extremely profitable few miles of line that should be theirs. Thus, they bought out the Imperial and Gulf Railroad when it barely had gotten under way and at a good profit to its owners. Meanwhile, W. F. walked away with a good deal of water stock from the Imperial Land Company.

The Southern Pacific completed the railroad line to Imperial February 13, 1903, just a little over a month after T. P. was required to take Grandma Allen across the desert from Flowing Well to the Banta home in his spring wagon. By April 1903, the cash receipts from this railroad line were $10,000 for the month and by October they were averaging $15,000 per month, putting Imperial in eighth place among all S. P. lines in Southern California. Plans were proceeding to run the line to Calexico.

T. P. could see that Holt was amassing a substantial number of shares of water stock. He saw that W. F. was betting his entire poke on the future of its value.

1903 saw many new homes built in Imperial as well as large brick commercial buildings. It was announced toward the end of the year that the old canvas and wood hotel would be torn down and replaced with a modern brick hotel. In November, the first creamery in the Valley was opened. During the summer, a group of business men organized the first Imperial Chamber of Commerce.

In October, thirty editors from all over the country were invited by the Imperial Land Company to visit the valley and see what had been accomplished. All thirty arrived in Imperial by train. They couldn't believe all that had been done in three years; four thousand head of cattle, six thousand hogs, Water delivered to one hundred thousand acres, crops being sown and reaped everywhere water was available and a future full of promise to the four thousand inhabitants. The editors took the amazing story back to their papers and the valley was given its first truly big newspaper publicity. To the delight of the Imperial Land Company, this resulted in a large increase in prospective settlers in 1904.

W. F. Holt had plans of his own concerning the valley that would enrich his own estate. He was an excellent business man and as any true entrepreneur, he intended his work to enure to his own benefit rather than the benefit of the California Development Company and the Imperial Land Company. He recognized the terrible financial condition in which the California Development Company found itself. He realized that the Imperial Land Company was not being obstinate in refusing to improve Imperial, but, instead was financially incapable of doing so. This meant that anyone with the financing to develop a city other than Imperial in the center of the valley could make a fortune as the Imperial Land Company simply did not have the money to make the City of Imperial competitive.

His plans were well formed in his mind. He had received a

large amount of water stock from the telephone franchise, the church building and the railroad bluff the California Development Company and he had put over on the Southern Pacific. In addition, he had made a considerable amount of money in the sale of the railroad rights to the Southern Pacific. These things he decided he would invest in his own stake in the valley. He found land on the east side of the valley to which the California Development Company believed that it was impossible to bring water since the land was higher than the level of the Alamo channel which was being used by the C. D. Company to carry its irrigation water to farmers on the east side.

W. F. had determined a way water could be brought to this property through a means not apparent to the Company. Thus, the Company welcomed his proposal to buy at a very low cost 14,000 shares of water stock to be applied to this land. These were in addition to the shares he already owned. They agreed that he could start his own water district on this land with the water stock he owned. With the C. D. Company's approval, he started offering water stock to settlers at very advantageous prices, even putting the settlers on the land with no down payment for the water stock. Poor settlers flocked to this land and soon the population in Irrigation District #7 boomed, making it a successful settlement.

The settlement's farmers needed a town, as the City of Imperial was too far away to be a practical source of needed supplies. On this land where he had obtained the water stock for next to nothing, W. F. bought a townsite and platted out a town. The Imperial Land Company bitterly contested his right to build a town in the Imperial Valley but were unable to stop him. He, then, built several buildings and established the town of Holton, shortly renamed Holtville.

The settlement's farmers needed a connection to the Southern Pacific Railroad line running down through the Imperial Valley. This spur line met the Southern Pacific main line at a junction called Niland which was ten miles north of the old mule train junction of Flowing Well. By July 1904 the spur line through the

Imperial Valley was completed all the way to Calexico. The residents of Imperial and the Imperial Land Company thought the line from Holtville to the Southern Pacific line, which W. F. was financing and building, himself, would connect with the main valley line in the City of Imperial. Much to their surprise, W. F. constructed the line to intersect the main valley line four miles south of Imperial on a townsite he had purchased.

The first mention of this junction appeared in the Imperial Press of July 16, 1904. The name the junction was given at that time was Cabarker which it is interesting to note was a combination of the name C. A. Barker, a wealthy friend of W. F. Holt from Redlands. W. F. had induced Mr. Barker to come to the valley in August of 1903 hoping to get him and his syndicate to invest in the valley. This junction was the investment area in which he hoped he could induce Mr. Barker to join him. Naming the new townsite after Mr. Barker could have been the bait W. F. was using to lure C. A. Baker into the investment.

In this inauspicious mention of a new junction in the valley, unnoticed by all but those involved, lay the beginning of one of the bitterest battles ever conducted in our country between two cities desiring to be the county seat of the yet to be formed Imperial county. Later this townsite passed to the Redlands syndicate which organized a new corporation with W. T. Bill as president, and the townsite was placed on the market as El Centro.

T. P. dearly missed, and had been in constant contact by mail with, his younger brother, Robert, and his family. T. P. realized that the Banta farm on the marginal land along the Aqua Fria Creek could never support his youngest brother's family other than on the ragged edge of poverty. A young son, Fred, had been added to Robert's family of three daughters. Robert was also ready to give up any hopes he might have had on making his farm a successful venture.

T. P. begged Robert to come to Imperial. He promised to build him a house in his tract close to where he had built this own house. T. P. went to his friends in the California Development

Company and arranged to have a job for Robert with the irrigation project if he would come to Imperial. T. P. finally convinced
Robert to come to the Valley in 1904 and built a house only a few
blocks from his own house for Robert, Mary his wife, and his
children, Grace, Myra, Pearl, and baby Fred. The two brothers
were delighted to live near to each other again. They had always
been so very close. Now their families would grow up as friends.
They visited each other on a daily basis and the cousins became as
dear to each other as brothers and sisters. Robert went to work for
the irrigation project, a job he enjoyed for the rest of his life though
under various managements.

When T. P.'s brother arrived from Stodard, Arizona, with his
family, T. P. and Carrie threw them a marvelous party to introduce
them to all their friends in the Imperial Valley. Papa was delighted
to have his closest and youngest brother with him in the valley.
With his brother and his family as well as Grandma Allen now in
Imperial, T. P. and Carrie truly felt the Imperial Valley was their
home. Papa felt exuberant that all the family's problems had been
resolved and that he could now devote all his time to the many
excellent business opportunities that were opening before his eyes
in this desert valley that was turning a verdant green and was so
rich with promise.

In April of 1904, a sadness came over Imperial that especially
affected the Bantas. Tom Beach, their next door neighbor and good
friend, had a tragedy strike his family with the death of Cameron
Beach, his three-year old daughter. Her death was caused by Diph-
theria. The disease also attacked her older sister but she was strong
enough to through it off. On the frontiers of America, such epidemics swept through pioneer communities, taking the lives mainly
of the very young and the very old. Cameron was the first baby girl
born in the valley and the darling of everyone who had come to
know her. The Bantas would especially miss her sweet laughter
which had become a part of their lives. She had been named after
Cameron Lake where T. P., Tom and Mobley had first met.

During the several days little Cameron struggled with the illness before her death, Carrie had spent most of her days and nights assisting the stricken Beach family, cooking the dinners and keeping the house. This was not only because of her compassion and love for the Beaches, but because this was what was expected from all neighbors on the frontiers of our country. Mama had no fear for her own health, or the health of Papa and the boys, for the young and the strong were usually able to throw off these illnesses that ravaged frontier settlements every few years. She did worry about Grandma Allen contracting this contagious disease. She need not have worried, though, for although Grandma Allen was ninety-three, she had a constitution like a mule skinner and had not been sick a day since she had joined the Banta family.

Politics seemed to be at the heart of everything and as Justice of the Peace, T. P. was in the middle of it. During the summer of 1903, a group of businessmen, including T. P., organized the first Imperial Valley Chamber of Commerce. Eighty-four businessmen signed up as members. E. F. Howe, the editor of the Imperial Press, was elected President and Leroy Holt was elected Treasurer. T. P. ardently believed in the Chamber of Commerce and worked on its various appointed committees.

Next on the political agenda of the Imperialites was to have the town of Imperial incorporated as a city of the sixth class. In January 1904, E. F. Howe, the editor of the Imperial Press, started a petition for the city's incorporation. Eventually he obtained the signatures of fifty residents of Imperial including that of T. P. Banta. This petition was published in the newspaper as the first intention to incorporate the city. Two months later, an election was held March 3, 1904. Thirty-seven votes were cast although the town had eight hundred inhabitants. Many of the towns inhabitants were ineligible to vote as they were not residents or were women or underage. When the returns were canvassed by the San Diego Supervisors it was found that some of the signers of the original petition were not qualified voters and the election was annulled. A new committee was appointed by the Chamber of Commerce, consisting of editor Howe and R. D. McPherrin, to circulate a new petition making sure that all who signed it were registered voters.

With the empty coffers of the Imperial Land Company, T. P. and his friends recognized that if the city was to prosper and grow, its citizens would have to pull themselves up by their own bootstraps. They had to wean themselves away from dependence on the company and build the city themselves. The California Development Company, because of their terrible financial condition, did not oppose this group of citizens but instead cooperated with them.

T. P., heading a group of five other Imperialites, issued the following call for a public meeting which was published in the newspaper along with an article about the upcoming meeting:

PUBLIC MEETING

Tonight June 18, 1904: At City Hall over Clark's Hardware store, at eight o'clock. Notice is hereby given that a mass meeting of the citizens of Imperial will be held at the above hall this evening at eight o'clock for the purpose of nominating candidates for the various city offices to be voted for at the coming election, June 30th. The meeting will endeavor to nominate a ticket composed of representative citizens, who if elected will act for the best interest of Imperial. Let every citizen attend who feels an interest in the advancement of the city's welfare.

Signed: T. P. Banta, J. B. Parazette, Wilber Clark, S. W. Mitchell, Paul S. Anderson, Laurence Harris.

The meeting was called to order and Judge Farr, the principal attorney for the California Development Company, was elected as chairman of the meeting. He pointed out to the more than one hundred citizens present that he took for granted that those present stood for "certain good features of a local platform espoused by the signers of the call." These were graded streets, sidewalks and street lights and, also, public ownership of light and power. Those in attendance warmly applauded these sentiments, especially those concerning public ownership of utilities. They appeared to be unaware of the fact, or simply accepted it as the best course of action, that this course would remove the Imperial Land Company from the duty of building the city's infrastructure and would put their costs on the taxpayers.

Judge Banta, as T. P. was called by those living in the valley, moved for a committee of five men to be appointed. The motion carried and the chairman appointed the committee. T. P. was named as one of the five men. The committee selected a slate of nominees for the various offices. A committee on resolutions was also appointed. Following a recess the committees reported their nominations and resolutions. A full slate of nominees was reported to the meeting. The Resolutions Committee reported its resolutions to those in attendance and all were voted on and passed. The Resolutions Committee recommended that this slate of nominees be called the "Citizens' ticket" and the meeting adopted that name.

July 1, there was a second meeting of the "Citizens" ticket supporters in the old drug store building on eight street. Brawley, a new Imperial Land Company townsite in the northern most part of Imperial Valley, had been growing rapidly as the new railroad ended there. Brawley had started a brass band of which it was very proud. The Brawley band supplied music for the meeting adding to the festive air and excitement. Supporters overflowed the hall and were standing outside the door and windows to hear the speakers. Judge T. P. Banta chaired the meeting and introduced Judge Farr, the exponent of the "Citizen's" platform. The Imperial Press reported in its next edition on Judge Farr's remarks as follow:

> Judge Farr paid a handsome tribute to the pioneers of the Imperial Valley. He believed in municipal ownership of public utilities, especially water and light plants and believed that the time would come when the government would own all railways and telegraph systems. In words of warning, he called the attention of the voters to the danger of the town from fire at

the present time, with the water plant in control of a corporation. Painting the future of Imperial, free from the domination of outside interests, in glowing colors, . . .

T. P. closed the meeting with timely words on the principles for which the "Citizens'" ticket stood and was warmly applauded. Judge Banta was so proud of his activities in the politics of the prospective City of Imperial that he had Mama, Grandma Allen (though being deaf she didn't hear a single word), and the boys attend this very successful meeting.

In the hot desert weather of the Imperial Valley, liquor was a dangerous drug that took all ambition out of pioneers whose lives depended on energy and clear thought. Thus, a second ticket was put in the race by a rival faction. It was wet while the "Citizens" ticket was dry. The drys won by a vote of eighty-two to seven and the city was incorporated and liquor was outlawed. Leroy Holt was elected treasurer and T. P.'s old friend Tom Beach was elected Marshall, William A. Edgar, foremost of the four Edgar Bros. who owned the Edgar Bros. Merchandising Company, was selected by the new board of trustees to be the city's first mayor. T. P. and his friends had triumphed and the entire slate of the Citizens' party was elected.

T. P. thought it was strange that though Leroy Holt had been very active in the political process of making Imperial a city, even being nominated and running for and winning the office of treasurer, W. F. Holt was conspicuous by his absence and inaction.

All the businessmen were surprised when Editor E. F. Howe announced his resignation as president of the Imperial Valley Chamber of Commerce. He had sold the Imperial Press to Charles Gardner who had recently arrived in the valley from Pasadena. The members of the association voted editor Howe a complimentary resolution of regret and thanks to be entered into the minutes of the next meeting.

R. D. McPherrin, the popular attorney and T. P.'s long time friend who had come to the valley in 1900, was elected the new president of the Chamber. To T. P.'s delight and pride he was placed on the board of directors along with Charles A. Gardener, who had purchased the Imperial Press from Editor Howe, and F. G. Havens, who was the U. S. Land Commissioner and who would shortly buy the Imperial Press from Mr. Gardener.

Mr. Gardner in a very short while sold the paper to five men, four of whom were working for Government control of the irrigation system under the Reclamation Department. These men and many others in the Imperial Valley wanted the Reclamation Department to purchase the Imperial irrigation project from the California Development Company and operate it as a part of the Laguna Dam project at Yuma. They planned to use the paper to forward their opinions to the paper's readers. It was but a few months before they resold the Imperial Press to W. F. Holt, the entrepreneur who had so impressed T. P. but who failed to have any interest in the political campaign to make Imperial a city.

Other townsites similar to Holtsville were being laid out by the Imperial Land Company. Newspapers started up in two of these new cities, Calexico and Brawley, in competition to the Imperial Press. A newspaper also began publishing in W. F. Holt's townsite of Holtsville.

In 1904, Imperial was wired for electricity during the summer. An oil burning engine was used to drive a dynamo. The rate was $1.00 per month per lamp, or twenty-five cents a kilowatt, the customer to install the meter. T. P. had electricity run to both his home and his real estate office. What a novel and delightful experience it was to simply turn a switch and have Edison's wonderful invention flood the room with light on the darkest night.

In December, T. P. was surprised to learn that W. F. Holt had purchased the ice and light plants from the Imperial Light, Water and Power Company for $35,000. One of the principal planks in the Citizens' party platform was the municipal ownership of public utilities. This had been pushed by Judge Farr who was one of the lawyers for the California Development Company. Yet the Imperial Land Company and its parent, the California Development Company were in dire need of cash and were forced by their financial condition to sell the plant to Holt. W. F. had by this time considerably increased the original $20,000 he had when he came to the valley. The City of Imperial having just been chartered was in no position to make a counter bid for the utilities.

W. F. had discovered a very inexpensive way to generate electricity. After irrigating the farms in Irrigation District #7, he had water left that was going to waste running down a forty-foot embankment into the Alamo canal. Holt had heard of water turbines connected to dynamos generating electricity. Promoters see things that can make money that other men would not notice. W. F. began to wonder if the water couldn't work for him. He harnessed a turbine to a pipe carrying the falling water down the forty feet to the bottom of the Alamo canal and generated electricity free of cost except for the maintenance. He had put a water power plant on the desert floor and produced enough electricity to light the district. T. P. realized that W. F. was becoming a very powerful man in the Valley and one that undoubtedly had a master plan behind his many moves on the chess board of the Imperial Valley.

1904 was a boom year in construction within the City of Imperial. Many new homes were built. The new Imperial Hotel was completed and had its grand opening on June 19. The new hotel boasted the first curb and sidewalk in the City of Imperial. A dozen new brick commercial buildings were erected. Several new businesses had started up each month. The city was off and running. It was the most successful year the city had seen and everyone looked forward to the future of Imperial as the central city of the amazing Imperial Valley. Everyone, that is, except W. F. Holt and the group of businessmen in on his plan.

A lawless element had been drawn to the bustling new city. Several brothels had commenced doing a rousing business drawing upon the many single male canal workers and farm hands for its clientele. The law-abiding citizens were jolted to action and called a mass meeting to consider the suppression of vice when an ugly incident occurred. William P. Hays was murdered by Lee Dees in a drunken brawl in the street in front of one of the brothels.

George Banta, age 9, on the Banta ranch, Imperial Valley, 1904

By coincidence, little George Banta had been walking home and saw the incident. George was only nine at the time and observing a murder left him terribly shaken and frightened. T. P. was very worried about the effect this had on his youngest son. George had always been an outgoing boy. Now he was frightened to leave the house and would under no circumstances go out of the house alone when it was dark. T. P. was furious that this lawless element was ruining the peace of the valley and had caused such a destructive change in George's personality.

Judge T. P. Banta, as Justice of the Peace, and other law abiding citizens of Imperial brought heavy pressure to bear on the city council to pass a strong liquor law and on the constable to close down the brothels. At the same time he gave serious thought to how he might bring George around to being the fearless young boy he had been prior to witnessing the murder. After serious thinking, Papa decided on a plan that would cure George or, perhaps, make him more fearful than ever. There were no books on how to raise children in the early 1900's. Parents handled such problems by the seat of their pants, trying to solve each child's problem as best they could. T. P.'s plan involved George's fondest wish and request. He had seen a pony across town that he would give anything to own. He had talked to Papa about the pony and told him he would do anything he asked if T. P. would buy him the pony. George was talking about extra work and extra chores when he made this proposal to Papa. T. P. saw George's desire for the pony as a way he might get George to face and defeat his fears, thus, he made him this proposal.

"George," he said, "you want that pony, and you said you would do anything to get it. Tonight I'll walk you up close to that old abandoned adobe house just outside of town that you told me you thought was haunted. I'll walk you to within fifty yards of that old house and if you will go from there into that broken down old wreck and holler loud enough for me to hear 'I ain't afraid of anything or anybody in this place.' I'll buy you that pony."

George trembled with even the thought of that old house he was sure was haunted.

"Papa," George said, "I'm so fearful right now that I can't think. Can I go to my room and have some time to think it over."

"Sure you can." Papa said. "Let me know when you've made up your mind."

George went to the room shared by Al and himself and closed the door. He thought of the pony; then he thought of the haunted house. Then he thought of the haunted house, and then thought of the pony. He thought how that house had ghosts and spirits for sure. He thought how much fun it would be to ride the pony to school and how all the other children would ohh and ahh when they saw him ride up on his own pony. He thought back and forth and back and forth again and again. He couldn't go into that house, but he had to have that pony. Finally, the pony won out. Maybe the goblins wouldn't eat him and would let him go, and he would have his pony. If they ate him, that would be that, and Papa would cry and feel real bad that he had made his youngest son march into that old building to his death.

George came out of his room and announced to T. P., "Papa, I'll do it."

"George," T.P. said "you know I love you too much to have you do anything dangerous. There are no spirits in that house. I know it, and after tonight you'll know it too. Tonight you're going to find that most fear has no basis in fact, and when you face up to false fear it melts away like ice on a hot wagon bed."

Night was soon upon them and T. P. took George by the hand and led him out to within twenty-five yards of the old abandoned house though it seemed two hundred yards to George.

"O. K. George, go earn your pony," Papa said.

George ran to the house, pushed open the old broken door and shouted at the top of his lungs, "I ain't afraid of anyone or anything in this place, I'm the bravest boy in Imperial Valley, and I'm going to stand here and give you a chance to get me, cause I'm just not afraid."

IMPERIAL

A SUNDAY TRAGEDY

William P. Hayes Fatally Stabbed by Lee Dees in Drunken Quarrel

Assailant Bound Over to Superior Court in the Sum of $1,000 on Charge of Homicide

Sunday afternoon this peace-loving community was horrified to learn that a murder had been committed in its vicinity.

William P. Hayes, a barber employed by Phillip Strickler, was fatally stabbed by Lee Dees, a laborer, at a disreputable camp about three-quarters of a mile north-east of the city. This camp, consisting of a tent well-hidden and shaded by mesquite bushes, was recently established by two Mexican women, Rosa

instance, they were ordered to leave camp and went away a few yards.

Here there is conflicting evidence, certain witnesses declaring that Hayes picked up a beer bottle and threw it at Dees, hitting him on the left side of his head. Others state that Hayes struck Dees with a bottle, holding it in his hand, while again others assert they saw no bottle used at all.

The fact remains that Dees has a severe cut on his head that may easily

LITTLE GEORGE WITNESSED THIS VICIOUS MURDER
Recovered from microfiche

The last part he made up himself and with trembling legs he stood there for what he thought was ten or fifteen minutes when T. P. came crashing through the door. He didn't give George credit for having that much nerve and thought that maybe a drifter had been sleeping in the building and had grabbed George. George laughed uproariously to see his Papa had fear too. He didn't understand at such an early age that it was a different kind of fear his Papa had. Not fear for himself, but fear for his son and that a father would charge into hellfire itself to save his son even if it meant his own death.

This time, T. P. had done it right. It might not have worked for other boys but it worked for George. George was free from the fear that had infected him since he had witnessed the murder.

From that day forward he only feared real things. Imaginary things never frightened him again for he had called their bluff, and found they just weren't real. The next night when George returned from school there was the pony he wanted so badly waiting for him in the corral. T. P. had taken part of the day off from work to make sure the pony would be there for such a brave boy.

The Colorado River is a very unusual river in as much as its high and low water seasons are reversed. Summer is the time of high water and winter is the time of low water which is completely the opposite of most of the other great rivers of the world. The summer water that flows through the Colorado River in the arid Great Basin comes from the snow capped mountains surrounding its northern half. The water from this snow on the sides of the mountains facing the Great Basin in Idaho, Montana, Wyoming and Colorado melts in the late spring and summer months causing a rise in the flow of water in the river. These were the high water and flood months for the great river prior to its taming by the Hoover Dam. This reversal of flood and low water seasons was ideal for the Imperial Valley Irrigation Districts as the high water came just as the farmers needed the water for their spring and summer crops.

During the winter months the arid Great Basin receives very little rain in comparison with the rest of the country. It is almost entirely desert. Thus, the winter months are the low water months for the Colorado River. Very few floods had been observed since records of winter floods had been kept. Many years would go by between winter floods on the Colorado river.

During the winter of 1903, insufficient water had been available to meet the demands of farmers planting winter grain crops. The cause of this was the silting up of the main canal in its first four miles from the Chaffey gate. For these first four miles, the canal paralleled the Colorado River and the grade was very slight.

As you recall, Rockwood erroneously thought the bottom of the Chaffey gate had not been built low enough for the low water months. He was not aware that Chaffey had built the gate with a two-foot-high sand board that could be removed to lower the level of the floor of the gate during low water. To supply water to the farmers, the Company had cut a by-pass alongside the Chaffey gate. Even so, relief did not come in time for some of the farmers to save their crops. Because of this, more than a quarter of a million dollars in law suits had been brought against the Company.

Chief Engineer, C. R. Rockwood could not let this happen again. In 1904, the by-pass alongside the Chaffey gate was cut in September in ample time to provide the additional water it could supply. In addition, at the order of the president of the California Development Company, Anthony Heber, Rockwood made a 3300-foot cut from the Colorado River in Mexico immediately above the main canal to the Main canal. He made this cut through very soft alluvial fill without building a head gate. The drop of the cut from the river to the main canal was sufficient to allow ample water to flow to the main canal without silting up the cut.

Heber had worked out a contract with the Mexican government, ratified by the Mexican Congress, for diversion of water from the Colorado River in Mexico. Many historians believe, backed by Chaffey's contention as written in the "Life of George Chaffey," that the cut was not made to supply additional water. Their belief is that Heber ordered the cut to thwart the Reclamation Service and the War Department in their statement that the Colorado River was a navigable river and that, therefore, filings under state laws for irrigation purposes were null and void. The Secretary of the Interior recommended that those who had constructed canals should have those canals protected, but that extensions should be made only with the consent of the Secretary of the Interior.

In the Arid Lands hearings in Washington during the spring of 1904, Mr. Heber found himself all alone in battling the Reclamation Service and the War Department. In an effort to save his Company, he said his chief engineer was ready to make a cut on Mexican soil eliminating the need for permission of the United States Government to remove irrigation water from the Colorado River. In an impassioned statement at that hearing he declared, "It

is my earnest desire to worship at our own altar, and to receive the
blessings from the shrine of our own government, but if such
permission is not given we shall be compelled to worship elsewhere."
This statement was made by a lone man against the power of the
United States Government in an effort to save his company from
ruin.

Whether the cut in Mexico was made for political reasons or
to provide more water for winter farming during the low water
months of the Colorado river or for both reasons is moot. The cut
was made in September 1904, unprotected by a heading gate.
The contract between Heber and the Mexican Government provided for permission to build gates in Mexico with the approval of
the Mexican Government. Because of government red tape, permission for building the gate had not been received by the CD
Company, but the company attorney in Mexico City wired Heber
it was forthcoming and to proceed with the cut.

Rockwood and the other engineers on the river did not consider the cut to be a danger as they had studied the records of the
past twenty-seven years. In all these years there had been only
three winter floods of any size and no year had two floods. They
thought it would be a simple matter to close the cut in Mexico
well before the summer high water. Thus, the die was cast that
resulted in the multi-million dollar disaster which without the
intervention of the Southern Pacific Railroad would have inundated all the farm land in the entire valley under a gigantic fresh
water lake.

CHAPTER 30

1905, THE SOUTHERN

PACIFIC IS IN. ANTHONY HEBER

IS OUT. THE FLOOD BEGINS.

Meanwhile the Banta family was involved in personal problems of their own which were demanding immediate solutions.
Earl should have started high school in 1901. Yet, at that time
in the valley, there was no high school or plans to build one.
Four years had passed and one had not been started even by
1905. Papa knew that he had been unfair to Earl to deprive
him of schooling simply because the family needed him on the
farm. He and Mama determined that this situation had to be
resolved.

T. P. decided that Earl had to complete his education. He
hired a foreman to manage the ranch and relieved Earl of the task.
Since there was no high school in the valley, Carrie decided Earl
would have to leave the valley and attend prep school as a boarder
wherever the best high school was available. Mama wrote to every
boy's prep school in California and reviewed the material they sent
her to determine which school would be best for Earl. Earl had
given up much for the family and was entering high school at
nineteen because the family had needed him. Now, she wanted
the very best for her oldest son. After careful study, Papa and
she decided on the Washburn Boarding School in San Jose,
California.

Earl looked forward to the excitement of leaving home and being on his own. He had always been a bright student and enjoyed learning. He looked forward to the challenge of high school and then college. Both the family and he were delighted when the problem of the ranch management had been resolved. Yet, when the time came for the packing of his suitcases and the purchase of his train tickets, the Banta family took on the appearance of people attending a funeral. Papa and Mama tried to make light conversation and laugh a lot, but it was impossible to mask the fact that this pioneer family which had grown so close together, building their new home and farm by the sweat of their brows, was losing what had been one of its most essential members. By the time Earl was ready to leave on his new adventure, he realized that he was just as sad to leave the family that had filled every day of his life as they were to lose him.

But, just as from the ashes left from the fire that consumed the old mythical Phoenix, the new Phoenix arose, from the young men and women leaving the warmth of their families arose the families of the next generation, and the world was reborn in the eyes of the young who see every thing from a new and different prospective. Thus, every new family formed is destined to dissolve.

Al felt especially grieved as he and Earl had always been so close. George, in his eyes, was just a little boy and with the five years difference, they had little in common. Al knew that Earl would be back in nine months for summer vacation but that was little comfort with Earl leaving him for a school so very far away. Both boys promised to write to each other regularly.

When Earl mounted the steps to the vestibule of the railroad passenger car, there were tears in the eyes of all five Bantas and Grandma Allen. The tears turned to joy with the receipt of Earl's first letter home. He had made new friends and was very happy with his new studies and school.

It's very hard to understand how a great river could change its course because of a half mile cut from that river to the source of the Alamo Channel that is dry most of the year. We have included in this book two maps that help visualize the conditions that made this possible. It will be helpful to refer to these maps as we discuss the topography that made this feasible.

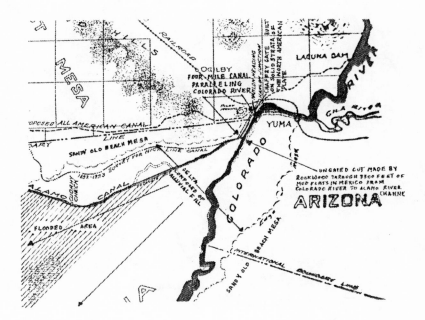

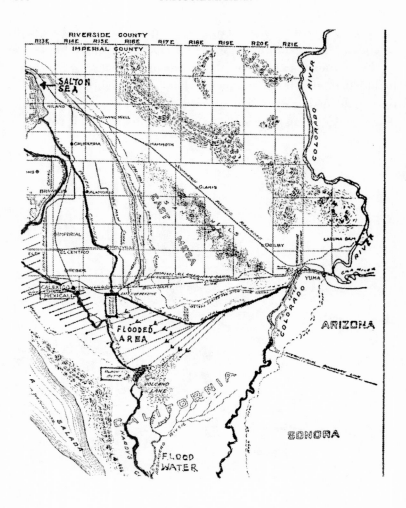

   The Chaffey Gate had been built on solid strata of the North
American plate just south of Yuma at Hanlon's landing. It had to
be built east of where the river started to flow over its delta which
had been created by the dumping of its alluvial fill into the Gulf of
California. In an earlier chapter we described how the river's delta
finally cut the Gulf of California in half, The northern portion
becoming the Imperial valley. This alluvial fill was nothing but silt

and could not provide a sound footing for a gate used to divert water from the river to the valley. This fact was understood by all the engineers. The fact that by diverting the river's water only a half mile to the north, the water could be made to flow down the north side of the delta into the Imperial valley rather than flowing in its normal course down the south side of the delta through the Alamo channel to the Gulf of California showed them how critical was the equilibrium of the river as it first flowed onto its delta. It was walking a tight rope and could as easily fall to the north as to the south with a very minor change in conditions.

The river had filled the Gulf of California with silt to such a depth and length that it formed a plain that was almost level, with only the slightest incline in any direction. As silt was deposited across the crevasse which was the Gulf of California, it created a forty-five-mile flat plain across the Gulf of California with only the slightest incline in all directions away from the tip of its delta. On such a level field of play the river could easily change its course always seeking the lowest area, The river had changed its course many times over the millennia as new silt was deposited causing its then present course to be higher than the surrounding plain.

During flood stage, the river would overflow its self-made levees and flow to the north into the Alamo River Channel. This is how the Alamo Channel was created. The California Development Company used the Alamo Channel as its main canal after the first four miles of dredged canal from the Chaffey Gate to the beginning of the Alamo Channel. The water was then diverted at Sharp's heading just south of the International Border into the main canals of the irrigation district.

At flood stage the river overflowed its banks to such a degree that the Alamo Channel could not carry all the water and water flowed down the slight incline to the west until it reached the Cocapah Mountains on the west side of the Gulf. Water running in this direction traveled at such a slow pace that it spread out as a flooded area covering the plain with water only inches deep until it reached Volcano Lake forty miles to the west at the foot of the

Cocopah Mountains. Water reaching Volcano Lake formed a body of water that discharged its overflow in a strange manner.

At the far western side of the lake, stood a rock formation known as Black Butte, which caused the water overflowing the lake to split in half. One half of the water flowed north into the Imperial Valley which created a waste water channel down the west side of the valley known as New River. This is the channel in which Cameron Lake lay and where the Construction Camp of the California Development Company had been established when the Banta family first came to the valley. The other half of the overflow from Volcano Lake flowed south into the Gulf of California.

Thus, we see that flood water from the river entered the Valley by two sources during flood stage. The first source of water flowing into the Imperial Valley from flood overflow of the Colorado River took a direct route. It flowed in the Alamo flood channel northward until it reached the Salton Sea The second source flowed west across the flat plain for approximately forty miles to Volcano Lake. The outflow from the lake split against Black Butte into two streams. One stream flowed to the Salton Sea down the western side of the valley in a drainage gulch created by erosive forces of thousands of previous floods and was known by those who lived in the valley as New River. The other stream flowed into the Gulf of California.

When Rockwood was ordered by Anthony Heber to make a cut of 3300 feet through the soft alluvial fill from the Colorado River to the head of the Alamo Channel he did so only because it was a temporary stopgap which he felt he could easily close before the spring rise in the flow of river water caused by the melting of snow in the mountains surrounding the northern half of the great basin. He had checked the flow of water in the Colorado River during the winter months for the twenty-seven years for which he had records. These indicated there had been few winter floods, none of which would have posed a serious problem for the un-gated cut he had made through the 3300 feet of alluvial fill. Thus, he followed Anthony Heber's orders and made the cut fifty feet wide and eight feet deep from the river to the Alamo channel by-passing the four silted up miles of the canal from the Chaffey gate at Hanlon's landing. He did this to insure ample water for the valley's winter crops.

Unfortunately for the California Development Company, this winter season would prove that twenty-seven years of statistics could not predict what this river, known to the engineers as the "Yellow Terror" because of its yellow color from the silt it carried and its affinity to multiply its flow many times in a few days, might do in any particular year. How the Yellow Terror must have laughed at these puny engineers, who thought they could understand its nature from a quarter century's statistics. It knew, from the hundreds of millions of years it had flowed its varying course across the great basin to the Gulf of California, that it was terrifyingly unpredictable.

The first flood of the 1904-05 winter season came in February 1905. It caused no damage other than some silting of the cut. Two weeks later a second flood hit, followed three weeks later by a third. The third flood considerably widened the intake cut and substantially scoured out the bottom of the channel. This force-fully brought to Rockwood's attention that an unusual winter season was upon them. Since the summer flood season was rapidly approaching, he decided to close the intake as quickly as possible.

As the engineers were preparing to close the intake, a dire crisis, as to whether Heber or the Southern Pacific Railroad would be in control of the California Development Company, demanded Rockwood's immediate attention. The gist of the matter revolved around a proposed desperately needed loan for $200,000 by the company from the Southern Pacific Railroad with control of the California Development Company being turned over to them until the loan was repaid. The Company was in such dire financial straits that survival likely depended on this loan. The railroad demanded that Anthony Heber resign as president and no longer be connected with the company in any capacity if the loan were to be made. They also insisted that a controlling portion of the company's stock be signed over to the Southern Pacific Railroad until the loan was repaid and that three of the five directors of the company be appointed by the railroad. Anthony Heber obviously opposed this entire proposal. Rockwood, recognizing the pending bankruptcy of the company if the loan was not secured, favored the plan though Heber was unaware that he did.

In order to protect his interests, Rockwood had to leave the closure of the intake to his assistant C. N. Perry and rush to Los Angeles to rally his forces in order to oust Heber at the upcoming company annual meeting. This internal company hiatus will be further discussed later, but, for now, it is enough for us to understand how this political struggle within the company caused those at the top to almost lose sight of the critical conditions at the heading.

Perry prepared to close the intake in the usual manner. Piles were driven across the intake with woven brush mats placed at both ends. On these mats were placed ten-thousand sacks of sand to hold the mats in place. The water was confined to a thirty-foot channel in the center of the intake. Long timbers were placed across this gap and woven brush mats placed on top of these timbers. The timbers were shattered by explosive devises attached to them and the mats permitted to fall into the thirty-foot gap closing it to the intake of any further water. Just as the workmen finished this part of the closing and before they could complete the closure by filling the intake ditch for several hundred yards behind the brush mats, the fourth flood came down the Colorado, undermining the mats and washing them completely away.

Perry, Beach and his co-workers were badly shaken by this and at this point became fully aware that bad luck had brought them a season for which their twenty-seven year statistics had left them completely unprepared. Their foe, the old Colorado River, was unforgiving and unpredictable when they threw away their sound engineering practices and tried to take it on with unprotected intakes through soft alluvial fill.

A dredge was brought in and a second dam was started upstream in the gateless intake but the water was so swift that the engineers soon abandoned this second attempt.

Perry, on his own responsibility, went to Los Angeles to demand the attention of those in charge of the company. This insubordination by Perry elicited the desired effect and the factions met in a diligent effort to try to determine a means of effectively meeting the crisis at the heading. No money was available from the company but the stockholders of Water Company #1 finally came to life recognizing the seriousness of the situation and raised $5,000 which they loaned to the company to stop the flood through the un-gated heading in Mexico.

Returning to the heading in April of 1905, Perry, with William Best as foreman, continued his attempt to close the gap. The water was barely beginning its rise from the snow which was beginning to melt on the slopes of the mountains in the northern states surrounding the great basin but Perry continued to sink a large number of brush mattresses, woven together with steel cable, and then pinned them in place with piles driven through the mattresses into the alluvial fill. By June, the work had proceeded in a very satisfactory manner though the water was at summer flood stage.

At this point Rockwood returned victorious in his quest to drive Heber from the presidency of the company and the company itself. Epes Randolf, a trusted assistant to president E. H. Harriman of the Southern Pacific Railroad, was now president and general manager of the California Development Company. Rockwood was his assistant and chief engineer of the Irrigation Project and as such in charge of closing the gap. He ordered Perry's third attempt at closing the breach abandoned. The question continues to this day as to why he did this as many engineers believed and many historians agree that Perry's mattresses might well have provided a good foundation on which to build a successful dam. This seems quite plausible since the breach was still not more than five hundred feet wide. Rockwood's contention was that the water at that time was too high and was flooding the surrounding countryside.

As a third attempt at closure, Rockwood decided to attack the river itself. The intake had been cut opposite an island in the center of the river called Disaster Island. The island ran from several hundred yards north of the intake to perhaps half a mile south of the intake and divided the river into two streams, one to the east and one to the west of the island. The intake was cut into the half of the river running to the west of the island. Rockwood decided to close off the half of the river flowing to the west of Disaster Island, forcing the entire river to flow down its east side. The ungated intake would then be attached to the dry west fork of the river and the flood through the intake would be stopped. He planned to put the entire river in its east channel by creating a 3000 foot jetty running parallel to the west shore above the island to the northern tip of the island. He thought that running the dam in this manner would put the least force against it as the water would be running parallel to the dam rather than directly toward it.

Rockwood put Thomas Hind in charge of building the 3000 foot jetty. The jetty was to be constructed of brush and piling connecting the Mexican mainland to the northern point of the island. The work was very easy till all but one hundred feet of the jetty was completed. When the jetty was completed to this point, the velocity of the water flowing through those last one-hundred feet increased tremendously as well as the velocity of the water flowing parallel to the jetty. This added to the corrosive force of the river's water to such an extent that within a few hours gigantic gaps were beginning to appear all along the 3000-foot jetty. The torrent of water pouring through the last one hundred feet to be closed was so great that it was impossible to do any work in it at all. On August 3, all work on the Hind Jetty was abandoned.

Puny man's brush mats and piles were but toys in the hands of the great river. It dared men to try to close the gap they had so impudently cut into the mud flats it had created. It laughed at their tinkering with the precarious equilibrium of the delta it had built of soft alluvial fill. It thought them fools to have left the

security of the Chaffey Gate anchored in solid strata to tempt tragedy by drawing water through an unprotected cut in its mud flats.
Then, with a mighty roar it tore their flimsy mats and sticks away
and the two streams of the Colorado River, flowing both to the
east and the west of Disaster Island, combined into one stream
which rushed through the intake now almost one thousand feet
wide, leaving its old beds on both sides of Disaster Island dry
gulches. The water from the entire Colorado River again started to
fill the Imperial Valley through the Alamo Channel which at that
point was also the main canal of the Imperial Irrigation system, a
course which for thousands of years it had not been allowed to
flow.

Randolph insisted that a workable plan be proposed and acted
upon immediately. On August 5, 1905, Rockwood made the
following proposal known as the "Rockwood Gate" which was
accepted by Randolph. He would cut an intake for a bypass at a
position high on the Alamo canal, which was now the runaway
river channel. The bypass would parallel the Alamo channel for
several hundred yards. He would then cut the bypass's outlet several
hundred yards down the Alamo Channel. The majority of the river's
water would then be caused to flow through the bypass. In the
nearly dry Alamo canal section between the intake and outlet of
the bypass he would construct a coffer dam surrounding an area in
which he would construct his Rockwood Gate. This would leave
the space inside the coffer dam as a dry dock. With the river water
flowing through the bypass and with a minimum amount flowing
around the coffer dam, he could build his Rockwood gate capable
of carrying 10,000 second feet of water in the newly dried-up
area. After his gate had been built, he would remove the cofferdam
and open the gate. After this, rock fill dams would be constructed
from the edges of the gate to the sides of the Alamo canal forcing
all water still flowing through the canal to flow through the
Rockwood Gate. He would then close the bypass sending all the
rivers water down through the Rockwood Gate. By slowly closing
the gate, the river would be denied access to the valley and would

be once again forced to flow in its old channel to the gulf of California. This was the plan as of September 1, 1905.

At this time, Rockwood found the work of managing the company and also acting as its chief engineer was "too much for one man." Mr. Randolph agreed and appointed F. S. Edinger of the Southern Pacific Railroad as engineer in charge.

Edinger lost faith in the Rockwood gate and as a fourth attempt at closure talked Randolph into letting him pursue a different plan of constructing a 600 foot jetty similar to the previously tried 3,000 foot Hind jetty. Construction of this jetty was well under way when on Thanksgiving Day a gigantic flood swept down the river with a wall of water ten feet high carrying trees, logs, pilings, and other trash and dead animals on its crest. This wall of water completely demolished Edinger's dam. Disaster Island was washed away and the entire river continued to flow down the main irrigation district canal which was also the old Alamo Channel.

The Alamo Channel was not large enough to contain the entire flow of flood stage of the Colorado River. Waters were overflowing it and inundating thousands of acres of land south of the border and ultimately finding their way westward across the delta to New River. Heavy March rains fell making this entire area a vast lake. Some of the flood water reached New River by crossing the delta and flowing into Volcano Lake. Here, the overflow split into the two channels already discussed with some going to the Gulf of California and the remainder flowing into the valley through New River.

Other flood water entered New River by flowing across the alluvial plain north of Volcano Lake but south of the border. This incredibly large and dangerous amount of water accumulated in several sloughs which over flowed covering miles of delta before finally finding its way into the New River. During the remainder of 1905, all the flood water was accounted for by the above means without the flood impinging on the irrigation districts in the Imperial Valley.

With the failure of the Edinger jetty and the entire Colorado

River flowing into the valley, Rockwood again assumed command of bringing the great Yellow Terror under control. He believed that the only hope of containing the river lay in his "Rockford Gate" plan and returned to it at once. Things had, however, changed since he had first proposed the plan. The island had been swept away in the Thanksgiving Day flood and the Alamo flood channel was now 900 feet wide. Nonetheless, his plans were again approved December 15, 1905 and he immediately began the work of constructing his gate.

Though the great Colorado River had broken out of its old bed flowing to the Gulf of California and it's entire flow was descending into the valley through the Alamo and New River and in spite of the fact that much of the land below the border was a flood plain, the residents of the valley did not seem concerned with the disastrous situation on the river. This was undoubtedly caused by their ignorance of the seriousness of the potential catastrophe facing the future of the valley and each one of them. Concerned or not, in fact, they were so helpless that there was nothing they could do but leave the matter of the river to the California Development Company. Yet, if they had as a group demanded the Company assert far greater efforts to control the river much earlier in the river's rebellion the disaster currently occurring might well have been avoided.

The Los Angeles Chamber of Commerce sent a carload of business men to the valley in April 1905, and at that time the country was unaware of the seriousness of the problem. On their return to L. A., they gave out interviews highly praising the Imperial Valley. In June, a train bearing the house and senate public lands committees arrived in the valley. They were shown maps, prepared by the government after the survey which resulted in Circular #9. Areas declared infertile by the government were now completely covered with lush crops. They were surprised and delighted by what they saw. They, too, were not told of the problems at the ungated intake.

The Valley's newspapers largely ignored the disaster as it did not affect any inhabitants during 1905 and the editors did not understand the nature and seriousness of the river breakthrough. Several articles were written about the problems of crossing the high water in the Alamo and New River in addition to articles about the high water in the Salton Sea. The waters of the Salton Sea were lapping at the footings of the Southern Pacific Railroad by the end of the year but this was treated as if it were only a temporary matter.

As the river raged and tore at the puny efforts of the company's engineers to bring it under control in 1905, life in the Valley continued as if no problem existed. Crops were sown and reaped, buildings continued to be built and new businesses continued to open their doors. New immigrants were still arriving in large numbers.

Anthony Heber, prior to his ouster as president of the California Development Company, decided he could not continue to act as president of the Imperial Land Company due to the many hours he was spending on political affairs with the Federal Government over Colorado River water rights. He, therefore, appointed F. C. Paulin as its president.

T. P. knew F. C. well due to his many contacts with him in Paulin's former position as manager of the Imperial Land Company. It chaffed T. P. that last year Heber had sold to the Emerson Realty Company an exclusive franchise to sell town lots in Imperial, Calexico and Brawley. That company had sold $98,000 worth of lots during the last year. He induced F. C. Paulin to buy back this franchise from Emerson so that all real estate men could sell lots in these towns once again, and make their commissions. Though T. P's primary real estate business consisted of large parcels of undeveloped land and developed ranches, he also bought and sold many town lots. He had in fact developed his own subdivision in Calexico known as the Banta Tract.

T. P. spent a good deal of his time in his duties as Justice of the Peace. He was, also, very involved in circulating a petition to the government for a resurvey of the valley. There were such great discrepancies in the old survey that the government withdrew much valley land from final entry. This directly effected his real estate business and his daily sales activity. The valley had to be re-surveyed, and it had to be done quickly. T. P. had yet to learn that the wheels of government move exceedingly slowly, and it would be years away with much suffering and cost to the farmers before anything would be done by the United States Survey Department. He would have been very depressed if he knew that the resurvey would not be completed for four years due to government procrastination.

So much land had been brought under cultivation in the valley that the Southern Pacific freight receipts at Imperial reached $70,000 in May putting the Imperial in third place on the Southern Pacific's western line behind only Los Angeles and San Pedro.

The ramada shed and tent that had served as George and Al's grammar school was abandoned at the beginning of the 1904-05 school year and replaced by a frame school building. Student enrollment at the beginning of the school year was 105 students. Al and George were very happy that they no longer had to endure the freezing winter mornings in the open ramada shed but they missed the wonderful things they could observe from their open air classroom. When school got boring they could watch the eight mule team freighter wagons go by with their cacophony of squeaks and rattles almost drowning out the shouts of the mule skinners to their mules. They also missed the view. For in any direction you could see miles and miles of miles and miles from the ramada schoolroom.

New business and buildings opened up in Imperial and new houses were built. 1905 continued as a building boom for Imperial though there was considerably less building in 1905 as compared to 1904. A new newspaper, the Imperial Standard was started in Imperial by Heber, Dool, Lawrence and Perry, all California Development Company men. This surprised the town folk who could not understand why the city needed two newspapers. Former U. S. Land Commissioner and, as we recall, the man whose name was transposed with T. P.'s in the 1902 election, F. G. Havens, had taken over the Imperial Press. A new newspaper was also started in Holtsville called the Holtsville Tribune.

Meanwhile, four miles south in the new township of El Centro amazing things were happening. W. F. Holt had worked closely with the men in charge of the Imperial Land Company and realized that though they were charged with developing the towns in the valley the parent company, the California Development Company, was in such dire financial condition that no money was available to build an infrastructure to support their towns. At the vote for incorporation of Imperial, the platform of the Citizens' party shifted the cost of building such an infrastructure to the taxpayers of Imperial. Holt recognized that this platform adopted by the party put his new city of El Centro in the driver's seat. Being a true entrepreneur, W. F. realized, that with sound financial backing, he could build and control the business and financial center of the entire Imperial Valley. If he supplied a solid infrastructure for a township near Imperial, the businessmen would desert Imperial and flock to his township for they were sick and tired of the dust and unkept promises of the promoters of Imperial. The Imperial Land Company and their city of Imperial were not in a financial position to compete. There would undoubtedly be much bluster but no real competition.

As we have already read, W. F. Holt and C. A. Barker bought three hundred and twenty acres four miles south of Imperial at $40 per acre in 1904. Holt ran his spur railroad from Holtville so that its junction with the Southern Pacific rail line from Niland to Calexico met in these three hundred and twenty acres. They in turn sold the property to the El Centro Townsite Company for $125 per acre.

In June 1905, articles of incorporation of the El Centro Land Company were filed by W. T. Bill and four other men with a capital stock of $10,000. Two weeks later The El Centro Hotel company filed articles of incorporation with $50,000 of capital stock with the same directors. Almost immediately, the new townsite started drawing business people from Imperial and the Thelma rooming house announced they were moving to El Centro. The hot summer months of 1905 were spent by W. F. and his business associates making preparations for building the improvements that would change El Centro from the farmland it was at that time to the future business center of the Imperial Valley.

In October, laying out the town started in earnest. Main street was graded and laid out for two miles east and west. Other streets crossed it at right angles forming blocks. Family dwellings were to be constructed on these streets with the commercial buildings on Main Street. W. F., learning from what had most disturbed the residents of Imperial, had a carload of oil delivered to El Centro which he had spread on the streets to eliminate the dust.

He also had a quarter of a million feet of lumber delivered which would be used to erect his opera house as well as store buildings on the south side of Main Street on what he called the Holton block. In addition, he completed the Holton Power and Ice company building in December of 1905. He had purchased these utilities from the California Development Company right out from under the newly elected City of Imperial officials. Power lines would be extended from the Holton Power Company to Imperial, Brawley and Calexico. Contractor J. L. Travers came down from Redlands to construct the new buildings and planned to have ample skilled labor for the expected boom in new construction. Seven new frame houses were constructed by the first family residents of the new city. A lumber yard and hardware store were also opened.

Holt heard that the Southern Pacific Railroad was lending the California Development Company $200,000 to save it from insolvency. This did not bother him in the least for he knew that this entire amount would have to be spent to meet the obligations of the Development Company for new canals to supply water to the many farmers who had bought water stock but still didn't have water delivered to their land. He recognized that none of this money could possibly find its way into the hands of the Imperial Land Company. He knew that the City of Imperial could not compete financially with his new town of El Centro.

T. P. and other business men who had large amounts of money invested in Imperial clearly saw the challenge Holt had cast before them. T. P., being a true entrepreneur, admired what Holt had planned and carried out. T. P. recognized that Imperial was at a tremendous disadvantage in the upcoming struggle for supremacy between these two cities. The men of Imperial had to come up with a plan to outwit W. F. or they stood to lose much value of their Imperial land if El Centro proved to be victorious.

T. P. recognized that it would be the investors in the City of Imperial who would have to bear the entire cost of the battle as the Imperial Land Company's coffers were empty and the California Development Company was struggling to stay afloat in spite of the $200,000 dollar loan from the Southern Pacific. That sum would barely cover the costs of the new canals necessary to satisfy their commitments to the holders of their water shares. Now, with the Colorado River running amuck, it would take that much to bring the river under control.

The bitter facts were, as the men of Imperial knew, that the California Development Company, by selling the Power and Ice Utilities to W. F. Holt, had cut the throat of the City of Imperial because they needed the $35,000 so badly. Now they would have to contend with these major utilities, with their buildings and employment opportunities, being located in the competition's city. What was needed was a plan clever enough to outwit W. F. Holt and his Redlands syndicate in spite of the tremendous advantage in capital they had available for the upcoming battle. The men of Imperial met to devise just such a scheme.

CHAPTER 31

1906, THE 5TH AND 6TH

ATTEMPTS TO CLOSE THE BREAK

FAIL. HARRIMAN SAYS, "WE QUIT."

December 15, 1905, with the failure of the Edinger Dam, Rockwood was recalled as Chief Engineer. He immediately requested authorization to proceed with his plan for the Rockwood wooden headgate even though the super-flood that had washed away the Edinger Dam, had widened the intake from 200 feet prior to the flood to 900 feet after the flood. Because of this widening of the intake, Rockwood decided to increase the width of the gate to two-hundred and forty feet

He immediately received authorization from Mr. Randolph and construction of the earlier described cofferdam, which is on the same principal as a dry dock was begun on January 7, 1906. The cost of the coffer dam was very expensive and time consuming but when it was finished, work on the gate was quickly completed. From inside this water-tight Dam, completely surrounding the work area for the Rockwood gate, water was pumped and mud was dredged. The gate was built on three rows of thirty foot piles which were faced with water-tight planking. The gate, itself, was 240 feet long, 25 feet high and ten feet wide. The gate was completed April 18, 1906. C. R. Perry had drawn the plans which called for a great amount of rock to be dumped at both ends of the gate to anchor it in place and give it added stability. For some reason, this was never done.

The river was at the beginning of the spring—summer flood season. Water was pouring down the channel at the rate of 20,000 second-feet. This was a volume of water with which the engineers did not feel comfortable because this would be the low point from which the volume of water would increase as the flood season progressed. It, therefore, was decided to wait until the summer flood season had subsided.

During this waiting period, Rockwood again resigned as General Manager. His reason was that he found it impossible to handle things in a manner with which he felt comfortable. He complained that he was not permitted to implement his own ideas. On April 19, 1906, Epes Randolph appointed H. T. Cory, one of his trusted advisors, to take Rockwood's place as General Manager and Chief Engineer. During the prior year, Mr. Cory had made frequent trips to the area of the break and was well acquainted with Mr. Rockwood and his gate. Mr. Rockwood agreed to stay on as his advisor.

The day before Mr. Cory's appointment, the great earthquake struck the city of San Francisco. Mr. Cory went at once to San Jose to see for himself the condition of a giant clam shell dredge that had been ordered by Edinger during his time as Chief Engineer. The dredge had not been damaged though the buildings in which it had been manufactured had been demolished.

Incredibly, Epes Randolph had secured from Harriman a $200,000 appropriation to close the break while Mr. Harriman was standing among the earthquake and fire-ravaged city that was the hub of his great railroad empire. The securing of this appropriation as Harriman examined his terribly crippled railway facilities, not knowing whether the great tragedy would cause the collapse of his life's work, was according to Cory, "the most remarkable accomplishment of the entire matter."

Mr. Cory decided that a railroad line to the Rockwood gate was absolutely necessary. This line would start at Hanlon's Landing on the Southern Pacific line past Pilot Knob, a rocky mound just south west of Hanlon's Landing, to opposite the break at the

Rockford Gate. At Rocky Knob, he developed a massive stone quarry as quickly as possible. Just south of this railroad spur, he located clay soil and built a pit where large steam shovels could quickly fill railroad gondola cars with enormous amounts of dirt.

Mr. Cory was leaving nothing to chance. Prior to this, every engineer "knew" it was futile to try to close the break with rock as rock simply endlessly disappeared into the soft mud at the bottom of the channel. However, until this time they had no money to build a railroad line to carry vast quantities of rock to the scene of the break. For this reason they had to rely on pilings and brush mats to dam the river without sinking out of sight in the muddy bottom of the channel. Cory had the money and foresight to recognize the absolute necessity of such a spur line to where the closure would be attempted.

When the river's water had dropped to twenty-five thousand cubic feet per second, the task of closure was begun. Ample workmen and materials were rushed to the scene by the Company's steamer, Searchlight, in early August. The river channel which had been enlarged to almost a half mile by the summer floods was narrowed by jetties to six-hundred feet. A trestle was built over the sand bars left by the summer floods on a bed constructed of brush mats sunk by rock from the quarry and dumped by car loads. The coffer dam in which the Rockwood gate was built was removed and all the river's water that was bypassing the gate was forced to flow through the gate.

By October 10, nine-tenths of the water was flowing through the gate. On October 3, the earthen dike at the north end of the gate suddenly settled. This caused the gate to buckle up about four inches in the middle. This allowed water to get under the gate greatly weakening it. Rock was rushed to the site of the trouble with a new trestle quickly built by the railroad men. When a train load of rock was pushed onto this trestle, the trestle settled and the train was lost.

Without any warning, the gate broke in two and drifted about two hundred feet down stream. The wall of water released when

the gate went out eroded the pilings of the railroad trestle that
were located three hundred feet below the gate. The trestle failed
so quickly that a train was almost lost except that the locomotive
engineer hurriedly rushed his train across the trestle to the north
side of the channel in order to not leave it stranded. He brought
his train across the trestle one minute before it was destroyed.
Thus, the fifth attempt at closure of the break failed.

The rock-filled diversion dam used to force the water through
the Rockwood Gate was left unscathed while the gate, itself, failed.
This caused the engineers to examine this rock filled gate built
without the use of pilings or mattresses. They became convinced
that such a dam at the mouth of the break could close the break
without pilings and brush mats if rock were poured into the gap at
a fast enough rate. Now, with the railroad spur and the rock quarry
they were convinced that this could be done.

From this diversion dam, the Hind Dam, whose construction
was conceived and directed by Thomas Hind and was built without the use of brush mattresses or pilings, the trestles used for the
Rockwood Gate were rebuilt. The workmen started dumping rock
at a furious rate building up a series of three rock dams. By October 29, these dams had raised the water to the point that it started
flowing down its old channel to the Gulf of Mexico. The water
flowing into the Valley had been stopped.

The problem now facing the engineers was that almost no
water was flowing through the headings into the valley's irrigation
canals. The engineers solved this problem by rapidly dredging out
the bypassed four miles of the main canal from the Chaffey Gate at
Hanlon's Landing to the Alamo Canal. By doing this as quickly as
possible, the valley never suffered from the lack of irrigation water.

The river had been returned to its old channel for but seven
days when a great flood came down the Gila River into the Colorado and then hit the newly erected Hind Dam. Within a day's
time the flood breached the levee being erected alongside the dam
and the entire river was again flowing into the Imperial valley. The
sixth attempt at closure had failed.

The railroad had already advanced $1,532,000 to the California Development Company in six attempts to put the Colorado River back in its old banks leading to the Gulf of Mexico. This, along with the other bonds and damage claims which the Company owed amounted to more than $4,000,000 in liabilities. The company had only $2,000,000 in actual assets. Mr. Cory could not see how the Company could repay its debts out of current income and more money would be required to again try to close the breach. In addition, the company would be faced in the future with heavy costs to avoid a repeat performance by the untamed river. With such figures before him, Mr. Cory could not do other than recommend to Mr. Randolph that all advances to the California Development Company stop immediately. Mr. Randolph agreed with Mr. Cory's appraisal of the situation and so reported to Mr. Harriman. Around the 8th of December, the settlers in Imperial Valley were advised that no more money would be advanced by the Southern Pacific to close the breach.

Early in the year of 1906, the settlers were not impaired at all by the antics of the river. Water was building in the plains behind Mexicali but none had as yet entered the valley except through the Alamo and New River channels. This was but a minor nuisance and the folks in the valley left the problem of the river to the engineers.

In the Imperial Press now owned by F. G. Havens, an editorial comment appeared in the February 10, 1906 issue:

> In the promotion of the town of El Centro, an entirely new departure in town making has been followed . . . about all other schemes have been promoted by getting the public to buy on promises of what would be done. In El Centro it is different; the capitalists who are building it up are investing more than $100,000 in substantial brick buildings and in the establishment of industries before advertising it or making any effort to sell lots. In this connection we may add that Mr. W. F. Holt, more than anyone else, is due the credit

for this great development. As the organizer of the Holton
Power Company, he is causing the expenditure of $300,000.

It is obvious from this article that Mr. Havens had joined Mr.
Holt and his associates. It is also obvious that Mr. Heber, while
still President of the Imperial Land Company had good intelligence
in the enemy camp and was aware that Mr. Holt had great plans
for the future of El Centro as the principal city in the Valley and
that these plans did not include Imperial or the Imperial Land
Company. He learned that Holt had every newspaper in the valley
in his hip pocket. In the coming battle for the supremacy of these
two cities, Mr. Holt would have complete control of the only media
available to mass-distribute information to the people in the valley.
With such control of the media, the contest between the two cities
would be whatever term was used in those days to describe a "slam
dunk."

In an attempt to provide a more level playing field, Mr. Heber
and his friends started the Imperial Standard. The answer to the
question as to why Imperial needed two newspapers was now answered. Mr. Holt purchased the Imperial Press from Mr. Havens
and moved it to his new city changing it's name to the Imperial
Valley Press. The first issue published in El Centro came off the
presses on March 1, 1906, with F. G. Havens as editor. E. F. Howe,
former editor and publisher of the Imperial Press, purchased the
Imperial Standard and announced that he would make it a daily.
Clearly, he would be the voice of the City of Imperial and the
Imperial Land Company.

By April, El Centro had changed from being a barley field to a
city. 1,700,000 bricks and 1,050,000 feet of lumber had gone
into buildings. These buildings were being filled with Imperial
businessmen moving to the new, glamorous city. Water lines had
been laid in the streets and the first domestic water tank was erected.
In June, El Centro freight shipments exceeded those of Imperial.
The new Ice plant came on line in July, storing huge quantities of
ice. In August, the offices of the Holton Power Company moved to

El Centro. The men of Imperial were seeing the results of the
California Development Company's decision to sell these utilities
to W. F. Holt. They felt betrayed.

Holt's plans had been set long before the Yellow Terror jumped
its banks and flowed into the valley. His plans had to go ahead in
spite of the new developments at the heading. There are those who
talk of the courage he had in continuing building El Centro during the time of the errant river. When the Southern Pacific took
over the task of making the closure, everyone in the valley, including W. F. Holt, could not but believe the problem would be solved.
Very few settlers discontinued investing in the valley during this
time and fewer still left the valley because of the river. Their reasons were the same as Holt's. The problem would be solved and
besides, what were the alternatives?

Mr. Holt must be given the highest plaudits for being a most
intelligent entrepreneur and businessman. He had great vision and
creative ability. But his greatest ally in his success was the
Government's actions in destroying the financial stability of the
California Development Company. In his fight to establish El
Centro as the principal economic center of the valley, W. F. Holt
was the matador in a bull fight where he had only a wounded cow
for an opponent. Under these conditions, those who had a large
investment in the city of Imperial could not win.

The businessmen of Imperial, including T. P., met to devise
some scheme that might give them some chance against such overwhelming odds. They knew that the Imperial Valley must become
an independent county for the current County Seat of San Diego
was days away due to the coastal mountain range that separated
them. They decided their only chance for survival was to advance
the vote for county division and county seat to a date well before
Holt had had a chance to complete his development of El Centro.
If the vote for County Seat occurred while Imperial still had an
advantage in registered voters, perhaps Imperial could prevail. As
County Seat, Imperial would have all the county buildings which

would even out the capital being poured into El Centro by W. F. Holt and the Redlands syndicate.

The question will arise in the mind of the reader: Why were the settlers in the Valley so calm despite the calamities that were befalling the engineers at the river breach? The answer lies in the remarkable design of structures that held the key to the water that flowed through the irrigation system and provided the water that kept Imperial Valley from returning to its prior primitive desert state. The structures of which we speak diverted the water from the Alamo channel to the irrigation canals that delivered irrigation water to all the farms in the valley. These structures held throughout the flood despite their carrying several times the flow of water for which they had been designed. These engineering marvels were the Alamo Waste Way and Sharp's Heading. The structures were designed by engineer C. N. Perry.

The Alamo channel was used by the irrigation project as the main canal to Sharp' Heading which was in Mexico about one mile south of the border and about six miles west of Calexico. The water in the Alamo channel was raised by means of the Alamo Waste Way which was a weir across the Alamo channel. A weir is a dam who's waste way can be raised or lowered. When the waste way was raised, water in the Alamo canal was raised to the point where some water was diverted into the irrigation canal intakes. Had these structures failed, the Imperial Valley would have returned to its prior desert state in a few weeks. They did not fail and, therefore, the valley pioneers never suffered from lack of irrigation water throughout the flood.

In the spring of 1906, the settlers were awakened to the hazards of the Yellow Terror changing its course and flowing into the valley. The water that had been overflowing the Alamo channel well south of Sharp's Heading and flowing eastward across the delta began to rise covering much territory south of the border and flooding much of Imperial Water Company # 6. Mexicali, the sister city south of the border opposite the city of Calexico in the Imperial Valley, saw the flood water approaching its outskirts. The flood waters were also approaching Calexico. It looked as if every thing south of the main canal two miles north of Calexico would be flooded. T. P.'s farm lay just north of the main canal.

Calexico was in imminent danger of being flooded with several feet of water. Every able-bodied man and boy in Calexico as well as many others in the valley, including T. P.'s brother Robert, turned to building levees to protect their cities and three farms that lay in harms way. Many homes and buildings in Calexico were at risk. They built a wall of earth six feet high and a mile long. This levee held back the waters of the flooded lands on its other side for weeks. Then a resolution of the problem of the standing flood waters appeared to the south. The flood waters started to enlarge and cut back the New River channel down stream toward the Salton Sea. The gradient steepened as it went south. The soft soil and erosive action of the water formed rapids in the channel that speedily cut an expansive channel back toward the giant lake that lay around Calexico. It became a race between the cutting back of the channel which was moving south at the rate of a mile a day and the water rising over the top of the levees.

The men from the railroad and men from the valley went to the aid of the cutting back of the channel by using dynamite to hasten the cutting back. Soon the channel would be cut back to where it would drain the water building south and west of the main canal. Then on April 1, a gale as had been seldom seen in the valley, came in from the west raising waves on the lake west of the levee thrown up by the men of Calexico that lapped at the top of the six-foot high and one mile-long levee. A call went out for volunteers and T. P. went to Robert's house to pick him up and they both responded as did almost every able-bodied man from Imperial south to the border. When T. P. climbed on top of the levee to help the men closing breaches in the levee as quickly as they opened, he saw a terrifying sight. Wind whipped water reached as far as the eye could see toward the coastal mountains. It looked as if the entire valley south, west and north of the levee was one vast lake. The wind blew for three days as these exhausted men fought the waters lapping at the top of the levee. T. P.

and Robert, the Dutchmen whose great, great, great, great, great-grandfather had come over to New Netherland from the dikes on the delta of the Rhine river in Holland, were, figuratively speaking, holding their fingers in the dike protecting Calexico on the delta of the Colorado river.

Meanwhile, men in rocky row boats, at the peril of their lives, were dropping sacks of powder in the channel and detonating them to hasten the progress of the cutting back of the channel. Among the men manning the row boats was Marshall Mobley Meadows, one of the first friends T. P. had made when he came to the valley. The race between the cutting back of the channel and the rise of the water above the levees was a close one but finally the cutting back of the channel won and the waters surrounding Calexico were sucked into the giant gorge that replaced the former channel that was New River and the waters began to subside. Exhausted men mounted their horses and rode them home while others drove home in their wagons, victorious despite overwhelming odds against the flood and the three-day gale that blew the water perilously close to destroying the levee. After catching only cat naps for three days, they had much sleeping to do to catch up on the three nights of lost sleep.

Upon reaching home, T. P. told Carry, Grandma Allen and the boys that he was too tired to tell them the perilous story he had just endured. He told them that he would relate the story in full as soon as he awoke from a good long sleep.

At the same time the men of Calexico were building their levee that was six feet high and one mile long, the men and boys of Imperial and El Centro were strengthening and raising up the west banks of the canal opposite their cities. This levee alone was protecting the towns from the flood water west of the main canal which had built up two feet higher than the tops of the canals themselves. They had to build foot bridges across the canal in order to carry material to strengthen and raise the height of the levee west of the canal. T. P., Al and George worked hard on this task. The boys in the grammar school were dismissed from their classes to help their fathers with the emergency. The same chasm that finally reached the water around Calexico and sucked it down to the Salton Sea sucked all the flood water west of the main canal opposite Imperial and El Centro into its thirsty gorge. Within a week the business men and farmers in the valley had returned to their normal duties and again the problem of the river was forgotten and left to the experienced engineers of the Southern Pacific Railroad and the California Development Company now controlled by the Southern Pacific.

One continuing problem of the flood could not be forgotten as it was happening before their eyes. That problem was the great chasm that was eroding along the course of the New River channel ran close to the tracks and buildings of the Southern Pacific as well as a few frame dwellings in El Centro. As the great chasm eroded its way through this area, it sucked everything in its path into it's rushing water and carried them down to the Salton Sea. The Southern Pacific buildings and the frame houses were dismantled and saved before the chasm reached them. The chasm also eroded its way through Mexicali where the buildings were constructed of adobe. These could not be moved and were lost. Hundreds of acres of valuable farm land were also devoured by the chasm.

In spite of all the destruction caused by the chasm, the net results were positive for the valley. The channel of the New River prior to the great flood was sufficient to handle the waste water from the irrigation district at that time. However, in the years to come when the irrigated land increased multi fold, the old channel would have been grossly inadequate to carry off the waste water running through the irrigation canals.

The businessmen and farmers continued investing in the Valley throughout the remainder of 1906, completely believing that the railroad and the engineers would solve the problem of the errant river. Imagine their surprise and chagrin, when on December 8, 1906, the Southern Pacific advised the pioneers in the valley that no more money would be advanced to close the break.

CHAPTER 32

SAVE OUR VALLEY !!!!

When the word reached the valley that Harriman and the Southern Pacific were quitting their attempt to put the mighty Colorado back in its old banks, the settlers were shaken to their bootstraps. At first, there was disbelief for they saw what a bonanza the valley's produce was to the railroad. Disbelief was replaced with utter despair. Despair was replaced with feverish activity by the pioneer settlers in their attempt to determine and set in motion a plan to save the valley.

T. P. had paid little attention to the river's antics except when it was threatening to flood Imperial and Calexico. When the giant Southern Pacific stepped into the role of protector of the valley he had no doubt that they had the ability and determination to tame the river. With their sudden departure, he decided to carefully study the entire problem of the breakthrough and the conditions that had brought them about. He and Carrie thought about all the sacrifices their family endured in those impossible days when they first came to the valley with the wagon train from Mesa, living in a small tent through the terrible sand storms. They recalled the family's delight when the land was first patented. They remembered the unbearable heat of that first summer when ignoring the one hundred and twenty degree days they leveled the land and planted the first crop. They remembered the pride the family felt when their ranch sold the first cash crop grown in the valley. They remembered all those endless days of struggle they had endured to bring the valley to the successful enterprise it was in

December of 1906. "This just can't and won't be the end of our valley and our six years of hard work," Carrie remonstrated.

"Damn," T. P. said to Carrie, "It was those no-good Federal Government people that brought us to this state of affairs. The Agriculture Department with its Circular # 9 started the whole thing. Then the Reclamation Department's jealousy of free enterprise for stepping into their domain kept it going. And finally, it was the War Department's joining with them, to declare the unnavigable Colorado River navigable resulting in Heber making the un-gated cut, that caused this disaster. The California Development Company didn't have a chance against the Federal Government. They were the ones that pushed us off the cliff."

T. P. had no ill feelings for Rockwood or the California Development Company. He understood capitalists. He could understand their motivation. They were out to make money. That's why they did what they did. Knowing a man's motives made it a fair game. Under such circumstances you could usually figure out what he was going to do. Politics were different. Incompetence in the free enterprise arena meant a man would go broke and that would be that. In politics, you could be wrong a dozen times and you still had your job. Look at those two young fellows that did the research for the Agriculture Department's circular # 9. They began the ruination of the Imperial Valley and, yet, they still had their jobs. And what motivated the Reclamation and War departments. There was no money in it for them to destroy the Imperial Valley. What motivated people in Government bureaucracy was an enigma to T. P.

Why had the Southern Pacific pulled out? He had to find out for himself. He knew that their motivation had to be that the costs exceeded the rewards. That was a capitalist's motivation. He had never been down to the site of the river breakthrough. Tom Beach had been and had described it to him. He had to see for himself and decided to ride his horse down to the break the next day. He packed his saddle pack for a two-day trip and told Mama that he would leave from the ranch the next morning. Because the ranch was more than five miles closer to the break than their house, he would stay with the foreman and his family that night.

Early the next morning, he saddled his horse and started his journey down into Mexico to the site of the break. When he arrived there, he examined the wreckage left from the six attempts that had been made to close the break. He could see for himself what a foolish move it had been for Heber to have ordered the cut to the Alamo through the soft alluvial fill without building a gate. "Well," he thought, "hindsight is always 100 percent."

Tom had told him that most engineers felt that the Colorado River, the Yellow Terror as they called it, would have broken through and started to refill the old fresh water lake within the next two or three decades whether the cut had been made or not. The equilibrium of the river's flow was at such a critical point that natural forces would have caused the river to change its course and flow into the valley in the near future. Heber's cut, along with the unseasonable series of floods, simply precipitated the event. From his own observations, he could see that this was so.

To his own satisfaction, he had solved the problem as to why the Southern Pacific was pulling out. This change in the course of the river was not just a temporary, one time thing the valley was experiencing. This was to be a constant battle forever or at least until the Colorado River was tamed by engineers building dams to control the surges and ebbs of the river's flow. This changed his prospective of the matter for the costs would be staggering, and more than even the great Southern Pacific Railroad could bear. If the Government wanted to stick its nose into the valley's business, as they had done with such devastating results in the past, perhaps the Federal Government's desire to be active in valley affairs could be diverted by the settlers into more positive channels such as the taming of the great Colorado River at a point well above the Imperial Valley. This had to be the ultimate solution to forever stopping the river's urge to refill the ancient fresh water lake that had once occupied the Imperial Valley. He clearly saw that the Federal Government had to be weaned from being the settler's antagonist

CONQUEST OF A CONTINENT 439

and guided toward being their savior. He returned from his trip revitalized.

Upon his return, he found the people of the valley organizing themselves to make a united front to save their valley. At first, pledges were solicited from the valley's organizations and individuals in an attempt to close the breach with money from within the valley. W.F. Holt was among the first in the valley to pledge one hundred thousand dollars through his Holton Power Company. The directors of the Mutual Water Companies pledged five hundred thousand dollars. Many other important enterprises in the valley pledged money and soon nine hundred and fifty thousand dollars had been pledged. Far more money was needed than could be raised from those in the valley using the valley's limited resources. These pledges were never collected. Instead the settlers decided on taking another tack.

The settlers had decided to appeal to President Theodore Roosevelt. T. P. had come to the same conclusion during his trip to the breach. He reasoned that it was the deviltry of the U. S. Government starting with Circular # 9 that had put the California Development Company in such tight financial straits that they had no money to do the things that had to be done. Just as the valley's promoters were getting financially well, Circular #9, the Reclamation Service and the Department of War knocked the props right out from under them. For this reason, he felt no hesitation in forcefully bringing to President Theodore Roosevelt's attention that a very important fertile valley was about to be covered by one of the largest fresh water lakes in the world. President Roosevelt was, after all, the great conservationist. He couldn't help but see the government's responsibility to save this great national treasure from inundation. When T. P. found that the other settlers had come to this same conclusion, he joined them and soon this was the wheel to which everyone in the valley applied his and her shoulder.

The Southern Pacific's pulling out from the battle to return the Colorado to its old banks was precipitating a national catastrophe that was on the front pages of every major city's newspapers. As such, the President had to be aware of what was happening and its ramifications. The men of the valley decided to send a committee to talk directly with the President to enlist his aid in returning the great river back into its old course into the gulf of Mexico. At the same time they organized a telegram and letter writing campaign to the President. As a result, the President was not only deluged with telegrams from throughout the country, but he also met with valley settlers who were very convincing in their arguments that the river had to be put back into its old bed.

The President explained his dilemma in his meeting with the committee of valley settlers. Congress would have to appropriate money for the expenses involved in such a large undertaking, and congress was about to recess. He agreed that something had to be done and had to be done quickly. In thinking the matter over he came to realize that the only solution was for the Southern Pacific to re-engage themselves in the task of harnessing the run-away river. Here, he was on the horns of a dilemma because, but a short time before, the president had quarreled with Harriman after years of friendship and he had denounced Harriman as "an undesirable citizen," "a corruptionist," and "an enemy of the republic." Nonetheless, he took the matter up by wire with Harriman. Harriman responded that this was a job for the Federal Government and the Reclamation Service. The President explained that the Reclamation Service could not act without authority from Congress which had just adjourned that day. He, also, explained that the Federal Government could not do the work involved in closing the break in Mexico without an arrangement with the sovereign nation of Mexico. Such arrangement would take time and would cause a fatal delay in closing the break. The President assured Harriman that the government would reimburse the Southern Pacific for all the costs the Railroad would incur.

On December 20, fifteen days after the Southern Pacific pulled out, Harriman agreed to re-undertake the closing of the break. He issued an order to Epes Randolph to "Close that break at all costs!"

Epes relayed the order to Mr. Cory and immediately went to the scene of the break. That same day, December 20, the seventh and finally successful attempt to close the breach was begun.

With the plight of the valley so clearly brought to the President's attention by the valley's settlers, and his immediate action in placing pressure on Harriman, the re-engagement of the Southern Pacific in the closing of the break happened so quickly that all equipment was still in the field. Therefore, it was just a matter of assembling a work crew to restart the project. This was done in a remarkably short period of time. Rock again was quarried in unbelievable amounts and shipped by flat cars and gondola cars to the work site. Freight trains carrying this rock were given priority over crack passenger trains. Workmen worked around the clock with a new crew relieving a working crew with no delay whatsoever. At night the crews worked in the eery light of giant searchlights

Parallel trestles were constructed concurrently using five pile drivers. The work was terribly dangerous especially on a floating pile driver which was located in a central position between the two trestles. Two boats were kept at the ready in midstream to rescue the men on this pile driver if it should topple over while moving the ninety foot piles into place. Two extra pile drivers were ready to take over the task if the floating pile driver was lost. During the building of these two trestles, which would carry the trains that would dump the rocks, gravel and clay to create the dam across the break, freshets brought large amounts of debris against the bents and three times portions of the trestles were lost. When a portion of a trestle was lost, it was quickly rebuilt and on January 27, 1907 the two trestles were completed.

During the next fourteen days, the trestles were never empty. Six hundred men dropped car after car of rock, gravel and clay into the yellow swirling water of the Colorado river. Finally the rock began to appear above its surface. February 10, at eleven o'clock the break was repaired and the Colorado returned to its old bed flowing to the Gulf of California. In fourteen days they had dumped two thousand and fifty-seven carloads of rock, 221 carloads of gravel and 203 carloads of clay into the breach and stopped cold the errant swirling waters rushing down to the Salton Sea.

The railroad men didn't trust the wily Yellow Terror for a second. The workforce continued to work on the levee system for the summer floods of 1907 threatened to break through again. By constant vigilance of the work crews, the river was forced to stay in its old bed. Workmen constantly patrolled the levees and with fifty thousand sacks, fifty thousand cubic yards of rock and six steam shovels at the ready, aborted any attempt by the muddy Colorado to again flow to the Salton Sea. The Southern Pacific had not only done what the President asked them to do in closing the break, but also strengthened the levee system to reduce the possibility of breaks in the future.

Unbelievably, except to politicians, when congress assembled for its new session, the house refused to honor the President's commitment to Harriman. They offered only to reimburse 20 percent of the Southern Pacific's cost of closing the breach. The house reported, "We oppose this proposed gift to the Southern Pacific Railroad Company, as well as all other gratuities to private enterprise." Go figure politicians!

In a report to congress in which he outlined the circumstances leading up to his promise to Harriman to reimburse the Southern Pacific for closing the breach, the President severely criticized the California Development Company implying that they had made improper use of money from the sale of water stock. He said that the Reclamation Service should take over all responsibility for construction of irrigation projects involved in supplying water to the valley. "In order to accomplish this," he said, "the government should acquire all rights to the California Development Company . . . upon such reasonable terms as shall protect the Government and the water users."

George Chaffey was appalled by the many erroneous statements and innuendos in the President's message. He wrote to the President asking where he had obtained such false information. The President immediately responded and sent George Chaffey the document on which he had bases his remarks. Charles D. Wolcott, Chief of the Reclamation Service, had written the document which revealed the department's obviously bias. In the controversy that ensued, George Chaffey clearly delineated the jealousy and obstructionism of the Reclamation Department toward the California Development Company. He more than upheld his side of the story in the press.

In his address the President had also said, "The Imperial Valley will never have a safe and adequate supply of water until the main canal extends to the Laguna Dam. As each end of this dam is connected with rock bluffs, it provides a permanent heading founded on rock for the diversion of the waters." T. P. totally agreed with the president on this matter and would spend many hours in the coming years working for its fulfillment, but he was equally opposed to the Reclamation Department taking over the control of the valley's irrigation system

Though the break was closed, the California Development Company was destroyed financially. Cory, of the Southern Pacific, was General Manager of its shell. Roy D. McPherrin was Assistant General Manager and controlled its affairs in Calexico. T. P. had been Roy's close friend since he had come to the valley in 1901. Roy had come to the valley in 1900. He was a graduate of the law school of the University of Nebraska and his first business opportunity was as a part of the surveying crew of the California Development Company. Almost immediately, he had filed on one hundred and sixty acres of land near Blue Lake. As a landowner he became engaged in all of the farm owners problems.

As the Assistant General Manager of the C. D. Company shell, he was responsible for all of its daily activities from when the Southern Pacific took over the company until 1910. He did a magnificent job in keeping all sides (the valley settlers and water users, the creditors, the plaintiffs in suits against the company) reasonably happy. With the many lawsuits against the company, the California Development Company applied to the Superior Court of San Diego county to be declared insolvent and to have a receiver appointed. The court declared the company bankrupt and appointed W. H. Holabird as receiver in 1910. Under Mexican Law, a receiver was needed to handle the affairs of the Mexican company. General A. F. Andrade was appointed receiver for the Mexican Company.

With the impending demise of the California Development Company after the expenses incurred in the closing of the breech and its resulting insolvency, it is a proper time to reflect on the two men responsible for bringing the dead Colorado desert to life. We are speaking of C. R. Rockwood, though he will return briefly latter in our story as an employee of the Imperial Irrigation District, and Anthony A. Heber. Their foresight, dedication and undying belief that this desolate, inhospitable desert could be made to bloom and turn a verdant green, was wholly responsible for the creation of the Imperial Valley. These men have been center-stage in our story since the Imperial Valley was just a gleam in their eyes.

Rockwood began his saga to create the mighty Imperial Valley in 1891 and had spent his last sixteen years first surveying the dead world of the Colorado desert, then years of frustration finding financial backing, finally, seeing this brain child of his come to fruition under his company, the California Development Company. Now, he witnessed its collapse leaving only the shell of his once proud company. The dream had come true but fate and the U. S. Government had robbed him of his reward. The reward would go to another who was in the right place at the right time with ample capital behind him. Rockwood and Heber now move off into the wings, but their contributions cannot be forgotten or diminished. T. P. had always looked up to them because the development of the valley had been from the very beginning a cause which they believed in with their whole hearts and souls; although as all capitalists they expected reward for their risks.

After his ouster as president of the California Development Company at the Annual Meeting of 1904, Mr. Heber became interested in property in Goldfield, Nevada. On November 17,

1906 while a guest in the Goldfield hotel, newly erected and the pride of Nevada, it caught fire in a strong wind storm and burned to the ground. A. H. Heber was trapped in his room and burned to death. T. P. felt a great personal loss at hearing of his tragic death for he had always held him in his highest esteem. C. R. Rockwood severed all connections with the California Development Company in October 1906.

Their corporation had been destroyed but the Imperial Valley lives on as a monument to their foresight and perseverance. The Imperial Valley is one more example of the building of this new nation by gritty men and women who were willing to bet their blood, sweat and pocketbook on what other's thought was only a daydream and a delusion. Unfortunately, there is no natural law which says that if you are right in your assessment of the possibilities of a great project and work hard to turn it into a reality, you will succeed financially. Man doesn't operate in a vacuum, but operates in interaction with other men. Sometimes, the actions of others from motives that can't be explained, yank the rug out from under what should have been a financial success.

Those capitalists who had done the work to bring the Imperial Valley into being were completely wiped out. The California Development Company's creditors controlled its future and were trying to determine how to get as much of its debts paid as possible from the shell of this once promising corporation.

CHAPTER 33

A TALE OF TWO CITIES IMPERIAL

BATTLES EL CENTO FOR SURVIVAL

The battle for County Seat of the newly proposed County of Imperial—between the two cities of Imperial, the oldest city in the valley, and El Centro, the valley's newest city, continued unabated during the crisis with the errant Colorado River. The demise of the California Development Company under Rockwood or Heber eliminated the company from having any proprietary interest in the City of Imperial. The Southern Pacific railroad had no desire to be involved in valley politics. Its interest was solely in protecting the valley from the river so that it could continue to profit from the shipping of the valley's produce. Imperial was on its own. The Citizens Party of Imperial and their resources were left with the responsibility of protecting the city's interests.

This was to the benefit of W. F. Holt and the Redlands syndicate. They couldn't have hoped for a better outcome. The demise of Rockwood and Heber meant that their chief financial adversary, the California Development Company, was no longer involved in the battle for County Seat. W. F. Holt's and the Redlands syndicate's financial backing were infinitely greater than the financial backing of those behind Imperial's bid for County Seat. They had the money to buy the electric and power utilities from the California Development Company when it was in such dire financial straights that they got them for next to nothing.

They also had the resources to purchase and move the Imperial

Press from Imperial to El Centro, and had purchased or started newspapers in Calexico, Holtsville and Brawley. Imperial's backers only had the new Imperial Standard newspaper to carry their side of the story. The fact that W. F.'s foresight and resources got control of all but one of the valley's five newspapers, gave his City of El Centro a tremendous edge in the upcoming battle for county seat. The slings and arrows of outrageous fortune that brought Rockwood and Heber to their knees put W. F. Holt in a position to reap the reward from the creation of the valley that these two men so richly deserved.

T. P. and the men from Imperial realized that they had an uphill struggle if they were to win the county seat for Imperial. At this point, Imperial had two very important factors in its favor: First, it had far more registered voters than the upstart El Centro. However, many of Imperial's registered voters were toying with moving to the city of El Centro because of its well-maintained streets and brand-new buildings, and the many employees and their residences that its ice house and public utilities would bring to that city. Second, those voters north of Imperial also outnumbered those to the south of El Centro. It would be reasonable to assume that voters would vote for the city that was closest to where they lived. These demographics were bound to change dramatically in the near future in favor of El Centro. The glamor of the brand-new city with its new buildings, streets and employment opportunities were bound to draw population to it. If Imperial was to prevail in the election for County Seat, time was of the essence.

This, T. P. kept forcefully bringing to the attention of the men backing Imperial. "If we can't cause this election to be held almost immediately, we will lose it," he hammered home to Judge Farr, F. C. Paulin, R. D. McPherrin, Leroy Holt (yes, the battle of the cities found the two brothers on different sides), Rev. Charles Wentworth, Arthur Edgar and all the other fellow backers of Imperial. Upon his urging, Imperial made the first move. Invitations were mailed to one hundred leading citizens of the valley in which they were invited to attend a meeting to be held in Imperial on May 2, 1907.

Almost all one-hundred invitees assembled at the assigned place and time. R. D. McPherrin was elected chairman and recognized Judge Farr who introduced a resolution calling for the division of San Diego County and the creation of a new Imperial County. The resolution called for the chairman to appoint a committee of three from each precinct to conduct the campaign. Professor McCully, of Calexico, called to the attention of those in attendance that this meeting was not representative of all those who lived in the valley. Nonetheless, the resolution carried and the campaign was on. Imperial had started its master plan for an early election to win the county seat for Imperial, and they had won the preliminary skirmish.

Holt and his contingent were taken aback by this preemptive strike by the men of Imperial. They needed to take control of the timing of the election for they, too, knew that if the election could be delayed long enough, victory would be theirs. Time was in their favor for the demographics that were now against them would shift their way as voters moved to the new City of El Centro. They met to develop a counter strategy to that being employed by the men of Imperial. They decided to make every effort to stall the election until late fall. The Holt faction called for a meeting of all who were opposed to an early election to be held in El Centro May 8. The turn out for the meeting far exceeded the meeting caller's expectations. The meeting was held in the Masonic Hall in El Centro. The Hall was filled to overflowing with two hundred and seventy-three citizens.

News of the meeting reached the ears and eyes of T. P. and the other Imperial men, and they were ready for the challenge. They spread the word among all those who were after an Imperial victory, and the call was out to pack the El Centro meeting. The Reverend Charles Wentworth, of Imperial, was elected chairman. The chairman permitted all who wished to debate for and against delay to have their say. The debate went far into the night; but chairman Wentworth knew how the vote would ultimately turn out for the Imperial men had counted the house and knew they had a victory. Finally there was a call for the vote and the vote was taken. Much to the surprise of W. F. and contingent, they discovered that the Imperial men had outwitted them again right in the meeting they had called. To their surprise the vote for an early election was 156 to 117. They had been bested a second time by T. P. and the Imperial men. W. F. realized he had underestimated his foe and made a solemn promise to himself never to allow this to happen again. His city's fate hung in the balance and he was determined to win the battle at all costs.

From this moment forward through the election, the battle for County Seat between these neighboring cities became the bitterest, dirtiest and most intense struggle for County Seat in the entire west and probably anywhere in the entire nation. When El Centro pulled out all stops to win victory, Imperial followed in a like manner.

Chairman McPherrin, elected at the Imperial meeting, took the vote as a mandate to go ahead appointing the campaign committee as he had been directed to do by the resolution passed at that meeting. T. P. was honored to be one of the twenty men Chairman McPherrin named to serve on the committee. The committee's responsibility was to circulate a petition among registered voters calling for a county division and the formation of a new county to be named Imperial. After collecting this list of voters on the petition, the committee presented it to the Board of Supervisors of San Diego County. The petition contained the names of more than eight hundred registered valley voters. The Board of Supervisors heard the petition at their meeting of July 5, and granted it, calling the election for August 6.

Elections were immediately called in the various precincts in the valley. Each precinct elected delegates to represent its voters at a non-partisan convention of delegates to be held July 15, in Imperial. This convention would nominate candidates for the various county offices. T. P. was again honored to be elected by his precinct,

Imperial, as one of its twenty delegates. He arrived early for the convention to try to determine the sense of the delegates' positions, however; he was unable to determine from the sixty some delegates which way the convention was leaning. Both Imperial and El Centro had tickets with slates of candidates for the various county offices.

The meeting was called to order by R. D. McPherrin. Imperial and El Centro immediately tested the flavor of the delegates in the election of the convention's chairman and secretary. C. H. Day of Brawley was elected chairman and O. B. Tout, editor of the Calexico newspaper, was elected secretary. T. P. was disappointed with this outcome; as both of these men were in the El Centro camp. W. F., he thought, had learned his lesson and had done a good job of buttonholing the uncommitted delegates. The sleeping lion had awakened and it wouldn't be as easy to win skirmishes in the future as it had been at the last two meetings. From the two tickets proposed by Imperial and El Centro, the delegates nominated one non-partisan ticket. These candidates were almost exclusively from the south end of the valley, another defeat for Imperial!

T. P. and the Imperial men were very discouraged by the outcome of the convention and realized that W. F. and the El Centro contingent had the money and the determination to win this battle. The only money available to the men of Imperial was their own; and, though they stood to lose if Imperial did not win the election for County Seat, none of them would be seriously hurt. On the other side, he could see that his opposition's determination was brought about by their very substantial investment. The syndicate stood to lose a great deal of money if El Centro lost in the coming election. They had the money to make sure it didn't. They had the newspapers. They had the men, time and motivation to campaign vigorously and, T. P. knew they would do just that.

The Imperial men didn't own the City of Imperial and were not as motivated as W. F. and the Redlands syndicate. They were working men and could not close down their businesses to conduct a campaign. The battle they could mount would be amateurish compared with the professional campaign that would be mounted by El Centro. For the next two weeks, from July 15 to August 6, the campaign assumed the bitterest and dirtiest course ever observed in valley politics. As was expected, the Imperial men found themselves out-gunned not only in time and men to campaign, but in money and most important in the media. The media in those days consisted exclusively in the newspapers, and as has been already said, four of the five newspapers, with the lions share of readers, were in W. F's hip pocket. When inaccuracies and innuendos were published in these papers, there was no way to get the correct information out to the voters.

The rhetoric in the opposing newspapers became bitter and hostile. The El Centro contingent decided to frighten the Imperial men by causing the arrest of editors E. F. Howe and S. J. Ulrey for criminal libel. Instead of frightening the men of Imperial, this infuriated them. "We don't have to take this type of intimidation," said Clark Bradshaw, one of the more hot-headed Imperial men. T. P. tried to quiet him down but to no avail. Clark saddled and mounted his horse, and with a gun strapped to his saddlehorn, rode down to El Centro. When he arrived there, he asked where he could find "that no good varment, Denver D. Pellet." Pellet was the editor of the Imperial Valley Press, the paper W. F. had bought out from under the City of Imperial and then moved to his City of El Centro. Fortunately, Pellet was warned in time and hid out until Bradshaw came to his senses.

W. F. Holt and the Redlands syndicate had the money, men and time to mount a formidable campaign during the two weeks between July 15 and August 6. W. F. and his men borrowed the only automobile in the valley, owned by C. H. Day who lived in Brawley but was in the El Centro camp. H. C. Day was infamous for his causing the arrest of the Imperial Standard editors. The El Cento syndicate used it to tour the valley. He and his men, driving this unusual vehicle never seen before by most valley residents, drew crowds of voters wherever they went. Then they spoke at these meetings from sun up to late at night in all parts of the valley every day for the two weeks prior to the election.

T. P. and the Imperial men tried to do the same thing in a horse and buggy in the limited time they could spare from work. The modern, new fangled automobile of W. F. and his men as compared to the stayed, old fashioned horse and buggy of the Imperial men accentuated the new modern City of El Centro as compared to the older conservative city of Imperial. This was just the comparison between the cities that W. F. wanted to make.

After the railroad reached it in the fall of 1903, Brawley, a townsite that had been laid out in that same year was the northern entryway to the valley from Los Angeles. It had grown because the immigrants first look at the valley was Brawley, and this was the first place where they saw crops growing in abundance in the middle of the desert. Many stayed right there and this was good for the new townsite. Some Brawley businessmen thought that since they had what was said to be one more voter than Imperial they should be the new County Seat and held a meeting to try to persuade the men of Imperial to unite with them. Four hundred and fifty Brawlyites joined together for this end.

T. P. and the other imperial men called to their attention that because they were located so far north in the valley, the entire south of the valley would unite in favor of El Centro which was also in the south. The honor of being county seat would have to go to a centrally located city. There was simply no hope for Brawley to gather enough votes to win. They convinced them that to split the northern vote was to assure a victory for the south end of the valley. El Centro was the city that favored the south end and they would win bringing the south a victory and would control expenditures for roads and other public services unless Brawley threw its weight behind Imperial.

W. F. saw that El Centro could lose the election if Brawley in the north of the valley, was not neutralized. With 430 voters, Brawley had the largest contingent of voters in the valley. This was one more voter than Imperial. W. F. found that no argument he could produce could sway these Brawley voters to vote for El Centro because they were closer to Imperial; therefore, he decided on a plan from the political bag of tricks. He would wait until a few days before the election and then counter the Imperial men's arguments by convincing the leading men of Brawley that their city could win by declaring their city in the running for County Seat. With W. F. controlling all the papers but one, the Imperial men wouldn't have enough time to counter this move.

The night before the election the El Centeo syndicate would help fund the greatest rally the city of Brawley, or the valley for that matter, had ever seen to convince the voters of Brawley that they had a real chance of becoming the county seat. This would neutralize the Brawley vote and stop Imperial from winning the election. Timing the rally for the day before the election would leave the Imperial men no time to counter this move. W. F. knew that Brawley had no chance in the election but he knew this staged rally would enthuse them to the point where they would think they did.

When the sixth of August was just three days away, eighteen leading men of Brawley announced that they would support only Brawley for County Seat. Imperial sent its first line, including T. P., to talk sense to the Brawley leaders. T. P. thought he had cleared their minds so that they saw that a vote for Brawley was in actuality a vote for El Centro. Imperial had to have Brawley's support or El Centro would win the election. The entire south of the valley was solid for El Centro.

Brawley in the north was Imperial's ace in the hole except that this ace in the hole was in plain site of the El Centro men. The Imperial men thought they had prevailed but as soon as they had left, the automobile full of El Centro syndicate men were making arrangements for the big rally the day before the election. Brawley was very proud of its band which had played at the Imperial meeting which T. P. had chaired when Imperial had become a city of the sixth class. Brawley named its band the "Submarine" band because it was a marine band and Brawley was below sea level. Bunting had been ordered and arrived in time to hang it from all the electric light poles and building fronts which would proclaim "Brawley, Imperial County Seat."

On August 5, the bunting was up, the band was playing and refreshments were served. The residents of Brawley found the moment magic and patriotism flowed in every red blooded Brawley man. Don't tell them Brawley couldn't win. Brawley would win and every man jack of them would vote solidly for Brawley. The Imperial men weren't even aware that the rally was taking place until it was too late. There was no chance to talk sense to the people of Brawley, nor would they have listened if one was brave enough to try. On August 6, the men of Brawley who were in the valley during this, the hot season, which was about half of the registered voters, rose early and with great patriotism and fervor cast his vote for Brawley for County Seat. W. F.'s plan had worked. One hundred and ninety-five for Brawley, eleven for Imperial and eighteen for El Centro.

Thirteen hundred and twenty six votes were cast in total in the valley. County division carried almost unanimously, eleven hundred and twenty for and eighty eight against. El Centro won the battle for county seat with 563 votes, Imperial had 455 votes and Brawley had 222. W. F.'s plan had succeeded. Brawley's votes held the key to the election and Brawley's votes had been nullified. The Imperial men were furious at the ploy that had been played on them but all is fair in love and politics. The votes were in and counted and El Centro had won. T. P. was secretly impressed with the cool calculated manner in which W. F. had won the day. It wasn't the end of the world for the Banta family. His tract just outside of Imperial's west city limit would wither on the vine, but he had his very successful tract in Calexico, his ranch and his very profitable real estate business.

"You know," he told Carrie and the boys, "it's really for the best. Those Redlands people have the money and can build a first class city. We men of Imperial don't have that sort of capital. I'm going to forgive and forget. We're all in this scalding valley together and I'm going to work with the winners to make it work. It didn't turn out the way I wanted, but I'm not going to be a sore loser." Mama and the boys were proud to have T. P. for a husband and a father.

The entire slate of El Centro candidates, as chosen at the July 15 convention, also prevailed. No quarter was given to the Imperial men.

CHAPTER 34

PEACE AND PROSPERITY COME TO

THE VALLEY AND THE BANTA FAMILY

During the years of the great flood and the year following with its political chaos, the day to day living of the Banta family continued like a play within a play. During the years of 1904 through 1907, the family continued in its normal daily life. George attended the local grammar school and was in the sixth grade in 1908 when the valley finally settled down to a normal life of peace and well-deserved prosperity. Al had graduated from the local grammar school and was attending the Imperial High school which opened its doors in September, 1907. He entered as a freshman that year along with his cousin grace. In 1911, they were in the first class to graduate as students who had attended Imperial High for all four years.

In 1907, a personal tragedy, that was not unexpected, struck the family. Grandma Allen simply slipped away during her sleep one night. At the age of ninety-eight, this ancient pioneer slipped her earthly bonds and went to her eternal reward. She had been born in Vermont in 1810 as Margaret Laughlin, two years prior to the war of 1812 when the British burned our White House. On April 14, 1831 she had married George Allen, the son of Barna Allen who was either the legitimate or illegitimate son of Ethan Allen (This matter was never settled to Carrie's satisfaction), a patriot of the American revolution. The couple had two children,

Oscar and Mary. Grandma Allen had out lived her husband and both of her children.

Her daughter, Mary, was Carrie's mother. When Mary passed away, she took the trip related earlier in this story to join her granddaughter's family on the west coast of the country that she had seen grow from swaddling clothes to maturity. As has been related, she spent the last five years of her life on the hot Colorado desert, the nation's last frontier. This old lady, who was the last of the baby boomers from the revolutionary war, died just as the last frontier was changing from being a frontier desert valley to a successful farming community. T. P. buried her in the Imperial Cemetery with a funeral and burial service befitting her 'larger than life' stature.

Earl completed the curricula of the Washburn Preparatory school in San Jose and graduated with honors in June, 1909. He was accepted as a Freshman at Stanford University and enrolled there in the fall, taking up residence in a dormitory on campus.

T. P. and Carrie, with Al and George, continued to live in the little house on Eighth Street just one block from T. P.'s office in the city of Imperial. Though most well off valley families sent the women and children to L. A. or the coast for the hot months of the year, T. P. and Carrie were in the land business together, and he did not make an investment without consulting her. Thus, she did not want to leave the valley for six months out of the year, and T. P. did not want her to go. Carrie was one of the few women to stay in the valley all year. Most left by the end of May and did not return till November. During the bleak days of the flood, many farmers were selling their farms and leaving the valley. Because buyers were almost nonexistent, T. P. and Carrie were able to buy property at bargain basement prices.

After the great battle with the Colorado river, the bitter contest between Imperial and El Centro for the County Seat and the insolvency of the California Development Company, 1908 brought a new day of peace and prosperity to the hard-working valley settlers. As we recall, the great Southern Pacific Railroad was stuck with the remaining shell of the company. Its management was handling matters of the C. D. Company's operation under Mr. Cory, whom the railroad had appointed as its General Manager, and R. D. McPherrin, T. P.'s friend from the early days, who it had appointed as Assistant Manager. Mr. McPherrin was officed in Calexico and was in charge of daily matters. Mr. Harriman, President of the railroad, had been stuck with the operation of the company as the result of being its Good Samaritan, saving it and the valley from the ravages of the wayward Colorado River. He made it abundantly clear that this was a task the railroad was undertaking reluctantly, for, as he often said, the railroad's business was the transportation of people and goods. It was not and did not want to be in the business of selling water rights and water to farmers.

The farmers, on the other hand, were very happy with the new owners of the California Development Company for Roy McPherrin was handling with dispatch the difficult tasks of keeping its water users, creditors and plaintiffs reasonably happy. He used diplomacy, tact and good common sense in directing its day by day operations. Thus, under the wing of the great Southern Pacific Railroad, the valley farmers and businessmen began to reap the rewards from their hard work of transforming the dead Colorado Desert into the lush green valley that was Imperial. Credit was now easily available and new farms and buildings were being established at a pace that would have been thought unimaginable but two or three months prior.

During the flood years of 1906 and 1907, the population of the valley actually decreased. In 1908 the population swelled as new settlers came in droves to the valley. T. P. and the other early farmers had settled the matter of which crops were the best to grow in the valley and the matter of controlling the river had been solved at least for the near future. During the years of 1908, 1909 and 1910, the valley and its inhabitants, saw property values go up at a pace that had never been seen before and would never be seen again. Property values doubled in 1908 and rose another fifty

per cent in 1909. Those who had stuck it out through the flood
were amply repaid for their intestinal fortitude.

The Banta family was in a most advantageous position; T. P.
had been buying out the quitters at very low prices. Now he was
in a position to offer farms to new settlers who were willing to pay
top prices for them. T. P. and Carrie had been well-to-do prior to
the river's ravages; now they had become very wealthy. The years
of 1908, '09 and '10 were years that brilliantly repaid those who
had stuck it out through the dark days of the flood. T. P. and
Carrie's faith in the valley, by buying farms that had become almost worthless during its darkest days, repaid them ten fold now
that the problem had been solved. The Banta family had become
one of the wealthy valley families, certainly not as wealthy as W. F.
Holt who had become a millionaire, but very wealthy. Everything
had worked out far better than T. P. or Carrie's fondest expectations. All the years of hard work were quickly forgotten as their
family found themselves able to afford and to do all the things that
they couldn't even dream of doing in years past.

In 1909, Carrie and T. P. began to recognize that they were
becoming very wealthy. With that wealth they realized that it was
no longer necessary for Carrie to stay year round in the valley. In a
family discussion, the matter of buying a house in Los Angeles to
let Carrie avoid the terrible summer heat was considered. Most
other families had been sending the women and children to the
coast during the hot months for the last several years. Carrie was
an important part of the family's success with its investments. T. P.
consulted her before every major decision and their investments
were team decisions. "Well," she said, "with the telephone I'll always be available to talk things over. We can afford a lovely house
in the West Adams district we both so admired when we went to
L. A. in 1904. We've all dreamed of the day we could escape the
unbearable summer heat. Maybe we should cash out of our valley
investments and all move to L. A. We've certainly have enough
money to retire. Papa, you're fifty-five and you have worked unbe-

lievably hard to get where we are. Why not enjoy the fruits of our labor?"

"Carrie," T. P. replied, "I'm not ready to retire yet. There's too much money to be made in this valley and too many things to be done. We've got to provide a more permanent solution to the irrigation gates on the Colorado River. I'm up to my ears in working toward the valley obtaining water from the Laguna Dam in Yuma instead of continuing to rely on Hanlon's Landing and the Rockford Gate. I just can't quit while there's so much to be done. I've got lots of energy and I've got to see this thing through till the valley's water supply is safe. There's no need for you and the boys to suffer the valley heat. We'll buy that house in L. A. and you and the boys will stay there during the hot months and I can visit you on week ends."

T. P. got in touch with a real estate agent he had known for years in Los Angeles. This agent had sent him many prospective buyers for valley property. He called him on the telephone and described what type of house he was looking for. He told him that Carrie and he had decided on the West Adams district as the area where they wanted to buy their house. A short time later, the agent called him back and told him that he had a distressed listing of a house for sale that he thought would be perfect for the Banta family.

The next weekend, T. P. took Carrie and the boys to Los Angeles to see the property. This time they could stay at the best hotel for with their new found wealth they could afford the best. The house was everything the real estate agent had told T. P. it was. It was a six thousand square foot craftsman style house on the north side of 24th Street in the 2000 block which was in the center of the stylish West Adams district. The mansion was on a large well landscaped lot with a covered patio and stable that had been converted into a three-car garage. Automobiles were quite popular with the wealthy Los Angelinos.

The owners wanted to sell the house with the carpets, drapes and furniture though some rooms were sparsely furnished and additional furniture would be needed. George and Al looked at the magnificent estate and still being unaware of their family's new wealth thought the chance of their living there was equivalent to that of a snowball in the August valley heat. Much to their surprise, T. P. bought the house with the carpets, drapes and furniture in early 1909 and Carrie moved into the new mansion in May, in time to beat the oppressive summer valley heat. She went to the Barker Brothers' furniture store and completed furnishing the house so that it was completely furnished by the time school in the valley let out for summer vacation and George and Al joined her in Los Angeles. George graduated from the eighth grade in June and Al finished his second year at Imperial High School.

When Earl returned on summer vacation from Stanford where he was going to college, he joined T. P. in the valley. Thus, the family was split during the dog days of summer in order to give some respite from the heat to those whose presence was not absolutely necessary. At every opportunity that his real estate business would allow, T. P. and Earl would take the train to Los Angeles to bring the family together and escape the terrible valley heat.

In September of 1909, George would start his first year of high school and Mama felt that he would get a better education at the highly rated Los Angeles High school than at the high school in the valley. After all, George was still her baby who Papa had purchased at the cost of her trip to Michigan to see her mother. Therefore, she decided that she and George would stay in Los Angeles for the full year. T. P. was not happy with this decision and felt that an adequate education could be achieved at Imperial high school. Carrie ultimately won out in the debate for Papa realized what a high price Carrie and George had paid in creating the wealth they had accumulated in the valley. His wife and family had been courageous in living through the first decade of the Imperial Valley's rise from a deadly desert to a lush green valley of plenty. Now that the family was very wealthy and could afford the best he decided that they should live up to what they had earned by the sweat of their collective brows. For this reason, he saw that his insistence on their living in the valley was selfish. He wanted what was best for them even though it would be emotionally difficult for him.

Al was asked if he would like to complete his junior and senior year at the Los Angeles high school. Al was dead against this as he had all his friends in Imperial high plus the fact that he was a star athlete on the varsity teams. Most of all he resisted moving because of his serious romantic involvement with the campus beauty, Jewel Gallaher. Jewel and he had been going steady and young love being what it is, he couldn't bear to leave her. Thus, Mama and George stayed in their big new mansion in Los Angeles all year round.

The valley and the little valley house became very lonely for T. P. Where just over two years prior he had Carrie, George, Al and grandma with him all year and Earl with him three months of the year, now he only had Al with him all year and Earl with him during the summer. As a man who idolized his family and who had worked so closely with them in turning the desolate Colorado Desert into a garden, the lone-liness over missing Mama and George was overwhelming. At every opportunity he and Al, and during summer vacation Earl, were on the train to Los Angeles but his business forced him to stay in the valley most of the time. It was also a shock for Mama and George in Los Angeles for they missed Papa, Al, Robert and his family and all their other valley friends. They were frontier people, after all, and not prepared for the modern cosmopolitan city folks they were to associ-ate with on a daily basis. Their neighbors considered these people from the frontier to be hicks not up on the ways of the big city. Carrie, being raised in Lansing and a college graduate, better edu-cated than most of her neighbors, recognized that her boys were rough at the edges. This was a major reason she wanted George to go to the prominent Los Angeles High school. He had spent his entire life until now barefoot and in bib overalls. She longed to give him lessons in the ways of city folk.

Papa had grown up on the farm and had always been one of the frontier people. He loved the country folk and didn't see the necessity of changing for his city neighbors. Though he had a gardener to take care of the grounds around the big city house, he continued to love to work in his new estate's magnificent gardens. Thus, when he and Al came to L. A. on weekends, he would get up early in the morning and put on his bib overalls to putter around the yard. This bothered Mama who recognized that her neighbors thought of the Banta family as frontiersmen out of their element and in the wrong neighborhood. Thus, she would upbraid Papa for wearing his overalls and plead with him to please dress in slacks and a shirt as did the other gentlemen in the neighborhood. This, of course, was to no avail as T. P. was well-set in his ways.

One day, a neighbor lady, who had not been introduced to T. P., on one of his weekend visits, mistook him for the gardener on a Saturday morning. She watched him with rapt attention as the old farmer worked around the garden. After watching him for a considerable period of time and noticing his skill around the well-manicured garden, she finally approached him.

"My good man," she started, "I've admired these beautiful gardens surrounding the Banta house. I've also been watching your tending of the plants with such tender and loving care. If you will come to work on my garden, I'll pay you twice what Mrs. Banta is paying you. By the way what is she paying you?"

"I accept your offer," said T. P. "But she doesn't pay me anything in cash. She just lets me sleep with her." This was excellent farm humor but didn't go over well with the cultured big city folks.

During that summer, though the boys came from a completely different background, they made many friends in the neighborhood and Carrie became better acquainted with the neighbors on 24th Street. Soon everyone in the 2000 block of 24th Street discovered she was a well bred and well-educated women and not the country bumpkin they first suspected. When they heard the story of what she and her family had been through to gain their wealth, they found new respect for her and her family.

In September George entered Los Angeles High and made many new friends. Instead of alienating George from his new classmates, the life he had lived on the desolate desert made the stories of his childhood on the frontier exotic and absorbing to these city boys. The stories George told of carrying water to the Indians as a water boy of five years of age held his classmates spellbound. The story of his seeing a man killed in a brawl in front of a brothel and his earning a pony by losing his fear through going alone into a haunted, deserted house at mid-night, sounded to his new friends like a story out of a Western pulp novel.

T. P. on the front porch of the Banta's 24th Street house

George missed the frontier life he had known. In the big city there were to be no more rattlesnake killing contests or five mile walks to school across a desert and alongside a canal. Here he simply climbed aboard a streetcar for a few minute ride to Los Angeles High. The fun and freedom he had known in the valley were replaced by a different kind of fun and much less freedom due to the more restrictive rules and manners of society in a big city. These were exactly the rules and manners Mama wanted George to learn. She wanted to wean him away from his frontier custom, manners and way of talking. Surprisingly, these were the very attributes that made him popular with his new found schoolmate friends. His new friends had never met a boy who had seen and done the things that George had. George, as a freshman, became acquainted with many in his class. In no time, the family became well integrated into the neighborhood and he into Los Angeles High school.

Papa, on the other hand, found it difficult to adjust to the lonely life of coming home to a house with no Mama or George each night. He had never had a life outside of his family. Success had taken his wife and son from him. He felt guilty resenting their happy life in L. A. far away from all the hard life he had chosen by continuing to live in the valley. He knew it was his own decision but that made it no easier. Both his sense of responsibility for solving the water problems still facing the valley and his greed for making the money that was waiting for any entrepreneur willing to endure the rigors of valley living made it impossible for him to do other than stay. Lonely as he was, he couldn't shake the fever that kept him tied to his valley. He was glad he had Al with him and Robert and his family only a few blocks away.

In 1910, at the request of all parties, the creditors, the Southern Pacific Railroad and the valley settlers, the court relieved the Southern Pacific from its duty of operating the shell of the California Development Company. Mr. Cory and Mr. McPherrin had done an efficient and exemplary job of running the insolvent company during its two most difficult years. Now, everyone decided, it was time to close out its affairs as fairly as possible by the court declaring the California Development Company bankrupt and then finding a buyer or buyers for its substantial assets.

Since the company's business involved operations in both the United States and Mexico, the laws of both countries required separate receivers be appointed to look after the best interests of the citizens of each country. W. F. Holabird was appointed receiver for the American company while General A. F. Andrade was appointed as receiver for the Mexican company.

Col. W. H. Holabird did a superb job in maintaining the water distributing system in spite of the demands of the receivership's creditors whose interest was to get every dime they could from the defunct company and who couldn't care less about the interests of the farmers. Col. Holabird, on the other hand, had a terrible temper which made him unpopular with water users and creditors. Fortunately, he named Mr. J. C. Allison, who had worked on the closure of the river into its old bed, as Chief engineer and Assistant Manager of the receivership. He was eminently well qualified for maintaining the irrigation district and the levees along the untrustworthy Colorado River. Unfortunately, Mr. Allison was the object of many slings and arrows hurled Col. Holabird's way due to his irascible personality. As a result of the management of the receivership by these two men during their tenure, the Valley had its greatest advancement and lowest water rates up to that time.

T. P. was lonely without Mama in the valley. He coped with his situation by immersing himself totally in the Valley's business. He made money while the sun shone, and the sun shone every day of the year during these days following the rivers closure. On every major investment he called Carrie on the telephone and discussed it thoroughly with her. Every investment and every day found them growing wealthier and wealthier.

T. P. was into many businesses beside real estate and farming. He was involved in warehousing and shipping fruits and vegetables from the valley where he owned his own warehouses and railroad siding. He was also into brokering cotton which was becoming a

major crop in the valley. Valley cotton was of excellent quality and
was dearly sought by both American and European mills.

With Mama away, T. P. spent his evenings with His brother
Robert and his family as well as other old friends in the Valley. Al
and he were invited out to dinner most nights, Because his neighbors
knew that he didn't know how to cook. One family with whom
the Banta family had become close friends was the Weaver family.
Wiley Weaver Sr., and his wife and young son, Wiley Weaver Jr.,
had arrived in the valley in 1904. Mr. Weaver had introduced
sheep into the valley in 1905 and had raised them on his three-
hundred and twenty acre ranch in the Mesquite Lake area. T. P.
had met him through his real estate business at that time.

The Weavers son, Wiley, Jr., was the same age as George and
the two boys had become close friends which also drew the two
families close together. Though close friends, Carrie and T. P. always called the Weaver's by their last names. The Weavers always
called T. P., Judge Banta, and they called Carrie, Mrs. Banta. This
was a rather formal arrangement for two close families but it was
the custom that had grown up between the two families.

T. P. had come to admire Mrs. Weaver for her business ability.
She was very active in the valley community, being involved in
promoting the valley through valley fairs and other activities. She
seemed to be involved in everything to do with promoting the
valley. Judge Banta thought she had a shrewd head for financial
matters. The gossip in the valley was that he was "sweet" on her.
However, this had no basis in his actual feelings for her. Instead,
he sincerely admired her ability to make friends and to cooperate
in getting a task finished. With his wife in Los Angeles, she felt
sorry for T. P. and had Al and him over to dinner quite regularly.
Carrie and she were best friends and Carrie appreciated the Weaver's
concern for T. P.

The Weavers and T. P. had many conversations about all sorts
of things as friends do. In one conversation Mrs. Weaver had told
T. P. that, in her opinion, a sure way to make money was in valley
cotton futures. She had invested in them with surprising success.

Because of her success, T. P. became interested in cotton futures and watched them carefully. He felt he understood them sufficiently to make a killing by investing in them. He talked the matter over with Mama, but Carrie told T. P., "Papa I'd rather we not get involved in anything speculative. We've made our fortune, and there is no reason for us to gamble in hopes of getting even richer. If the future market interests you why don't you just invest a small amount for the sport of it." She hadn't said an outright no, but he knew better than to press the subject further.

T. P. valued Carries judgement but he also admired the judgement of Mrs. Weaver. Each time he and Mrs. Weaver met they talked about all the money that could be made in cotton futures. Mama was right, he thought. The family had all the money they needed and they were making more each day in their valley businesses and the Banta ranch. They were independently wealthy but why not try for more when it was a sure thing. Carrie had said he could dabble in futures and this he did, each time making a handsome profit,

Aside from his personal business, T. P. heavily involved himself in the matters of how the valley irrigation system would be owned and operated. Also, how the system could guarantee that its heading on the Colorado River would hold and that the valley farmers could in the future be sure that their supply of water would be there. These matters were primary concerns of all businessmen in the valley for the certainty of water was essential to the sale of real estate. Any doubt whatsoever was disastrous to T. P.'s real estate business. It was his belief that the matter would not be solved until the heading for the valley's irrigation system was the Laguna Dam at Yuma. This was the end to which he constantly worked.

Another matter pressing-in on the valley was who would own and operate the valley's irrigation system. Here was an extremely valuable operation that was being managed by receivers due to the bankruptcy of the California Development Company. It didn't seem sensible to put the irrigation district in the hands of private enterprise since that method had already failed. In 1910 the President of the Southern Pacific again reiterated that the railroad wanted no part of operating the irrigation district as a permanent part of its business, so they were out of the picture. The Federal Government could not take over the system because of its international nature. By elimination, public ownership became the focus of the valley people.

In 1910 the valley lost a formidable and brilliant friend when W. F. Holt decided to expend his considerable talents on a new project. The Chandlers, owners of the Los Angeles Times, owned tens of thousands of acres of irrigatable land south of the border. They wanted W. F. to work with them on establishing an irrigation district similar to that in the Imperial Valley on their land in Mexico. W. F. found the opportunities offered by the new venture too promising to turn down and thus his brilliant days in establishing the valley as a living reality came to an end.

A new name and face was to replace that of W. F. Holt in the politics of the valley and became the backbone of the valley's battle for a solution to a sound heading and guaranteed water supply for the Imperial Irrigation System. The newcomer's name was Phil Swing. He, and T. P. thought alike on how the footing for the district's main heading had to be built on bed rock and the water supply had to be constant despite the ebb stage and the flood stage of the great Colorado River. Phil and T. P. became close allies in protecting the irrigation system from the catastrophes that almost brought the Imperial Valley to it's knees.

The majority of people had decided that public control of the irrigation system was the only prudent way to proceed. The question was, how should this be accomplished? John M. Eshelman, M. W. Conklin and Phil Swing, all lawyers, made a study of state law to find the best vehicle for public ownership. After studying the Bridgeford Act which was already on the statute books, they determined that with certain amendments, it offered the ideal method of ownership by the public. They, along with other prominent men of Imperial, brought the public's attention to the benefits of the act if modified with proposed amendments and suggested that the matter of forming the Imperial Irrigation District under the Bridgeford act be put on the next ballot. The proposal was passed at the election held July 14, 1911.

The matter of the amendments to the act was taken to the legislature in Sacramento and was promptly passed. Phil Swing had been District Attorney for Imperial County at the time of the chartering of the Imperial Irrigation District under the California Irrigation District Act which was the name given to the amended Bridgeford Act. Since its organization well over one hundred other irrigation districts operate under its authority. The district held its first meeting July 25, 1911 and Phil Swing counseled it during its earliest days. He was defeated for District Attorney in the next election and then became Chief Council for the district carefully walking it around pitfalls in its infancy.

The Imperial Irrigation District, which continues in existence to this day, is imbued with powers similar to that of any city or county. The powers of the District under the act include: the right to purchase the systems owned by the California Development Company, the right to levy assessments, the right to condemn property and do many other things similar to those of a city or county government. Attorneys Eshleman, Conkling and Swing had found the perfect vehicle for the people's ownership of the irrigation district.

T. P. was delighted that one of the first acts of its board of directors was to ask the Department of the Interior what actions the district would be required to take, and what would be the terms of securing water from the Laguna Dam at Yuma. The securing of water from an invulnerable source was essential to the peace of mind and security of the people living in the valley. Though he was never a member of the board, he personally knew every member and was ever active in advising members on matters that would effect the district and the valley. They, often asked for his counsel and opinions as well.

The subject of an All American Canal which would cross the sand hills north of the border was mentioned for the first time at the Board meeting of March 23, 1912 in a discussion as to how the district might eliminate the Mexican Receiver. The idea of an All American Canal was so popular that it was a topic of discussion at every following meeting of the Board. T. P. also became very a active supporter of an All American Canal.

The discussion of an All American Canal was the embryo that ultimately ended with the birth of the Bolder Canyon Project Act. This act passed by congress in 1928 authorized the construction of Boulder Dam to control the ebbs and flows of the lower Colorado River and the construction of the All American Canal. Both of these projects were essential to the safe future of the Imperial valley. While the act provides protection for all irrigation projects along the lower Colorado and the production of enough electricity to provide power to much of the west, it was the brainchild of valley men who deserve every credit for conceiving the idea and making realities of Bolder Dam and the All American Canal. This saga of epic proportions will be touched upon in the later pages of our story. Phil Swing more than any other man can be called the father of the Bolder Canyon Project Act and its resulting projects.

Although the district was organized in 1911, it wasn't until 1916 that it purchased the remains of the California Development Company from the Southern Pacific Railroad. The Southern Pacific had purchased the property at Receiver's sale under the court's authority. The old California Development Company was now owned and controlled as a public authority.

CHAPTER 35

BUSINESS AND PLEASURE. THE

IMPERIAL BEACH SUBDIVISION AND

THE COTTON MARKET FOR PAPA, AND A

TRIP AROUND THE WORLD FOR MAMA.

It was November of 1912 when a new idea for a business venture struck T. P. like a thunderbolt. It actually became a fixation pushing all his other business activities into the background. He had become interested in a new railroad that was in the process of being organized and whose promoters were singing the praises of the future of its stock. The new railroad was to be called the Arizona and San Diego Railroad. Its road bed would not follow the tortuous automobile road from the Valley to San Diego which currently took almost a half day to transverse if an automobile of the day was strong enough to make it at all. The present highway to San Diego, if you chose to call the primitive mountain road a highway, ended at the northern end of San Diego where Mission Valley met the sea. The new railroad proposed to take a different route which would require the digging of several tunnels. It would cross temporarily into Mexico and then return to California just east of Tijuana and south of San Diego. It would then follow the coast line north to San Diego.

Since it was November and valley families were returning from their summer residences along the cooler California coast, the topic of conversation all over the valley concerned the high cost of rentals in the various coastal areas used by valley residents to escape the unbearable Imperial Valley summer heat. T. P. realized that since the building of the Arizona and San Diego Railroad was just becoming a reality, real estate near where the railroad reentered California from Mexico would be dirt cheap. Yet in the future, with the automobile road being so treacherous, he felt that most valley people would use the new railroad to escape to the cool coast during the searing valley summer heat. Promoters, recognizing this fact had named the beach area just north of the Mexican border Imperial Beach.

T. P. moved to San Diego for several months during which time he made a thorough search for a parcel of land large enough for a good sized subdivision. He found just what he was looking for along the southern ocean front of Imperial Beach. It was about forty acres of beach front surrounded by tidal canals similar to those that currently surround Balboa Island in Newport Beach except that one side of this island was the Pacific Ocean. He was convinced that if this land were to be improved with streets platted and with water and power to each lot and if the lots were reasonably priced, the Valley residents would flock to have their own reasonably priced summer homes and he could make a handsome profit. He was convinced the lots would sell out almost immediately if he financed them with easy payments and kept the prices reasonable.

He was so convinced of the practicality of his idea that he mortgaged some of his valley land to buy the forty acres, build a causeway across the tidal canal to the island, lay out the streets and bring water and electricity to them. The streets were all named for valley cities and towns. The main street was Imperial and cross streets were named for other Valley cities or towns. By the time that all the surveying and construction work were completed it was March 1913. On March 8, 1913, T. P. kicked off the opening of the new subdivision with a full page add in all the valley papers that read as per the following article inside the quotation marks.

The ad is copied verbatim as it tells how T. P. was thinking in his own words. The ad appeared as if it were a typewritten letter from T. P.'s own typewriter.

OFFICE OREGON HOTEL

El Centro, Cal, March 8, 1913

To the People of Imperial Valley

Being one of the earliest settlers in the "Hollow of God's Hand," and with the full appreciation of the necessity of a summer resort of easy access for the settlers and residents of this, "the greatest valley in the world," and further realizing the vast amount of money taken from the people here to secure summer vacations, I conceived the idea that if I could find such a retreat, at a low cost, I would not only make a little money, but at the same time confer a blessing on my friends and neighbors.

My mind naturally turned to Imperial Beach, The first beach reached by the San Diego Railway, soon to be made easy of access from the valley by the 1000 men now working on its construction. With this in mind I made a trip to San Diego to look over the situation. I was successful beyond my fondest expectations in finding forty acres of beautiful land at the mouth of the Tiajuana river, just off the ocean sands; high and scenic, with a fine loam soil, which I purchased. I have just had it platted and the streets well graded, as they must be to be accepted by the Supervisors of San Diego County.

To my surprise, I found Imperial Beach has the best climate in the world, both in summer and in winter, and not only is it the best beach for bathing within forty miles of San Diego, being free from seaweed, undertow, and stingarees; it is one of the best Ocean Beaches in the whole world.

This unsurpassed Beach property will be open for

purchase Monday, April 14th, and I am offering these lots at prices which will insure the sale of every one within 60 days.

I will have a representative in every town in the valley, so that you can take advantage of this opportunity. In the meantime reservations can be made by letter or telephone, or by a personal call at the office of the Eastside Reality Company, my representatives at Holtsville, where plats can be seen and full information secured. The prices, including water piped to the tract, range from $70.00 to $350.00 a lot.

These prices give you a chance to own a beautiful beach lot at a small cost, any one of which I believe will be worth $1000 as soon as the San Diego and Arizona railway is completed. As I look back over the twelve years I have spent here, during which time lots on the beaches around Los Angeles have advanced from a few hundred dollars to as high as $30,000 a lot, I feel the above prediction is too conservative, and that these lots will prove to be one of the best investments you have ever made.

I have also made arrangements for you to obtain, if you wish, portable houses fully equipped, at a very low cost. This will not only enable you to spend this summer on your own lot, but to construct, while on your vacation, a permanent home to which to take your family and friends when you go to the Panama-California Exposition at San Diego in 1915.

Very truly,
T. P. **Banta**

T. P. was selling the lots for twenty-five dollars down for the least expensive lots and up to seventy-five dollars down on the most expensive lots with easy payments for the remainder of their cost. By May he had sold more than one hundred lots.

Interest was high among many prospective buyers but they wanted to see the property with their own eyes. T. P. recognized this as a sensible request and planned a caravan of valley residents who would travel by car or buggy over the treacherous mountain road from the valley to San Diego. He felt sure that the journey would reemphasize his argument that the new railroad that was being built was the only sensible way for valley residents to commute to San Diego.

A very large contingency of valley residents signed up for the caravan. Since several of the new owners of lots planned to stay during the hot summer weather in one of the "portable houses fully equipped" T. P. had mentioned in his opening advertizement, T. P. called the organization that was to supply these portable houses and made arrangements to have them delivered to the owners lots two or three days before the caravan was to arrive. These houses were similar to today's trailers except that instead of wheels they had sleds beneath them and were delivered by flat bed trucks with special equipment to unload them on a lot. T. P. also arraigned to have a picnic lunch for all who would be in the caravan.

EL CENTRO, CALIFORNIA, MONDAY EVENING, DECEMBER 29, 1913

ANGES IN BASEBALL COACHING

Dec. 29.—Baseball coach-conference colleges may ecided change after next he result of "Big Nine" ment, according to state-by University of Chicago cials. The Maroons an-y would use their influ-or of modifying the cur-l of baseball instruction, lieved they will urge the rd to vote on the matter meeting.

'ay agitation took visible .he "Big Nine" professors .heir resolution to the ef-coaches be permitted to t in the conduct of inter-ames, but be required to tands with the spectators ames are in progress."

Chicago professors think' r is too radical, they favor proposition contained in ion.

all, who is known as an baseball fan, declares the me needs to be differen-

T. P. BANTA HAS NOT LOST GRIP ON VALLEY AFFAIRS

Fariss Ta
(By United Press)
Los Angeles, Dec
Fariss today denied t ments that Rena H county is the girl I San Francisco and I(he robbed trains to told a pitiful story I declaring the first "g cept his own famil; was an eighteen-year in a Los Angeles da: he took her to San Fr with her there. He and robbed trains. H girl was "good" an(have married her.

Superior Judge C sented to hold argun the death sentence in

Los Angeles, Dec. ; father of Ralph Far Pacific bandit and s Los Angeles from B: day, accompanied by younger brother of tl ter an affecting meel demned man in his (jail at once began a life of his son.

T. P., THE TYCOON
FRONT PAGE, IMPERIAL VALLEY PRESS, EL CENTRO
DECEMBER 29, 1913
recovered from microfische

The day the caravan was to leave the Imperial Valley was Saturday of the last week-end in June 1913. Everyone going on the caravan was in a holiday mood, most intending to purchase a lot after seeing the new Banta subdivision at Imperial Beach. The caravan was made up of dozens of Ford Model T's plus autos of every other make under the sun. Many were going by horse and buggy. They left at six in the morning to avoid the heat of the day and to

have the whole day to travel as the road through the coastal mountains was so primitive that it was impossible to determine an accurate estimated time of arrival. Every one had packed a basket lunch
to be eaten on the trip to the subdivision even though T. P. had
arranged a fine picnic lunch for every one once they arrived at the
subdivision.

As was expected, the caravan was plagued with flat tires, en-
gines boiling over plus assorted other mechanical difficulties. As
was the custom of the day, other motorists pitched in to repair the
mechanical problem of those unfortunate motorists suffering difficulties. Automobiles were so new in 1913 that making emergency
repairs was a challenge and part of the mystique of being a motor-
ist. The caravan proceeded in a carnival atmosphere until they
reached the Banta subdivision at two in the afternoon. The cater-
ers were there with tables set up for the picnic T. P. had arranged.
Everyone sat down to eat at the tables that had been set up. All
were delighted with the forty acres on which the subdivision sat.
Being on an island with a causeway over a canal to reach it, made
the streets of the Banta tract even more appealing.

Everyone was having so much fun and was so excited that it
was a full half hour after the caravan had arrived that one of the
three families who had made arrangements with T. P. for a temporary house brought to his attention that there were no temporary
houses anywhere on the tract.

"Damn it." T. P. said, "Those scoundrels I contracted with for
the temporary houses must have forgot to deliver them. I'll find a
telephone and call them right away. If they can't deliver them
today, I'll pay your lodging till they are delivered." With this he
had to leave his own sales party and search for a telephone in the
nearest town. When he reached a phone and contacted the firm
who was to deliver the temporary houses, he was told that the
houses had been delivered the day before and placed on the lots as
he had directed them to do.

"Well, they are certainly not there now," he informed the firm.
The owner of the firm came onto the telephone and informed T. P.

that they had been delivered into his care, custody and control as per his instructions and if they had disappeared he was responsible for their cost.

"What the hell could have happened to them?" T. P. exploded.

"If you ask me," the owner of the firm replied, "since your tract is just across the river from Tijuana, the Mexicans in Tijuana saw them out on that island and figured that since no one was around they were deserted and theirs for the taking." Sure enough, when T. P. returned to the tract, he along with the other men in the caravan searched for traces of what had happened and found wagon tracks leading from the three lots on which the temporary houses had been deposited which led to the causeway and from the causeway south toward the Tijuana river which was the border to Mexico.

"By gosh," T. P. exclaimed, "They got us stupid gringos this time. But the real question is how are we going to protect our property in the future. The only police protection we have out here is the County Sheriffs and they won't keep a man out here on a permanent basis. The Temporary Housing firm agreed to deliver three new houses today for the three families that intend to stay here for the summer and I'll pick up the cost for the stolen houses but from now on the lot owners will have to protect their own property by having at least one family living here while the houses are here."

Everyone agreed that this was fair but they wondered about what would happen when they built permanent homes. If all the owners of lots in the Banta tract were in the valley, who would protect them from vandalism and theft? T. P. assured them that when sufficient homes were built, someone would be on the island at any period of time. At the same time when a larger amount of personal property was at risk, the Sheriff's Department would keep it under closer surveillance. The Achilles's heel of T. P.'s wonderful plan for a summer getaway for valley residents was clearly exposed to everyone there. Since the tract lots were to be sold exclusively to Imperial Valley residents to avoid the impossible summer heat, for a good part of the year it would be deserted or almost deserted making it prey to vandalism and theft.

Needless to say, the caravan that appeared to be a potential bonanza to the selling out of the Banta tract lots, became a disastrous backfire. Very few lots were sold that day and the reports of the day's events circulated widely throughout the valley. The sale of additional lots slowed to a trickle. The setback of the Imperial Beach Banta tract was not a disaster to the Banta fortune but it did hurt and was more than a mere slap on the wrist. Being an entrepreneur, T. P. realized that every venture undertaken would not succeed and that failures were a part of the game.

With their new found wealth, T. P. and Carrie realized that they could do and have just about anything they wanted. After buying and magnificently furnishing the beautiful city house, T P. was looking for new toys of the rich. For his first major toys, T. P. purchased two of the most expensive motor cars, the Franklin, with an air-cooled gasoline engine. One was kept in the valley for his use down there. The other was kept for the family's use in the garage behind their home in Los Angeles.

After the cars, with the money rolling in beyond their fondest dreams, T. P. and Carrie's thoughts went to non-material things that had to do with education and building the family's cultural horizons. In the wealthy West Adams neighborhood that was now home to Carrie and George, the most cultured thing a person could do was to take a trip around the world. In those days only the richest of families could afford such a luxury. As the family's fortune mounted, T. P. and Carrie realized that they were in a position where they could afford such a luxury. When the subject was brought up by Mama, T. P. Said, "There is no way that I can get away from my businesses in the valley, Mama, especially with my involvement with the Banta tract at Imperial Beach, but such a trip would be a great investment in George's education. He was raised on the frontier and knows little beyond the ways of the valley. He will graduate from high school in June of 1913. Why don't you and he take the trip?"

George was the apple of Carrie's eye. T. P. had purchased him at the price of a trip for Carrie to go home to Michigan to visit her mother when she had been lonesome for her family way out in Mesa. George was so young when he came to the Imperial Valley that he barely remembered anything but the frontier. Both T. P. and Carrie realized that from a cultural viewpoint George needed to shave-off his rough edges and broaden his cultural horizons. Carrie jumped at the chance to show George the entire world and immediately started planning for the trip. She visited many travel agencies and brought home loads of travel literature. By January of 1913 she was well into planning her itinerary. In the year of 1913 up to the day in September that George and she would start the trip, she was completely wrapped up in travel arrangements. Papa and George were equally as excited with the prospect of the extended trip.

The most prominent travel agency of that time was Thomas Cook and Company. They had facilities around the world where Carrie could go to change arrangements and to pick up tickets. The trip was a family affair and she talked over every minute detail with Pa and the boys. It was soon apparent that a trip around the world would take an extended period of time. At a minimum, the trip would take five to six months.

As the time for the trip drew near, The itinerary was carefully and clearly laid out. On a trip of this stature careful planning was a must. Even so, a delay along the way or a missed sailing of a steamer or a train could destroy the entire remainder of Mama's and George's scheduled reservations on modes of travel. The travel agency suggested that reservations be made only on modes of travel because accommodations in first class hotels would always be available at the point where they were needed.

They planned their final itinerary as follows: From Los Angeles, they would take a train to New York, then a ship to

England, landing in Plymouth and visiting London. Next they would take a steam ship to France and visit Paris; then, onto Germany by train, visiting Bremen, Frankfort and Cologne; and on to Holland and Belgium, visiting Rotterdam and Antwerp. Next, they would sail through the North Sea, the English Channel and the Bay of Bisque, through the straits of Gibralter, visiting Gibralter, and on into the Mediterranean Sea.

Their steamship would arrive at Genoa, Italy. They would travel by train to Milan, Venice, Florence, Rome, the Vatican City, and Naples, spending Thanksgiving Day in Pompeii. From there, they would then board a steamship for Alexandria, Egypt and travel by land conveyances to Cairo, Port Said, Jerusalem, Bethlehem, Jericho, and Jaffa, at which point they planned to go back to Port Said and board a passenger liner for Ceylon, then to sail through the Suez Canal and the Red Sea to Aden, Arabia, and sail across the Indian Ocean to Colombo, Ceylon. They would spend both Christmas and New Year's Day on the steamer to Ceylon.

Carrie Banta and son George, age 21,
on their trip around the world, 1917

Boarding a steamer in Colombo, their next stop would be Bombay, India. They planned to travel by train on the Indian subcontinent to Delhi, Agra, to see the Taj Mahal, Benam, the Ganges River, and Calcutta. There they would board a steamer for Rangoon, Burma.

Once again, they would board a passenger liner for Penang, Malay States and would travel by steamer to the following ports of China: Singapore, Hong Kong, Canton, Macao and Shanghai.

From Shanghai they would steam across the Yellow Sea to Nagasaki, Japan. In Japan they would travel by train to Kobe, Kyoto, Nara, Mianashita, Hakone, and Tokyo. After touring Japan they would board an ocean liner to cross the Pacific to the Sandwich (Hawaiian) Islands, stopping at Honolulu. Their final ocean voyage would be to San Francisco, planning to arrive in Los Angeles by train around the middle of March 1914.

This is the magnificent trip around the world the Banta family planned for Mama and George which they would undertake in late September, 1913 following the summer after George's graduation from High school. Earl and Al were jealous of George, of course, but that did not stop them from sharing in the planning and excitement with the rest of the family. This was a well-deserved vacation for Mama, and George was lucky enough to be the one to accompany her.

To George, it was like when he had been a small boy waiting for Christmas. Never before had he experienced such excitement and anticipation. The days before his graduation in June of 1913 seem endless. He had to summon up all his self discipline to study for his final high school exams with such an exciting adventure awaiting him. Finally, graduation day came and passed and he began the endless summer of preparing for the trip Mama and he would take around the world.

The summer finally came to an end. The last minute rush and excitement were compounded by the "going away" party planned by Pa and the boys. Los Angeles and valley friends were at the lavish party to wish them Bon Voyage. Carrie and George were exhausted by the time they got to bed so it was easy for them to fall asleep. It seemed but an instant till it was morning. They had to arise at five in order to be at the train station at eight in order to have time to check their luggage and find their Pullman sleeper. They were accompanied by Papa, the Moons (Los Angeles friends who would house-sit the Los Angeles home while they were away), T. P.'s sister Madge (the

Medical Doctor) and Carrie's best valley friend, Mrs. Weaver. At 9:00 A. M., to great shouting and waving by Ma and George matched by those on the station platform, the train pulled away from their friends and Carrie and George began the mother of all journeys. After the train pulled out of the station, T. P. treated all those who had seen Carrie and George off to a lunch in the station dining room. Then, he and Mrs. Weaver caught the train to Imperial and Madge and the Moons headed back to L. A.

On the trip to Imperial, the subject of cotton futures again came up between T. P. and Mrs. Weaver and they had a great deal of fun discussing every aspect of the matter. "You know, Mrs. Weaver," T. P. said, "I'll bet I could recover all that I lost in the Imperial Beach tract. Maybe we could even corner the valley cotton market if we tried." With Carrie on her way around the world, this was the first oral mention of an obsession that was to take over T. P.'s mind for the next year.

Cotton had become the major valley crop. The Imperial Press carried little financial news except daily quotes on cotton futures. This was because cotton futures were vital information to the farmers growing cotton. T. P. and Mrs. Weaver were watching the futures daily and buying and selling futures in a small way on a regular basis. The market for futures was very strong as demand always seemed to exceed supply. Valley cotton was harvested about two months before the cotton crop in the south matured and therefore, while supplies were at their shortest.

T. P. seemed to have a feeling for cotton futures. He seldom lost money. He could see that not only the U. S. market was expanding but the European market seemed insatiable in their demand for cotton for their mills. With demand constantly increasing, he would buy way out in the future and hold the contract till the crop came in. Seldom did he lose money. He almost always made money. It seemed like an almost foolproof way to increase the value of his estate. He couldn't understand Carrie's fear of the market. She always said that the market is swayed by forces beyond his control and that to do other than dabble in it was taking an unnecessary risk with their assets.

The final death knell of the Banta Tract at Imperial Beach tolled with the announcement by the San Diego and Arizona Railroad Company that because of the difficult work, including the drilling of eighteen tunnels through the mountains, the railroad would not be completed before 1917. Actually it was completed in 1919 because of the ensuing World War I. Even the date of 1917 was beyond what the purchasers of the tract lots were willing to endure. Travel by the difficult auto highway was not an acceptable alternative to the expected railroad. Purchasers simply quit making payments on their lots and they reverted to the Banta Tract Corporation. Though T. P. had formed a corporation as owner of the tract, he had mortgaged his holdings to acquire the corporation's paid in capital and those mortgages had to be paid off. This had been an expensive venture for T. P. and he was looking for a way to recoup his loss.

During the fall and winter of 1913, the valley newspapers were full of news of cotton. Everyone was talking about this wonderful crop that was bringing such wealth to the valley farmers. Mrs. Weaver and he talked about cornering the valley cotton market constantly, but T. P. was limited in the amount he could play with; all his property and businesses were in the joint names of Carrie and himself. If he were to go heavily into cotton, he was certain he could recover that part of his fortune lost in Imperial Beach but he would need a power of attorney from Carrie so that he could borrow the money he needed.

He decided he would write to her and tell her of the bankruptcy of the Imperial Beach Tract. He would tell her he had done so well in valley cotton futures with small investments that he felt sure he could recoup his losses if he could make larger investments but that would require borrowing against some of their holdings and that he needed a signed power of attorney from her to do that. He wrote a letter to her attention making his case and mailed it to the post office in Naples. By the itinerary she had left with him, she and George would be in that city on November 25.

He had been writing to her every three or four days and she had always gone to the post office in each city on her itinerary and picked up the letters. She had also written him at least twice a week and had commented on things he had said in his letters so he knew his mail was getting through. He picked Naples because he knew that it would be the next city she and George would visit where there would be sufficient time for his letter to arrive before she did. He also knew that the next Capitol she and George would visit after leaving Naples would be Rome so he suggested she execute the power of attorney at the American Embassy in Rome and have them send it to him.

In the diary of her trip around the world, she noted on November 25, 1913, "We went to Aselmeyer's and got our letters. 2 from Pa, 1 from the boys and one from Frank Klyne." Then on the 28th of November she wrote, "Drove to American Consulate to execute a Power of Attorney to send to T. P. It cost $2.17." T. P.'s letter was persuasive and he had Carrie's permission to invest further in valley cotton.

T. P.'s letters to Carrie were filled with news of his business and social doings in both the valley and Los Angeles. He had no reservations about letting her know about the bad news as well as the good. He was so close to Mama that he knew she wanted to know everything and that it would not interfere with her enjoying her magnificent trip.

Carries letters to Pa were filled with her impressions of the wonderful places she was visiting: England with all it pomp and circumstances, France with its beautiful capital filled with world-renowned sights, Germany with its clean old quaint and new modern cities, Gibraltar under British rule but containing elements of both Africa and Europe.

She also told him of her becoming infected with the flu on November 9th as she and George sailed across the Mediterranean sea on their way to Genoa, Italy. She told Pa how she seemed unable to shake its symptoms and how caring George was in taking care of her during her illness. She told him that undoubtedly one of the reasons she was unable to shake her sickness was that she was unable to stay in bed with all the wonderful things to be seen in Genoa, Milan, Venice, Florence, Naples, Pompeii and Rome; cities they had visited since she had become sick. She wrote of her personal audience with the Pope arranged through the good offices of Bishop Conaty. He had given them a letter addressed to the Vatican requesting such audience be granted. In her letter to pa concerning her audience with Pope Pius X (Now St. Pius X, Ed.) she wrote:

Thursday, November 20th 1913

Dear Papa:

I had a bad night the night before we were to have our audience with the Pope, and I arose feeling badly but we got ourselves into our good clothes. (George went out and bought a silk hat.) We had no time to eat breakfast but, I didn't want any anyway. We got to the Vatican a little before eleven A. M. There was a large room full of those on the same mission.

We were directed to the throne room, a beautiful large room, all in embossed cardinal, marble floor inlaid in fancy design and the wonderful gold throne, all too beautiful for description. There were also beautiful paintings and frescos. After awhile we were all taken into another room where we stood around the wall. The Pope came in attended by guards and officials. He is a fine looking old man, not strong, with a kindly face and manner. He was dressed in pure white with a red cape and hat.

He came inside the room and we all knelt and received his blessing. One little lame girl kissed his ring and he patted her head kindly.

He then passed to another side of the court of the Vatican where a large crowd from some outlying district was waiting. He came out on a balcony and blessed those gathered. We went out there so we received two Papal blessings. The band played and the crowed cheered. He has many dignitaries about him in elegant and beautiful uniforms.

We got a rosary for Joe, a little crucifix for Mrs. E. and I wore Mrs. Weaver's scarf. They were all blessed by the Pope.

We returned to the hotel and after lunch we went to Dr. Brock, an Englishman. He prescribed for me and told me to go to bed as I have influenza and a temperature. I certainly feel like staying in bed only it makes me nervous. I intend to stay in bed all day tomorrow.

We are seeing and doing wonderful things but being sick is such an inconvenience and waste of valuable time.

George and I miss you and the boys more than words can express. I hope my descriptions of our day's adventures let you share in your minds all the wonderfully exciting things we are seeing and enjoying.

Love, Carrie

T. P. received Carrie's Power of Attorney in December 1913 and started buying future crops from valley cotton growers on a direct basis. He would agree to pay them the going futures prices carried in the local papers for the crops they would plant in early spring and which would be harvested in August and September of 1914. This took the risk out of raising the crop for they knew what price they would receive for whatever cotton they would harvest. T. P. knew most of the farmers and contacted them personally purchasing many of their future crops at around thirteen and a quarter cents per pound which was the futures price for August, September and October 1914 cotton. These were the months that much valley cotton was harvested. Since valley cotton was harvested about two months before cotton from the cotton belt, it was in short supply and he knew he could make a nice profit selling it to those in the futures market that had sold short. The spot market was usually higher at that time of the year than the futures price had been. In order to have the cash available for the cotton futures contracts, T. P. went to the Peoples Loan and Trust Company with the power of attorney executed by Carrie and borrowed a large sum of money using the Banta Ranch as collateral.

By the time Carrie and George returned from their trip around the world in March of 1914, he was heavily invested in the 1914 crop of Imperial Valley cotton which would be picked in July, August and September. The demand for cotton from American and European factories was constantly exceeding supply and prices were holding steady or rising. T. P. had made money through this method for the last several years on a small basis and this year looked very good. If he controlled a large enough supply of valley cotton, he could control the market by withholding it from sale until prices rose. By the time Carrie and George returned from their trip things looked very promising.

The Mulkern's home on 24th Street

CHAPTER 36

THE WORLD GOES TO
WAR AND A NEW FAMILY MOVES
ONTO THE 2000 BLOCK OF 24TH STREET.

When Mama and George returned from their fantastic trip around the world, over a third of the year, 1914, had already passed-by. T.P. had much to tell Carrie about social and business events both at home in L. A. and in the Imperial Valley where he spent most of his time. Their letters were always delayed by as much as a month and a half, and letters don't compare to face to face conversation because if you have questions, it took as much as three months to get an answer. After the disastrous failure of the Banta Tract Corporation in Imperial Beach, T. P.'s luck had changed and his numerous other business ventures were doing very well. He had purchased future cotton crops from valley farmers in large quantities and at good prices. He was sure he would make a killing on the spot market in August, September and October. Carrie was delighted to hear that his businesses were doing so well.

Carrie and George had many colorful stories of their adventures in far away places all around the world. They kept Papa and the boys' rapt attention for hours listening to all they had seen and done in those exotic lands across the oceans.

Homecomings are wonderful, but after two or three weeks everything settled down to the events of everyday life. Earl had graduated from Stanford in June of 1913 and was undecided as to what he wanted to do. George was ready to start college in September. With advice from Papa, George decided to enter law school in September. After family discussions, Earl decided he too would like to spend his life practicing law. All of Papa's lawyer friends in the valley seemed to be in the middle of everything that was exciting and Papa often wished he had studied to be a lawyer.

The thought of both Earl and George becoming lawyers pleased Papa very much. He urged both of them to register for the University of Southern California Law School. Earl and George followed their father's advice and applied to be admitted for the Fall semester at the U. S. C. School of Law. Both were accepted.

. Robert and Mary announced to T. P. and his family that their oldest daughter Grace had accepted the marriage proposal of Ober Fries, a prominent grocery store merchant in Imperial and that the wedding ceremony was set for the second Saturday of May. T. P. was happy for the young couple. The young man was well thought of in the community, but, he thought, "Good heavens, she's only a baby." This would be the first marriage in either family and it shocked him to think of the children as being old enough to get married.

Then Al further shook-up Papa by announcing that he and Jewel Gallaher were to be married in June. Jewel had accepted his proposal and her mother was preparing to have the ceremony in their family's church in Imperial. T. P. loved Jewel but he had hoped that Al would go on to college before he married. Al, in spite of Papa's pleading, showed no desire for higher learning. T. P. thought that after a few years in the college of hard knocks he would come to his senses but the marriage at this time made a higher education for Al look improbable. Since birth control was by now a common and successful practice he persuaded Al that after his marriage it would be wise to delay starting a family for a few years. Al had graduated from Imperial High in 1912 and had worked with him on his valley business interests since that time. This would permit Al a few more years to think about getting a college education.

Both Robert and T. P. and their spouses were experiencing that moment in every parent's life where they are confronted with the fact that a new generation is emerging. Parents generally are amazed when they find that their little boy or girl is old enough to start the ministry of procreation. In T. P. and Carrie's case this was doubly so since their oldest child, Earl, had shown no indication of being interested in marriage. Earl had been dating for years but as yet had not settled down to serious interest in a single girl. This new revelation enlivened the lives of both families, and for the next few months nothing mattered to the families, especially to Carrie and Mary, except the upcoming marriages.

The two mothers' lives were completely involved with planning for the ceremonies and all the preparations that go with them. Carrie moved down to the valley house to help the Gallahers with the various tasks involved in any way she could. Being mother of the groom simplified her responsibilities; but Mary, being mother of the bride had the pleasant burden of making all the plans for the service and the social events.

Both events were the talk of the Imperial since both families had been in the valley since its earliest days. It was obvious to everyone that both couples were very much in love and devoted to each other. May and June were wonderful months for the two Banta families. Both events were confined to family and close personal friends with the receptions held in the involved families' valley homes.

Papa decided it was time for him to move to the West Adams home and conduct his business by commuting and by phone. This would leave the valley house for Al and Jewel. He would stay with them when it was necessary to stay overnight in the valley. Having a home already furnished was greatly appreciated by the newlyweds.

Grace's husband was a successful valley merchant and had built his own home so it was merely a matter of Grace's moving her belongings into her new home.

The two couples, who were close before the ceremonies, became the best of friends now that they were newlyweds and socialized together often. T. P. and Carrie were delighted with their new daughter-in-law and Robert and Mary felt the same about their new son-in-law This was the happiest of times for both families.

"Mama," T. P. said, "How could things be better. Earl and George have been accepted to U. S. C. and will be starting in September. Al is married to beautiful Jewel, and my cotton futures are doing splendidly. We're living in this lovely home. These will be the best years of our lives." It would do little good to remind T. P. at this moment of euphoria that a beautiful sunset precedes the darkness of night.

An event that would change the life of George and enliven all the families that lived on 24th Street for the next seven years occurred in July of 1914. A large Irish family by the name of Mulkern moved into one of the large homes just across the street from the Banta estate. At first the neighbors thought that perhaps two families had moved into the house. There was an elderly lady in her eighties, two women who appeared to be mothers and five children whose ages ranged, as near as the Bantas could estimate, from thirteen or fourteen to the early twenties.

They only had to wonder about the new family until the next day when the youngest boy rode his bicycle over to their house to get acquainted. George was out on the front porch when he rode up. He called to T. P. and Carrie to come out and meet the youngest of the new neighbors. They found that the neighbor boy's name was George, so the two Georges had something immediately in common. Young George was friendly and talkative and soon the Bantas knew all about their new neighbors. They were the Mulkerns from Chicago. The elderly woman who was living with them was Mrs. Mulkern's mother, Grandma McGarigle.

His mother, Mrs. Mulkern, was the thinner of the two middle aged ladies who appeared to be in their fifties and was taller by one inch. She was five feet two inches with her shoes on. The other lady was George's maiden aunt, Mary McGarigle, who had devoted her life to helping to raise Katie Mulkern's large Irish

Catholic family of nine children. Four of the children had left home and five children, two girls and three boys, were still living at home.

George Mulkern invited the Bantas over to get acquainted. They declined because they thought it would be an imposition the day after the new family had moved into their new house. George insisted that it would be no problem because the ladies had the house in quite presentable order. Thereupon Mama went to the kitchen and brought out a chocolate cake she had ready for dinner and the three Bantas went across the street with the cake to meet their new neighbors.

Katie Mulkern met them at the door and introduced them to the other members of her family. They met Aunt Mary, the maiden lady who had helped to raise the family, Grandma McGarigle, Katie and Mary's mother, Violet, the oldest daughter, Mary, the next oldest, Johnny, the oldest of the boys who had just finished high school and was still at home, Hugh, who was in high school and of course they had already met George who was in the eighth grade. It was hard to tell by Katie's accent that she was Irish, for she had the broadest of Scotch brogues. She and Aunt Mary had been raised in Glascow, Scotland. Her family had been forced to leave Ireland and immigrated to Scotland during the potato famine in the 1840's.

Aunt Mary prepared a large pot of tea and put the Chocolate cake on a large cake plate. Then she set the dining room table with dessert plates and cups and saucers for eleven, eight in the Mulkern clan plus the three Bantas. "This is too much," said Carrie. "Entertaining the first day after moving."

"It's nothing at all." said Katie. "When the whole family was together, we had fourteen at the table morning, noon and night. Grandpa and Uncle Tom also lived with us until they passed away. I recall one time when we had a new ice man, he came in at lunch time and remarked, 'I see you're having a party.' Aunt Mary told him, 'It's this way every meal and it's no party!'"

Katie and Aunt Mary had wonderful senses of humor and

entertained them with stories of the family's life in the mid-west before their recent trip to California where they intended to make their new home. She also told them of her four children who had left the nest. Ben, her oldest, had contracted infantile paralysis when less than a year old and had to walk with a brace on his left leg all his life. She said he had a beautiful Irish tenor voice and was gifted at playing the piano. He was now an entertainer in the Klondike. The Bantas didn't say a word, but each was wondering where a piano player and singer would entertain in the Klondike in 1914, outside of bars and brothels.

Her next oldest boy, Jimmy, was in real estate and investments in Santa Monica. Vi, her oldest daughter, had become sickly in the cold winters of Chicago and moved out to live with him while she recovered her health. Her letters home about how wonderful the California weather and countryside were led the family to take the big step of moving to California. Now Vi was living at home with the family. Tom, her third oldest boy, was married and still living in Chicago. Margaret, the one girl who was not living with the family, had a job in Dallas, Texas.

Bernard, her husband, she said, worked as a specialist in the steel mills and his work caused him to move around from mill to mill as his services were needed He would be home shortly and they would meet him then.

There was an immediate attraction between George and the second oldest daughter, Mary. She appeared to be in her mid-twenties while George was only eighteen but the age difference made her only more attractive as she appeared so poised and sure of herself. She had a regal statuesque beauty which had been rec-ognized formally in Chicago where she had won a citywide beauty contest. George wanted to get to know her better but was a bit shy about starting a conversation with such a beautiful girl.

While the older set sat around the dining room table getting acquainted, Vi went to the Victrola and put on a popular dance record. Mary broke the conversational ice by asking George if he liked to dance. "Yes," he assured her, "I do, but unfortunately I have two left feet. If you'll excuse my clumsiness, would you like to dance."

"That was sort of the concept," Mary replied. She and George started to dance around the parlor. Soon Vi was dancing with her brother, Johnny, with Hugh and George cutting in for their share of the dancing. John got bored after a while and went over to the piano and started to play some of the latest rag-time music. Soon all the young people were over at the piano singing along with the old and new sing-along songs. This was turning into more of a party than the older folks could resist. Even grandma came over to join in the singing. Before anyone realized it, it was seven P. M.

"My goodness," Carrie said, "we've got to get home for dinner. I've had a pot roast cooking all day. Its got to be good and tender by now. We've taken up most of your day but I can't remember when we've had more fun." With this the Bantas bid the Mulkerns goodbye and crossed the street to their home.

When the Bantas returned home after the get acquainted party over tea and cake followed by dancing and singing, they couldn't stop talking about this unusual new family that had joined their neighborhood. What an addition to our neighborhood this new family is," Mama said. "I guess we find them just as unusual as our neighbors found us when we first moved here."

T. P. Banta, age 60

George's head was spinning by the beauty of the two daughters but he was especially taken by Mary. He had never been in love before but the raging hormones of an eighteen year old told him that what he was feeling had to have something to do with love. He could hardly wait to see Mary again.

It wasn't long before the entire street was captivated by the Mulkern's friendliness and hospitality. The Mulkern home was the center of a party of some kind almost every night and anyone in the neighborhood was invited to attend. None of the neighbors ever complained of the noise from the Victrola, piano and singing that often went on til well after midnight because if there wasn't someone from the neighbor's family in attendance, someone had been there the night before or intended to be there a following night. There was never any liquor. Katie wouldn't allow it. But liquor wasn't needed in the Mulkern home to have all the fun anyone could wish for.

In late July, the first cotton crops in the valley started to be harvested. As expected, T. P. made money on his futures contracts by selling the harvested bales on the spot market. Things were going just as he had planned as these were the first of the cotton crops to be harvested in the United States in 1914 and cotton was in short supply.

An arch-duke had been assassinated somewhere in eastern Europe and the papers were full of speculation about a war that would involve the entire European sub-continent. T. P. saw no connection between war in Europe and his cotton futures contracts.

In early August, war was declared between the Allies (Great Britain, France, Russia, Belgium and Serbia) and the Central Powers (Germany, Austria-Hungary and the Ottoman Empire). Great Britain Immediately declared a blockade against the central powers and declared that any ships trying to run the blockade would be warned by shots being fired across their bows. If they refused to stop they would be sunk. This effectively stopped all commerce between the Central Powers and the United States including the Central Power's imports of American cotton.

One fourth of the American cotton crop had been bought by the nations composing the Central Powers. In an auction market such as the cotton market, this meant that supply now greatly exceeded demand and thus the cotton market crashed. As early as August eighteenth, cotton farmers were calling on the government to appoint fiscal agents to care for the cotton crop. Cotton which had been selling for thirteen to fourteen cents a pound dropped to seven and one half cents a pound and even at that price buyers were scarce. T. P. had stumbled into incredibly bad luck. His plan that had seemed so sensible when he embarked upon it turned to disaster from conditions completely beyond his control. Though Mama had warned him against investing in the cotton market she never once said, "I told you so," for she realized that his plan was sound and that no one could have predicted the terrible turn of events that turned his plan into a catastrophe.

"Mama," T. P. said, "I turned sixty last December and I've semi-retired from my valley businesses and have Al handling the things that needed immediate attention. Now I've got to go back to the valley to recoup as much of the money I've just lost as I possibly can. Between Imperial Beach and cotton futures, I've lost about forty percent of our capital. We've taken chances at every point in our career. That's what capitalists do every day of their lives. We've won a lot more than we've lost. It's just hellish that I took two such big losses towards the end of my career. I don't think I've got time enough left to ever get back to where we were."

T. P. took the train the next morning to El Centro. Al met him at the station with the Franklin and drove him to the family home where he and Jewel were living. "How are you newlyweds doing," Papa said to Al.

"Great," Al said. "We couldn't be happier, and I'm not going to kid you by telling you that Jewel is happy about this arrangement of you living with us on a semi-permanent basis, but I'm happy you're here to help me resolve this problem. Frankly, I don't know how we'll get out of losing a lot of money."

"We won't," T. P. said. "I took a risk and I lost."

He and Al sat up most of the night planning their strategy to bail out of this expensive adventure with the least possible loss.

Carrie Banta, age 58, 1913

"I'd bet my last dollar that cotton will be up to twenty-one cents a pound within two years but that won't do us any good now. We're stuck with seven or eight cents now and the average I paid was about thirteen cents a pound. I'm going to end up filling my warehouses with my own cotton and I'll not only lose on the drop in cotton prices, but I'll lose storage rent that I could have collected."

Al responded, "Every farmer in the valley that didn't sell his cotton under a futures contract is in the same boat we are, except that unlike us they have nothing else to fall back on. Most of them won't have enough money left after selling their crops at today's prices to live through next year yet alone plant next years crop."

"It's crazy," T. P. said. "The valley went so heavily into cotton because it was such a profitable crop to grow. Yet cotton is the only crop that went to hell in a hand-basket with the start of the war in Europe. Beef, pork, wheat, oats and every other commodity, has stayed steady or risen in price and here in the valley we're stuck with this damn cotton."

T. P. was right that there was no way around losing money. They had to take their losses just like every capitalist who guesses wrong in spite of all his studies. Any time there is a good reward from an investment there is a significant risk. Still they had substantial holdings in the valley, and they loaned money to those farmers who required it—cash to do next year's planting as did Leroy Holt and all the valley bankers. T. P. was right also about the future prices of cotton. By 1917, cotton was up to twenty-one cents a pound but T. P didn't have one cent invested in cotton futures that year.

Grace and Ober Freiss came over regularly to visit Jewel and Al. They didn't wait to start a family, and it was apparent to T. P. that Grace was pregnant. Although it was at his suggestion that Al and Jewel were holding off starting a family, T. P. couldn't help but be jealous of his brother, Robert. Robert and Mary were going to be grandparents while such an event was nowhere in sight for Carrie and himself.

T. P. spent many evenings with Robert and his family. Myra had finished high school and was ready for college. T. P. suggested that she could come to L. A. and live with them while she attended Los Angeles Normal College which was just a few blocks from his 24th Street house. This sounded like a wonderful idea to Robert and Mary.

T. P. stayed in the valley tying up loose ends concerning the cotton contracts and the storage of the cotton he had purchased under them. Meanwhile, back in Los Angeles, Earl and George started law school classes at U. S. C. T. P. had dreams of them coming to the valley and opening a law practice when they received their law degrees in 1918.

Ober Freiss's business was going splendidly and the newlyweds and expectant parents were deliriously happy in a manner that only a young couple in their position could be. They had fixed up a room in their house for the new baby and were anxiously awaiting its arrival. At every meeting of the Bantas in the valley, the new baby was the center of conversation. Would it be a boy or a girl? Ober wanted a boy and Grace wanted a girl but neither would admit it. All that they would say was that all that mattered was that the baby was healthy.

Carrie came down from Los Angeles and threw a baby shower for Grace. It was a big success with all of Grace's school chums envying her because she was one of the first in her graduating class to be expecting. All of Carrie and Mary's lady friends were in attendance. It was the talk of Imperial.

Ober always closed his store after the banks had already closed their doors. He was afraid to leave the day's receipts in the grocery store because he had been robbed twice. For this reason he would take the cash home with him and keep it under his pillow along with a thirty-eight-caliber revolver. Unfortunately, This practice had become known to others in Imperial, and he was fearful that the bad element that had robbed his store twice would come to his house and rob him again.

Grace, being pregnant, had to go to the outhouse several times during the night. Ober told her that no matter how tired he was nor how late he came home to promise him she would never get up to go to the out house without waking him. This she promised him she would do. However, in October Ober came home about midnight after taking inventory and was dead tired. He woke Grace and told her he was home. She felt sorry for her hard-working husband and saw how he fell asleep as soon as he had put the money under his pillow and laid his head down.

About two in the morning Grace awoke and had to go to the outhouse. Ober was breathing heavily in the deepest of sleeps. "He's so sound asleep that there's no need to awaken him. He's had such a long hard day that I'll let him sleep," she thought. She arose and slipped out the back door. When she returned, she opened the door as quietly as she could but she stumbled as she crossed the raised threshold of the back door. Ober awoke with a start and saw a figure entering the bedroom. Half asleep, he thought it was the bad element in town coming to rob him. So certain was he that this was the case that he pulled his revolver from under his pillow and shot Grace through the abdomen. She let out a shriek and he awakened to realize he had shot his expectant wife.

Distraught with anguish, Ober dropped the revolver and threw on the light beside their bed. As he rushed to her side, he could see that she lay in an ever increasing pool of blood. Grabbing the sheets from the bed he held them against the bullet hole to stop the flow of blood.

"My God, Grace, how could I have done such a thing," he wept. "I've got to get you to the hospital."

As he was grabbing up the blankets from the bed and surrounding her with them to keep her warm on the way to the hospital, Grace was still alert and said to him, "Darling, It's not your fault. I should have awakened you, as you asked me to do, before I left the room." She felt she was near death and wanted him to know if she died that she did not hold him responsible.

Ober picked up his critically wounded pregnant wife and carried her to the bed of his grocery delivery truck where he made her as comfortable as possible with pillows and blankets. He cranked the motor of the truck and as soon as it started, drove her as gently as possible to the hospital in El Centro. As soon as they arrived at the hospital, the entire staff went to work to stop the blood flow and see if they could reverse her extremely critical condition. Four doctors were called in and were with her continually in their attempt to save her life.

At his first opportunity, Ober rushed to a telephone and called Robert and his family getting him up out to a sound sleep. Robert was wide awake in an instant when he was told of the terrible tragedy and awoke Mary, Myra, Pearl and Fred. The family that had been so happy at the thought of the coming birth of the next generation were shocked into a state of numbness by the terrible news. The family got dressed as quickly as possible and rushed to the hospital to be at Grace's side. They found Ober unconsolable in his grief as he told them in detail the story of the disaster that had overtaken his wife and unborn baby.

"I'll never have a gun in my house again," he told them. "Let the scoundrels steal the money. If God will give me my wife and baby back, money will never again be my first concern."

The four doctors worked throughout the day to save Grace's life. Robert called T. P., Al and Jewel and told them the awful news. He asked T. P. to relay it on to Carrie, Earl and George. T. P. promised to do so and after calling them, Al, Jewel and he rushed to the hospital to be with Grace and her grieving family.

At four in the afternoon the doctors knew they were losing the battle to save Grace's life and called the family into her hospital room to see her for the last time. Ober was already there and was holding Grace's hand. Grace had slipped into a coma thirty minutes earlier and was breathing very hard as is often the case just prior to death. The family gathered about her bed quietly weeping while Ober kept repeating over and over, "I love you, Grace, I love you. Please don't leave me." Then, with a final gasp, Grace breathed her last breath and was gone. Ober let out a mournful moan and pressed his head against her breast sobbing uncontrollably.

Robert and Mary embraced each other as tears rolled down their sun worn faces. "We've lost our beautiful Grace, our beloved first born," Robert said to Mary in a wavering voice. "And our first grandchild, too," Mary said quietly.

T. P. went over to his baby brother and Mary and put his big, strong arms around both of them. There was nothing he could say but he thought to himself, "I don't think I could take it if I lost one of my boys. Robert and Mary are enduring the most difficult of all losses, the loss of their child. I'm not the most religious of men, but I thank God my loss was only money."

Ober had lost his beloved wife and unborn baby. Carrie, George and Earl arrived too late to say goodbye to Grace but were there to offer their support to her husband and her family. The funeral was packed with their Imperial friends. The bond between this loving couple had been severed in a most terrible way and their promising life together terminated by this ghastly mistake in a dark bedroom.

Pearl Banta and Grace Banta, Imperial High School

Left to right, Myra, Robert and Pearl Banta
at their home in the Imperial Valley

Fred Banta

Grace was laid to rest in a family plot in the Evergreen Cemetery in El Centro.

Al and Jewel realized even more acutely how precious their love was now that their dearest friends had been separated by death. T. P. also realized that his company in the house caused the young couple to have an ambivalent feeling towards his living with them. A visit was one thing but he had been in the valley three months and having Papa around even if it was his house isn't what a newly married couple finds the most desirable of arrangements.

It was now November and all of his contracts for cotton had matured. He met all his obligations and had disposed of most of the bales of cotton he had purchased under them. His losses had been heavy but by every ethical means he had kept them to a minimum. His estate had suffered heavily, but by any standard he was still a very wealthy man. It was time for him to return to Los Angeles and leave the cleaning up of the remainder of matters to Al.

The death of Grace had forcefully brought to his attention how important these first years of marriage were to a young couple. He would stay with Al and Grace when he came to the valley on business but he knew that living with them as a permanent resident was a strain on the newly married couple. Beside that, he missed Carrie, Earl and George. Earl and George had started law school in September and he wanted to hear all about their studies from them directly each night, not just by telephone. So in November, T. P. again returned to semi-retirement in Los Angeles leaving the business matters that required personal attention to Al. He continued going to the valley on a weekly basis to go over business matters with Al.

George and Earl were doing splendidly at U. S. C. They loved the University and had become avid members of the student body. Their law classes were not held at the campus on University Avenue just a few blocks south of Adams Boulevard. Law school classes were held in a building on Spring Street in downtown Los Angeles. Both boys commuted by streetcar. Earl had been away from home for such a long time that he found it stifling to live at home as a child of his parents and was talking of renting an apartment of his own.

Everything else at the mansion in Los Angeles remained as it had been when he had left three months earlier. The Mulkern family had become the center of social life on 24th Street. Margaret had returned home from her job in Texas and she was as pretty as the other two Mulkern girls. Most parties weren't planned but with all the children bringing home their boyfriends and girlfriends, they just happened. When a party was planned it was a corker to use the slang of the day.

In January, Earl found an apartment in Long Beach just off the ocean front. Transportation by the big red streetcars brought him within a couple of blocks of the Law school. T. P., Carrie and George would drive down to his place on weekends and spend a day at his apartment or on the beach under a big multicolored beach umbrella.

George loved to swim and was a very strong swimmer, often swimming out of sight scaring Mama almost to death. She would watch carefully until he came back into sight. Then as he left the surf and dried himself with a beach towel she would berate him and swear that if he did that again she simply wouldn't come to the beach again. She repeated this each time and the next time they went to the beach he would do it again getting the same lecture.

In the valley, Al kept the family's businesses moving efficiently. The family's yearly income was still substantial in spite of the two recent financial disasters. While Al took care of the valley businesses, T. P. remained involved in politics. He was still deeply involved in the organization of the new irrigation district and the attempts by the district to contract with the United States Government for the rights to take water from the Laguna Dam, because it was built on bed rock while the heading at Hanlon's Landing was far mor precarious. The valley would never be safe from the ebbs and flows of the Colorado River until such a contract was in effect.

After negotiations, the irrigation district and the Southern Pacific Railroad agreed that three million dollars would be a fair price for the C. D. Company property. The District called an election for a three million five hundred thousand dollar bond issue. The election was held in late October of 1914 and carried by a vote of 3278 to 330.

The receiver's sale was held by the court in February of 1915 and the Southern Pacific purchased the property of the California Development Company. They then bought three million dollars of the irrigation district bond issue. The money from the sale of the bonds was paid back to the Southern Pacific under a contract which conveyed the C. D. Company's irrigation works to the new irrigation district. This contract between the Imperial Valley Irrigation District and the railroad marked the actual beginning of public ownership of the valley's water distribution system by the Imperial Valley Irrigation District.

The thought of building an All-American Canal arose with the settlers who questioned continuing to deal with the Mexican Receiver. Mark Rose, who owned a 400 acre farm in District 7 on the "East Side'" was an early leader in the fight for a canal from Laguna Dam to the valley built entirely on this side of the border. He brought the idea of an All-American Canal to the attention of the Imperial Irrigation District Board of Directors and kept it constantly on their minds.

His idea was to build a concrete canal from the Laguna Dam across the sand hills to the east of the Eastside Mesa and then across the Eastside Mesa to the Imperial Valley. He and a group of his friends, including T. P., formed the Imperial-Laguna Water Company. He was interested in the farming potential of the Eastside mesa land across which the proposed All-American Canal would flow. Mark led these men in a campaign to have Secretary Lane of the Department of the Interior restore the Eastside Mesa to entry. Mark succeeded in talking the Imperial Irrigation District Board into making such a request of the Secretary. This however was unsuccessful. The men, including T. P., who made up the Imperial-

Laguna Water Company then claimed a prior right to enter these lands when they were restored and with this as a primary motivation, continued an unrelenting campaign to get water to their land.

Mark even went so far as to obtain a contract from Secretary of the Interior Lane to permit he and his associates to construct such a canal which would bring water from the Laguna Dam. The Irrigation District opposed this; they did not want to be placed in a secondary position concerning water from Laguna Dam. This opposition plus the difficulties in arraigning financing of the canal made this project unrealistic.

Mark then set about to get the Board of the Imperial Irrigation District to promote the idea of an All-American Canal with the Federal Government. He proposed lobbying for a law through which the Federal Government would provide the financing. Some members of the Board did not agree with this position which caused him to join with other citizens who were unhappy with the composition of the board in demanding the recall of two Board members. Though the recall failed, it did cause the resignation of the entire Board in 1916. Even the new Board was not ready for his All-American Canal proposal. So, he and the Imperial-Laguna Water Company continued to pound away until the Board finally relented and asked the Reclamation Service to determine what it would cost to build such a canal if such a canal could be built at all.

The idea of petitioning the Federal government to build an All-American Canal continued to be a matter that was discussed at every irrigation district board meeting. Such a canal would cross the sand dunes that lay between the Laguna Dam at Yuma and the Imperial Valley. It would then flow across the Eastside Mesa land which had been the shore line of the ancient fresh water lake that had filled the valley in prehistoric times.

United States Government surveyors divided newly surveyed areas into townships. Each Township was six miles by six miles square. The township was divided into thirty-six sections of one square mile. One section (one square mile) in each township was

declared to be school land. School land was sold to the highest
bidder rather than being opened to entry under the Arid Lands
Act and the money paid for the land was to be spent on schools for
the new settlers. These school land sections were available for purchase even if the area was not open to entry. Mark Rose saw the
possibility of these school land sections being used for the construction of towns when the new land was opened to entry. A full
section would provide ample land for a town site.

Mark and thirty-six other Valley business men, of which T. P.
was one, purchased the school land sections. They then formed
the Imperial-Laguna Water District and asked the Imperial Valley
Irrigation District to include their school land purchases within
its boundaries even though the the the rest of the Eastside Mesa was
not yet open to entry. At their request, the district ordered these
privately owned school land sections admitted. While the Eastside
Mesa land has never opened to entry, these school land sections on
the Eastside Mesa are part of the district to this very day.

Although the principal purpose of the demand for an All
American Canal was to avoid the precarious political unrest in
Mexico through which the International Canal ran, the real push
for its building came from the owners, the Imperial Laguna Water
Company, that owned the Eastside Mesa school land and claimed
first entry to the rest of the Eastside Mesa land. They stood to
profit from the availability of water to the Eastside Mesa as the All
American Canal ran across it.

The split of responsibilities for the Banta ventures in the valley worked very well. Al took care of the day to day business while
T. P. worked on new projects such as acquiring the Eastside mesa
land and the building of an All-American Canal. He remained
involved in the political activities of making the irrigation water
source truly safe from the Yellow Terror, the Colorado River. Al
was bright and skillfully handled matters requiring immediate attention so that T. P. could resume his position of semi-retirement
and still be active in valley affairs.

On March 25,1914, Al suddenly appeared at the front door

of the Los Angeles house with Jewel assisting him from the taxi to the front porch. Mama met them at the front door and her face turned ashen as she saw her son writhing in pain. "Land sakes," Mama exclaimed, "you look terrible, Al. What is it? What has happened to you?"

"All I know, Mama, is that I'm too sick to work any longer and I thought the best place for me to recuperate would be with you and Papa. I've had the most awful pains in my stomach," Al responded.

Papa came downstairs from his study and was shaken to see how sick his son was. He had seen him just the week before and he had been in the best of health. When he heard Al's story, he said, "You and Jewel did the right thing. You couldn't keep working, and the best place for you right now is here with us."

Mama went upstairs to prepare the bedroom where Al and Jewel always stayed when in Los Angeles while Al rested in the parlor with Papa. Jewel went upstairs with Mama. When they were alone she said in a frightened shaking voice, "Mother, I'm really worried about Al. The doctor in the valley thinks its cancer of the stomach. He said we should come to Los Angeles for further diagnosis. Al doesn't think it is cancer and said he doesn't want to go to the hospital, though he will see Aunt Madge. I think he's in denial. The pain just won't go away and its truly unbearable." Aunt Madge was T. P.'s sister who was the medical doctor and who was now living in Los Angeles.

Carrie's face again went ashen. Al had always been the picture of health. His only previous illness was the result of an accident. A mule had kicked him in the side of his face when he was fourteen and he had been unconscious for several hours. A doctor in the valley who knew nothing of plastic surgery had sown up a terrible gash in the side of Al's face left by the horseshoe leaving an ugly scar. Other than that Al had never been sick. The news that her son might be terminally ill caused her to be light-headed. Her legs became so weak that she had to sit down on the bed or she would have collapsed to the floor.

When Mama had composed herself and her pioneer spirit again took over her body, she said, "Jewel honey, We've got to think the best and consider its just an ulcer or some other thing that isn't so fatal. We can't think that only the worst thing can be true. You and I will nurse him back to health with milk toast, Cream of Wheat and other foods that are easy on the stomach."

Al got undressed and went up to his bed. As soon as she could get T. P. alone Carrie told him what Jewel had told her. Tears came to the old frontiersman's eyes and he struggled to maintain his self-control. "I'll call Madge to come over and see him right away," T. P. said. T. P. rushed to the phone and called her. She listened as he told her the story and the symptoms Al was displaying. "I'll be over as quickly as I can get there," She told T. P."

Madge was over in less than an hour. She immediately went upstairs to examine Al. "Al," she said, "let me have a look at you. I understand that you're in unbearable pain."

"Aunt Madge," Al responded, "you know I can tolerate a great deal of pain so when I tell you this pain is intolerable you know it has to be bad."

Madge chased Carrie, Jewel and T. P. out of the room as she completed her examination of Al. Then she said, "T. P. will get you some medicine from the drug store that will ease your pain. In the meantime I'll be in regularly to see you."

"Can you tell what it is?" Al asked.

"It's to early to make a diagnosis," Madge said, "but a few days should give us a better picture of the problem."

Al and Jewel Banta

When she opened the door to Al's room, T. P. greeted her with the same question and she gave him the same response. "But we can control the pain," she said. "T. P. run to the drug store and get this medicine for Al," she continued as she wrote out a prescription.

When George came home from law school, he too was shocked to see how sick Al had become. They called Earl that evening and told him of his brother's condition. Earl had always been very close to Al and came to see how he was doing each night before going to his Long Beach apartment. Mama and Jewel did everything they could to make Al comfortable. Mama spent hours cooking bland food prepared and served the way she knew Al liked his meals but Al could hardly eat a thing. Often when he would eat, he couldn't keep the food down and would throw-up.

After two weeks at home, Al wasn't any better. Madge would not give Al or the family a definite diagnosis though she was almost sure it was cancer of the stomach. Thus, Madge decided that he should be admitted to the Good Samaritan Hospital on Wilshire Boulevard. By now, Al welcomed the idea of going to the hospital. Though the pain had been alleviated by the medicine, he was ready to get an answer to his physical problem. Madge called the Good Samaritan and told them she was admitting Al immediately. While Mama wrote a note to George, who was still at school, telling him they had taken Al to the Good Samaritan Hospital, Papa started the Franklin and brought it around to the front porch. Papa and Jewel assisted Al onto the front seat. Then Jewel and Mama climbed into the back seat.

When they arrived at the hospital and entered the lobby, the staff had a room ready and he was immediately escorted to it. A team of doctors decided that an exploratory operation was not necessary. Al definitely had inoperable cancer of the stomach and it had spread to other organs. He had but a short time to live. He was released the next day.

After staying two weeks at the Los Angeles house, Al decided he would like to spend his last days at the beach by the ocean. After growing up on the stark Colorado desert, being by the ocean seemed as close to paradise as Al could imagine. Papa told him to find an apartment that he and Jewel liked and that he would pay the rent whatever it was. Al and Jewel moved in with Earl in his Long Beach apartment for one week until Jewel could find their own apartment. She found just what they wanted at the Sea Breeze Apartments on the ocean front.

Ever since Al had left the hospital, he was unable to eat. When he tried he couldn't keep anything down and it just made him feel worse. Jewel and the family watched him as his body wasted away to a shadow of its former athletic self. By the time they moved to the Sea Breeze Apartments he was too weak to go for a walk on the beach. Jewel and he would sit at the window facing the beach and watch the breakers roll onto the sand. The best part of their day was when the sun set over the blue Pacific. While it can be very foggy and overcast in May, this year, the sunsets were spectacular and the newlyweds would sit hand in hand as the sun dipped below the horizon and the clouds turned a brilliant red.

"After growing up on the desert, it just doesn't get any better than this," Al said to Jewel as they watched the sunset on May 9. "I love you, Jewel, and I know I don't have much time left. Every time you look at a sunset think of me and I'll be there."

Al passed away on May 10, 1915, a week after they moved into their own apartment and a month and a half after coming home ill to the Los Angeles house. T. P. learned first hand that the loss of money is insignificant as compared to the loss of your child. The loss of a child leaves a darkness in a parent's life that no light can ever penetrate. Even time can not erase this kind of broken heart.

In less than a year after their weddings, the two young couples' marriages had been torn asunder by the tragic deaths of Grace and Al.

With Al's death, Jewel moved back with her parents and returned to Imperial High School to do postgraduate work while T. P. moved into the valley house to again resume managing his valley interests. He would spend five days of each week in the valley and weekends in Los Angeles.

Business wise, 1915-16 were good years for the Banta ventures. T. P. was back to work as hard as ever in the valley with the

passing of Al. He had taken the load off of T. P.'s back but now T.
P. was fully back in the saddle.

As was previously discussed, the board of the Imperial Irrigation District, as then established, was not fully behind changing
the source of river water from Hanlon's Landing to the Laguna
Dam. Mark Rose's Imperial Laguna Water Company insisted that
the Valley would not have a safe supply of Colorado River water
until Laguna Dam was its source.

As one of the thirty-six Valley men who composed the Imperial Laguna Water Company, T. P. was on the side of Mark Rose.
His company was pressuring the Irrigation District to make water
available for the Eastside Mesa from Hanlon's landing until water
could be obtained from a deal negotiated with Secretary Lane for
water from the Laguna Dam.

Because the board could not reach an agreement as to whether
or not a contract with the government should be pursued for use
of Laguna Dam as the source of all the Valley's water, the entire
board agreed to resign so that harmony could be restored. The
new board with, Leroy Holt as president, was fully in favor of a
contract with the Secretary of the Interior which would permit the
Irrigation District to use the Laguna Dam built on bed rock as the
source of its Colorado River water.

Mark Rose pressed the new board concerning an immediate
canal right of way from Hanlon's landing to the Eastside Mesa.
The new board's attitude towards the Eastside Mesa was made
clear through a resolution they passed which stated that the board
was in favor of the earliest possible development of the mesa land if
the prior rights of the developed lands was assured and the Irrigation
District assumed no additional burdens or debts.

CHAPTER 37

THE UNITED STATES ENTERS THE
WAR GEORGE AND EARL FALL IN LOVE

Earl and George were spending all of their time studying law. When they weren't studying, they were discussing and arguing points of law. T. P. was sure they would be good lawyers as their favorite pastime was debating any issue. It didn't really matter what their true beliefs were for if one made a positive statement about anything the other would automatically take the opposite position. George joined the debate society at U. S. C. for to him debating was a sport and he loved it dearly. He won several medals on the debate team.

By the end of 1916, things were heating up between him and Mary Mulkern. He absolutely adored her and she thought he was the smartest boy she had ever met. Since she was seven years older than he was, she saw no future in their dating as far as marriage was concerned. Not so with George. Being the baby of his family he loved being mothered. Mary being the older sister, had raised her four youngest brothers and was an expert at mothering.

The more George saw of Mary the better he liked her as a person and the more beautiful she became both inside and out. There was just one thing about her of which he did not approve. She was a Catholic and more than that a very religious one. With his family's background of being ardently protestant, though they didn't go to church, this was a major impediment in romantic relations in 1916. At that point in time interfaith marriages were almost non-existent and reluctantly sanctioned by rabbis or clergy.

T. P. knew little about Catholics other than that he had been told that they had caused serious trouble for Christianity and that Martin Luther had put the faith back on the right path by leading the protestant revolt. He had never known many Catholics but was quite prejudiced against them and hoped that none of his boys would, heaven forbid, marry one.

Carrie had been raised in Lansing, Michigan, and intermingled with many Catholics in that city. She was not religious though she believed in God. She, T. P. and the boys had never joined any organized religion though they attended various revival meetings over the years where the itinerant preacher told his congregation that hell-fire and brimstone awaited sinners unless they repented. She always left these revivals in fear of hell and repenting any sins she might have committed. At the same time, she had great respect for the Pope and considered him to be a holy man.

George never brought up or mentioned to Mary his concerns about this religious conflict since he was infatuated with Mary and didn't want to disturb their relationship. During 1916 they became quite an item. Except when he was studying, wherever Mary was you could be sure he was close by. They dated regularly and became not only boy-friend and girl-friend but best of friends. Whatever one would say the other would swear to it.

One warm summer evening, they were passing the time playing croquette as a pair against George Mulkern and Vi on the broad grass lawn that surrounded the Mulkern house. The light was beginning to fade as the game was coming to its conclusion. George Banta was clear across the court and had only to go through the last two wickets and hit the post to win the game for Mary and himself. If he missed, it would be George Mulkern's turn and he was just outside the wickets with an almost sure shot at going through them and hitting the post and thereby winning for Vi and himself.

George Banta made a major production of looking at the shot

from all angles, carefully taking in consideration the slope of the lawn and testing to see the heaviness of the grass. As he did this it was getting darker and darker. Finally, he took his stance and hit the ball squarely toward the target. Wham! It hit the post.

"We win," Mary said. "It went right through the two wickets before it hit the post."

"The heck it did," said her younger brother who was closer to the wickets. "It went beside the wickets and hit the post. Vi, you saw it . Don't you agree?"

Vi honestly said she wasn't watching that close.

"O. K.," little George said. "You hit it, George. Did it go through the wickets?"

"If Mary said it did, then it did." George replied, "and we win."

"Holy smoke," little George said. "You're some pair. One lies and the other swears to it."

Brother George picked the perfect time to confront Mary as to her honesty in the matter. He waited until Mary had just returned from eight-o'clock Sunday Mass where she had just received Holy Communion. Then he cornered her. "O. K. Mary, You've just received Holy Communion. Did that croquette ball go through those two wickets?"

"This isn't fair," Mary said.

"Answer me," George demanded.

"Well, it was getting awfully dark and I can't say for sure," Mary confessed.

"Ah ha," George laughed with glee. "Then you forfeit the game and we won."

Little George knew that in the Baltimore Catechism taught in all Catholic schools, one of the questions was:

Q. When should you tell a lie?

A. You should never tell a lie, in fun or in earnest, or to save yourself or others from harm.

He had timed it perfectly. Mary couldn't lie. Not right after going to Holy Communion.

Earl, too had fallen in love with an Irish Catholic girl. There is something about forbidden fruit that has tempted mankind from the days of the garden of Eden. The Irish had immigrated from Ireland during the 1860s because of the terrible starvation caused by the potato blight. This blight wiped out the principle diet that sustained the Emerald Isle resulting in the death of one fourth of the Irish population. A second fourth of the population migrated to countries around the world to avoid the famine. America was a favorite among the emigrants with hundreds of thousands passing through Ellis Island. The population of Ireland dropped from four-million to two-million during that terrible tragedy.

The Irish moved mainly to the larger cities where they began their careers as common laborers. Through hard work and intelligence they took advantage of the freedoms offered to all men in this new country. They had a knack for entrepreneurship and some moved from the lowest class as new immigrants to captains of industry. Many entered the middle class as business men and foremen in the factories. Since Protestant England under the house of Orange, which originated in Holland as we recall, occupied their homeland and exported crops from their island for a profit while one million Irishmen died of hunger, their Catholic religion was more than a religion to the Irish. It was their badge of defiance to Protestant England.

1916 was close enough to the potato famine that these stories were relayed by parents and grandparents to the younger generation born in America. Again this was a wedge between inter-marriage between the Irish Catholics and the Protestants. Yet love is blind and young lovers find ways around any obstacle.

Earl had met Mary McLeod, whose mother's maiden name was Mary Murphy through T. P. and Carrie's good friend, Mrs. Weaver. She had been raised in a convent school much of her life and followed her mother's Catholic faith. Earl at an early age had been frightened to death by the itinerant revival preachers teaching that the "wages of sin" was to be damned to eternal hell fire. Therefore, he consoled himself by declaring himself to be a free thinker which in layman's language meant he didn't quite know what he thought though he had read the Bible from cover to cover many times.

He found many places where there were apparent contradictions in the good book. When he needed guidance from conflicts of conscience he always chose the passage that worked in his best interest and justified what he wanted to do. Being a free thinker had many merits in its behalf. Being a free thinker, he felt Mary had as much right to believe the way she wanted to believe as he did, as long as it didn't infringe on his free thinking.

Mary, as we have related, met Earl through Mrs. Weaver, who was a good friend of her Aunt Liz who lived in the valley and whom she visited frequently. Mary lived in L. A. with her Aunt Trace. Aunt Liz thought the world of Earl and was delighted to see that they were infatuated with each other. Aunt Trace, on the other hand, didn't care for Earl, who she referred to as "that Banta boy." None the less Earl and Mary dated regularly and fell in love.

Since both Banta boys had fallen in love with Irish Catholic girls named Mary, a means had to be worked out to differentiate between the two when they were in the same room or were being talked about.

Mary Mulkern, being first on the scene, decided that she should be called Mary while Mary McLeod would be called Marie. Mary McLeod didn't care much for this arrangement but could think of none other that would solve the problem. Thus, from now on in this story , Mary will refer to Mary Mulkern and Marie will refer to Mary McLeod.

George and Earl were now spending every minute with their new sweethearts that was not spent studying law or debating points of law.

Ever since the sinking of the Lusitania by a German submarine, America had grown more distant from Germany and closer to England. The sentiment in the United States had swung dramatically in favor of the Allies. The Germans had defused the Lusitania disaster by declaring that they would not indiscriminately sink Allied passenger ships. The British took immediate advantage of this limited submarine warfare and transported much war material on passenger ships.

Because of this, at the end of 1916, Germany declared unrestricted submarine warfare. On April 6, 1917, the United States retaliated by declaring war on Germany. The nation by this time was fully behind this action. Posters appeared everywhere saying, "Uncle Sam Wants You!" with a picture of Uncle Sam pointing a finger at whoever was looking at the poster. The draft had already started and draft boards were filling their quotas with intense ardor.

Those in universities were deferred until graduation. Thus, George and Earl were deferred until June of 1918. While other boys were being drafted or enlisting in the various services, George and Earl continued with their study of law. It was embarrassing when strangers on the street asked why such a big strong boy was walking the streets of L. A. while their son had been shipped to the front lines in France. Earl and George could hardly wait to graduate so that they too could fight the Hun.

Upon graduation in 1918, both boys enlisted immediately: Earl in the tank corps and George in the Army Air Corps. Both commenced to write their sweethearts regularly.

Mary always promptly answered George's letters and was vitally interested in everything he was doing as he went through cadet pilot training. She knew it was very dangerous and as a good Catholic prayed fervently that nothing bad would happen to him.

Earl on the other hand received no letters of reply from his sweetheart Marie. He was heartbroken that she had dumped him while he was training to fight for his country. It just didn't seem fair to him and after a dozen unanswered letters he gave up writing her. Soon he was through with his training and on his way overseas with his tank corps.

George's training as a pilot required more time and after months of training in a Jenny, he was given his wings and commissioned a Second Lieutenant. Upon graduating, he was given a two-week leave prior to being sent over seas. He caught the first train to Los Angeles to see his family but especially to see his sweetheart, Mary, for absence had made the heart grow fonder and he had decided to ask her to marry him before going overseas.

What a welcome Mama and Papa had for this handsome young pilot in his Air Corps uniform sporting those wings that made the young girls' hearts beat faster. They invited all of their friends and neighbors to a party in his honor and had things planned for the entire visit. George thoroughly enjoyed the party but had other plans for the rest of his leave. He and Mary were inseparable. T. P. and Carrie understood young love and though they longed to spend more time with George, they knew that he preferred to spend his leave with his sweetheart.

Mary always had thought George was handsome but she simply swooned when she saw him in his uniform. She couldn't take her eyes off of him. When he proposed and offered her a ring, she accepted immediately. Both the Bantas and the Mulkerns couldn't have been happier for the young couple, for the Bantas had grown to love Mary and the Mulkerns had grown to love George. All of their friends said it was a perfect match.

When George left Los Angeles to head for New York, which was his port of embarkation for the western front, Papa was proud but Mama wept bitterly for she knew the high percentage of casualties that were being inflicted on the young airmen of both sides. She wondered if this was the last time she would see her baby. Mary had already been praying for his safe return since he first started flying for there were so many of the young pilots who were killed in training. The two young lovers embraced as he boarded his train for New York and both wondered if this might be the last time they would ever see each other again.

"Mary," George said, "we'll get married as soon as I get back!"

"Yes," Mary said as the two sweethearts broke their embrace and George hurriedly climbed aboard the railroad car's vestibule, for the train had started to move slowly ahead, "and I'll pray for you every minute while you are away."

This was on November 5, 1918.

George Banta and Mary Mulkern, 1918

While these things were happening to the family in Los Angeles, T. P. was spending his time in the valley trying to recoup his
losses from the cotton futures fiasco. Since he had been burned in
the futures market, he was frightened by it and could not force
himself to invest in cotton futures even though those who were
investing in them were making a good profit.

With America's entry into the war, wool prices had gone through the roof for the Government had to outfit the ever growing army with woolen uniforms. T. P. found a sheep rancher in Mexico who was willing to sell him a flock of one thousand sheep at a very reasonable price. In the U. S., the wool from those sheep would bring a handsome profit and would help to outfit our troops. Thus, he went down to Mexico to work out a deal with the Mexican sheep rancher.

The Mexican sheep rancher said he would herd the sheep to the Mexican border if T. P. would pay him in advance fifty percent of the price he was asking for the sheep and then pay him the remainder when he delivered the sheep to the border. T. P. agreed and paid him the asked price. The Mexican sheep rancher then said he would contact him as soon as he had the sheep at the border. T. P went back to the Valley to await word from the rancher. In a few weeks he received a phone call from a man he did not know telling him to meet the rancher in a bar in Mexicali concerning the sheep. T. P. thought it was strange that the rancher did not come to his office to make arrangements for the transfer of the sheep, but he went to the named bar at the specified time as instructed.

The bar in Mexicali was a typical border saloon, poorly lit, dark and dingy, with about a dozen Mexicans inside sitting at tables and drinking beer as a mariachi band played. Two men were dancing with bar girls while other girls sat on a line of chairs by the band awaiting customers. T. P. did not feel uncomfortable since he had often been in such bars but thought what a strange place it was to conduct business. When his eyes adjusted from the bright sunlight outside to the dimness of the light in the saloon, he noticed the rancher from whom he had purchased the sheep sitting at a table in a dark corner. Even in the darkness, he could not help but see the terrible state of attire in which he found the rancher. His clothing was torn and covered with mud. In the torn places of the clothing he could see that the rancher was scratched and bleeding. His hair and face were matted in mud. He was a wretched mess.

T. P. walked over to the table and the rancher motioned for him to sit down and then called for the bartender to bring T. P. a beer.

"What in the name of God has happened to you?" T. P. asked as he pulled the chair from under the table and sat down.

"Oh, Senior Banta, I have just endured the most terrible experience of my life in herding the sheep from my ranch to the border," the rancher replied. "I had no idea of the treacherousness of the path I had to take."

"Treacherousness? What do you mean treacherousness?" T. P. asked in a doubting voice for he smelled a rat. "How many sheep are you delivering from the flock of one-thousand I purchased from you?"

"Before I answer that, please let me tell you of my experiences on the trail." the rancher requested and he immediately began to relate the story. "It was bad luck from the very first. I started the journey with my well trained border collies that all the world knows are the best sheep dogs in the world. They were eager to start the trip, full of energy and eagerness.

"It was a beautiful sunny day when we set out but within several hours the rain clouds began to build up and as we left the plain to cross some rugged bad lands the clouds turned into thunderstorms. The rain and hail beat unmercifully on the sheep, the dogs, my horse and myself. As the dogs were driving the sheep across a gully a flash flood came down it with a wall of water six feet high carrying logs and brush on its crest. Senior Banta, it was the most awful thing I have ever seen. In that one flood you lost four hundred of your sheep and I two of my sheep dogs."

"Well then, you have brought me Eight-hundred sheep," T. P. said in astonishment. I'm not paying for those lost sheep. I've already paid you for six hundred sheep and I'll pay you for two hundred more. That's all you are going to get."

"That was not all," said the rancher. "Let me continue the story of my journey. With two less dogs it was hard to herd the sheep and keep them in control. We came to a cliff and the remaining dogs did their best but those foolish sheep walked right up to its edge and the ones behind were pushing the ones in front over the cliff. We lost another two hundred sheep over that two-hundred foot cliff before the dogs brought the herd under control."

"You mean I have only six hundred sheep left out of the thousand?" T. P. asked incredulously. Then I will pay you nothing more. The half of the original payment that I already paid you is all you'll get.

"I wish it were true, but let me finish my story," the rancher continued. "Next, we came to the marshy land along the river. My dogs were doing wonderfully well in checking the ground for firmness but those stupid sheep could not be controlled and wandered into quicksand. In minutes three hundred sheep and the rest of my sheep dogs that were trying to save them sank out of sight."

"Look," growled T. P., "let's cut out all this stuff you're feeding me. How many sheep have you delivered?"

"Senior Banta," said the rancher, "the last sheep fell into a hole and disappeared only five miles from here. There are none left."

"What?" T. P. bellowed. "And you expect me to believe all this?" T. P. was very agitated and was becoming very loud. The others in the bar glared at him and he could see they were not on his side.

"Senior Banta, You do not believe me. Look at me. I am battered and bleeding from trying to deliver your sheep to you," the rancher said in a hurt tone of voice.

"No, I don't believe you. You muddy and scratch yourself up and feed me this cock and bull story. If you had not come, I could have gone after you for not fulfilling the contract but this way I must dispute your word and the court will not be on my side," T. P. said quietly for he knew the dumb gringo had been taken again; first, it was the portable houses in Imperial Beach and now, half the price of a thousand sheep. What in the world would he tell Carrie and the boys? He couldn't bear to face them.

He quietly left the bar and headed back to the house on Eighth Street.

CHAPTER 38

T. P. AND THE LAGUNA DAM CONTRACT

T. P. knew he had been unlucky or had been taken in his business dealings since he had turned sixty. Now, in 1918, he was sixty-five and as one of the thirty-six business men in the Imperial-Laguna Water Company, he stood to make back all he had lost and a substantial amount more. When the Eastside Mesa Land would be opened by the Department of the Interior, he had first rights to the land and already owned land in the school sections which would be used as townsites for the new settlers.

Mark Rose was a man of unbelievable energy and persuasion. He would make the dream of the All-American Canal and the opening of the Eastside Mesa become a reality. He had complete faith in his abilities.

In November, 1917, the Directors of the Imperial Water District passed a motion made by Director Nickerson which requested the Secretary of the Interior to make an immediate survey to determine the cost and feasibility of connecting Imperial Valley with the Laguna dam by means of an All-American Canal. The secretary accepted the Boards recommendation if the district would agree to pay $30,000 of the cost while the Government would pay $15,000. The Board agreed to accept the Secretary's proposal and sent Attorney Swing, Engineer Grunsky and Director Holt to Washington to work out the details of the contract.

These men were instructed by the board that all electrical power generated by the project should enure to the District. If it didn't, then the district should receive a credit. The final contract as submitted by Secretary Lane was not acceptable and a second committee consisting of Leroy Holt, Phil D. Swing and T. P. Banta was sent to Washington to procure an acceptable contract.

T. P. had always remained in the background in All-American Canal matters but this was a matter of such significance to the future of the valley that he stepped forward into the limelight. On June 4, a new contract was forwarded to Secretary Lane. The contract was put before the people in the valley and approved by a vote of 2535 to 922.

It was important to have the support of department heads prior to the next session of congress. For this purpose, Attorney Swing was sent to Washington. In a letter of instructions drafted by the those in the Imperial-Laguna Water Company, he was told not to bring up the subject of storage of water for flood control of the lower Colorado River for fear that it would kill the proposal for the All-American Canal. The report of the All-American Canal engineering board was a shock to everyone in the Valley. The estimated cost for building the All-American Canal was placed at $30,000,000.

Representative William Kettner met with the Imperial Valley delegation and together thy wrote H. R. 6044, the Kettner Bill, the first bill addressing taming of the Colorado River and protection of the valley. Everything looked like it was going in favor of the Imperial-Laguna Water Company and water for the Eastside Mesa. It looked like, at last, one of T. P.s investments was going to pay off.

Once again bad luck crashed down on T. P. This was 1919 and the G. I.s were returning from the war. The new organization, the American Legion, suggested that it would be in the interest of these young men to make the new land that would be watered by the new canal on Eastside Mesa, open to them for first filing.

· The small group of men who made up the Imperial-Laguna Water Company had pushed the building of the canal from the beginning on the understanding that they would have first rights of entry on the mesa land. They also saw that the Kettner Bill

would have a much better chance of passing if the returning service men were to gain from the opening of this land. These men,
recognizing the great benefits the valley would gain from controlling the Colorado River and the All-American Canal, put their self
interest aside and threw their full support behind the proposal
that the service men be given first rights to the Eastside Mesa land
and continued to be leaders in the struggle to protect the Valley
by river control and the All-American Canal.

With this, the last opportunity for T. P. to recoup his losses
evaporated. With no one to champion the opening of the East
Mesa land, it was never opened to entry and today the only land
on the mesa which is owned privately and is in the Imperial Irrigation District is that school land purchased by the thirty-six men
who made up the Imperial-Laguna Water Company. The land has
never been improved and much of it is still owned by the descendants of those thirty-six men who keep it in memory of a great
dream that lingers only as a nightmare.

CHAPTER 39

THE WAR ENDS.

GEORGE AND EARL COME HOME.

George Banta arrived in New York, his point of embarkation to Europe and the front lines, on November 10, 1918. When he arrived, he found all the headlines in the New York newspapers were about an imminent armistice that was being arranged between the two warring factions. The articles stated that Germany was about to unconditionally surrender. Was it just talk or was the war really coming to an end just as he was leaving for the front?

The next day, November 11, 1918, the city and the nation went crazy with emotion as the news was released that the war was over. Giant headlines covered the entire front page of the papers across the nation. "**WAR ENDS**" they announced to the world.

Earl had already been shipped over seas in October with Company C, 335th Battalion of the Tank Corps and was on the verge of entering into combat. Because of this, he was not returned to the United States until May 5, 1919. George, since he was still in New York, received his discharge within a couple of weeks and returned home to resume his normal life. The very first thing on his mind was his sweetheart, Mary. T. P. had come up from the valley to be at their Los Angeles home when George arrived. When he got home, George just took time to kiss his mother and father before he was across the street to the Mulkern's home.

Mary was delirious with happiness. She had prayed day and night for the war to end before George had to fly in combat, and she thanked God for his deliverance from that awful task. When she saw him coming across the street so very handsome in his uniform, she ran out to the driveway, and they embraced in front of the whole neighborhood much to the delight of Carrie who was watching through her front window.

"Mary, lets get married right away as soon as we can get the license," George said as their lips parted.

"Wonderful," Mary said. "Can you come with me to the church right away to see the priest and make arraignments?"

"Sure," said George. "Let me go tell mom and dad. I'll get the car and we can drive over to the church. I'll be right back."

George ran across the street and flung the front door open and with a beaming face announced to T. P. and Carrie that he and Mary were going to the Catholic church to make arrangements with the priest for their coming marriage. Carrie's face showed her delight at what George had just said, but T. P.s face looked agitated. "Just a minute, George," T. P. said.

"What's the matter, dad." George said. "Mary's waiting in the driveway across the street for me to come with the car. Can't this wait til later?"

"No," T. P. responded. "We've got to talk about this right now. Carrie, go across the street and tell Mary, George has been detained and will see her a little later."

"Papa, what's got into you?" Carrie asked. "Mary's waiting for George. Why must I tell her he'll be over later."

"You'll hear as soon as you get back. Please do this for me. It's important to me that you do as I ask."

As Carrie went out the front door, George stood with his mouth open in shock and surprise. He thought he knew his father but realized he didn't know him as well as he thought he did.

When Carrie returned, T. P. asked that George and Carrie sit down with him in the parlor for an earnest talk. When they had settled themselves, T. P. arose and walked back and forth in front of them. Then he said, "George, there is something that I've been thinking about since you and Mary started seeing each other regularly but up til now I've put off discussing it because it is so distasteful. Mary is a Catholic, and Catholics don't believe in birth control. You've seen her family, nine children. Mr. Mulkern isn't working in a different city for economic reasons. He's deserted the family because it was more than he could bear. He sends his pay home each month, but they are not sure where he is. Margaret was looking for him when she was in Dallas. The news is all around the neighborhood."

George broke into T. P.'s story to ask, "Papa, what has this to do with Mary and me?"

"Just this," T. P. answered. "I was one of nine children, myself. Life is hard in such large families. Mama and I had to give up intimate relations because there was no good method of birth control when we were young. It was either that or to have nine or ten children. Now there are good methods available but Catholics are forbidden by their church from using them. I can't let you suffer as I did when I was a young man. Marriage is hard enough with intimacy. It's near impossible without it.

"You've got to tell Mary she has to give up her religion if you are going to marry her. I'm your father and I know what's best for you. Right now you are too much in love to think clearly. If she remains a Catholic, it means that either you end up with ten or twelve children or, as did your mother and I, you will have to give up intimacy. Either choice is impossible. Science today makes such a choice unnecessary. Explain this to her. Tell her we all love her, but this thing of Catholics and birth control is unrealistic."

Carrie remained silent and George didn't speak either. He had thought about this in an off hand way but dad had clearly stated what had entered only the edges of his mind. Could he bring up such a matter with Mary? She was so religious that she might break off their engagement.

"George," T. P. went on, "I've planned on your taking over my business in the Valley as a young attorney building his practice. I can support you and Mary but I don't see why I should extend myself to a family while you're getting established. If you want my continued support, you must follow my wishes in this matter."

There it was. If he didn't do as Papa wanted him to do, he and Mary were on their own. He had no job and would need dad's help for the first few years while he set up his practice.

"All right, dad," George said. "I'll tell Mary she must give up these silly ideas on birth control if we are to get married. I might as well get it over with. I'll go over right now and tell her."

Though she said nothing, Carrie's face fell. What would she do if she were Mary with Mary's faith and she was confronted with such a choice? She knew what she would do and she knew Mary would do the same thing. She truly loved Mary and the thought tore at her heart.

George went across the street and rang the doorbell. When Mary answered the door, her face showed her concern over his not coming right back with the car. She could tell by the expression on George's face that he was in deep distress.

"Mary, could you come out on the front porch? I have something I must say and it's private between you and me," George said in a soft but strained voice.

"Of course, George," Mary answered. "What's happened? You look pale as a ghost. Aren't you feeling well?"

"No, I'm not feeling well. I'm feeling awful but I've got to talk to you about a very private matter. I guess the best way is to come right out and tell you what dad has been saying to me," George went on. Then he told her his father's words almost verbatim.

Mary tilted her head up to look at George and a tear rolled down her beautiful cheek. "George, I love you with all my heart but I can't give up my religion," she said as she removed his ring from her finger and put it in his hand. She then quietly turned without a single additional word and went back into her house.

George was crushed. He returned to his house and went directly to his bedroom without saying a word to mama or papa. His heart was in his throat. He lay down on his bed with a terrible sick

headache and fell fast asleep to block what had just happened
from his mind.

The next morning George found that it was not the end of the
world. The sun was up and shining brightly. The hurt from the
night before was still there and he felt miserable, but he knew he
must face the new day. He arose, showered and shaved, brushed
his teeth, dressed and went down to tell his mother and father
what had happened.

When he arrived in the breakfast room, he found T. P. and
Carrie already there finishing their breakfast.

"Let me fix your breakfast, George," Carrie said. "And tell us
what happened last night. We know it wasn't pleasant when you
came in and went directly to bed. I felt so sorry for you and wanted
to talk with you and comfort you but I knew that was not the
time for me to get involved. Mary broke off the engagement
didn't she?"

As mama went to the kitchen, George sat down heavily at the
breakfast table. And put his face in his hands. "Yes, mama,," he
answered. "Mary didn't hesitate a minute or argue with me. She
just returned my ring and went back inside. My mind tells me I
was right in doing as Papa said but my heart told me I had made a
terrible mistake."

"Hold on, George," T. P. broke in, "Wait a spell before despairing
of your romance with Mary. She's probably at the breakfast table
in her house across the street crying to her mother and Aunt Mary
and telling them she had made a mistake. Don't go over there on
your knees. You made a sensible request. Her mother and brothers
and sisters are probably telling her that you're a handsome catch
and to not be silly and let you get away."

"Papa, you're very smart in things of business," Carrie inter-
rupted as she brought George his breakfast, "but in this matter
you're wrong. I agree with your position on birth control, but
Mary is not going to cave in. George had better get use to a broken
heart and start looking at other young ladies. Mary is not the old-
fashioned girl who could be pushed around by the man she loves.

She is one of the modern young ladies with a mind and feelings of her own. I don't agree with her thinking but I knew she would take this stand and admire her for it."

George sat glumly, picking at his breakfast with a look of hopelessness on his face.

T. P. looked sternly at George sitting so dejectedly across the table and said in a soft but firm voice, "Son, though this minute you feel miserable, you made the right decision, and you've saved yourself from a lifetime of regret. In time you'll forget about Mary, but if you'd have gone ahead with the marriage you'd daily face the problem of raising a family of ten children with a limited income. Start dating other girls right away and get this potential mistake behind you."

Across the street in the Mulkern household, Mary was eating breakfast with her family. She had told them last night what George had said and her mother and she had talked late into the night both weeping at the broken romance. This morning, things seemed to have lost their luster and though most of the family agreed with Mary, they had grown fond of George and the Bantas and hated to see her lose him. Now, it was as if a wall had been built in the middle of the street between their two houses over night. These close neighbors failed to recognize or talk to each other when in the yard or passing on the street.

After two weeks the tension became unbearable for young George Mulkern. He decided to take matters into his own hands. When he knew that T. P. had returned to the valley, he walked over to the Banta house and rang the bell. Carrie answered the door.

"Mrs. Banta," he started, "is George home. I'd like to speak to him."

"Why, yes he is," Carrie responded. "Go into the parlor and I'll call him down from his room. George," she called up the stairway, "George Mulkern is here to see you."

George Banta came down the stairs and both Georges shook hands which turned into a contest to see which could squeeze the hardest. This had become a ritual with the two men. George Banta always won but as little George grew older and stronger, it had become a real effort. With this, they both started laughing as they withdrew their hands.

"What's up, George," George Banta asked.

"Well," little George replied, "You're a great guy and Mary's a great girl and you make a perfect pair. I've come over because you can cut the tension between our two families with a knife. I've talked to Mary and she won't budge. I've got to get you two together again so I've come over to reason with you."

"I've been miserable," George Banta said, "but my dad is right about this. I don't know what to do. I can't bear to loose Mary and I can't go against my father."

Carrie had been standing in the foyer listening and at this point interjected herself into the conversation. "Son," she said, "what do you think your father would have said if his father had put the same question to him? He would have told him he respected him but he loved me and it was his life to lead. Don't worry about papa. Do what you think is right for you. You've been moping around the house for two weeks. It's time to act if that is your choice."

"George, mother, thank you both," George said with a sigh of relief. "I had come to the conclusion I was wrong in what I asked of Mary but didn't know how to approach the subject with you and dad and going over to the Mulkerns to beg Mary' pardon seemed impossible."

"Come on back with me," little George said. "It'll be easier that way. I'll tell them I talked you into it. That way you won't have to lose face."

"You're a real pal," George Banta agreed and they both went arm in arm across 32nd street to the Mulkern's house.

Little George threw open the front door to his house and hollered up the stairs, "Mary come on down. I've talked George into caving in. You win and you've got your little brother to thank for it." Then he laughed uproariously as George Banta's face turned red. He could have killed little George until Mary came down the steps, and then he could have kissed him if he hadn't been busy by that time kissing Mary.

"Mary," George said, "I never should have put you in the position between your religion and me. If you'll still have me I'll raise all ten kids Catholic."

"George, I love you with all my heart but where did the ten kids come from."

"Let's go find the priest right now and you'll find out."

They were married on December 26, 1918, by her priest in a private ceremony in the garden of Mary's parish church and honeymooned on the Balboa Peninsula in a hotel near the Pavillion.

When T. P. learned what George had done, he was furious but he also knew Carrie was on George's side and was smart enough not to stand in the way of the two young lovers. He told George that he still would set him up with his Law office in El Centro where he could also handle the family's property in the Valley. He told the young couple that they would live in the Banta house in Imperial where Jewel and Al had shared their short life together.

The newlyweds had moved in with the Bantas until arrangements could be made for their move to the Valley. T. P. had them both sit down in the parlor and laid out to them his plans for their future.

"I'll pick up all your bills until you've developed a practice that can support you. You'll take care of our business and live free of charge in the house. Mary, you'll be given an advance for living expenses but you must keep track of all you spend. Write the costs down or give me the bill and I'll reimburse you."

Mary was taken aback. They would have no money of their own in the form of a salary. She would be beholden to T. P. for every cent she spent.

"That doesn't sound fair, dad. You paid Al a salary. Why must we be put on such a plan?" Mary countered.

"I didn't have to rent a Law office for Al. Al worked strictly on my business. This is a fair arrangement. When Earl comes home, he will come to live with you and both of you boys will build your Law practice together."

Mary saw that T. P. was punishing them for going against his will, but she said nothing for as a new member of this wealthy family she felt she was in no position to battle the master of the family. So, she and George moved down into the Valley in January of 1919 where she made the best of what they had been given and George set up his Law practice.

"I really don't think you can take the heat of summer here in the Valley," George told her. "In June you will have to go back to Los Angeles and live with your family or mine. The heat here is unbearable"

"No," Mary said. "If Jewel could take it, I can too. That's no way to start a marriage, seeing each other only on weekends. I'm tough. I can take it." But Mary had no idea of the heat in the Valley during the hot months.

When they moved to the Valley in late winter, the weather was perfect and they were in their own little house. Life was beautiful for the young couple. George had furnished and opened his Law office in El Centro and drove to it each day in the Banta's Valley car. Then he would return in the evening to their little love nest to tell Mary all that had happened during the day.

Building a practice in an area where the family had been established for nineteen years sounded like it would be easy. But this was not the case. Most businessmen had used the same tried and true practicing lawyers for years and were loath to change. They offered George minor cases but the larger problems they took to those who had come through for them in the past. George knew he would have to gain their trust and he expected this. Starting from scratch, money came into his practice very slowly. First he had to work the hours. Then he had to bill the hours. Months later money came in for what he did today and since he hadn't been there previously, nothing came in from what he had done last month or last year. They were absolutely dependant on the money T. P. had put in a bank account for them.

After two weeks of living in the Valley, Mary put all the bills she had paid in an envelope and mailed them to T. P. for reimbursement. She hated living off of George's parents but there was no other way til George built his practice. Then two days later, after T. P. had received the mail, she received a telephone call from him.

"Hello," she said when the call came in.

"Hello, Mary, this is dad. I got your letter with the bills today."

"Is everything in order?"

"Well, that is why I'm calling. There isn't enough detail."

"Why? Doesn't each bill tell you what it's for?"

"Only in general. As an example, here is one for a dollar and thirty cents and all it says is 'groceries'"

"That's right. It was for groceries."

"You have to explain what groceries."

"You mean like 2 cents for a bunch of carrots and 2 cents for a bunch of beets?"

"Now you have it."

Why do I have to do that? Don't you trust me? Do you think we will be living too high off the hog?"

"Don't be silly, Mary. That's just the way business is done. We must be business like."

Mary was miffed with T. P. but also scared to death of him so she answered as a dutiful daughter-in-law should by saying, "All right, Father. I'll do it that way."

When George came home that night, she told him of the indignity she felt T. P. had imposed on her.

"I agree with you. It's ridiculous, but can't you go along with him? It's unnecessary, but it's not unacceptable. I'm glad you didn't challenge him. I think he's getting back at me for my not following his wishes." George confided to her. So Mary kept track of everything she bought down to the penny but it was a lump in the middle of their love nest.

March, April and May were beautiful months in the Valley. The weather couldn't have been more perfect except for the occasional dust storm when everything in the house would be covered with a layer of dust. George worked at law while also tending his father's business. They both made new friends and George rekindled old ones. They became close to Uncle Robert and Aunt Mary but Pearl, Myra and Fred were away most of the time. Mary became active in the Catholic church and George became best friends with the priest.

In May, Earl had been discharged from the army and came down to live with them and to become George's law partner. While it was not what a new bride would choose, Earl and Mary had always been fond of each other and got along beautifully. A little money was coming in from the law office but now new business had to be split two ways when there really wasn't enough to keep one busy.

By late May, Mary was beginning to see what Valley summers were going to be like. The nights were delightful but the temperature was over a hundred degrees by noon. Each week seemed to get hotter and hotter until the summer temperatures were daily over one hundred and ten degrees sometimes exceeding one hundred and twenty. She never experienced anything like this. She had heard how the dry heat made the temperatures more bearable but she couldn't imagine them being more unbearable. It was like living in a sauna. She realized that she had misspoken when she said she could take the heat if Jewel could. Jewel had been raised in the valley and though no one ever got acclimatized to Valley summers, those who had lived here all their lives were better able to tolerate the heat.

George and Earl went of to their offices each day and with the heat Mary didn't feel like going anywhere. It was simply too hot. All she could do was to swelter and wait for the boys to come home. When they did, she knew that it wouldn't be long until the sun set and temperatures would drop to tolerable levels. She was lonely and miserable during the long summer days. In addition to the heat, she had to put up with T. P.'s tight fisted hand on the money strings. In spite of this, she tried to keep the boys happy with a clean house and clothes while having a good dinner prepared for them when they came home.

They always wanted desserts and she always tried to have a nice dessert after dinner while keeping the food costs at a level where T. P. wouldn't complain. This wasn't easy and she tried every way to have a tasty dessert without running up the food bills. One day she saw the grocery store had day-old bread on sale. Mary had always been a business woman before she was married and hadn't spent a great deal of time in the kitchen. She did recall, however, how Aunt Mary stretched the food budget in feeding the large Mulkern family by using stale bread to make bread pudding. Here, she thought, was a wonderful way to have a dessert she always had liked and save money at the same time. She bought four loafs for two cents a loaf and two quarts of milk. Then, with her other purchases, she headed home to make George and Earl a wholesome dinner with a tasty dessert.

When she got home she immediately went to the kitchen to prepare dinner. First on her mind was the bread pudding. She took a large bowl out of the cupboard and placed it on the sink and then proceeded to break the four loafs into small pieces. She found that the four loaves when so broken filled the bowl to over-flowing and since she didn't have a larger bowl decided to make the bread pudding in the porcelain face bowl. She realized that she had probably bought too much bread but knowing how tight T. P. was with two cents, she couldn't force herself to throw two loafs away.

Next, she poured the milk into the face bowl and started gently to turn the bread so that it could absorb the milk. The milk only barely moistened about one half of the bread but caused it to rise alarmingly. She could afford no more milk, so she decided to dilute it with water. Soon the wet bread swelled up until it was overflowing the face bowl. She rushed out and found the washtub and dumped the concoction into it. Still it continued to expand until it completely filled the washtub.

"Jesus, Mary and Joseph," she prayed, "Please help me get out of this mess. What will T. P. say when he hears about this?"

Immediately she thought of the chickens. She thought it was an answer to her prayers. They had a very large flock of chickens. She would feed the washtub full of bread and milk to the chickens, except for a small amount she would save and bake in a small bowl for dinner. She carried the wash tub out to the chicken coop and poured it out on the ground in the middle of the chickens.

"Thank God for the chickens," she thought as the chickens walked up to the mess and gave it a couple of pecks. Then they just walked around the pile of bread pudding, looking at it with one eye and then the other but not eating any of it. After about a half hour of making clucking sounds and saying in a high voice, "Here chicky, chicky, chicky. Eat the good food." Mary determined that chickens don't like bread pudding.

Now what was she going to do? It had to disappear before the boys got home. They would think it so funny they were bound to let it slip to T. P. She had to get rid of the evidence. So she went to the garage and got a shovel, dug a big hole just outside the chicken coop and buried it. She was so distraught that she didn't even save the small pot full for that night's dessert. She wanted no evidence whatsoever of her debacle. Now all she had to do was to find where she could hide the cost of the bread and milk among her other expenses when she sent her grocery list to be reimbursed by T. P.

By November the valley was cooling, and George and Mary found they were expecting their first child in March. Mary had been in the valley ten months and the income from the law office was miserably small. She was still dependent on T. P. who was pinching pennies tighter than ever. She knew that she had made it into the cool months but also knew that she faced the same problem of living in an oven seven months later. She was discouraged and saw no way out of her despondency. It was obvious to Uncle Robert and Aunt Mary that she was very unhappy.

They went to Los Angeles on weekends to see their families. There, too, everyone saw that Mary was despondent. T. P. was not happy that Mary was pregnant. She had thought that when he found out he was to be a grandfather, he might loosen up the purse strings, but this only further convinced him that he had been right about the ten children. She confided her feelings with her mother and Aunt Mary. Everyone in the Valley and in West Adams knew she was unhappy. Christmas only made her more miserable for even their gifts to each other were bought with T. P.'s money.

George waited until they were alone one day in the valley and sat close to Mary in the front room of the Valley house. He took her hand in his and looked into her eyes and then said, "Mary, everyone says that you're going to leave me. Please don't. I just can't bear to loose you."

"No, George. I'm not going to leave you. But we are leaving the Valley and you are going to get a job in Los Angeles. The baby is due in March and we can't raise it depending on handouts from your father."

"Sweetheart," George said, "if that's what it takes to keep you, I'll leave the firm to Earl. We'll pack our things and move to the L. A. house as soon as I can get things at the office in order."

In January, they moved back to Los Angeles and George started looking for a job. T. P. was furious, but Carrie told him he had no one to blame but himself for he had pushed the young bride to far. He offered to put them on a salary but it was too late. The die had been cast and neither George nor Mary would go back to the Valley. George found a job with the Security-First National Bank of Los Angeles at their home office and they moved into their own rented cottage on the Avenues not far from the Banta and Mulkern families.

While T. P. was hostile to Mary, Carrie could hardly wait for the blessed event. She and Mary became very close. Mary had not spent much time in the kitchen; she had been a buyer for a large department store prior to her marriage. Thus, she spent time in the kitchen with her mother-in-law learning the art of cooking what George liked. One day, as they were working together in the kitchen, Mary told Carrie that George had said he had been baptized as a Baptist, yet Mesa was in the center of a Mormon settlement. She asked how Carrie had found a Baptist church.

"Land sakes, Mary," Carrie said, "we were so busy then that we didn't have time to get him baptized."

"You mean George has never been baptized."

"That's right. He was never baptized. It never came up and I guess he just assumed he had been Baptized in his father's religion."

"Holy Mother," Mary exclaimed. "Then we are legally married but not married in the rules of the Church. The Church permits us to marry baptized Christians but a special dispensation has to be obtained before a Catholic can marry a pagan."

"Mary," Carrie said, "You've got to attend to this right away. You're pregnant and we've got to make sure this baby is legal not only in the eyes of the law but in the eyes of your Church."

Mary drove immediately to her parish church and asked to speak to the pastor. When he came into the room, she told him her sad story. "Look, Mary," he said in a calming voice. "Don't get so upset. I'll write to the diocese immediately and get the dispensation. George may not be baptized, but he's one of the finest men I've ever met. I just wish we had more Christians with all his qualities."

The priest did as he said he would do, and a dispensation by the Bishop was received shortly. Mary and George went back to her parish church and were married a second time. This time, with the full blessing of her church. "You had your chance to get out of this marriage by church law, Mary," George chided, " but now by the laws of the church you're stuck with me for life."

In carrying her first child, Mary acquired Albumen poisoning and became very ill. Because of the sickness, she couldn't keep anything on her stomach and developed double vision, which gave her vertigo. Because of this she was in bed most of the time and had to wear a patch over her right eye. Aunt Madge administered to her but was unable to prescribe anything that would lessen the problem. Although Madge was not a religious woman, she knew the power of the mind and suggested that Mary pray for a cure since she had such a strong faith. Mary was feeling so sick that she jumped at the suggestion and asked George to take her to a little Catholic church that was dedicated to St. Ann in Santa Monica. There were stories of miraculous cures that had taken place in the church. Though George was a non-believer, he dutifully drove her to the church and helped her up to the altar.

Mary knelt at the altar and prayed, "St. Ann, mother of our Blessed Virgin, please hear my prayer and cure me of this illness that might hurt my baby. Please, please. If you will cure me, I will offer up my baby to the service of the church." Then she took her eye patch off and was convinced that Ann had preformed a miracle. Her double vision was gone and she felt her normal self again.

After her cure in the winter of 1920, the young couple couldn't have been happier. The problems of their newlyweded life had all been eliminated in their major decision to leave the Valley and because of the unhappiness of the last year, their new life together was all the more delicious. In March, a little girl was born to the happy couple. Carrie and Katie were thrilled to death with their new grandchild and Carrie couldn't be with her enough. The baby girl was named for Carrie's mother and was christened with her mother's maiden name with Ann inserted in the middle because of the miracle Saint Ann had preformed. Thus the baby gitl's full name was Mary Ann Allen Banta. Mary thought of the name Ann as a token of her thanks to the good Saint.

In the Fall of 1919, Carrie met Marie McCleod by chance in the grocery store. Carrie told her that Earl had been crushed by her not answering his letters while he was in the army. Marie was flabbergasted for she had received no letters from Earl and had been hurt that he had sent her none. It didn't take long for the two ladies to figure out what had happened. It was apparent to them that Marie's Aunt Trace had filed all his letters in the waste basket because she did not like "that Banta boy."

"Marie," Carrie said, "Earl will be home from the Valley this weekend. Come on over and talk to Earl. Tell him what happened. We can't let Aunt Trace get away with such a terrible thing."

Marie got her hair done, bought a new dress and as planned showed up at the Banta's house the next Sunday. Carrie had not told Earl of their plans and he was completely surprised when Marie showed up for lunch. Earl's heart raced when he heard the voice of his sweetheart when Carrie answered the door. He rushed over to see if it was really she and there stood the girl he thought was the most beautiful in the world.

EARL BANTA AND MARIE MC LEOD

Carrie laughed with glee as she saw how happy the two young lovers were at this first meeting after months of despair and two broken hearts. Aunt Trace's dirty trick only made the meeting and renewal of their romance all the sweeter. Their romance flourished over the next two years as Earl continued to try to make the law office in the Valley profitable. Marie was not happy with the arrangement T. P. had with Earl and was not going to let herself be trapped in the same situation Mary had found herself. She would not marry Earl until he was self supporting or had changed employment. She was open with Earl in her feelings about the Valley. It was just too hot and she was used to the big city.

T. P. realized he had alienated his son's desire to carry on his legacy in the Valley and began to liquidate some of his Valley holdings. He was still very active in Valley politics but he longed for the life of a farmer nearer to the big city. All of his adult life since accepting the job as foreman of the McCord ranch in Mesa, Arizona, had been spent in irrigation farming so when he heard of a new irrigation project alongside the San Gabriel River in what is now Pico Rivera he went to look at it. He was not happy in the big home in the West Adams district and here was many acres of sandy loam being opened to irrigation farming near Los Angeles where the weather was cooler and he could get back to his first love, farming.

"Mama," he said to Carrie in 1920, "I know how happy you are in this beautiful home in the West Adams district but I'm not. I'd love to get back to my roots and again live on a farm. The Valley's too hot but would you agree to developing a farm near Los Angeles? That way you'd have your city life close by and I'd be a farmer again."

"Papa, you've left the Valley for your family and I know how much you loved it and every minute of your life there. We're getting up into our sixties and you are still active. I think it's the perfect compromise. Why don't you look into buying land alongside the San Gabriel River? We could sell this house and have enough to purchase a farm there."

With Carrie's blessings, T. P. went to the developers of the new irrigation district and purchased seventy acres of prime sandy loam alongside the San Gabriel River just south of where the Whittier Narrows Dam now lies. Here they built a farm house and developed a walnut farm. Once again, they lived in a true ranch house with a windmill to provide household water and a large red barn. He planted the seventy acres in walnuts. T. P. was the happiest he had been since moving from the valley. He was fully involved in managing the ranch and supervised every aspect of its development.

Carrie realized she, too, had missed the life of frontier woman. She had become accustomed to being a country housewife, and this year was one of the best in their life together. The family was raised and the struggles of getting ahead were past. They had nothing to prove to the world any longer. T. P. was now a gentleman farmer looked up to by all in the new irrigation district. Now, they could reap the benefits of a lifetime of building, kick back and enjoy life.

In 1921, just as the development of the ranch was completed, T. P. began to feel severe pains in his abdomen and sister Madge was again called to diagnose his medical problem. Madge made arrangements for T. P. to be admitted to the Good Samaritan Hospital on Wilshire Boulevard in Los Angeles. Here it was confirmed that T. P. had terminal cancer of the stomach just as had Al.

When T. P. was told he had cancer and had only a few months to live, he became a different person. He had always been able to use his brain to control what was happening to him but now he realized his future was being decided by forces beyond his control.

"Mama," he confided to Carrie, "I'm leaving this world shortly and I haven't finished my work. The crowning work of my life has been to guarantee the water supply to the Valley. We've tied the irrigation system up to the Laguna Dam which means the heading is secure but I'll never live to see my All American Canal and the opening of the Eastside Mesa. It's going to happen because we have good men in Washington who will make it happen. With the unrest in Mexico, the valley will never have a truly safe irrigation water supply until a canal is built that flows from the river to the valley and lies entirely within the United States."

"T. P.," Carrie replied, "you can go to your reward knowing you helped build the Valley from a desolate desert to the nations salad bowl. They will never let what we've done in the Imperial Valley turn back to what it was when we arrived in 1901. The canal will be built and I feel sure you will know about it in heaven for you've lived a good life."

"Generally speaking, that's true," T. P. responded, "But there are some things now that I wish I could have seen differently for now that I'm dying I can see them so clearly."

"What in the world are you talking about? Everyone has regrets but you've always lived your life trying to do your best." Carrie asked.

"Well for one thing, there was that birth control thing with Mary. With my life ending, I now see the beginning of new life in a whole new perspective. Al is gone, and Earl doesn't seem in a hurry to get married. Where a dozen little Bantas seemed like a tragedy yesterday, today it seems like a beautiful miracle."

"Another thing, Carrie," he continued, " did I do right to sell the city house and move you way out on this ranch so far from all your friends?"

"Don't be silly," Carrie answered, "I've been a farm girl a lot longer than I've been a city girl. My friends will enjoy coming out to this farm and I will visit them often in the city. The walnut ranch is in and running smoothly. We've built a small house for the new Mexican foreman we've hired and he's doing a fine job. The ranch gives me something to do and think about. The boys will make sure things go well and get done. You've made them good business men."

Once again the family went through the torments of losing a loved one. T. P.'s cancer was very aggressive and his health deteriorated quickly.

During these very trying days, his two boys, Mary and baby Mary Allen were with him much of the time. As his life neared its end he realized that nothing he had done mattered as much as Carrie, his two boys and his little granddaughter. T. P. became very attached to little Mary Allen and he became sick at heart for treating her and her mother so shabbily. One day toward the end of his illness as he was sitting up in his bed at the Good Samaritan Hospital, little Mary Allen was crawling over his stomach and around his bed. He suddenly realized how much this little grand-daughter meant to him and he said to Mary, "Mary, there will be more won't there?" This was as close to apologizing as T. P. could bring himself.

Mary was so upset over the treatment T. P. had made her endure that though she was then pregnant with her second child she answered, "No, Dad, this is all that there will be."

With this reply, T. P.'s face dropped and lost all its freshness. Suddenly, he looked like a very old and sick man.

On the day before Christmas, 1921, at the age of sixty-eight, this eighth generation pioneer and frontiersman on the American continent breathed his last. There would be no further migration by the Banta family to the newest frontier because the continent had been conquered and the Pacific Ocean ended their two hundred and sixty-two year western migration. The family had pioneered the opening and settlement of the new continent from Flushing, New Netherland, on the shores of Long Island to the Imperial Valley, California, an unexplored continent away. T. P. had helped conquer one of the world's most inhospitable deserts, the Colorado Desert, and had shared from the beginning in its being turned into the lush, green Valley it is today. He had lived through the Colorado River disaster and profited by his will to stay when everything told him it was time to get out. What his family had endured is beyond the comprehension of most of today's American citizens yet without the sacrifices of such pioneers our great nation's infrastructure could not exist. Yet, as he breathed his last, only his family really mattered.

Though he did not live to see the ultimate fruits of the early Valley pioneer's labor, he was part of those who worked endlessly for a safe heading to the Valley's water supply. T. P. was among those men who never gave up until the Federal Government under the Swing-Johnson Act built the All American Canal across the sand dunes and the East Mesa to the safe heading at the Laguna

Dam. Attorney Phil Swing was elected United States Congressman representing the Eleventh District which included Imperial County. He and State Senator Hiram Johnson introduced and passed a bill whose official title was "Boulder Canyon Project Act." This bill passed the House and the Senate and was signed by President Calvin Coolidge, December21, 1928.

Work on the project was begun July10, 1930, nine years after T. P.'s death. The Valley team had not only succeeded in successfully introducing and passing an act to build the All American Canal but also included in the same act was the authority to construct the great Boulder Dam. This, the most successful economic venture ever undertaken by our Government, was the direct result of the Valley pioneers. Today, it provides a water supply and generates low-cost electric power to the booming southwest. Its primary purpose in being built, however, was to tame the lower Colorado River, the Yellow Terror of the early twentieth century, and to turn it into the well-behaved river it is today. One of T. P.'s fondest dreams never came to reality. The Eastside Mesa was never opened to settlement.

The Boulder Dam and the All American Canal are two tangible bits of evidence of the foresight of these nine generations of pioneers who, through their indomitable spirit, gave our nation the best infrastructure of all the nations on our beautiful planet. T. P. left his boys of the ninth generation educated. Earl's son, Art, and George's children, brother Mike (that's me, the author) and sisters Pat and Fran of little Mary Allen, of the tenth generation, were prepared to be what has been called the greatest generation. Although, after reading the story of the previous nine generations, we wonder if that designation could really stand an impartial test.

Nonetheless, this tenth generation would live through a terrible depression that would test the soul of free enterprise and they would survive it. They would then fight a vicious world war pitting democracy against the tyrannical totalitarian dictators and win it. They would, through social reforms and economic strategies, develop a gentler and kinder free enterprise system. Next they would engage in a cold war between communism and free enterprise. With the fall of communism, while leading most of the world to democracy and free enterprise, they would see the United States become the world's one great superpower. The tenth generation would live to enjoy the fruits of the labor of these fearless frontiersmen who constructed our nation from a hostile new continent and prepared the United States of America to be the richest, freest and strongest nation on the earth.

The End.

A PARTIAL BIBLIOGRAPHY

Akers,Vincent. *The Low Dutch Company. A History of the Holland Dutch Settlements of the Kentucky Frontier.*, Series of Articles from the Holland Society's Magazine, De Halve Maen

Archives-Library Ohio Historical Society. *Atlas of Montgomery County, Ohio, byTownshipsc1830*

Banta, Elsa M. *Banta Pioneers,* Prepared by Elsa M. Banta 1983

Banta, Theodore M. *A Frisian Family. The Banta Genealogy.* New York 1893

Berry, Ellen T. and David A *Early Ohio Settlers, Purchases of Land in Southwestern Ohio, 1800-1840,* Genealogical Publishing Co. Inc. Baltimore

Conover, Robert Alan. *The Low Dutch Company: An Ethnic Experiment.* Race and Ethnic Relations, Sociology 532, December 12, 1977. Unpublished

Copies of Original Documents. *Tract Book and Entries. U. S. Lands West of Miami River and Between the Miamis,* Auditor of the State Unpublished

Copies of Original documents. *Record of Preempted Land, Symes Purchase, Proceedings of U. S. Commissioners (1801),* Auditor of the State of Ohio Land Office Record Book

Copy, *Preble County, Ohio, United States Land Entries,* Unpublished

Crout, George C. *Butler County, An Illustrated History,* Winsor Publications, Inc Woodland Hills CA 1984

Demerest, Rev. J. K. D.D. *History of the Low Dutch Colony of Conowago,* Unpublished

Earle. *Home Life in Colonial Days*

Fabend, Firth Harling. *A Dutch Family in the Middle Colonies 1660 1800,Rutgers University Press*

Fiske, John. *The Dutch and Quaker Colonies in America, Vol. I, The Riverside Press, Cambridge*

Fodor's. *Holland, Past and Present*

Gates, Paul, Review: Swenson, Robert. *History of Public Land Law Development, Public Law Commission*

Griffis, William Elliot. *The Dutch of the Netherlands in The Making of America, Holland society of New York September 1921*

Harvey, Cornelius Burnham. *Genealogical History of Hudson and Bergen Counties, The New Jersey Genealogical Publishing Co. 1900*

Henstell, Bruce. *Los Angeles: An Illustrated History, Knopf, New York*

Hill, Laurance Landreth. *La Reina—Los Angeles in three centuries, Los Angeles Security First National Bank*

Howe, Edgar F. and Hall, Wilbur Jay. *The Story of the First Decade in Imperial Valley, CA, Edgar F. Howe & Sons, Imperial 1910*

Irving, Washington. *Knickerbocker's History of New York,, Frederick Ungar Publishing Co, New York*

Koehler, Francis C. *Three Hundred Years, The story of the Hackensack Valley, Its settlement and Growth, Printed in Chester, N. J., U.S.A*

List, Howard M. List Family Notes, With Data on Banta and Demerest Families, 1986

Lowry, R. E. *History of Preble County, Ohio, Cook and McDowell Publications, Owensboro, KY 1915, Available through Preble County District Library, Preble County Room.*

Faragher, John Mack. *Daniel Boone, Henery Holt and Company*

Mellick, Andrew D. *The Story of an old Farm, The Unionist-Gazette, Somerville, NJ 1889*

Merk, Frederick. *History of the Westward Movement*

Mulkern, George. *Eleven to One. The Mulkerns, Unpublished*

News Paper Articles. *re. San Diego Arizona Railway. On the Right track, San Diego Union-Tribune, Nov. 23,1997, Auction boosts Plan for S. D.-Baja Train Link. Los Angeles Times. August 21. 1997*

No Name. *History of Preble County Ohio, 1798-1881, H. Z. Williams Bros., Publishers, Available through Preble County District Library, Preble County Room*

Original Records. Land Purchases and Sales, T. P. Banta, Imperial Valley.

Original Records. Imperial Water Company #1, Recorded Deeds. etc.

Original Records. Original Filings with U. S. Land office for John F. Leighton, Margaret Allen and others

Overton, Jacqueline. Long Island Story, Garden City, Doubleday Doran & Co.

Petro, Jim, Auditor of State of Ohio. Ohio Lands, a Short History, State of Ohio

Riegel, Mayburt Stephenson. Early Ohioans' Residences from Land Grant Records, Unpublished

Riker, James, Jr. The Annals of Newton in Queens County, New York. D. Fanshaw, 108 Nassau-Street 1852

Roosevelt, Theodore. The Winning of the West

Ross, Peter. History of long Island from its Earliest Settlement to the Present Time 1902, Lewis publishing Co.

Ruehrwein, Dick. Discover Fort Howard, Fort Harrod, Creative Company, Cincinnati

Sarapin, Janice Kohl. Old Burial Grounds of New Jersey, A guide, Rutgers University Press, Van Brunswick

Schlotterbeck, Seth S. Y Old Mill Streams, Preble County, Available through Preble County District Library, Preble County Room

Smith History Library, Oxford, Ohio, Research by Gayle Brown and Pages Sent from the Following Books. History of Ohio, History of Montgomery County.

Tenzythofff, Gerrit J. PHD. The Dutch in America, Lerner Publications Co. Minneapolis

Thompson, Benjamin F. History of Long Island, New York, Robert H. Dodd 1918

Turner, Frederick Jackson. Frontiers in America

Van Winkle, Daniel. Old Bergen, History and Reminiscences, Harrison, John W.

Van Valen, J. M. History of Bergen County, New Jersey

Winfield, Charles H. History of the County of Hudson, New Jersey,

New York: Kennard & Hay Stationary Mfg and Printing Co. 1874

Meyer, Nancy. *Hanging Grove Township, 1853-1965,*

Preble and Other Indiana Counties, Dates of Purchase of Public lands. Including Part of Section, Section, Acres, and Name of Purchaser, Unpublished, Preble County Library

Tout, Otis B. *First Thirty Years in the Imperial Valley, Otis B. Tout, Publisher*